W9-BRE-806

Red Sky at Night—
Lovers' Delight?

By JANE AIKEN HODGE

FICTION

Maulever Hall
The Adventurers
Watch The Wall, My Darling
Here Comes A Candle
The Winding Stair
Greek Wedding
Marry In Haste
Savannah Purchase
Strangers In Company
Shadow Of A Lady
One Way To Venice
Rebel Heiress
Judas Flowering
Red Sky At Night—Lovers Delight?

NON-FICTION

Only A Novel—The Double Life
Of Jane Austen

Jane Aiken Hodge

Red Sky at Night
Lovers' Delight?

Coward, McCann & Geoghegan, Inc. New York

First American Edition 1977

SBN: 698-10841-8

Library of Congress Cataloging in Publication Data

Hodge, Jane Aiken.
Red sky at night—lovers delight?

I. Title.
PZ4.H6866Rg3 [PS3558.0342] 813'.5'4 77-6351

PRINTED IN THE UNITED STATES OF AMERICA

Chapter 1

The heat of the summer day had ebbed and the sunset faded. Already, lights here and there below on the marsh showed work continuing at the Tidemills down by the shore. Soon it would be dark. And time to be getting home. The solitary rider took a last look at the great pale sweep of Glinde Bay, then turned uphill into a shadowed lane over the shoulder of the down.

"Who goes there?" Rough hands caught the horse's bridle and pulled it to a halt.

"What in the world?" The young rider sounded more surprised than alarmed, peering down at the two masked men who had emerged so suddenly from the hedge. "Quiet, Boney." A gentle hand soothed the fretting horse.

"Boney!" The man who held the bridle glanced quickly up at the many-caped figure above him. "There's only one horse named for Bonaparte in this district. It's never—"

"Of course it is." Amused. "And you're—"

"No names!" It was he who sounded frightened now, as he glanced sharply across the horse's back to his silent companion. "And be off with you home, for God's sake. Not across the long meadow."

"No?" A laugh in the confident young voice. "You tempt me vastly, my nameless friend. What would I find there, I wonder? A waggonload of tea? We could do with some of that up at the house, and so you might tell your friends from me. Oh, very well." Sensing something strangely like danger in the air, the rider suddenly capitulated. "Since you ask me so civilly, I'll go round by the park wall. *If* you'll be so good as to let go the reins." And then, turning back as the horse moved forwards: "The best tea, mind!"

"You should a' knocked un out." Left alone, the silent man turned on his companion. "He knew you!"

"That's my business. 'No violence' was the word, and no violence it is. As for that young varmint . . . I'll see they get their tea up at the house, all right and tight, and no harm done."

"Which house?"

"That's my business, too. You're a stranger here, friend, and the less questions strangers ask, the better for us all. You gave the password: good. Did I ask where you come from? No. Ah! There's the signal." An early owl had hooted from somewhere towards the cliffs. "Meeting's ready to start. You'd best come along with me. They're a mite leary of strangers."

"And leave no guard?"

"You surely do think us a lot of country clogheads." He whistled softly and then addressed a third figure who emerged from the thick-set hedge. "Keep good watch, Tom."

"Yes, Sam, I'll do that." The youth spoke more broadly than his companion. "You said 'Boney'?" he asked. "That was never—"

"No names, Tom!"

The third man laughed sardonically. "No names! 'Tom' and 'Sam' and 'the house.' I could unravel your little mystery in five minutes if I put my mind to it."

"No doubt you could, stranger. But I don't advise it, I surely don't. Not if you want a chance to speak at our meeting, and ride safe back to London in the morning."

"And that I do." Well aware of the threat behind the words, the stranger yielded gracefully, merely adding, "Can't blame a man for being curious. Spunky young varmint, that! Not a scrap of fear, and us coming on him so sudden."

"Be curious, *if* you like, but ask no questions, you'll be told no lies. And a hell of a lot safer."

Meanwhile the "young varmint" had emerged from the deep lane and obediently turned left to take the long circuit around the wall of Hawth Park, instead of the shortcut across the meadow. Tedious, but a gentleman's word was his bond, and it would only put half an hour on the ride home to Warren House.

But the evening's adventures were not yet over. Hawth Park had stood empty and desolate ever since old Lord Hawth had died, full of age and dishonour, in Trafalgar year, and there was no other house but the Warren this side of the county town of Glinde. So what were a parcel of children doing, coming chattering down the lane?

A quick gesture, and Boney came obediently to a halt, his rump to the park wall, straddling the path. "Well?" His rider surveyed the children, who had rounded the curve of the wall and come to a surprised stop at sight of the horse. "What, may I ask, are you doing out so late? And where the devil do you come from?"

"That's no way to speak!" The girl's voice was at once haughty and frightened. "Father would have you whipped for talking to us like that."

"Oh, would he? And who, pray, *is* father?"

"Lord Hawth, of course." A hint of bravado in the girl's tone now.

"We're exploring." This was a younger boy, twelve or thirteen perhaps, who had moved forward to run a friendly hand along Boney's nose. Contact thus established, he looked up. "Only . . . we seem to have lost ourselves."

"Nonsense!" said the girl sharply. "It's merely to keep going along the park wall and there's bound to be a gate. Isn't there?"

"Well, yes." The gate was back down the lane, the other side of that sinister ambush. "But it's a good way to walk. You'd best go back the way you came."

"But we *can't,*" wailed the third and youngest child, a girl. "We can't get back in," she went on to explain tearfully. "And I know it's an adventure, but I want it to stop. I want Nurse Simmonds, and my tea."

"What kind of an adventure?" The question was addressed impartially to the two older children. And then, as they hesitated, "I do think you had best tell me. I promise I'll help, and not tell tales unless I must. To tell truth—" leaning down in the saddle to be nearer their level—"I quite long to know how you got out of the park. I grew up just across the downs, and I could have sworn there wasn't an entrance before the main one in Glinde."

"So there isn't," said the boy.

And, "I think we'd better tell him," said the older girl.

"I'm sure you should." The rider dismounted, looped the reins over an arm and held out a friendly hand. "Kit Warrender, very much at your service."

"How do you do." Her small hand was cold, and trembled just a little. "I'm Sue Chyngford." The note of bravado was back. "And this is Giles. And silly little Harriet, who is crying."

"I'm not," said Harriet.

"Well—" the rider had bowed courteously to the two younger children—"if you've got to walk all the way back to Glinde, I'm not sure that I blame you. It's five miles if it's a step."

"You'll be able to get us in," said Harriet. "Sue and Giles weren't strong enough to move the stone, but I'm sure you can."

"Stone?"

"It's the secret passage," explained Sue.

"We found it," interpolated Giles.

"Good gracious me! You never found the secret passage." No mistaking the note of genuine respect. "We looked for it—always—my brother and I." The light voice shook a little on the word 'brother.' "Never found it. And you've been here—how long?—and found it already."

"Two days," said Sue.

"It's easier from inside," said Giles fairly. "That's the trouble. It comes out in the ruins up the hill there. A big stone. Opens at a touch from inside."

"And closes after you," added Sue.

"And we can't get it open," wailed Harriet.

"We'd better go back and have a look hadn't we," said Kit Warrender. "Up you go, Harriet. Can you manage astride?"

"Course I can." The child dealt ruthlessly with muslin petticoats and settled herself in the saddle. "What's his name?" She leant forward to pat the horse's neck.

"Boney."

"But he isn't," protested Harriet. "He's beautiful."

"For the Emperor, stupid," said her older sister. "That's right, isn't it, sir?"

"Call me Kit. Yes, quite right. He was born in 1804. The year Bonaparte crowned himself."

"Seven years ago?" Sue Chyngford was showing off for the stranger's benefit. "Has he been yours always?"

"No." Shortly. "He was my brother's."

Something about the tone of the answer stopped the next question on Sue's lips, and they walked on in silence until a bend in the park wall revealed the ruins of the Saxon priory Cromwell's men had so thoroughly destroyed.

"I hope we can find the stone again." Giles looked about him dubiously in the gathering dusk. "It all seems different, coming the other way."

"Nonsense," said his older sister. "It's by a big yew tree. I marked it carefully, just in case."

It was a pity that there were several big yew trees growing among the ruined walls of the old priory. Harriet was beginning to sniff again when a cry of triumph from Giles proclaimed that they had found the right one. “You see, sir,” he showed it to Kit. “It swings out on a . . . a kind of hinge, only we couldn’t get it moving, Sue and I.”

“Well, let us devoutly hope that I can,” said Kit Warrender, “or we’ve a long walk ahead of us.”

The assumption that they were all in it together had a cheering effect on the three children. Harriet stopped sniffing and the other two worked with a will helping their new friend push and pull at the unyielding stone. In the end, Kit thought, it was more good luck than any particular strength or skill that brought the rock swinging out to reveal a dark, yawning hole.

There was a little silence, then, “I don’t like it.” Harriet summed up the feelings of all three children.

“We came this way, silly.” But even Sue’s voice was uncertain.

“At least the candle’s still here, and the tinder box.” Giles had been feeling around on the left of the entrance.

“Well of course they are,” said his older sister quellingly. “You don’t think dozens of people have come this way since we did, do you? But—is there enough candle left to get us back?”

“I expect so.” Giles sounded far from sure. “I say, sir,” he went on more eagerly. “You wouldn’t like to come, too? Just . . . just for a lark? To see the passage?”

“Yes, *do.*” No mistaking the appeal in Sue’s voice.

“Where does it come out?”

“Oh, that’s all right and tight,” said Giles. “It’s behind the panelling in Father’s study, and he’s away, visiting the Prince Regent at Brighton. He just brought us here, and dumped us, and went away again. He won’t be back for weeks. And he locked up the study before he left.” His voice dwindled and died.

“Then how did you get in?” asked Kit.

"We . . . we found the key. Nurse Simmonds told us about the secret passage, don't you see, and how it started from the study."

"They key was just hanging in the butler's pantry," explained Sue, in extenuation. "Oh, do please come, sir . . . Kit. It does look dark in there. We'll give you a fresh candle to come back with."

"Well, it is an adventure," Kit admitted fair-mindedly, lifting Harriet down and tying Boney to the yew tree. "You go first with the candle, Giles, you next, Sue, and I'll take care of Harriet. And the quicker the better, once you've lit the candle. What's the going like?"

"Paved." Now that he was sure of grown-up company, Giles was beginning to feel better. "It's easy, really."

"Then let's get started. It's time you three hellborn brats were safe home. Your nurse must be having fits."

"We're not brats!" Sue's indignation took her into the tunnel with not so much as a backward glance, and Kit gave a little laugh, took Harriet's willing hand, and followed. Better not ask how long the children had taken coming through. It would only remind them of that all-too-short candle stub. And though the floor was indeed paved, it would be hard going in the dark. But the air, surprisingly sweet and fresh, suggested that the tunnel could not be very long. It was rising steadily, presumably following the slope of the down. How far above the park wall did Hawth House stand? It had begun to seem very far indeed, and the candle was flickering dangerously low when Giles gave a shout of relief. "Here we are! I'm glad we left the panel ajar. I can see light!"

"Light?" asked Sue anxiously, and the candle went out.

Light indeed. The shining crack that showed ahead of Giles widened as he pushed the panel to reveal a brilliantly lit room, and a still figure, seated at a writing desk, gazing at the tunnel entrance.

"Father," breathed Giles.

"Quite so." Frowning under black brows, Mark Chyngford, second Earl of Hawth, rose and moved forward to help his reluctant son down from the tunnel mouth. "All my pretty ones, I see," he added sardonically, giving a hand to Sue. "And one extra." He gravely accepted Harriet from Kit, put her down and turned back to find that Kit had jumped lightly down and stood, chin up, to face him. Enormously tall, dark-haired and surprisingly elegant in the Prince Regent's gaudy uniform, Lord Hawth looked thoughtfully down at his unexpected guest. "I suppose I am to thank you for bringing my hellborn brats safe home," he said.

Sue let out a surprised giggle. "That's just what he called us!"

"I do not believe I asked you to speak, Susan." The black brows drew still closer together. "Giles, before you go to find what punishment awaits you, perhaps you will introduce me to your new friend."

"Oh, yes, sir. It's Mr. Warrender, Kit Warrender. We . . . we invited him to come, sir."

"Quite so. How do you do, Mr. Warrender." He returned Kit's bow gravely. "We meet under somewhat unusual circumstances, but I trust you will take a glass of wine with me before you leave. . . . Perhaps in a slightly more orthodox manner?"

"But his horse," wailed Harriet. "He left poor Boney tied to a tree!"

"I do not believe I asked you to speak either, Harriet." Hawth took a long stride across the room and pulled a bell-rope, then turned to gaze down repressively at his three scarlet-faced children. "You will wish to say good-bye to Mr. Warrender and thank him for his kindness in bringing you home, before you retire to your own quarters and the discomfort that awaits you there. Nurse Simmonds has left, by the way. She will not talk to you of tunnels again. Ah, Parsons." He turned to the door as a black-garbed butler opened it and trod softly into the room. "Our prodigals are returned, as you see. When they have finished saying good-bye to Mr.—ah, Warrender—you will have them taken back to their nursery, where they will stay. Then be so good as to send one of the men out by the sea gate to fetch a horse he will find tied in the priory ruins."

"Sir!" Speaking up, Kit half expected the same set-down as the children had received.

But, "Yes?" Lord Hawth's tone was at once courteous and quizzical.

"The Glinde gate would be better. There's something going on in the long meadow. Smugglers, I think. And a guard out in the lane. That's why I didn't want the children to come back that way."

It earned a sharp glance. "It seems I owe you more thanks than I had realised, Mr. Warrender. The Glinde gate, Parsons, and a supper for Mr. Warrender while he waits."

He watched impassively while Kit said a friendly goodnight to the three children, wishing in vain for some word of comfort. There was not much to offer. Giles was very white. Sue, scarlet with confusion, looked suddenly almost a young woman. Harriet was sucking her thumb. Kit bent to pick her up. "You were very brave, riding my horse, Harriet. And in the tunnel. I'm sure you're tired. Sue will carry you to bed." And, handing the child to Sue: "I think they're all exhausted, sir. It was quite an adventure."

"Was it?" Uninterested, he watched impassively as the butler led the three children from the room.

"You're hard on them." Once again Kit risked a set-down.

"Hard?" One black brow lifted sardonically. "I've owned them, haven't I? Given them my name. Brought them up. Fed them, had them taught manners. I thought." It reminded him of something. "Forgive me. Your coat, Mr. Warrender. Things are all to pieces here: no housekeeper, no staff to speak of . . ." He moved forward to help his guest out of the big, caped riding coat.

"I'll keep it on, thanks. That tunnel of yours was cold. And I mustn't stay. I'm . . . expected."

"A glass of wine then, to warm you." A half empty bottle on the writing desk suggested how he had been passing the time while he waited for his errant children. "Damnation!

There's only one glass." A furious tug at the bellpull produced a scared footman. "I ordered a supper."

"Yes, my lord. Directly, my lord." And then, greatly daring: "In here, my lord? Mr. Parsons was wondering . . ."

"Of course, fool. Where else, in this pigstye? And a glass, at once, for Mr. Warrender. And another bottle. Two more bottles." He sat down, rather abruptly, on the big chair behind the desk; then, remembering his manners: "A seat, Mr. Warrender? You must forgive me. You find me a trifle foxed. Blue-devilled, too. I'm glad of your company." He absentmindedly poured himself a full glass and drank it off. "Your health! Warrender, you said? From the house across the down? But, surely, young Warrender . . ."

"Died last year," said his guest. "I'm afraid I have no more right to be Warrender than those agreeable children of yours—forgive me—have to be Chyngford."

"Like that, is it? I'm sorry. Yes, I changed their names for them to please that bitch, their mother, and she thanked me by running off with the tutor. Said she was tired of acting housekeeper and nurse together. Said he was going to marry her. Fool of a woman. Believe that, she'll believe anything. Well—" his smile was slightly crooked— "she never did have any sense. Pretty as a picture. A dead bore, no more brains than a codfish. Know what she did? Wrote me a letter to say she was loping off. Forgot to post it. Went off with the damned tutor and all the money in the house. First thing I knew about it, that nurse of theirs turns up with the whole pack of them at my hired house in Brighton. Never felt such a fool in my life. And now what the hell am I going to do with them?"

"Have you really discharged their nurse?"

A rueful look. "Yes. Told you I was foxed, didn't I? Ah, here's your supper at last."

It was a simple enough meal of cold meats, and a game pie that Kit shrewdly suspected of having been intended for dinner in the servants' hall. "Bachelor's fare." Lord Hawth had dismissed the nervous footman and poured his guest's wine himself. "No kickshaws in the house, and not much comfort either. Gone to rack and ruin since m'father died. And, for God's sake, don't tell me it needs a woman's hand."

Kit laughed. "I wouldn't presume. But those venturesome children of yours will need one. Pluck to the backbone, sir . . . my lord."

"Hell's teeth, call me Hawth. Everyone does. Think I'm an unnatural father, don't you? Well, what in the devil's name have I got to be natural about? Pack of damned nuisances. Never really known them, scared to death of me . . ."

"Well, can you wonder? I'm scared myself."

"No, you're not. Surprised me. Most people are. Your age, anyway."

"I'm twenty," said Kit Warrender with some dignity. "And you must be all of forty yourself. An old man, you think?"

The habitual frown and crooked smile dissolved in a burst of laughter than transformed the saturnine face. "Forty-two, Mr. Warrender, and if all bastards are like you, I'll be proud of my brood yet."

"Call me Kit."

"I will. But you're drinking nothing!"

"I don't much. It's shameful, but I don't like it."

"Don't like it! Good God! You'll be telling me you don't like a wench, next."

"Well—" a note of apology—"I'm only twenty. We can't all be wicked earls, you know."

"Oh! So you know about me."

"Well, of course. Everyone knows about you. What I don't rightly understand is what you are doing here at Hawth after all these years."

"Wishing to God I was elsewhere. And wondering what in hell's name I'm to do with those brats of mine."

"Yes. Delicious pie." Kit finished a last mouthful and drank a modest sip of wine. "Do you know," deliberately, "I might have a suggestion to make about the children."

"Oh?" The dark brows drew together. "Might you? Got a starving mother somewhere in the county of Glinde?"

"My lord!" The wine glass went down with a sharp little click. "You insult me? In your own house?"

"Hell's teeth, boy—Kit—I'm sorry. Told you I was foxed. Told you twice. It's this damned tongue of mine. Made me more enemies than my money has friends."

"Money doesn't make friends," said Kit Warrender. "But it's useful. Perhaps you would be so good, my lord, as to enquire if those frightened servants of yours have brought back my horse yet."

"Up in the boughs, eh? Well, I don't blame you. But, dammit, boy, I've apologised, and it's not often I do that. Would you rather I fought you?"

"No, thanks. I'd be scared."

"Right to be. Come, sir, another glass to show we're friends, and tell me what you did mean when you said you'd an idea." He filled the glass, then looked across, dark eyes friendly under the black brows. "Sorry. Forgot you don't like wine. Absurd of me."

"But I do like this of yours. It's not just what I've been used to."

"My best burgundy. Can't stand claret. Run goods, of course. And that reminds me, you said . . . smugglers?"

"Yes. They had a watch out, down where the lane turns up from the marsh. Funny thing, *they* scared me a little."

"They did, did they? That's saying something. But they didn't hurt you?"

"Oh, no. I knew one of them. But I didn't much want to go back, not with three brats in tow."

"You knew one? Who?"

"You can't think I'm going to tell you?"

Hawth threw out a hand in apology. "Sorry! I'm making a right mull of things tonight. Wine's in, wit's out. But do you really know someone might take on my hellborn brats for me?"

"'Hellborn?' I like them. I'd be sorry to see them suffer. That's why—I did wonder—how much do you know of what goes on in these parts?"

"Not a great deal. Some talk gets to Brighton."

"So you know about Charles Warrender's death?"

"Yes. Damned untidy business." It had brought the heavy frown back. He drank and looked across the glass at his companion. "To tell truth, I was one of the men he lost to. The night before . . ."

"Before he killed himself."

"I'm sorry. Kin of yours. Not my fault. Fair play, and he wasn't up to it."

"No. Not your fault. But it happened. And—he had a wife and daughter."

"Yes?"

"They think—" A pause. "They think he was desperate. His son had died, lost at sea. The estate was entailed. There wasn't much to leave them. So—he played."

"And lost."

"And killed himself."

"And where does that leave the wife and daughter?"

"Penniless, Lord Hawth. The estate is entailed. Father to son, since God knows when. The heir's an American, arriving any moment to turn them out. They want to go first. Anywhere . . ."

"You can't mean?"

"Housekeeper and governess? Better than starving. Better than being beholden to a canting Philadelphia Quaker. I can't answer for them, but from what they've said to me, it might be worth your while just to go and ask."

"The Warrenders? But they're old as time and proud as the devil."

"And poor as death. I'm on my way there now. I'll speak to Mrs. Warrender if you like. Warn her to expect a visit. No harm done if you dislike each other on sight."

"Will we, do you think? What's she like, your . . . cousin, is it?"

"I'm fond of her. I doubt she's quite in your line."

Hawth laughed. "I wonder just how I should take that. A bluestocking, I collect: reads nothing but Mrs. Godwin and Mrs. More. Will she lecture me about the rights of women?"

"Visit her and find out."

"And the daughter? Another amazon? Mind you, that's what I need for those brats of mine. But they'll never do it. The Warrenders came over with the Conqueror, and everyone knows we Chyngfords are just eighteenth century dirt."

"Golden dirt. But suit yourself." Kit Warrender rose. "If you don't ask, they won't come. If you do, they might. Necessity is a hard master. I think Mrs. Warrender would give a good deal to be able to hand over the keys to the American heir and leave the house on the spot."

"Hard on him."

"You think so? Never answered a single letter. Never wrote when my—Mr. Warrender the younger was drowned; but turns up pat as bedamned when he learns he's inherited. Writes a lot of fudge about letters lost at sea, ships captured by the French."

"Well, they do, damn them," said Hawth. "How long's this war gone on? Almost twenty years, if you don't count that crazy peace in 1802. Things don't run easy, boy, not with a war on. One just about as old as you are. And now those damned Yankees taking sides with the French, lot of fuss about nothing: impressment, our right of search. Letters to the Yankee heir could easily *have* been lost."

"Yes, but if he hadn't heard something, what brought him to England so timely? Can't have it both ways, can he?"

"No. I see. Ah—" The butler had appeared to announce that Mr. Warrender's horse was waiting. "You're going to Warren House now? Give my respects to Mrs. Warrender and tell her I will do myself the honour of calling on her tomorrow. What will you tell her?"

"What should I?"

"Hell's teeth, boy, your idea. Tell her the lot. How you met those brats of mine. What a devil of a father I am. What they are. That's important, mind. Bastard brood of a jumped up earl and a bit of Bond Street ware. Tell her it all. House to rack and ruin, servants all nohow—what there are of them. All the money she wants to set things in order. Oh, my God!"

"Yes?" Politely trying to conceal impatience, Kit Warrender ran a hand through darkly curling hair. "What now?"

"The daughter. Miss Warrender. She'll set her cap at me. Bound to. They all do. God knows why."

"Something irresistible about bad temper?" suggested Kit Warrender with a gleaming eye. "Those romantic black brows of yours, *à la* Lord Byron, and your reputation? Do you write poetry, by the way?"

"No, Goddamn you! But what about it? What about the girl? Your cousin, too, I suppose?"

"Set your mind at rest." Kit Warrender held out a hand in farewell. "My Cousin Kate wouldn't have you if you were the last man on earth."

"Want to bet on it? No, I suppose not." He had caught the flash in his young guest's eye. "Got other interests, has she? Affections already engaged? Romantic young miss? Secret engagement? Pack of sentimental nonsense."

"Something of the kind," said Kit Warrender. "Visit them tomorrow, my lord, and see for yourself."

Chapter 2

"But where is she?" wailed Mrs. Warrender. "It's all very well to say, "Gone for a ride," Chilver, but where has she *gone*? And why isn't she back? It's dark, been dark for hours. She'll catch her death, or worse, out there careering about the countryside in that light habit of hers."

"Ahem." Chilver had been butler to the Warrenders ever since their marriage the year after the Bastille fell. "She's not exactly wearing her habit, ma'am, if that makes you feel happier about her. Which," thoughtfully, "maybe it should. She had Barnes saddle up with Mr. Christopher's saddle."

"Chris! She's never wearing his clothes again! Chilver, I shall have a spasm. I know it. I feel it coming."

"No you won't, ma'am," said Chilver with a kind of firm respect. "You never do, not when things is serious, you know you don't." He moved softly over to a side-table, poured a glass of cordial and handed it to her.

"And you think they're serious now?" She accepted the glass and took a sip, looking at him across it.

"I can't say I like it, ma'am. She's been gone a long time. It *is* dark. Has been, for an hour or so. She was in a proper tearer when she rode out. Well, you know that. *And* no wonder. It's enough to put anyone about. But it's not like her to worrit you. That's why . . ."

"I know," said Mrs. Warrender. "That's what's worrying me, too. Mind you." She took another hearty sip of the cordial. "I'm glad you told me she's in Christopher's clothes again, even if she did promise me she wouldn't. It does make her . . . make her seem safer, don't you think?"

"Of course it does, ma'am. She's likely down at the Bell in Glinde, like she used to go with Mr. Chris, and enjoying herself, I'll be bound. You know what Miss Kate's like, when she gets going."

She gave him a watery smile. "I do indeed, Chilver. Just the same, I wish she'd come home. She'll get into trouble one of these days, careering round the countryside like the boy she isn't. Poor lamb."

"Yes, ma'am." If he could help it, he did not mean to tell her about the rumour of a meeting in the long meadow. "She do miss Mr. Chris still, something dreadful."

"Don't we all, Chilver." A mechanical hand smoothed the heavy mourning she had worn first for her son and then for her husband, and the butler, looking with long affection at the curling, golden hair under the widow's cap, thought, as he had before, what a waste it all was.

There were many things he might have said, but in fact his head went up, listening. "There's a horse coming up the drive."

"Thank God, so there is! My goodness, won't I just give her a scold!" Mrs. Warrender hurried along the familiar maze of passages that led from her boudoir through the old wing of the house and so to the grand stairway, arriving just in time to see the heavy front door thrown open to admit her daughter. "Kate, you wicked child, how could you!" She ran downstairs as an impassive footman helped Kate Warrender out of her dead brother's many-caped greatcoat to reveal her every inch the slender country gentleman in blue coat and buckskins. "You promised me you'd never do it again!"

"I know, mamma, but I have had such an adventure. You will just have to forgive me, this once more." Half a head taller than her mother, Kate bent to place a loving kiss on her fair cheek. "You've not really been worrying, have you, darling mamma? I've had *such* a time!" A quick look for the loving, listening servants. "Come to your boudoir, and I'll tell you all about it."

"But you've not supped, child!"

"Oh, yes I have." Kate took her mother's arm and urged her up the sweeping stair. "I've been eating bachelor's fare with Lord Hawth."

"With—Kate, you're joking me." Mrs. Warrender put out a quick hand to steady herself on the banisters.

"Oh, no I'm not, mamma. Chilver—" He had been waiting, expressionless, at the top of the stair. "Has mamma got her cordial? Good. Then I'll have a bottle of the best burgundy."

"Miss Kate!"

"I've made a great discovery, Chilver. It's not wine I dislike, but claret and cordial. Father must have some good burgundy left in the cellar."

"Oh, yes, Miss Kate."

"And we don't want to waste it on the American heir, do we, Chilver, so—"

"Very good, Miss Kate." He retreated, disapproval in every line of his back.

"I ought to make you change!" In the privacy of the boudoir, Mrs. Warrender surveyed her daughter with a mixture of disapproval and resignation.

"Have a heart, love." Kate sat down and swung one elegant buckskin-clad leg over the other. "I am so comfortable like this, and I have had such an adventure, as the children would say."

"Children?"

"Lord Hawth's byblows. Oh, never blush and purse up your lips at me. You call a spade a spade when you want to. Just think of the things papa used to say. And Chris! Poor Chris!" A loving hand smoothed the neatly tied cravat that had been her brother's. "I could kill that George Warren for raking it all up again. A statement from you, indeed! What kind of difference is that going to make? There was no doubt at the time. If only there had been . . ."

"Well, of course not," said her mother sadly. "How could there be? But it was hushed up, you know it was. Your father saw to that."

"Yes indeed." Kate's eyes sparkled angrily. "After doing nothing for Chris, keeping him dangling at home without occupation, he must needs feel *himself* disgraced when his son was killed in a smugglers' affray."

"We don't *know* it was that," protested her mother.

"Naturally we don't, since father got his influential friends to make a state secret of it. Yachting accident, indeed! I'd have laughed if I could have stopped crying. Chris never went to sea but with his smuggling friends from the village. You know it as well as I do. And it was their kind of accident, too. You know. You saw the body. And I'll never forgive father for that either."

"After so long in the sea." Mrs. Warrender shuddered at the memory. "But a fight. It had to have been a fight. And his clothes . . . his watch . . . his poor face. I can give Mr. Warren the statement he wants easily enough, and you can see it would be awkward for him to have the least shadow of doubt over his claim to the estate."

"Warren!" fumed Kate. "As if Warrender wasn't good enough for him. And bringing his own man of business, too. It's an insult, mamma, to you and to Mr. Futherby. I look forward to saying a word or two to my cousin George Warren before we go."

"Oh, Kate, pray don't," begged her mother. "Besides, you know that's just the misery of it. There's nowhere *to* go. Poor papa, I am sure he would never have shot himself if he had realised that thanks to that wretched attorney even my jointure would be lost among his debts."

"I'm sure he never gave it a thought," said his daughter. "Let's not pretend with each other. You know as well as I do that he never thought of anything but himself."

"Oh, my dear." Mrs. Warrender bowed her head in the becoming widow's cap. "I do feel so dreadful that I cannot truly mourn for him. Do you know—" she put out a soft little hand to clasp her daughter's brown one—"once or twice receiving visits of condolence, I had to think of poor Chris in order to make myself shed a proper tear."

"I'm glad you told me that. Sometimes I was afraid you really were minding." Kate patted her mother's hand, rose to her feet and moved over to stand, as her brother used to, with one booted foot on the fender. "That makes everything much easier," she went on. "So you will have no objection to receiving Lord Hawth tomorrow?"

"Receiving Lord Hawth? But why should I?" Blushing with surprise, Mrs. Warrender looked hardly older than her formidable daughter.

"Object? Or receive him?"

"Well," said her puzzled mother, "both, I suppose."

"Pity," said Kate. "You didn't know. No need to have told you. But never mind. It seems Lord Hawth was one of the creditors," she explained. "He told me so, just now. He says there was no suggestion of foul play."

"Well, of course not," said Mrs. Warrender. "You know as well as I do that your father was a fool at cards."

"Yes," agreed Kate. "Chris and I used to beat him when we played for counters. He stopped playing soon enough. Said the luck was always against him."

"It always was. But, Kate, what's all this about Lord Hawth?"

"I was telling you. I met his three children on the path by the park wall. You won't believe it, mamma. They had actually found the secret tunnel, the one Chris and I used to look for. I helped them get back in." She laughed. "Lord, it was funny. Mind you, I didn't think so at the time. To tell truth, I was taken all aback. There we were, bouncing out into his study, and there *he* was waiting for us, like . . . like—" she groped for a description—"like a cross between the devil and Lord Byron."

"Good gracious! So what did you do?"

"Acted the man for all I was worth. Well, I was in good

form. The children had taken me at face value, bless their little hearts. Introduced me as Kit Warrender. No problem. He's *horrid* to them, mamma!"

"Kit Warrender, you said?"

"It all happened so fast. I didn't have time to think."

"Did he know?"

"About poor Chris? Yes. I'm afraid I said—" She smiled ruefully down at her mother. "I suggested I was in the same boat as his children."

"Kate Warrender!" Her mother drew herself up to her full five feet, reminding her daughter of nothing more than an angry kitten. "You never suggested you were one of poor papa's—" She stopped, blushing crimson.

"Byblows. That's just what I did do. Or, no, come to think of it, *not* one of papa's. I said you were my cousin. One of grandfather's lot, I suppose. Well: two of a kind, weren't they, and it's the greatest comfort that you admit it. And I will say," thoughtfully, "it does help to make my visits to the Bell possible. There seem to be so many of them. Tall young men with the Warrender nose. There must be a few girls somewhere, you'd think, but one doesn't seem to see them."

"Oh, Kate, I was such a failure as a wife."

"Nothing of the kind. Let's face it just this once, you and I. Papa was a disaster as a husband. And not much better as a father. It's a pity he left us with only my hundred a year between us and the poorhouse, but aside from that I simply cannot bring myself to mourn for him, and I don't see why you should any more than you think plain decent. You know as well as I do how much happier this house is now he's gone."

His widow nodded mutely, drying her eyes with the handkerchief her daughter had considerately left in her hand. "If only we could stay here," she said.

"And that we can't," said Kate. "Not a minute after you've handed the keys to George Warren and sworn whatever form of words he and his precious man of business have thought up. And that is why you are going to receive Lord Hawth tomorrow, mamma dear."

"You keep coming back to Lord Hawth."

"And his children. Don't forget the three byblows, mamma, and how unkind he is to them. He's out of all patience because their mother has run off with the tutor and left them on his hands. I doubt he'd have minded so much if she'd taken them with her. She sounds a dead bore of a woman to me. And an idiot. Fancy giving up Lord Hawth for the tutor. She has to be about in the head. But they're a nice lot of children. I liked them. Full of pluck. You'll dote on them, I'm sure."

"I?"

"Yes, ma'am. He's coming tomorrow to ask if you and I will come to Hawth Hall as housekeeper and governess."

"What?" It brought Mrs. Warrender to her feet, blue eyes sparkling. "He's doing *what,* Kate Warrender?"

"You heard me." From her place of vantage by the fire, Kate smiled lovingly down at her mother. "Hawth didn't think you'd be best pleased."

"Pleased! Housekeeper at Hawth Hall. Never!" And then, in explanation, "The Warrenders . . ."

"'Came over with the Conqueror.' That's what Hawth said. While the Chyngfords are nothing but eighteenth-century muck. But, think a moment. What good has being a Warrender ever done you? Besides, you're not, only by marriage. If I don't object to going as governess, why should you mind being housekeeper? At least," fiercely, "it gets us away from here. From Cousin George."

"Yes?" She thought for a moment. "Kate, dear, you can't have considered. Governess! I'd always hoped—in the end—a suitable marriage. You know, governesses don't . . ."

"I shan't marry. You must know I've seen too much of it. Besides, who should I marry? Who do I know? Father kept us cooped up . . . like . . . like a henhouse. And now Cousin George offers to introduce me to his friends—to a parcel of hawking, spitting Yankees like himself." She laughed angrily. "I collect he said that, just in case I had any idea of becoming Mrs. Warren. Lord—" the amusement was back in her voice. "Do you think he is married? Will turn up with a little dab of an American wife and expect us to introduce her into society?"

"I'm sure he's not. He would have mentioned it. And, Kate, dear, I had wondered . . ."

"If I might choose to change Warrender to Warren? What an incorrigible romantic you are! But, I thank you, no. I would rather earn my bread and scrape at Hawth Hall."

"Kate?"

"Yes?"

"You haven't . . . you can't have . . . you don't imagine . . ."

"Darling mamma," patiently. "What in the world?"

Her mother made a great effort. "Dearest, you haven't by any chance formed a *tendre* for Lord Hawth?"

"What?" Kate surprised and relieved her mother by bursting into an unladylike fit of laughter. Then, sobering up with an effort: "Don't fret. I told Lord Hawth I wouldn't marry him if he was the last man in the world."

"Kate!"

"He thinks I've formed a secret attachment. A pity, really. He offered to bet I'd set my cap at him. Stupid of me. I should have taken him: in sovereigns. Lots of them." She brightened. "Perhaps I'll pay him another visit, like this, and take his bet."

"Kate!" Her mother wailed again.

"Quite right, mamma. Not the action of a gentleman, certainly not a Warrender, even one from the wrong side of the blanket. Besides, if he's going to employ me as Kate, I think he'd better see no more of young Kit." She crossed the room to study herself in a gilt-framed looking glass. "What shall we do to make me look different tomorrow? These short crops are the devil."

"Kate!"

"Kit, if you please. I am having my last fling, mamma, before I dwindle into a governess. And here, in good time, comes Chilver with the burgundy. What happened to you, Chilver? Don't tell me you lost yourself in the cellar."

"No, Miss Kate." The butler was looking as ruffled as his

training would permit. "I was delayed. There was a person came to the back door asking questions. About you, Miss Kate."

"Questions?"

"If you'd had a guest here. A Mr. Kit Warrender. He wanted to speak to him. I said, yes, a gentleman had called, for a moment, but was gone. I said I did not know where he lived. I let it be seen that it was a matter I did not wish to discuss." Chilver was at his most stately, as he remembered the well-administered set-down. Then, human again: "I hope I did right, miss?"

"Quite right, Chilver. Thank you. But—what kind of a person? A servant, do you think? From the hall, maybe?"

"Oh, no, miss." Surprised. "Quite a rough fellow it was. A stranger. From London, I'd think, by his talk, or maybe even from farther north. Miss—" he had moved a mahogany wine table to her elbow and now poured wine into her glass—"you didn't come through the long meadow tonight?"

"No." She sipped, smiled her approval, and looked up at him thoughtfully. "I was—advised not to."

"By whom, if I may ask?"

"I think, best not." They were old friends, and the refusal held a note of apology. "Smugglers, I thought. I said we needed some tea. You might let me know if it comes, Chilver."

"It has," said Chilver. "He brought it. The stranger."

"Ah." It was a sigh of relief. "Then that's all right."

"Well, is it?" He had been debating whether to tell her this. "It's not the tea we generally have. That had come earlier in the evening. And before we expected it, too."

"Oh?" She thought about it for a moment, then went off at an apparent tangent. "The lights were on as usual at the Tidemills. You've not heard of more trouble there?"

"Not to say trouble, miss. Not more than usual, but they're not happy. I'd be lying if I said they were. Well, you know how it is, as well as anyone. Better than most. Times are hard, thanks to Boney. *And* those non-importing Americans. Prices high, wages bad. It was one thing when they had something to hope for down at the Tidemills. You'd be surprised what expectations was built on Mr. Chris, and then on you after he died. But Lord Hawth, he's another story. It was a bad day for the district when poor Mr. Warrender lost the mill to him. And he with no more sense than to go bullying down with talk of mass dismissals if trade don't look up."

"He's never done that?"

"Today."

"Stupid of him." And then, thoughtfully. "And the odd thing is, he's many things . . . a bully, oh, yes, but—stupid? I'd not have said so." She smiled at the butler. "Thank you for telling me, Chilver. We are expecting a call from Lord Hawth tomorrow. On my mother and Miss Warrender, of course. If he should happen to ask after the young kinsman who called here tonight, you will tell him he has left."

"Yes, miss." If Chilver was bursting with curiosity, he hid it well behind his impassive, butler's face.

"Lord, this is going to be a nuisance!" Kate was sitting at her mother's dressing table next morning while Mrs. Warrender enjoyed the luxury of breakfast in bed.

"What are you doing?"

"Plaiting my nut-brown hair. *Wasn't* it a good thing I saved it! There, mamma!" She turned round triumphantly. "Don't I look the most respectable Miss Trimmer that ever dragoned it in a ducal household?"

"Good God!" Mrs. Warrender looked at her daughter with undisguised horror. "Kate, you can't!"

"Oh, can't I!" She shook her head without disturbing the plaits she had pinned to hide every curl of her fashionable Brutus cut. "Admit it's a transformation!" Her mother groaned. "And only fancy my having kept such a dowd of a dress! I think I must have been ashamed even to give it away. This dun colour was all the rage Walcheren year, as I remember, and, mamma, just look at the quiz of a train. I do hope Lord Hawth is knowledgeable enough to know what a figure of fun I am."

"He'll know all right," wailed her mother.

"That's what I think. Now, I must go and warn the servants, or one of them is bound to betray me with a fit of the whoops."

"But, dearest, must you?"

"Indeed, I must. It's the children I'm afraid of. My lord was bosky enough to be no danger, but they are a sharp little set. Lucky for me they only saw me for a moment in the full light, and then they were well and truly minding their formidable papa. Besides, think a little. Now you agree we want to go to the hall—and I am so glad you do!" She crossed the room to give her mother an encouraging kiss across the breakfast tray. "We must apply our minds to getting the places. No use thinking we can make a dragon of you, love, so we must just do the best we can with me."

"Best!" moaned her mother.

"Let's hope that Lord Hawth has not already decided to cry off," said Kate, removing the breakfast tray and handing her mother the latest issue of *La Belle Assemblée*. "But whatever else he is, I take him for a man of his word."

Lord Hawth had indeed suffered from a good many regrets as he let his valet help him into impeccable morning dress instead of his usual country dress of riding coat and buckskins. "Trousers?" he considered his man's offering thoughtfully. "Do you think the old tartar will take me for a blood-red revolutionary? Well, maybe so much the better. The line is the Brummel look, I think. Quiet elegance, and the very best linen."

"Yes, my lord. But, if I may say so, your figure quite outshines poor Mr. Brummel's."

"Go to hell," said his lordship.

The carriage was stuffy. Morning calls were the devil. But his breakfast steak had been burned again, and Parsons had said something anxious about the children not eating their bread and water. He resigned himself to the interminable jouncing of the carriage ride. No use spoiling everything by swaggering in to call on the old dragon like a young blood, hot and sweating from driving his own curricle.

At Warren House he was obviously expected. The park, as he drove through it, had shown clear signs of neglect and of financial stringency: a wall collapsing here, a dead tree lying there and the shaws full of shaggy undergrowth. At the house itself it was a different story. Here, too, his quick, landlord's eye saw shabby paint and neglected pointing round the Tudor windows, but there was nothing shabby about the servants who received him. Could Parsons have held his own with the stately butler who was now conducting him to Mrs. Warrender's apartments? He wished his young friend of last night might be there, so they could have a bet on it.

But there were only two ladies in the comfortable, sunlit room into which the butler ushered him, and, looking at them, he wondered if he could have made some kind of amazing mistake. But, no, there could be no doubt about it. The tiny one in the heavy mourning, who was smiling at him, and blushing, and holding out a timid hand must be Mrs. Warrender. He remembered, now, with a silent curse, something sardonically gleaming in his companion's eye last night when he had described Mrs. Warrender as an old battleaxe. Well, no wonder. She did not look capable of scaring a kitten.

The daughter was something else again. Tall and handsomely built, she might, he thought, have been quite good-looking if she had made the slightest push at it, but her tightly braided hair and dun-coloured, outmoded dress made her almost a figure of fun. No wonder young Kit had looked so quizzical last night. It must be Miss Warrender, not her mother, who set up for a bluestocking. Well, so much the better. She did look as if she might be capable of knocking some sense into his three ramshackle children.

But could the shy little widow who could not get beyond a stammered, "Good morning, my lord," set his house in order? He very much doubted it. She looked incapable of saying boo to a goose, still less dealing with a good-for-nothing parcel of spoiled servants. His dark brows drew together in an unconscious frown as he bowed over the outstretched hand. A wasted errand. The devil could fly away with the children, but he must have some comfort at Hawth Hall now he was committed to living there.

Watching him, Kate saw and understood the frown. Presented to Lord Hawth by her mother, she held out an ungracious hand. "How do you do, my lord," she said. "You are thinking you have come on a fool's errand."

"I beg your pardon?" He gave her the look that had invariably reduced his mistress to tears.

Smiling, Miss Warrender was almost handsome. "And I yours. Should we have talked sweet nothings for ten minutes before we came down to business? It seems a waste of time to me. You are come for your own purposes and we are receiving you for ours. Why beat about the bush? Mrs. Godwin says facts should be faced, and I, for one, agree with her. Our fact is that we need employment, yours that you need a housekeeper and a governess. You are thinking that I am an odd sort of plain young lady who might not be able to teach your daughters the social graces, and that my mamma looks too gentle to keep order at the hall."

It was so exactly what he had been thinking that he actually found himself at a loss what to say, and favoured her with another quelling glance instead.

"Quite so," she said, as if he had spoken. "So how shall we set about convincing you that you are wrong?" She moved with a kind of angry grace across to an open piano. "Shall I favour you with my rendering of Herr Von Beethoven's newest sonata? No? You are perhaps not musical, my lord? How old are your children?" She asked it, surprising him, in Parisian French.

"The oldest, a girl, sixteen; the boy, twelve; little Harriet, ten." He retaliated in kind.

"Quite a little family." She switched to German. "The boy will need a tutor, I should think. My Latin is not bad, but I'm afraid I have no Greek."

"I shall advertise for a tutor." He said it in English, since, though he could understand German, he did not feel able to equal her pronunciation. Hoyden of a girl. And yet . . ."My daughters have plenty of airs and graces," he said. "It's backbone they lack. Discipline. Strength of character."

She surprised him again with a graceful curtsy. "And you think I might be able to inculcate those? I thank you for the compliment, my lord. I would do my poor best, though I should perhaps warn you that I have views about the position of women in society."

"I dare swear you have." He did not want to hear them, and turned pointedly to her mother. "But, Mrs. Warrender, forgive me." Despite himself his tone softened somewhat at the sight of the slender figure in its heavy mourning. "You have suffered a series of terrible misfortunes. Your bereavement is so recent. I was so sorry—" He had had a phrase of condolence ready-polished but the tartar of a daughter had got in first, and it came out awkwardly enough now, irritating him still further.

But the widow was smiling gratefully up at him as if he had done it just right. "You are very kind," she said. "It's been . . . a bad time." She produced a lacy scrap of handkerchief. Devil take her, was she going to cry?

She looked at the handkerchief thoughtfully and put it away again. "Are things very bad up at the hall?" she asked with a kind of shy sympathy.

"All to pieces." And then, angrily: "You've heard talk!"

"Forgive me! But my—" she stopped, exchanged a glance with her daughter and went on again—'my young kinsman said something. Just what you told him yourself. And then, I'm afraid, servants will talk."

"Servants?"

"Well," she blushed. "You're quite a stranger here, are you not, my lord?"

"What's that to the purpose?"

He was beginning to remind her painfully of her dead husband, who had often taken an equally impatient tone with her. But Kate wanted to get away from Warren House. She would do anything for Kate. She managed a tremulous smile. "You perhaps do not know that your butler and mine are first cousins?"

"Good God!" It forced an explosive laugh out of him. "I was just wishing that that young rascal of a Kit was here so I could wager him my Parsons could outbuttle your man any day."

"You'd lose your money." Her smile strengthened. "My Chilver is the older by several years. Perhaps you should ask him, my lord, whether I am able to hold housekeeping."

Like her daughter, she had surprised him by this insight into his doubts, but he found it more pardonable in her. "To tell truth," he said, "I had been wondering if it would not be too hard a task for you to bring things about at the hall. We are all at sea, I am afraid."

"I know," she said sympathetically. "A hogshead of strong and one of mild ale every day in the servants' hall, and I don't know how many dozen of wine. And best candles burning for their dinner! When Chilver told me that, I quite longed to pack my things and come at once. It's beyond permission! Oh dear!" She quailed at the furious look he bent on her. "I'm sorry. I didn't mean . . ."

"Servants' gossip," he said awfully. "You know more about my household than I do, it seems, ma'am. How long do you think Parsons will keep his position after this?"

"Oh, my lord, you couldn't!" In her horror she jumped to her feet. "It's entirely my fault, don't you see! Chilver and I have been friends for ever—since I came here as a bride. Of course he tells me things, and of course I asked him. Oh, please, my lord—" She gave up, quelled by his frown.

"You think, I take it, that I should make a friend of Parsons?"

She received it, as he had intended her to, as the most crushing of set-downs and began a pitiful "Forgive me," but was interrupted by her daughter.

"One can only ask oneself," said Miss Warrender, "whether Parsons would choose to make a friend of you."

"Kate!" Mrs. Warrender was suddenly and surprisingly dignified. "You will apologise to our guest at once."

"I will apologise to *you,* mamma." And then, with the smile that changed her face: "And to our guest, since you bid me. Forgive me, my lord." Another sweeping curtsy. "I am afraid I forgot myself. You will think me quite unsuitable now to teach your daughters manners."

It was indeed what he had been thinking and once again her quickness increased his anger. He rose to his feet, acknowledged her curtsy with a stiff bow, and turned to her mother, who was holding the lacy handkerchief again. "I am afraid I have wasted too much of your time, ma'am."

"Oh, dear," she said. "You don't want us. I can't bear to think of all those good candles . . ."

"Lord Hawth would prefer his discomforts to our company, mamma," said Miss Warrender. "We have not had a chance to explain to him that we would prefer to live in the Dower House."

"The Dower House?" he exclaimed. "What the devil do you know about the Dower House?"

"My lord." Her tone was tolerant. "It's plain to see you haven't lived much in the country. If you really propose to set up house at the hall you had best resign yourself to the fact that everyone in the district knows all about you, and always will. As to the Dower House, it's only common sense. If you were, for a moment, to entertain the idea of employing my mother and me, you most certainly would not wish to sit down at table with us every day, and you can hardly expect Mrs. Warrender to eat in the servants' hall. Or had you some idea of neat little trays in the housekeeper's room? The whole arrangement would cause talk enough in the district without our doing anything so idiotic as that. But I can see you have quite made up your mind against us. How are the children today? Pining on bread and water?" And then, throwing up a hand as his look blackened; "No, my lord, not servants' gossip; woman's intuition. Or do you like that less?"

"I don't like any part of it." The frown was heavier than ever.

"And no more do I." Surprisingly, Mrs. Warrender spoke up. "It was an absurd idea from the first. I cannot think why

I entertained it for an instant. I am afraid, my lord, you will have to make the best you can of bad children and spoiled dinners. I am sorry for the children, mind you. You cannot really be keeping them on bread and water? It's very bad for them, at that growing age." She rose with a little air of dignity that silenced him. "It was good of you to call, my lord. I am only sorry to have wasted so much of your valuable time. Yes, Chilver?"

"Ma'am." The butler actually looked human. "Mr. Warren is here."

"Mr. Warren?"

"Yes, he begs you will forgive him for arriving somewhat before his time. Oh!" Badly shaken now, "Here *is* Mr. Warren."

"Well!" She had no time to comment on the failure of manners that had brought the young American so hard on the butler's heels. They all three turned to look at the young man who was advancing with friendly hand outstretched. He was worth looking at. For one spellbound instant Lord Hawth caught Miss Warrender's eye, saw it sparkle, and wondered if she was quite the pillar of salt he had thought her. Mr. Warren had done his best for this, his first appearance in the home he had so surprisingly inherited. He must have combed London, Hawth thought wryly, to have found a tailor who would outfit him at once so expensively and in such deplorable taste. Where in the world had he found the material for the appalling black-and-white checked trousers? And as if they were not bad enough, he wore a grey coat and striped lemon-and-white waistcoat with them. Tall and handsomely built, but fair-haired, fair-skinned and blue-eyed, he looked like nothing more than a schoolboy who had helped himself at random from his father's wardrobe.

"Mrs. Warrender." The young American seized her hand and shook it warmly. "And my Cousin Kate." He turned towards her, but her hand was somehow not available. Withdrawing his own and looking a little foolish, he turned back to Mrs. Warrender. "I trust you will forgive me, ma'am, for coming on you unawares, and before my time like this, but I thought it my duty, in view of the news."

"News?" asked Mrs. Warrender, puzzled. And then, remembering her manners; "Allow me to present you to our neighbour, Lord Hawth. Our kinsman, my lord, Mr. Warren."

"Warren?" Lord Hawth's black brows rose. Here, too, there was no hand to be shaken. "I thought you were the heir in tail."

"Why, so I am." An apologetic glance for the two ladies as he coloured more highly than ever. "Oh, you mean the name. My grandfather changed it at the time of the Revolution. He was a true blue patriot and thought that Warrender smacked something of the aristocratic. Besides, there was a Warren came over on the *Mayflower,* I believe."

"Your American aristocracy?" asked Kate drily.

"Well, in a way." He looked from one face to the other, visibly taken aback by their cool greeting, and finally came back to Mrs. Warrender. "I take it you have not heard the news then?"

"What news, Mr. Warren?"

"I wish you will call me George."

"For Mr. Washington?" asked Kate.

"Of course." He was beginning to understand. "You think me an interloper. I am sorry. I had hoped . . . And I am afraid the news I bring will make matters worse."

"Perhaps if you were to tell us this news of yours," suggested Lord Hawth.

"I'm afraid it looks very much like war," said George Warren.

"War! But my dear fellow, we have been at war since 1803. Since 1793 really." Lord Hawth's tone was so patronising that the young man coloured more hotly than ever.

"With France! Of course! Everyone knows that! What brought me hurrying to my cousins' side was the news that war between America and England is all too likely."

"And we are supposed to lose sleep over that?" asked Lord

Hawth. "Surely you Colonials will not be so foolish as to risk a visit from our navy? Your seaboard cities would be in ruins before you had time to beg for terms."

"That's not just what happened last time, sir. Have you forgotten Yorktown? It almost seems you must have. I tell you, your Orders in Council are more than can be borne. You are driving us into the arms of the Emperor Napoleon." He pronounced it French fashion.

"And a very uncomfortable bed-fellow you'll find that jumped up Bonaparte. But why all the drama? What, if one may ask, has happened?"

"There's been a sea fight, sir—my lord—between our ship the *President* and your *Little Belt.* I'm afraid the *Little Belt* came off very much the worse."

"Afraid! Are you boasting, Mr. Warren?"

"Boasting! I'm warning Mrs. Warrender that I fear it may come to war between our two countries."

"And American troops will land in Glinde Bay and ravish her and her daughter in their beds? They must be deeply grateful, Mr. Warren, that you have come so swiftly to their protection. Or will you be guiding your ships to land?"

"Sir! Do you mean to insult me?"

"By no means!" Lord Hawth's tone was mocking. "I would surely never dare. Besides, as, I hope, a friend of these ladies, I must be grateful to you for your gallant offer of protection, even if I am not entirely certain of the need for it."

"It's not the Americans I fear," said George Warren, "as you must know as well as I, but the French. What of those camps the Emperor has at Boulogne? What of an invasion like the one you feared in 1804? I've heard alarming stories since I've been in London. Stories that an American is more likely to hear than an English lord. Stories of food and tithe riots. Of mobs setting their own price for bread."

"Mobs," said Lord Hawth reflectively. "You Americans are expert in mob rule, are you not? You look, I take it, for what you expect to find."

"At least I look," said the young American. "Lord Hawth."

Thoughtfully. "Of course. You own the Tidemills here in the valley. I'd watch for trouble there, my lord. My postilion said something, driving down."

"Your postilion?" Lord Hawth's tone was withering. "And what did the boots say at the hotel where you racked up for the night?"

Mercifully they were interrupted by Chilver with light refreshments and an apologetic aside for Mrs. Warrender. "Ma'am, Mr. Warren's man of business is in the study. He says he would be wishful to start back to town as soon as is possible."

"Oh!" said Mrs. Warrender.

"Forehanded of you, Mr. Warren," said Kate. "But I am afriad your man of business will just have to cool his heels while my mother sends for hers. You cannot imagine that she is going to give you the statement you so unreasonably demand, without her own representative being present. You would have done better to give us notice of your coming."

"So I am beginning to understand." His anger had risen to match hers. He turned, with a passable bow, to Mrs. Warrender. "My apologies, ma'am, for this unlucky intrusion. I saw a reasonable looking inn in Glinde—the Bell, I think. My man of business and I will await your pleasure there."

"Nothing of the kind," said Mrs. Warrender with unusual spirit. "This is your house, Mr. Warren. Your rooms will be ready for you by now, I have no doubt. As to any awkwardness . . ." She took a deep breath. "I think, Kate, you and I would be well advised to accept Lord Hawth's kind invitation." There was appeal in the quick look she flashed up at her first guest.

"Delighted," said he, gallantly concealing amazement.

Chapter 3

"Well, Mamma." Next morning Kate looked up, laughing, from the trunk she was packing. "I never thought you had it in you."

"Neither did I!" Mrs. Warrender laughed and blushed. "But what could I do? Much more of that kind of talk, and it would have been pistols for two. And I could *not* have it said that I had let the American heir get himself killed the first day he was here."

"Indeed no, even the second day would have been bad enough! And killed he would have been, no doubt about that. I'm sure Lord Hawth is a devil of a marksman. But tell me, how did you leave things, you and he? I was too busy with poor 'Call Me George' to hear what you were saying."

"And I was glad of it," said Mrs. Warrender. "I felt fool enough as it was. Imagine the effrontery of inviting ourselves to stay with that poor man."

"Well, he asked for it," said Kate. "But are we going as guests, mamma dear, or as housekeeper and governess?"

"I'm not quite sure," said her mother.

"On approval, perhaps. Like goods one orders from town and rather thinks one will not like when they get here?" She lifted a velvet pelisse from its shelf and folded it carefully. "You did burn our bridges with a vengeance, didn't you? What shall we do if we don't suit?"

"God knows," said Mrs. Warrender.

Her man of business, Mr. Futherby, rode up to the house before the last trunk was packed. He had already made clear his distaste for the whole affair, but as Kate said, he was not on very good ground, since it was his carelessness that had left Mrs. Warrender's jointure exposed to the demands of her husband's creditors. He listened now with patent disapproval while she made the statement the heir and his attorney, Mr. Coombe, had demanded as to the identification of her dead son. "Of course it was Chris," she said at last, breaking down into tears. "Who else could it have been?"

"There, mamma." Kate put a loving arm around her. "It is all over now, and Lord Hawth has been so good as to send his carriage for us. And a waggon for the luggage." She held out a cool hand to George Warren. "Good-bye, Mr. Warren. You will apply to us if we can be of service to you in any way. So far as the business of the estate is concerned, Mr. Futherby will be your guide. Come, mamma."

Left alone in the elegant if slightly shabby drawing room that was now his, George Warren turned savagely on his man of business. "You've given me nothing but bad advice from the start. And look what it has brought me to! As for that tailor you recommended! I cannot think why I did not realise sooner what a no-hope he was. Your cousin, perhaps?" He looked gloomily down at the disastrous black-and-white checked trousers. "You should just have seen Miss Warrender's expression when I was shown in. The glance she exchanged with that aristocratic friend of theirs! Well, no wonder!" He turned to Futherby, who had been making a little business of collecting his papers together at the other end of the room. "Mr. Futherby!"

"Sir?"

"Is there a tailor nearer than London? One who won't make a figure of fun of me?"

"Well—" Much though he disliked the whole business, Futherby had actually begun to find himself feeling sorry for the young American. "Mr. Warrender—*and* Mr. Chris—used sometimes to go to a man in Brighton. In an emergency, you understand."

"And this is most certainly that! You have his direction?"

The attorney smiled greyly. "I paid the bills. And, in that connection, I should warn you, I think, that he takes advantage of his position as the only man who can cut a coat this side of London."

"You mean his prices are high?"

"Quite shocking. And, I am afraid, there is worse."

"Worse?"

Mr. Futherby took out a smuggled bandanna handkerchief and mopped his sweating brow. "It's all happened so fast," he said. "No proper notice. Forgive me, sir." With a sideways glance for Coombe. "I have not even the figures to show you yet, but I think I should warn you that it is a sadly encumbered estate you are inheriting. And as for Snipe, the tailor . . . I am afraid there are a few bills still." He came to an uncomfortable halt.

"Outstanding?" said George Warren helpfully.

"Well, yes, sir. It seemed best to pay up where it would most immediately affect the ladies."

"Quite right. I wanted to ask you about their position. As to Snipe, if you will let me have his bills this evening, I'll ride in to Brighton tomorrow, settle them, and order myself some clothes I won't blush to be seen in. He'll make fast, I take it."

"For a consideration."

"Of course."

"But Mr. Warren!" Coombe had been dancing up and down on the sidelines of this conversation, trying in vain to get a word in. "You must not be settling the Warrenders' bills. And besides, you heard what Mr. Futherby said. What will you settle them with?"

"That, Mr. Coombe, is my affair. I have known you now, for, let me think, seven days. You have given me a great deal of advice and, so far as I can see, all of it has been bad. Thanks to you, I have made a fool of myself, alienated the relatives I wished to befriend, and look very much like losing my whole staff of servants. I've noticed their black looks, if you have not. Perhaps they will begin to think a little better of me when they see you pack your traps and start back to London."

"What?" Coombe was gobbling with surprise and anger.

"You heard me, Mr. Coombe. It's about time you listened to me. You have not asked me a single question, or listened to anything I said since we met. You have, in fact, treated me like the schoolboy I look. Well," ruefully, "my fault. I've behaved like him! In a strange country one goes carefully, takes advice, listens to one's friends. And you were all I had. To have made such a mull of things for me, you have to be either knave or fool. I want neither in my employment." He crossed the room and gave a firm pull at the bellrope that hung by the door. It was his first gesture as master of the house, and they were all three very much aware of it.

So was Chilver, who appeared almost at once. "Yes, sir?" His impassive countenance betrayed nothing of the furious discussion that was raging belowstairs.

"Ah, Chilver." George Warren had an attractive smile and a quick ear for names. "Mr. Coombe is leaving for London at once. Will you be so good as to have his things packed for him and order out the carriage." And then, on a comic note of doubt and appeal: "I suppose there *is* a carriage, Chilver?"

"Oh, yes, sir, two. Mrs. Warrender didn't take hers, you see. Lord Hawth sent for her."

"Good God!" He turned to Futherby, who was clearing his throat unhappily. "You don't mean to tell me I even own Mrs. Warrender's carriage?"

"You own everything," interposed Coombe with satisfaction. "I doubt if the ladies were entitled to take away so much as their bits and pieces. *As* I would have said, had I been consulted. And all through the careless drafting of Mr. Futherby here."

"So you have told me several times. I begin to think there are worse things than carelessness. Chilver, have Mrs. Warrender's carriage and horses sent after her to Hawth Hall with my compliments and apologies, and order out the other one to set Mr. Coombe on his way to London. He can hire in Glinde, I take it?"

"Yes, sir."

"Good. Add the expenses to your account, Coombe, and, good-bye."

"You'll regret this!" But Coombe found himself being inexorably shown the door by Chilver.

"So much for that." Warren turned with a smile to Futherby. "Now pray be seated, Mr. Futherby, and tell me all about this carelessness of yours. I do feel there has to be some kind of explanation."

"Of course there is." Futherby had watched the foregoing scene with a great deal of interest. "But Mrs. Warrender has been too kind to ask, and, to tell truth, I hardly liked to tell her."

"Mr. Warrender, eh?"

"Yes, sir. A very strong-minded man. Liked things done his way, and fast. I shouldn't have given way to him, Mr. Warren. You don't need to tell me that, and no one can blame me more than I do myself. But it was that or he would take his business away. And, truly, Mr. Warren, I was anxious for Mrs. Warrender . . . with a stranger . . . it might have been so much worse. And it was just for a few days, you see! How could I imagine what was going to happen!"

"How indeed! Does Mrs. Warrender know how bad things are?"

"Well, not entirely, or I am sure she would not have taken a stitch of clothing with her. Still less Miss Kate. They left all their jewels. Told me to give them to you when they were gone."

"Oh Jehosaphat!" His tone belied the mild phrase. "What the devil am I to do about that, Futherby?"

"No use sending them after, I'm afraid. It will be a miracle if Mrs. Warrender accepts the carriage. Or rather, she might, but I bet you any odds Miss Kate won't."

"Strong-minded is she? She certainly looks it. Ah." The door had opened to reveal Chilver and a footman bearing refreshments. "Thank you, Chilver. Perhaps you would be so good as to see that Mr. Coombe has something in his room before he goes."

"Very good, sir."

Alone with Futherby, Warren poured wine for them both. "One bridge crossed, I fancy. It looks as if I am not to lose my staff after all." He raised his glass. "May I toast my new man of business, Mr. Futherby?"

"Thank you, sir." The attorney gave him a straight look. "I'd be proud. Just so long as it don't conflict with Mrs. Warrender's interest."

"We'll see that it doesn't," said George Warren.

As Lord Hawth's old-fashioned carriage bowled up the long drive through Hawth Park, Mrs. Warrender's spirits sank visibly, and when they turned a corner to see the huge, ugly stone house looming before them she clutched her daughter's hand. "I must have been out of my mind!"

"Not a bit of it." Kate gallantly fought down her own qualms in order to comfort her mother. "Just much braver than usual. After all, we *could not* have stayed as guests of that . . . that . . . " She paused, vainly searching for a phrase.

"Your cousin, Kate," reminded her mother.

"Well removed, thank God. Now we have seen him, we must be grateful his father chose to change the family name." She choked suddenly with laughter. "Oh, Mamma, *wasn't* he a sight! I shall never forget Chilver's face as he showed him in. Do you think the servants have left in a body by now?"

"I do hope not. I urged Chilver not to, but I must confess I have my doubts. Poor young man, one cannot help but feel a little sorry for him."

"I cannot imagine why," said Kate. "Well, here we are. And at the front entrance I am glad to see."

"Well, I should hope so," said Mrs. Warrender, preparing to alight.

They were expected. Two footmen in shabby livery had flung open the big double doors at the head of a shelving flight of stone steps, and inside the butler waited to receive them in his immaculate black.

"How are you, Parsons?" Mrs. Warrender gave him her friendly smile. "Chilver sends his kind regards."

"Thank you, ma'am." The smallest hint of a reciprocal smile flickered across his face. "His lordship is awaiting you in the study."

"Oh?" Doubtfully. She had hoped for a moment to remove her bonnet and shawl and collect her wits.

"He leaves almost at once for London, ma'am." It was something between an apology and an explanation.

"Oh," she said again, and they followed him down a long, dark hall to the room Kate remembered so well.

Hawth was seated at his big, mahogany desk, writing busily, but rose when Parsons opened the door and ushered them in. "Welcome to Hawth Hall." He was in riding clothes, which suited him better, Kate thought, than yesterday's morning dress. Seating herself beside her mother on a faded damask sofa, she listened with reserve to the formal apology he was making. He had been summoned urgently to London. They must forgive him for playing the part of an absentee host. But perhaps in his absence Mrs. Warrender would have time to decide whether she really felt able to take on the formidable task of setting his household to rights. "You see now what it is like." An expressive glance flashed from cobwebbed cornice to shabby curtains. "And the servants the same. I shall be in London for the inside of a week. When I return, I hope you will tell me you can set all to rights for me."

"Everything?"

"Everything that needs it. I am contemplating marriage."

"But the lady—"

"No." He turned to Kate and changed the subject. "Miss Warrender, I have to ask a favour of you." He did not enjoy doing it. "The children . . . They seem to miss that nurse of theirs. Parsons tells me Harriet is not well."

"You've not seen them?"

"I?" Surprised. "No. They are in disgrace, and rightly so. Besides, what use am I to them?"

"I don't know." She looked at him thoughtfully. "Are they still on bread and water?"

He shrugged. "I don't know. I have not countermanded the order, but what those servants of mine are doing is another matter."

"Well, I declare!" Mrs. Warrender jumped to her feet. "If that isn't just like a man. Little Harriet—she is the youngest?—ill, and you don't even know if she is being fed! If you will excuse us, we will go to her at once. But first, if I may, I would like to give you my answer, my lord. What is the use of waiting a week to give it when, frankly, we have no option but to stay. I would say I was grateful to you for having us, were it not that you so evidently need us. And now, if you will have us shown to the children's rooms?"

"Immediately." He could hardly have looked more surprised, Kate thought, if one of the chairs had answered him back. But then, she was quite surprised herself. He had rung the bell, now turned back to her mother. "Knowles, my bailiff, will wait on you in the morning to take your orders."

"Orders?"

"For setting first the Dower House and then this barracks in order. He tells me the Dower House can be made habitable in a few days, but it must be done to your wishes."

"Oh." Now he had amazed her. "Thank you. But—this house—you will wish to be consulted."

"I? Good God, no." The door had opened. "Parsons, the ladies wish to visit the children. You will take care of them in my absence. Your servant, Mrs. Warrender, Miss Warrender. I shall hope to find you comfortably installed in the Dower House when I return."

"Well—" began Mrs. Warrender, safe outside the door.

"Hush!" said Kate.

And, "This way, ma'am," said Parsons.

The nursery wing was as far as possible from the study, and Kate found herself wondering if they would ever find their way back. "How is Miss Harriet?" she asked Parsons as he led the way down yet another long corridor.

"She's right down poorly, miss." He was suddenly human. "I'm glad you ladies have come and no mistake. Mrs. Simmonds, the nurse, had been with them all their life. She was—well, in some ways I reckon she was more of a ma to them *than* their ma. Stands to reason Miss Harriet's fretting. Of course his lordship don't understand."

"No. He wouldn't. Where's Mrs. Simmonds now?"

He turned to flash her a startled glance of complete understanding. "At Glinde, miss. She sent this morning to ask how they were."

"Good."

"Not very." His tone was a warning. "He won't have her back, miss, not nohow. What he does, he stands by."

"Very inconvenient," said Kate.

"But laudable in a way," said her mother.

The day nursery was a large, sunlit room with faded carpet and chintzes, and a huge antique rocking horse. When Parsons opened the door, Giles was riding listlessly on the rocking horse, while Sue sat on the window seat, deep in a book. They both looked up in surprise as Parsons ushered the two strange ladies into the room. "Miss Sue and Mr. Giles," he told Mrs. Warrender. And to the children: "It's Mrs. and

Miss Warrender, come to look after you." And then, on a much more human note; "How's Miss Harriet?"

"Asleep, I think." Sue looked wan and anxious, but made a graceful curtsy to the two ladies. Then, "Warrender?" she asked eagerly. "Are you—are you, perhaps, related to Kit Warrender?"

"Yes, dear." Mrs. Warrender bent to surprise her with a quick kiss. "Quite closely. He told us about you. That's partly why we have come."

"I'm so glad. We're worried about Harriet, Giles and I, aren't we, Giles?"

"Well, you are." He had descended from the rocking horse to make a somewhat ungracious bow. "I think we can do very well without old Simmonds. She does nothing but fuss."

"That's not a very pretty way to talk," said Kate, and met a black, challenging glance, very like his father's. It was odd how differently one got treated if one braided one's hair and dressed like a dowd. "Take us to Harriet, Sue?"

This won her a quick look of haughty surprise. Had Sue expected to be addressed as Miss Chyngford? But she put down her book and led the way through an inner door to the night nursery. "We were out late the other night," she explained, "and Harriet caught cold. She always does." She made it sound as if it was the child's fault.

"I see." Mrs. Warrender sat down by the bed where Harriet lay, flushed, snuffling and half asleep. "Good day, Harriet. We have come to help you get better." A gentle hand was on the child's hot forehead. "Yes, quite a cold, poor little thing. Parsons—" he had, surprisingly, lingered in the day nursery—"we need a doctor."

"I was afraid so, ma'am."

"Will Lord Hawth have left yet?"

"He was in a great hurry, ma'am."

"Yes. And of course he has no medical man of his own, being a stranger in these parts. So, if you will, Parsons, send a man to Dr. Thatchem in Glinde. My compliments, and I would be grateful if he would come at once." The child muttered something that sounded like "Simmonds." "Do you know where Mrs. Simmonds is staying, Parsons?"

"Yes, ma'am." He was looking at her with more and more respect.

"Then have her fetched. Or, better still, ask Dr. Thatchem to bring her in his coach. I won't waste time writing a note. He'll do it for me. And in the meantime, a fire in here, please, and I think I had best come with you and see what I can find by way of a tisane for the child. How long since there has been a housekeeper here, Parsons?"

He looked gloomy. "Board wages, ma'am."

"Quite so. Kate, dear, you stay here and see she does not uncover herself. I am afraid there is some inflammation on the chest. Sue will help you, I know, and Giles will come for me if necessary."

"Yes, mamma," said Kate meekly, taking off her bonnet and replacing her mother on the chair by the bed. And then, with a wicked smile, "I trust Lord Hawth *has* left!"

"I've no time for him now," said her mother.

All through that exhausting day, Kate watched her mother with amazement. What had happened to the timid wife who used to break into silent tears at the first cross word from her irascible spouse, and who had postponed every decision to his better judgment?

The doctor arrived at noon, bringing with him Nurse Simmonds, a buxom young woman with a roving eye and an instant, loving hug for little Harriet.

"We'll have you better in no time, my precious, you see if we don't." She looked a quick question from the doctor to Mrs. Warrender.

"The child really does need nursing," said Dr. Thatchem. "I'll apply a blister. She'll need constant care. Best from someone she's used to."

"Of course," said Mrs. Warrender. "I will explain to Lord Hawth when he returns."

Leaving Mrs. Simmonds once more in charge of the nursery, she proceeded to a whirlwind inspection of the house that left the small staff of servants awed and shaken. She was upstairs in the big linen room, looking for sheets fit for use on her and Kate's beds, when Parsons appeared to announce the arrival of her carriage, and give her George Warren's message. She stood for a moment, thinking. "Civil of him," she said at last. "I think it would be discourteous to send it back. Ask the man to wait, Parsons, while I write a note."

The result of this was the arrival, towards evening, of Parsons' daughter Betty, whom Mrs. Warrender had been training as housemaid at Warren House. Warren had sent her in his remaining carriage as soon as it returned from taking Coombe to Glinde, and the carriage was accompanied by a grinning stable-boy, riding Boney.

"Mamma, we can't!" Kate, who had protested in vain against the acceptance of the carriage, was angry now. "I won't ride him," she said.

"Then he'll be a great nuisance to Lord Hawth." Her mother had been reading the note Betty had brought. "Don't fret, child, it's not a gift, it's a loan. He asks what use he would have for a lady's horse, and begs you will exercise him."

"That just shows how ignorant he is," said Kate crossly. "Boney's no lady's horse."

"And sometimes I think you're no lady," said her mother. "You will be ruled by me in this, Kate, and if you refuse to exercise Boney, then I shall just have to."

"You, mamma!" It had long been a family joke that Mrs. Warrender was terrified of horses.

"Or Lord Hawth?" suggested her mother.

"What will he say when he finds his stables filled to bursting with our horses?"

"I doubt he'll notice," said Mrs. Warrender. "The size they are . . . " And went back to reading George Warren's note. "Good gracious! He's dismissed that Mr. Coombe and asked Futherby to handle his affairs!"

"Absurd!" said Kate. "Futherby will never consent. There's a clear conflict of interest."

"Oddly enough," said her mother, "Futherby has." She turned the page. "On the understanding that our interests shall be protected. There is a message from Futherby. He will call tomorrow to explain."

"He had better," said Kate.

Just the same, she could not resist the temptation to go and see Boney installed in his new stables, nor help being impressed by the shining order of the big stable yard. Lord Hawth might have let his house go to rack and ruin, but he or his head groom had seen to it that there was nothing wrong with the stables. They lay between the hall and the Dower House, which had been the original family home, before an eighteenth-century Chyngford made a fortune from the South Sea Bubble and astutely sold out in time. It was he who had celebrated his fortune by cannabalising stone from the ruined priory outside the park wall and commissioning young Lancelot Brown to design the hall to his own specifications. Between them, they had given it everything from Gothic turrets to crenellations and secret passage. They had failed, lamentably, to make it anything but a stylistic monstrosity.

Leaving the stable yard by the far gate, Kate was entranced by her first view of the Dower House. While Hawth Hall stood bold and ugly on the slope of the down, and, inevitably, caught every sea wind that blew, the Dower House was tucked away in a sheltered hangar and looked very much as if it had grown there. It must be older even than Warren House, Kate thought, its brick and tiles mellow and its timbers pale with age. Best of all, no one had ever improved it. It lay there snug and settled in its fold of the hills, its leaded casements gleaming red from reflected sunset, its chimneys twisting upwards as they must have when Elizabeth was queen. In the excitement and fatigue of the day, she had hardly had time to understand just how much she hated to leave Warren House, just how badly she was going to miss it. Now, her eyes suddenly filling with tears, she felt it all, and, at the same time, felt better.

"There you are, Kate." Her mother came along the path round the outside of the stables to join her. "They told me I'd find you here." If she saw the tears standing in her daughter's eyes, she gave no sign of it, but took her arm and stood silently for a moment also gazing at the house. "I like it," she said at last. "Don't you?" She loosened the string of her reticule and produced an enormous key. "I thought we'd have a look by ourselves first." She led the way across a cracked and weedy terrace to the front door.

"You think of everything," said Kate, following. "I had no idea. Did you know it was like this?"

"Like? Oh—old, you mean? Yes, I came here once, years ago, when I was younger than you are." She gave her shoulders a little shake and fitted the key in its heavy lock.

"Before you married Father?"

"Yes." She was struggling with the rusty key. It turned at last and she pushed open the door. "It's just the same—only dirty!"

"It was lived in then?"

"Oh, yes. Old Lady Hawth—and what a tartar *she* was." She lifted her muslin skirts clear of the dust and moved forward into the room.

"We'll get filthy, Mamma," protested Kate.

"Who cares?" said her mother. "There's no one to see."

Chapter 4

The Dower House was ready three exhausting days later, but Mrs. Warrender postponed the actual move until Harriet should be quite better. "I fancy I had best be at the hall to explain Mrs. Simmonds' presence to Lord Hawth," she told Kate, over a late luncheon in the morning room the servants had contrived to make habitable for them.

"I should rather think you had," agreed Kate. "Poor Mrs. Simmonds is in a perfect quake every time she thinks of his return."

"And so am I," said Mrs. Warrender. "But I do think he will find himself more comfortable, don't you?"

"I doubt he will believe he has come to the right house," Kate laughed. "It even smells different."

"So I should hope. Yes, Parsons?"

"Ma'am." Kate thought he looked anxious. "There's the overseer here, Mr. Bott from the Tidemills. He badly wanted a word with Lord Hawth. When I said he was from home, he asked to speak to you. There's trouble there, he says."

"Trouble?" Mrs. Warrender, who had coped with every

possible domestic vicissitude in the last few days, looked daunted at this external one. "I don't know . . ."

"You'd best show him in," Kate told Parsons.

"But what shall we say to him?" Left alone, Mrs. Warrender turned distractedly to her daughter.

"We will let him do the talking," said Kate. "But if there is trouble down at the mills, someone must do something. I know Lord Hawth owns them now, but after all, grandfather built them. Besides, Lord Hawth's not here."

"But what can we do?" wailed her mother.

"We'll see. Good afternoon, Mr. Bott." Kate smiled kindly at the anxious looking overseer, whom she had known from childhood visits to watch the great mill-wheels turning down in the tidal estuary.

"Mrs. Warrender. Miss Kate." He clutched his cloth cap in nervous hands. "It's good of you to see me. I'm sure I don't know what to do for the best."

"What is it, Mr. Bott?" asked Mrs. Warrender.

"Trouble, ma'am. Bad trouble if there's not something done quick. But who's to do it? His lordship's away, they tell me."

"In London," said Kate. "We could send there."

"No time, miss. They're out on the street already. Stopped the mill at noon, they did, and said they was having a meeting. Nothing I could say would get them back to work. Them as hung back got hard words, and worse. There's been a stranger in the village, Ned Ludd, he's called. He's been talking to the men, stirring them up. I blame him, miss. But what's the use of blaming?" He turned to Mrs. Warrender. "They sent me to speak to Lord Hawth, ma'am. Since he ain't home, I reckon I'd best give you the message."

"Sent you?" asked Kate, with raised brows.

"Just that, miss. I never thought I'd see the day. They had a hell of a long word I was to give his lordship. An ulti-something I was to say. Excuse the language, miss."

"Ultimatum?" suggested Kate.

"That's it. Either or, they said. Either he takes back what he said last week about sacking them if business don't look up, or they burns down the mill and that's an end to business."

"Burn it down? But it's their living!"

"That's what I told them, Miss Kate. Told them and told them. They won't listen. They've gone mad on the stranger. Well, treating them at the inn, talking of their wrongs. Bread so high, wages so low. The rich gets richer, he says, and the poor poorer. Justice, he talks of, and the rights of man. Jobs for all, and bread or blood. Fine speeches, he makes, miss, long words. But what use is long words, I said, if there's no food in the pot."

"And they—"

"Wouldn't listen. Nohow. Sent me with the message, like I said. They're all out in the streets. Waiting. And drinking, miss. He's got money, the stranger, and using it. I surely do wish Lord Hawth was home."

"I'd best come and talk to them," said Kate. "Explain."

"They'll never listen. Not to a lady. Not even you."

"Not even a Warrender? Then have you got a better idea?"

"Well." He cast an anxious glance at Mrs. Warrender, who had let out a squeak of horror at the idea of Kate's going down to the Tidemills. "I did wonder . . . if I might make so bold . . ."

"Yes?"

"It's the family, miss. You're right. They do reckon a lot to the Warrenders. If one of them was to come forward, listen to them, talk to them, give them some hope . . . It might keep them quiet till his lordship got back."

"You mean Mr. Warren up at the house?"

"The Yankee? Lord, no, miss. They wouldn't listen to a foreigner like him if he had the gift of tongues. No." His clumsy shoes shuffled on the Turkey carpet. "When I heard Lord Hawth wasn't home, I did make so bold as to wonder if you might chance to know where that cousin of yours was, miss."

"Cousin?"

"Well—" An anguished glance now for Mrs. Warrender. "There's a rumour going round that young Mr. Kit Warrender was in these parts the other night. The men reckon a good deal to him. They might listen to him. After all, he is family, ain't he? In a manner of speaking." Another apologetic glance for Mrs. Warrender, who was sitting very quiet, gazing at folded hands in her lap.

"Yes, I do see," said Kate. "How long can you hold them, Mr. Bott?"

"I don't know, miss, and that's God's truth. But if I told them—said Mr. Kit was coming . . ."

"Right." Kate rose to her feet. "Tell them Mr. Kit will be with them this evening, and that we'll send for Lord Hawth home from London. Because, whatever Mr. Kit says, it's what Lord Hawth does is really important, isn't it?"

"Yes, but they seem to think Lord Hawth might listen to Mr. Kit."

"Good gracious me, do they so?" said Kate. And after the man had gone, "No, don't swoon, mamma, there's not time. Do you write a note to Lord Hawth while I set about finding 'my Cousin Kit.' I wish I knew what I'd done to get him such a reputation."

"Kate, you can't!"

"I think I must. Just imagine what will become of those poor souls at Tidemills village if they burn down the mill that makes their bread and pays their wages. Oh, dearest mamma, how grateful I am to you for making me keep Boney!"

"But how are you going to manage?"

"I wish I knew. One thing's certain. I must have help." She chewed a thumbnail thoughtfully as she grappled with the problem. "I can hardly ride away from the hall on Boney in young Kit's clothes. But if I go through the tunnel, who will bring the horse round for me?"

"James," said Mrs. Warrender, then looked as if she would bite her tongue off.

"James?"

"He's the under groom." Mrs. Warrender looked guilty. "He's betrothed to Betty Parsons. He's—grateful to me just now. For bringing her here."

"I dare swear he is. Darling mamma!" A quick kiss. "What a miracle you are. Trust you to know all about everything. Who else is engaged to whom in the household?" And then, laughing; "No, don't tell me, there's not time. But be a love, send for Betty, tell her I am lending Boney to my Cousin Kit, and ask her to send James secretly to take the horse round to the priory ruins. Will he do it?"

"Oh, he'll do it," said Mrs. Warrender. "But Kate, I don't like it. Any part of it."

Nor did Kate much, but she put a brave face on it for her mother's sake. Luckily, a small unused room opened off the study and she was able to change into her brother's clothes there, rather than risk being seen by one of the servants as she walked through the house in them. "You'll have to stay in here while I'm out, mamma," she said, opening the panel. "Say you're busy planning the new decorations." She picked up her candlestick, put a spare candle in her greatcoat pocket, blew her mother a kiss and stepped into the tunnel before Mrs. Warrender could voice another protest.

She missed the children. Busy keeping their spirits up last time, it had been easy to forget about bats and rats, spiders and snakes. On one's own it was something else again, and she was glad of the need to hurry. She must be well away from the tunnel entrance before James arrived with Boney. Her mother had told him to wait outside the ruined chapel of the priory, which was some way from the tunnel, but she could not risk the chance of his wandering about to explore.

In fact, she had a short, anxious wait before she heard him come riding up the lane from the sea gate to the park—plenty of time to wonder whether something had prevented him from coming. When he came into view, she saw that he was riding one of Lord Hawth's horses and leading Boney. He touched his faded livery cap. "Mr. Warrender? Mrs. Warrender said I was to come with you, sir."

"Oh?" She thought about it for a moment. "Well, why not?" Clever of her mother. The Hawth livery would add weight to whatever she said. Just so long as she got a chance to say anything. "We'd better hurry." She used the moss-grown chapel step as a mounting block, settled easily in the saddle and led the way down the lane towards the marsh and the Tidemills.

When they left the woods along the park wall and came out on the open slope of the down, she drew rein for a moment to look towards the brick- and flint-built village below on the grey-green marsh. At first sight it seemed just as usual, lying there quiet in afternoon sun. At least no sign of flames, thank God, but, screwing her eyes against the sun's rays, she thought the little street looked too empty. Where was everyone? She was afraid they must be in the open space beside the mill, where in happier times the annual hiring fair was held.

"Quick!" She dug her heels into Boney's sides and led the way downhill at a pace that drew a silent prayer from James, guiltily riding one of his master's horses without permission.

When they rode into the village half an anxious hour later, it was to find it indeed unnaturally quiet and deserted. No children played in the street, and front doors that usually stood open to let sun and air into the tiny terrace houses were tightly closed. Only here and there an anxious female face peered out of an upstairs window. And now, from the far end of the street where the mill stood to one side straddling its tidal creek, she could hear the ominous hum of many voices. Some kind of meeting must be going on. Even the Ship Inn and the village shop stood empty and closed when they passed them. Every man in the place must be down by the mill.

No, not everyone. As they neared the turn in the road, where a huge warehouse blocked the view to the sea, Mr. Bott came anxiously round the corner. "Mr. Warrender!" His face lit up. "At last! They are holding a meeting. I persuaded them to wait to let you speak. It's—"if he had looked anxious up at the hall, he looked plain frightened now—"it's all so highly organised. They've closed the inn and the shop, told the women to stay indoors with the children. Mr. Warrender, do you think we should send your man to the barracks?"

"No use," said Kate. "We'd need a magistrate and the riot act read. Besides, they sound quiet enough now."

"Now. Yes. The man from London is speaking. Ned Ludd. They'll listen to him!"

"Well, let us hope they will listen to me. You had best take me to meet this sinister stranger from London. James, you hold the horses. If there should be trouble, ride to the barracks for help. If there is actual violence, the soldiers will doubtless come, but I devoutly hope it won't come to that."

"So do I!" Mr. Bott turned to lead the way round the corner into the mill yard. It was dusk, but not yet dark, and Kate was relieved to see that there were no torches yet.

The yard was full of silent men, standing pressed close together, listening to a speaker who was addressing them from a platform built up outside the entrance to the mill itself. It was the kind of stand used for hustings at an election, but the recently built village of Tidemills sent no member to Parliament. This scaffolding must have been brought and erected on purpose for the present meeting. Kate shivered. Mr. Bott had been right when he spoke about organisation. This was no spontaneously combusting riot. Well, at least it meant she had a chance of getting a hearing. But what in the world was she going to say?

"A way—" Mr. Bott had begun to push his way through the crowd. "A way there for Mr. Warrender."

As the crowd opened its ranks reluctantly, Kate took a deep breath of air and courage, and followed him. The crowd smelled. Sweat, and fatigue, and gin. It was unpleasant to feel it closing ranks again behind her. Unpleasant? Terrifying. The rigid set of Mr. Bott's back told her that he was frightened, too, but having started, he pushed his way firmly forwards through the crowd, which, in fact, did its best to open a path for them. There were murmurs of "Mr. Warrender," and even, "Let's hear Mr. Warrender!"

And all the time the man on the platform went on talking. Shorter than most of the crowd, and busy trying to make a way without causing the kind of scene that might be disastrous, Kate still contrived to catch a phrase here and there. "Brothers—" he called them brothers throughout—"are you men, or beasts?" It was not a local accent. "Will you let your women starve, while his lordship up the hill there buys and sells you as if you were cattle?" Kate lost a few sentences, then picked up the thread again as the speaker came to the heart of the matter. "Threatens to close the mill," he said. "Throw you all out of work. So: close it for him. Show the bouger what you think of him. Yes?" Kate could see him now in the half light as he leaned down from the wooden platform to listen to Mr. Bott. Dressed in a labourer's frieze jacket and breeches, he nevertheless wore them with something of an air, and the handkerchief tied round his neck was surprisingly white. "Mr. Warrender?" he said now. "With a message from his lordship? We will most certainly hear Mr. Warrender."

And that was both a surprise and a relief, thought Kate, letting Mr. Bott help her up on to the platform. It was surprising, too, to have her hand warmly shaken by the stranger, and then to have him give her a friendly shove towards the front of the platform. "Mr. Warrender," he told the listening crowd. "With a message from his lordship. We will hear Mr. Warrender."

It was an instruction, not a request. The crowd fell silent and Kate took a deep breath. What in the name of goodness was she going to say that would not make more trouble for everyone? "Brothers!" She made her voice as deep as she could manage, and got a very welcome cheer. It gave her both time and courage. "I do not exactly have a message from Lord Hawth," she went on, and got a groan. "But I promise you I will take a message from you to him. And make sure he listens to it. My family built this mill, *and* the village, to give bread and work to you all."

"Yes!" came a voice from the crowd. "And then what did you do with it!"

"Lost it at cards!" Another voice.

"To fat Guelph's friend!"

"Who'll see us damned before he raises our wages."

"Told us so, to our face."

Kate raised a hand for silence and, amazingly, got it. "True about us Warrenders, I'm afraid. We've not been much use to you. Why not give the new owner a chance? At least he's come here to live. Taken the trouble to come down to the mill."

"And promise us a sacking." Another voice from the crowd.

"Only if times get worse. And I've heard nothing about closing the mill." This was dangerous ground. "It's only because he doesn't understand," she hurried on, her clear voice sounding above some growls of "Times *will* get worse," and "Promised us a sacking." "I met Lord Hawth the other night. Talked to him a little. He's a man of sense. Put it to him right, he'll see it your way." How she hoped he would.

"And who's to put it to him?" She was beginning to recognise this voice, from the back of the crowd.

"He's been sent for. Should be here tomorrow or the next day. Send your leaders to speak to him, to explain . . ."

She was stopped by a great derisive cry from the crowd and realised her mistake. "Get them hanged . . . deported for life . . . breach of the Combination Acts . . . what kind of fools do you think us?"

This time her raised hand did not get her silence, but the previous speaker came to her rescue, pushing his way to the front of the platform and raising both his arms in a commanding gesture. "Let Mr. Warrender have his say," he shouted over the dwindling babble of voices. "He's young yet, he don't understand the risks we run. How should he?

But he took the trouble to come to us, so we'll hear him like reasonable people, won't we, brothers?" And then, as if the idea had just struck him: "Besides, who better for our messenger? He's a Warrender, ain't he? Kin to the man who built the mills. Knows Lord Hawth. Maybe his lordship will listen to him when he'd have one of us shown the door, or worse."

A roar of approval greeted this suggestion, and Kate listened with helpless horror as the meeting began a chaotic discussion of the message that should be sent. If there was one thing she did not wish, it was another encounter with Lord Hawth in her male disguise. But, listening, she began to realise that she was going to have to make the best of it. One suggestion, however, she did manage to veto. When several voices suggested that Mr. Bott accompany her, she negatived it firmly. "I must talk to Lord Hawth by myself, if at all," she said. "He's proud! It will be hard for him to go back on what he has said. If I am to persuade him, I must do it my own way."

The crowd divided on this, many of them wanting Hawth frightened rather than persuaded into compliance, and there were some vigorous suggestions about what should be done to make him see reason. "Burn his barns!" "Attack his carriage!" "Show the bouger!"

"No!" It was amazing how the original speaker could control the meeting. "We said we'd try reason first, brothers, and we are going to do it. The time for threats—and not empty ones—is later. But you'll tell him, Mr. Warrender, if you please, that there were votes for violence. He might as well know his danger."

"But no names!" The voice from the back of the crowd again.

Kate in turn moved to the front of the platform and looked out over the suddenly quiet crowd. "You know my name," she said. "You could get me in bad trouble for being here today. I don't know any of yours." It was not quite true, but it was as Kate, not as Kit Warrender, that she found several of the faces familiar. "I don't want to know," she went on. "A pack of fools who will destroy their own living! Burn the mill, you're paupers for life. My grandfather built the village for the mill, the mill for the village. How else would you live? By smuggling, and hang for it? Besides—" warned by an angry growl, she changed the subject—"your wives and children need the flour this mill makes. Lord Hawth will understand that. He's got children of his own."

"Pack of bastards," came a voice from the crowd.

"You say that to me!" She managed to sound quite convincingly angry. "And in the same breath ask *me* to be your messenger!"

"I apologise for them," said the stranger. "You're sorry, brothers? Good." Chastened now, the crowd was comparatively quiet while he spelled out the demands Kate must make of Lord Hawth. A promise that there would be no retaliation for this meeting. Guarantees of continued employment, no cut in wages and no increase in the price of flour.

Kate listened with a sinking heart. Hawth would no more make these promises than he would give the Tidemills away to the first person who asked for them. But useless, and dangerous to say so. "I'll do my best, brothers," she said, "but I warn you, it's a great deal you are asking. Times are hard."

"For Hawth? Who can win a fortune, *and* this mill, at a hand of cards! You tell him from us, Kit Warrender, that hard times is nothing in the kitty and nothing in the pot. Wages that won't buy bread for the children. And his with their own governess, and a tutor coming. Tell him to watch himself if he don't agree to what we say. *And* his children. What would he say if he woke up one fine morning and found them gone? Gone to work in a mill like this one, but far away, somewhere he'd never find them, sweating their little guts out like ours do."

Cold with terror at this new threat, Kate nevertheless managed a cool reply. "What would he say? Frankly, he'd say good riddance, and so I warn you. He doesn't give a damn for those brats of his, and so any of the servants at the hall will tell you. But I thought you said, 'No threats'?"

"You're right. It's early days for them. We count on you to make his lordship see sense. But if he don't, trust us to make him. And, a warning for you, Kit Warrender. We'll know when his lordship comes. Waste no time in seeing him. We'll be waiting and watching. Our eyes are everywhere."

It was all too obviously true. Kate had been appalled at how much he knew of what went on at the hall. "Watch too close, and you'll defeat your own ends," she told him now. "I've said I'll bear your message. Leave me alone to do it my own way, and tell your spies to do the same."

"Spies!" He seemed suddenly larger with anger, and the crowd sensed his change of mood and let out a growl. Then, surprisingly, he held out a friendly hand to Kate. "You've spunk enough for anything. Pity you're not the heir instead of that damned Yankee up at the house. Right it is, brother, we leave it to you." He moved to the front of the platform. "Meeting's over, brothers. Work as usual in the morning and keep it up till his lordship comes to tell us his answer. In person, mind!"

"He'll never do it," said Kate. "Not eat his words in person. You don't know him, or you'd not ask it. You'll have to take it—if you get it—in a message through Mr. Bott."

"Why not you?"

Why not indeed? What could she say? "Because I don't choose. Because I'm tired of being shouted at, if you like. Or, more to the point, because it's Mr. Bott's business."

"Spunk it is," said the stranger. "Bully for you, brother, and now, if you'll come this way, no need to pass through the crowd again."

"And no chance of recognising faces," said Kate, following him down the ladder at the back of the platform.

"What you don't see won't hurt you. But I wanted a word with you alone, now we've met at last."

At last? What could he mean? "Not now, I'm afraid," she said. "I borrowed Miss Kate's horse from the hall, and a groom. He's waiting. If I'm to be your messenger, I can't be seen apparently conspiring with you."

"True for you. I'm glad to have met you, Mr. Warrender.

We'll meet again. Soon, I hope. You'll find your horse down there." He pointed to an unsavoury lane that ran from the mill buildings along behind the terrace of houses.

"Thanks! I know my way. You'll not let them get dangerous drunk tonight and start some mischief that will make all impossible."

"Not on your life. Home to their wives is where they're going now. I've got them in the palm of my hand."

"So I saw," said Kate. "I congratulate you." And thought about it anxiously, all the way back up the hill. Behind her, James, too, rode silent and subdued. Even waiting as he had out of sight of the crowd, he had heard enough to make him realise just how serious the situation was. "I've got a cousin in the village." He moved forwards to ride beside Kate. "My Cousin Sarah. She opened her window and spoke to me while I was waiting. She's plumb scared. Says the men are neither to hold nor to bind since that Ned Ludd's been in the village. Funny sort of name . . ."

"Perhaps it's made up," Kate began, and then: "Listen!" They were coming up towards the place where the lane from Tidemills joined the one round the park wall, and she could hear a carriage coming swiftly up through the woods towards them.

"Christ!" said James. "If it's his lordship coming the short way from town, I'm out of a job."

"Does he?"

"Come this way? Often. Road's bad, but it spares him the holdup in Lewes High Street and by the bridge in Glinde. Can't bear waiting, can his lordship. Sir, if it is, you'll speak for me?"

"Of course, and so will Mrs. Warrender. Don't look so scared, man. He can't eat you." She wished she was sure.

"He can fire me, and that's worse. Oh, Gawd!" They had emerged from the woods in time to see Lord Hawth's light curricle come bucketing up the hill beside the park wall. He was driving, with his man perched up behind him. At sight of them, a quick word to his horses and a skilful touch on the reins brought them to a sweating standstill at the fork in the road. Then he sat there, sallow face impassive under the high crowned hat, and awaited their approach.

After the long strain of the errand to Tidemills it was almost too much. If she had been in petticoats, Kate would have burst into tears. As it was, she set her own hat at a slightly more rakish angle, muttered a word of encouragement to James, who had dropped behind her, and raised a friendly hand as she rode up to the curricle. "You are well met, my lord." She flung the cheerful greeting like a challenge at his stony stare.

"Mr. Warrender." The ground and the high perch of his curricle gave him a considerable advantage in height, and he looked down at her with the black brows hard together. "You are constantly surprising me. Or—"the hard looked moved over to James—"I do not recollect your name, but you have, perhaps, left my service and forgotten to turn in your livery?"

"Nothing of the kind," said Kate. "Mrs. Warrender very kindly lent me her daughter's horse, and your man to accompany me. I have been on your errand, my lord."

The brows went higher. "At my request? I must be growing sadly forgetful."

"At Mrs. Warrender's."

"That, naturally, explains everything. Then perhaps you will honour me with your company back to the hall, where Mrs. Warrender can enlighten me."

"I shall be glad to." Nothing was ever farther from the truth, but what else could she do? If only there was some way of warning her mother. "I wish we had known you were coming so soon, my lord," she said, as horse and curricle moved forward side by side along a grassy stretch of the lane. "It would have saved me an awkward enough mission."

"Oh? Well, Mrs. Warrender should know by now. I sent my man ahead. If he has dawdled on the way, he'll regret it. But, no, I see he has arrived." They had come in sight of the sea gate to the park, and the gates, usually kept locked, stood open. "After you, Mr. Warrender." He drew up his horses to let Kate ride first through the gate.

Riding ahead, Kate thanked goodness for the narrowness of the drive, which made further conversation impossible, and equally for the knowledge that her mother must have had warning of Lord Hawth's arrival. But she would hardly expect to have her come home with him. One way or another, she must be all to pieces with worry, poor darling. No chance in the world of getting together to concert their story. They would just have to brush through as best they might.

Chapter 5

As curricle and horse drew up side by side on the wide carriage sweep, the big doors of Hawth Hall swung open and Parsons came majestically out to greet his master. "Welcome home, my lord. Mrs. Warrender begs that you and Mr. Warrender will join her in the morning room."

"Morning room?" asked his lordship.

"Her late ladyship's, my lord. In the west wing."

"God damn it, Parsons. You think I do not know where my mother's morning room was! But whether it's habitable is something else again."

"You will find a few changes, my lord. Mr. Warrender," he came, surprisingly, down from the sloping steps to speak to Kate, with his back momentarily to his master. "Mrs. Warrender says not to worry. James!" raising his voice. "Make yourself useful for once. Take Mr. Warrender's horse." And was, somehow, between her and Lord Hawth as she dismounted.

That was a dangerous bridge crossed, but this time there could be no question of keeping on her greatcoat. She had to surrender it to a footman's willing hands, breathe a silent prayer and follow Lord Hawth down the long corridor that led to the west wing. Striding forward in formidable silence, his lordship cast, from time to time, a quick glance this way or that. Gleaming paint and shining wood challenged comment. He said nothing. Well, thought Kate, why should he? It was not Miss Kate but Mr. Kit Warrender who was following him.

The morning room was half lit by the afterglow of the sunset and smelled of lavender and beeswax. Rising to receive them, Mrs. Warrender looked pale, frightened, but not surprised. "Welcome home, your lordship." Her curtsy was graceful as a girl's. "I am so glad you have met Mr. Warrender. He has doubtless told you what he has been doing."

"Interfering in my affairs, I collect. No, we did not choose to discuss the matter on the open road."

"Very proper." She smiled her approval and gestured them to chairs. "So you do not know that I had Mr. Bott here this morning. Looking for you, of course. We—I sent for you urgently. You have, perhaps, met the messenger?"

"No. Merely came home sooner than I intended. So—what brought Mr. Bott here so urgently?"

"Trouble." She described Bott's errand briefly. "In your absence, he seemed to think Mr. Warrender might have a chance of making the men see reason. Did they?" She turned to Kate, colouring suddenly at the problem of what to call her.

"They won't burn the mill down tonight," said Kate.

"Burn the mill!" exclaimed Hawth. "Destroy their own livelihood! Are they off their heads?"

"Pretty well, I think," Kate told him. "And a stranger's there from London who can make them dance to his tune in a way I don't much like. He got me a hearing. Ludd, he's called. Ned Ludd."

"And you harangued them on my behalf? And expect me to be grateful?"

"Oh, no," said Kate. "I most certainly don't expect that."

"Though, mind you." Mrs. Warrender had picked up a

piece of embroidery and was stitching away at it in the failing light. "I did think it good of Mr. Warrender to ride down and confront the mob for you. As I recollect, the mill is really quite profitable in a good year."

"So why do the idiots want to burn it?"

"More profitable to you than to them," said Mrs. Warrender. "I've had servants with family there . . . heard stories I'd not dream of repeating to you."

"Afraid of shocking me?" His laugh was harsh. "If things are so bad there, ma'am, and you knew it, why didn't you speak to your husband?"

"Oh, I did." She left it at that.

He was silent, disconcerted for a moment, then turned to Kate. "So what did you say to those numbskulls?"

"Told them I was sure you had no intention of closing the mill."

"Closing! What lunacy is this?"

"You went down and made a speech there the other day. Your first visit? Perhaps not the ideal moment to threaten sackings if times did not improve. Gave the man from London a golden opportunity to make trouble. And—he's made it. You're going to be so angry when I tell you their demands that I'm plumb scared how to set about it."

"You sound it! so—to the worst of it. What promises have you made on my behalf?"

"Why, none. What right had I? Or, yes, I promised I'd bear their errand, which I suppose means I'd see to it you listened."

"I'm listening." With every exchange Hawth had come nearer to explosion point.

Mrs. Warrender jumped to her feet, letting embroidery silks fall where they would. "How could I be so stupid!" A vigorous pull at the bell. "You must both be parched with thirst. And hungry, too, I have no doubt. My dear father always said business went better over a glass of wine." A warning glance reminded Kate that she, like Hawth, must rise to her feet when a lady did.

By the time Parsons had ushered in a smartly clad footman with refreshments, the atmosphere had cleared perceptibly. Lord Hawth actually admitted to being hungry, congratulated Mrs. Warrender on the speedy service she commanded, and, reminded of his position as host, took wine with his young guest.

Kate was glad of the nourishing draft of burgundy. "I said you weren't going to like this." She plunged in, without further ado, to detail the rioters' demands.

"And if I refuse?" Hawth was looking black again.

"Various threats. The mill first. Then—some want to burn your barns, attack your carriage. And—I'm sorry—there were threats to the children."

"The children? What have they to do with anything?"

"The suggestion was that they should be kidnapped, sent to work in a mill in the north country. I took the liberty of explaining you wouldn't much care if they were."

"Oh, you did, did you?" Lord Hawth overrode Mrs. Warrender's horrified exclamation. "Taking a liberty, weren't you, boy?"

Kate finished her wine and rose to her feet. Any minute now, the candles must be lit. Time to be going. "It seemed a useful moment to tell the truth," she said. "And now, my lord, I have given you the message I was charged with, and will take my leave." She bowed over her mother's hand. "Many thanks for the loan of your daughter's horse, Mrs. Warrender."

It brought Hawth, still scowling, to his feet. "But how will you get home? You must take one of mine." It was the nearest he could get to apology or thanks.

"No, thanks. I've not far to go." She saw with relief that it was Parsons who had answered her mother's summons.

"This way." Once safe outside the morning room, he led her through a maze of stairs and passages that got her unobserved to her own room.

Thanking him. "How many of you know?" she asked.

"Only me and Betty, miss. Mrs. Warrender was so good as

to tell me, to ask my help. Told not to light the candles. It won't go no further, miss."

"Thank you." Alone in her room, she made the quickest possible change into her governess's drab, then hesitated. To meet Lord Hawth again so soon was to court recognition and disaster, and yet to leave her poor mother alone with him? But she thought she had best do so.

Her poor mother was letting Lord Hawth pick up her embroidery silks. When he had quite finished, she asked him prettily for just a drop more cordial. Then, having urged him to replenish his own glass, she smiled warmly at him. "Awkward, isn't it?" she said.

"Awkward! I don't know which is worse: to be told my own business by a boy young enough to be my son, or to have to take orders from a pack of rascally millhands."

"They've had a hard time," she said. "My lord," hesitantly. "Could you bear a word of advice from me?"

"From you!" For a moment she thought she had precipitated the explosion at last. Then, surprisingly, he dissolved into harsh laughter. "Well, for God's sake, why not? I've had it from everyone else. What advice have you to offer, ma'am, that I haven't had pressed down and running over already."

She took a deep breath. Then: "Get rid of Tom Bowles," she said.

"Tom Bowles? And who the hell is he?"

She smiled at him kindly. "You *are* a stranger, aren't you? Tom Bowles runs the shop down at Tidemills."

"Oh? Cooking the books, eh?"

"That's your affair. I expect he is. I always thought so. That's between you and him. Do you know how the hands are paid?"

"Paid? Weekly, I suppose."

"No, no." Patiently. "I can see you don't know. They don't get money, my lord. They get tickets on the shop."

"Convenient. It's the only shop for miles, isn't it?"

"Yes. So they are tied two ways. And what do you think they get? Mouldy bacon for the price of best. Meat that's nothing but bone. Cheese all rind. Do you know what happened last time a king's ship had her salt beef condemned down at the harbour?"

"No, what happened?"

"Tom Bowles bought it."

At Warren House next afternoon the Tidemills riot was being discussed, too. George Warren had ordered out a horse with the intention of riding the bounds of the sadly diminished estate he had inherited under the entail. An arduous morning spent with Mr. Futherby and his documents had left him with a pretty good idea of his boundaries and a passionate desire for fresh air. But the groom who brought out the horse he had selected from the Warren House stables looked anxious.

"You won't go down into the valley, sir?"

"I don't mean to. But why not?"

"There's trouble there, bad trouble. One of the girls was down to visit her ma and came back in tears."

"Oh?" Warren paused in the act of throwing his leg over the horse's back. "What happened? And why was I not told?"

"I don't rightly know what happened, sir. As to telling . . . well . . . I suppose Chilver . . . The old master didn't reckon much to what happened to us."

"Well, I do. Walk the horse for me, will you? I shan't be long." He was getting used to having the front door of his house swing open as he approached. "Send me Chilver," he told the footman who held it. "To the study." And, when Chilver appeared: "What's this about one of the girls coming back from the Tidemills in tears?"

"It was Lucy, sir. Lucy Penfold. Her mother lives down in the village. Father's dead, younger brother works in the mills. The old lady's—quite old. Mrs. Warrender gave permission, sir, when Lucy came here to work, for her to go home once a week and make sure all was well with her ma. I'm sorry, sir, I should have asked."

"Nonsense," said George Warren. "Of course the girl should go. What I want to know is why she came back in tears."

Chilver looked unhappy. "I don't rightly know, sir."

"If you don't know, you should, and if you don't want to tell, you're a fool. Send the girl to me, Chilver, if she's feeling up to it."

"Oh, as to that. She's only an under housemaid."

"So has no feelings? She's a woman, isn't she?" He sighed. "I see I must look about me for a housekeeper. And in the meantime, Chilver, everything that goes on in the house is my affair."

"Yes, sir. I'll fetch Lucy, sir."

Lucy was a surprise. Hardly more than a child, she was rapidly growing into a beautiful woman, would have been one already, Warren thought, if recent tears had not blotched the peaches-and-cream complexion. A golden curl escaped from under a hastily donned mob-cap, and she clutched her neckerchief round her shoulders with a desperate, dirty little hand.

"You're Lucy Penfold."

She had bobbed her curtsy and was casting a frightened glance round the study.

"Yes, sir." Another curtsy.

"No need to be afraid. I merely wanted to know what happened to you down in the village."

"Ooh, it was dreadful, sir." The strong local accent was a disappointment coming from her delicately shaped mouth. "But I mustn't tell, surely. He said if I told, things would be much worse for ma. And they're that bad already, sir, with two mouths to feed on a boy's wages. I . . . I wish now I'd let him, sir. Anything. He's good to them as does. Everyone knows that. I meant to, honest I did, sir, but then, when he got me in the back room of the shop, all among the flour sacks, I couldn't, sir. I scratched his face and ran for it. And he came after me, down the back lane, saying such things! I don't know what he won't do to ma, sir. And if my brother

Johnny hears of it, he'll try and fight him and get killed, most like. Or transported. Oh, sir," she put her hands to her mouth, "now I've told *you.* Oh what will become of us!"

George Warren stared at her, hardly able to believe what her incoherent speech seemed to suggest. "You mean, the shop keeper, down at the Tidemills—he attacked you?"

"Yes, sir. Tom Bowles. But not to say attacked, sir, not really. See, it's a known thing. He invites you into the back room, you go: vittles is better for the family. Only, I didn't seem able, sir, not when it came to the point. And now what'll happen to ma and Johnny?"

"Did you tell your mother what had happened?"

"Oh, no, sir. I couldn't. I was late already, see. I run all the way back here. If I lost this job we'd be in the basket and no mistake. Ooh . . ." She had suddenly remembered to whom she was talking.

"Never mind," he said soothingly, suspecting that his American accent had made her forget his position as her employer. "You'd surely not have lost your job just for being late?"

"Ooh, wouldn't I just! Chilver's powerful strict, sir."

"I shall most certainly have to get a housekeeper." Warren picked up his beaver hat and whip. "Now, quit fretting, child. I'll ride down to Tidemills and have a word with Mr. Bowles. And your mother, if you like."

"Ooh, sir. Would you really?"

"Yes, I really would. Now, off you go, wash your face and stop worrying."

Chilver was hovering in the hall. "I'm riding down to Tidemills." Warren could not quite keep a hint of defiance out of his voice.

"I wish you wouldn't, sir. Or wait till Mr. Futherby can accompany you."

"No. But I'll take a groom if it makes you happier."

"Yes, indeed, sir. Barnes would be best, sir. He was born at Tidemills."

"And got away as soon as he could, eh?"

"That's about the size of it. Sir?"

"Yes."

"You'll . . . you'll watch yourself? There was bad trouble down there yesterday. God knows what things are like today. And I hear Lord Hawth's back."

"What's that to the purpose?"

"They're his mills, sir."

"As if I'd forget that!" But it was with some slight, strange feeling of crossing a Rubicon that he jumped his horse over the hedge at the bottom of the long meadow that marked the boundary between his land and the fields Charles Warrender had lost to Lord Hawth along with the village of Tidemills itself.

At the village, everything seemed normal enough, with the splash and swish of the huge mill wheels speaking of work in progress, and women and small children here and there in the sandy street. But the shop, when they reached it, was closed, with a padlock on the door and a note in huge capitals: BACK WHEN I PLEASE.

"He'll be out collecting bad debts," explained Barnes.

"Then we had better hurry to Mrs. Penfold's house."

"It's at the far end, sir. By the mill yard."

That explained why Lucy had not even paused to warn her mother of trouble to come. Riding on down the narrow street, Warren began to fear that it had come already. There was too much noise at this end of the village. "What's going on?" he turned to ask Barnes over his shoulder.

"It'll be the day shift, sir, just out. Mill works twenty hours a day, see. They hold back the tide, so's to turn the wheels long as they can. So: two ten hours shifts. Depending *on* the tide."

"Long shifts."

"Yessir. Oh, blimey, a mill!" They had turned the corner into the yard where a rough circle of men had formed round a central space.

"A mill? Oh!" he recognized the unfamiliar term. "A fight, you mean?"

"Looks more like murder to me," said Barnes. "Young Johnny Penfold and Tom Bowles as can whip any two men in the village, and does, if they so much as breathe a complaint. He'll slaughter him, sir. He enjoys it, does Tom Bowles."

"Does he so? Keep close to me." George Warren pushed his horse through the crowd, which opened readily enough, assuming that the gentry had come to watch the fun. From their comments as he urged his horse forward, Warren, gathered that several rounds of the uneven contest had already been fought, and the betting was now on how many more young Johnny Penfold would survive. Reaching the edge of the circle, Warren drew a horrified breath. At one end of the improvised ring, a huge man was sluicing his bare, muscular back from a bucket held for him by willing hands. At the other, a fair-haired boy was crouched in the dust, blood pouring from above his right eye, trying vainly to wipe it from his face with his own floury shirt.

Tom Bowles wiped his face with a towel handed by another pair of eager hands. "Ready!" He moved forward into the ring, with the delicate, assured movements of a professional fighter.

"Ready it is," said a man at the far side of the ring whose clothes, less floury than everyone else's, suggested he did not work in the mill. "Come on out of there, young Johnny, if you're coming."

"I'm coming." The boy flung down the bloodstained shirt and rose shakily to his feet.

"Foul!" George Warren rode forward into the ring. And then, as Bowles and the referee gazed at him in open-mouthed astonishment; "What kind of British fair play is this? Who seconds the boy?"

"No one would, sir," explained the referee. "Not nohow. Not against Tom Bowles."

"Well, he's got seconds now. Hold my horse, Barnes." He dismounted and crossed the ring to where Johnny stood, weaving on his feet, helplessly brushing blood from his eyes.

After one look, “He’s not fit to go on,” he said. “Is there a doctor in the village?”

“Lord, no,” said the referee. “You’ll be Mr. Warren from the house.” A glance somewhere between servility and scorn took in the ill-fitting buckskins that were the best Mr. Snipe, the Brighton tailor, had yet managed to produce. “You wouldn’t understand, sir. My wife does the doctoring here in the village—when she feels like it.”

“Then she had better feel like it now. Which house is yours?”

“Why, the inn, sir, The Ship.” He was amazed at such ignorance.

“Fetch her, Barnes,” he began, but was shouted down by the crowd.

“Fight’s not finished!” “Betting’s still open!” “Out of the way, Yankee!” “No spoiling sport!”

“Sport!” exclaimed Warren. “Do you call it sport to see a boy half-killed?” Once again his voice was drowned by the increasingly angry shouting of the crowd. He took off his tall beaver hat and threw it into the centre of the ring. “If it’s sport you want, I’ll take on your bruiser, and back myself to have him crying for mercy in five rounds.”

“But, sir,” protested Barnes, as the crowd began loudly discussing this new proposition. “There’s not a man in the village can stand up to him. He’ll kill you.”

“I doubt it. He’s been cock of the walk here so long, he’s forgotten what a real fight’s like.” He laughed, stripped off his drab coat and handed it to Barnes. “Don’t look so anxious, man, I’ll not disgrace you! I learnt to fight the hard way, before the mast.” His shirt was off now, revealing a thin, wiry body whose deep tan had faded to a dull saffron colour. “But I’ll need you for a second. And one other. I’m not fighting by your foul Tidemills rules.”

“Let me!” Johnny Penfold was steadier on his feet now. “My wound can keep. And thank you, sir!”

“Thank him for nothing.” Bowles swaggered forward

from his corner. "Maybe you'd better send your man for a surgeon before we start. Two of the men will second you, won't you boys?"

"No, thanks." Warren cut short a sycophantic murmur of agreement, stepped out of his buckled shoes and spat on his hands. "Just tell me your rules, if you have any, and let's go!"

"For God's sake, be careful, sir." Barnes was in an agony of apprehension. "He reckons to kill you."

"Doesn't he just!" He moved forward as the publican gave the word, and spent a first round of delicate feinting, getting the feel of his opponent and his style of fighting. The crowd, excited by blood, booed its disapproval at this slow start, but Tom Bowles was beginning to look puzzled. None of his formidable blows seemed to connect with the opponent who danced around him like a gadfly. When time was called for the first round and Warren withdrew to his corner of the ring he recognized a change in the tone of the crowd. Bets were beginning to be taken both ways. He also saw that though he did his gallant best to conceal it, Johnny Penfold was half dead on his feet.

"We must get you to a doctor," Warren said, and went in for the second round. So far, he had been boxing right handed, like his opponent, now, suddenly, he switched to lead with his left, caught Bowles unawares, once on the right cheek, and then, as he staggered and recovered himself, hard on the right temple. "So much for that." He retired composedly to his corner as Bowles went down without even a groan, and the crowd burst into a great roar of applause. "Someone had better fetch the woman who doctors the village. He may be in need of her services. As for you—" to the publican, who had just finished counting Tom Bowles out—"You doubtless have a waggon of some kind?"

"Yes, sir?" Jewkes, the publican, though an old friend and associate of Tom Bowles, had recognized the change in the mood of the crowd. He left his friend lying senseless and gave a quick order to one of the bystanders. "At your service, sir."

"Good. I want young Johnny here and his mother taken up to Warren House without delay."

"And her bits and pieces, sir?"

"Bits?"

"Bowles had seized them for debt, sir. That's what this was all about."

"I see. Johnny."

"Yes, sir?" John Penfold pulled himself together with an effort.

"Does your mother care about her things?"

"Care?" The boy was beyond comprehension, and merely gazed at him dully.

"Oh, sir!" The crowd, openly delighted at the sudden fall of its tyrant, had helped the little old woman in black to push her way forward, and now she merged in front of Warren as if shot from a gun. Tiny and erect and bright-eyed, she swept him a surprising curtsy. "I don't know how to thank you, sir. You saved my Johnny's life. Do you really mean to take him to the house?"

"And you, too, if you care to come. I was just asking about your things."

"Let them lie in the dirt where he threw them." A savage shrug dismissed Tom Bowles. "You'll let me serve you, sir? And Johnny?"

He had been coming to one of his quick decisions. "There's an empty cottage up on the home farm," he said.

Chapter 6

"Pack of spiritless curs." Lord Hawth had surprised Kate by riding down to Tidemills to give his answer in person to his recalcitrant millhands. "Not a bit of fight left in them. Well, they'd had a busy day! That cousin of yours had been there, interfering in my affairs."

"Cousin?" Mrs. Warrender looked in puzzlement from him to Kate, demurely garbed now in governess's grey.

"The American heir. George Warren. Seems you were right in what you told me of Tom Bowles. Young Warren got wind of some of his doings—tampering with one of the girls from Warren House—went down there cool as be damned and found him in a fair way to slaughter her brother."

"Not Johnny Penfold!" exclaimed Mrs. Warrender.

"Got a pretty sister and an old mother that's seen better days?"

"That's the one. Oh, I knew I should have done something for old Mrs. Penfold."

"No need to fret, ma'am. Young Warren has. The village was buzzing with it. Walks into the ring where Bowles was having his fun with young Johnny, knocks him out cold as mutton and carries off the whole Penfold family to the house. A beauty, I take it, the sister?"

"Without two wits to rub together." Kate regretted the sharp comment the moment it was uttered.

"Oh, Kate," said her mother. "You know she always did her best."

"It sounds as if her best was good enough for George Warren." Hawth caught a flashing look from Kate and changed the subject. "Anyway, with Tom Bowles out cold and the stranger from town mysteriously vanished, I reckon I could have halved the men's wages and they'd have touched their caps and thanked me. Oh, well," tolerantly, "no doubt they threw a fright yesterday into that other young cousin of yours. He's only a boy after all," and again aware of the furious glance from Kate, "a game one, mind you, but I don't just see him knocking out Tom Bowles with a left-hander." He laughed his harsh laugh. "I can't decide whether I should call to thank George Warren for punishing my troublemaker, or complain of his stealing my hands. Seems he's to let the old lady help out at Warren House."

"Mrs. Penfold," said Mrs. Warrender. "What a good idea. She will manage admirably for him. It was a sad comedown, that marriage of hers, and I was always afraid not much good would come of it. She's not old, you know, not really: It was life with Job Penfold changed her so. I never did understand what possessed her to marry him. Or at least—" she coloured scarlet and was silent.

"Really, mamma!" Kate had followed her mother upstairs to her bedroom. "What with the things you let Lord Hawth say to you, and the things you say to him, you positively put me to the blush!"

"Shocking, isn't it?" Her mother smiled at her ruefully. "It's the strangest thing, Kate. He uses the most scandalous language, and glowers at one like a thunderstorm, and it doesn't trouble me in the least. I suppose it must be the advantage of being his paid servant. It makes everything so much simpler."

"I'm glad you find it so," Kate cast a furious glance at her reflection in the glass. "I confess I am getting a little tired of being the invisible governess."

Her mother laughed. "Just as well he doesn't notice you much. You should just have seen your expression when he said you weren't capable of knocking out Tom Bowles."

" 'Only a boy'!" quoted Kate angrily. "It'll be a long day before I meddle in his affairs again."

"Well, that's a comfort," said her mother. "I think young Kit Warrender had better emigrate to Australia or something, don't you?"

"Oh, nothing quite so drastic as that," said Kate. "I should miss it so. But maybe a trip to town . . . Besides, I have the most lowering suspicion that Sue has imagined herself into a *tendre* for young Kit!"

"No!"

"She keeps talking about him. Hoping to meet him again." Kate laughed. "If she only knew! Oh, well." She straightened her severe white collar. "Back to the governess's treadmill. I fear I must admit to being cured, don't you think?" She had, inevitably, had to feign illness the day before, while she masqueraded as Kit Warrender.

"My poor darling, do you hate it so?"

"Of course I don't." She gave her mother a quick hug. "I love the children. They're so quick, and bright, and funny. Besides," one last rueful glance in the glass, "*they* see me." And then: "Don't you think it is time we moved to the Dower House, mamma? You heard what our lord and master had to say about George Warren and Lucy Penfold. We hardly want him talking about us in similar terms."

"I should rather think not." Mrs. Warrender bridled like a furious kitten. "I will give the orders at once. Thank you for putting it in my mind, dear."

"His lordship will then be able to give free rein to his bachelor habits again, which must have been sadly curtailed by our presence. Do you think he will invite George Warren to bring Lucy Penfold to dine?"

"Kate!" But Kate had given a rather bitter little laugh and left her.

It was good to be welcomed with such glee, on her "recovery," by the children, and to find how painstakingly they had done the work she had set for them to do while she was "ill" the day before. Only Sue seemed quieter than usual, and Kate's suspicions as to the reason for this were confirmed when Giles began to tease her. "Sue's cross," he said. "She thinks Kit Warrender should come visiting us as well as papa. As if he would trouble about a parcel of children. A man like him who goes and faces the crowd at Tidemills."

The frank admiration in his tone was balm to Kate, but she must do her best about the complication of Sue. "I believe my Cousin Kit has gone away for a while," she told her. "No doubt he had a great deal on his mind when he came to see your father yesterday."

"Of course he did," said Giles. "They might have torn him limb from limb, James says. He was scared silly for his own skin. He told me so himself. And Kit Warrender up on the hustings, bold as brass, lecturing that crowd. I just wish I could have seen him, Miss Warrender."

"It's high time we got on with our lessons," said Kate. Listening to his recitation of the Latin verbs she had set him to learn, she worked away at the puzzle his words had summed up for her. After her own stormy reception by the Tidemills crowd the day before, Lord Hawth's walkover seemed altogether too easy. It was both puzzling and a little frightening, almost as if someone behind the scenes could manipulate the Tidemills crowd at will. But that was absurd.

She and her mother moved to the Dower House next day, and she was grateful for the freedom to be herself, instead of the stiff governess figure she had invented and now found so constricting. And there was one major advantage about the Dower House. Lying as it did on the far side of the stable yard, it made excursions as Kit Warrender possible without the hazard of the secret passage. At first, since the lodge gates were locked at night, she was compelled to confine her rides to moonlight explorations of Hawth Park itself, but on one of these she found a place not far from the sea gate where the wall had collapsed for several yards and been repaired with hurdles. Quite sufficient to keep sheep in and Tidemills children out of the park, they were nothing to Boney, and she was free of the marsh and the downs once more.

Once or twice, taking Boney over the hurdles, it struck her that they had been moved, and she wondered whether she should mention this to Lord Hawth or to Knowles, the bailiff. But Hawth was off on one of his long visits to the Prince Regent's lively court at Brighton, and she did not much like Knowles. He had been, in her opinion, altogether too obliging over the arrangements for the Dower House, and had made it rather uncomfortably clear that it was her taste and convenience rather than her mother's that he consulted. If Lord Hawth did not see her at all, she was afraid his bailiff saw her very clearly as a possible step up in the social scale. He missed no chance of hinting at what a warm man he was, and even went so far, one fine September Saturday, as to invite Kate and her mother to call and see the improvements he was making on his own house at the other side of Glinde.

"It will make an outing for you two ladies, and my sister will be only too happy to receive you." He had found them in their little paved garden, cutting late roses for *pot pourri,* and now managed a languishing glance for Kate. "Will you favour me with one of your roses, Miss Warrender?"

"I am afraid we have none to spare," Mrs. Warrender answered for her daughter, "and as for visiting, it is kind of you to suggest it, but we are far too busy getting things in train here before the winter sets in."

"Jams and jellies." There was the hint of a sneer in his voice. "It must make quite a change from the social life you have been used to enjoy. That's why I thought Miss Kate might fancy a little holiday."

"Miss Warrender is occupied with the children."

"Oh, bring the brats, too, if you like," he said carelessly. "There are plenty of trees for Giles to fall out of, and we might even find a young spark for Sue."

"That will do, Mr. Knowles." Mrs. Warrender put down her basket. "Come, Kate. How Mr. Knowles chooses to speak of his employer's children is his own affair, but I see no reason why we should listen to him. Good day, Mr. Knowles."

Safe indoors, Kate kissed her mother warmly. "Bless you for that setdown. I was afraid if I tried to speak, I would say too much."

"So was I. Poor man, if looks could petrify, he'd be stone by now."

"Yes, but he takes no notice," said Kate furiously. "I've tried every way I can to depress his unspeakable pretensions, and he seems to take my snubs for compliments."

"I expect he doesn't know any better," said her mother.

"Or doesn't choose to." Kate sighed. "And the infuriating thing is that he is right in so much of what he says. We're a proper pair of social outcasts, aren't we? I met Lady Beston who used to toady you so when I took the children into Glinde the other day, and she looked right through me as if I'd been a chimera."

"Well, said her mother, "a governess is just as bad. And as for housekeeper . . . 'Jams and jellies,' indeed!"

"And very good they are, too!" At this sign of gloom on her mother's part, Kate rallied gallantly. "I'm sorry, mamma! Who am I to grumble? It was my idea in the first place."

"And you were quite right," said her mother. "Let's never forget that, Kate. When I got that dismissive letter from your great uncle, the only relative we have in the world, I cannot tell you how glad I was to be able to write back and say we need not to be a trouble to him."

"Which he didn't intend anyway," agreed Kate. "You're quite right. We have chosen our bed, and really it could be a great deal less comfortable." She laughed, a little wryly. "But Great Uncle Frank isn't in fact our only relative. How do you think Cousin George Warren is getting on in his den of iniquity?"

"The less said about that," said her mother, "the better."

Busy from morning to night in trying to settle the chaotic affairs of his dead relative, George Warren had no idea of the gossip about himself and Lucy Penfold. Characteristically, Charles Warrender had left no will, but he seemed to have left no legitimate relatives either, except, of course, for his wife and daughter, and this made the settling of his estate a good deal easier than it might have been. While creditors came forward in swarms, there were no unexpected claimants to the estate. After several visits to a London solicitor recommended by Futherby, George Warren returned to Warren House one fine September evening with a waggonload of luggage and good news for Futherby, there by appointment to greet him.

"I think we are out of the wood at last." He had poured wine for them both. "I'm grateful to you for recommending James Martin, Futherby. I'd not have thought we could have brushed through the intestacy so well."

"And the debts?" An honest man, Futherby had done his best to persuade George Warren that he was under no obligation to settle these, but had yielded with relief to his angry retort that if he did not do so, the creditors were bound to come down on Mrs. Warrender.

"Oh, those debts!" George Warren laughed a shade grimly and refilled his glass. "What a muddle of a man, Futherby! Do you know, what irked me most of all as they came streaming in, with their claims for this hunter and that high perch phaeton, was that there was not so much as a fiver spent at Rundell and Bridge on trinkets for his wife and daughter."

"That," said Futherby, "I can well believe."

"How are they?" asked Warren.

"Well enough. I thought Miss Kate a shade blue-devilled

when I last called, but that's understandable. It's a dull life for a high spirited girl like her."

"High spirited? That's hardly how she struck me. Why, one of our Philadelphia Quaker young ladies would have more looks and more conversation. Perhaps she's just bored from her own lack of resources. Now the mother's something else again. I warrant you she's carrying out a root and branch shakeup up at the hall, just the way Mrs. Penfold is here, God bless her."

"Yes," said Futherby. "The Penfolds. There was something I was wishing to say to you . . ."

But as he searched for the tactful phrase, his employer interrupted him. "I've a commission for you, Futherby. One I hope you will enjoy. You are to call on Mrs. Warrender and tell her that a small part of her dowry escaped her husband's creditors. A mere £500 a year in the funds, but it should make a considerable difference to their situation."

"It should indeed." Futherby gave him a very straight look. "If I can just convince them they are entitled to it. They're not fools, you know."

"But nor are you, and I think you owe it to them—if you will forgive my saying so—to make a good job of it. You've no idea how hard Martin and I worked to make it all watertight for you."

"It's very generous."

"Generous! When I am living in their house, using their carriage, enjoying what should be theirs! I only wish I could make it more, but Martin thought it the most we could get away with. I hate to think of them dependent on that cross-tempered, bad-mannered earl of theirs. Do you know I ran slap into him in St. James's and received the nearest thing to the cut direct I ever hope to suffer? A kind of raising of those black brows and the slightest tilt of that aristocratic head of his and he was safe away without so much as pausing in his conversation."

"Talking, was he? You don't chance to know with whom?"

"Why, yes. Mr. Perceval, the first minister. I'd have liked to have met him. There is a thing or two I think he should know about our feelings over in America. What are you laughing at?"

"Forgive me!" They had become very good friends in the course of the summer. "But the idea of Lord Hawth—a Whig and a member of the Prince Regent's set—the very thought of him presenting a young American revolutionary to the Tory first minister!" He took snuff and laughed some more. Then, more seriously: "In fact, I find it odd enough that you should have seen them together. Lord Hawth does not often move in government circles."

"Oh, your English politics." Impatiently. "I'll never understand them. Whig or Tory, what's the difference? All they care about is their own comfort, their hunting and shooting, their parties of pleasure. And not an honest day's work done among the lot of them. What do they care if the crops fail and the poor starve? They're riding for a fall, I tell you. I heard some stories about doings in the north when I was in town would fair make your blood curdle. Mr. Madison's non-importation act has hit them hard up there in the cotton trade. Mass unemployment and starvation wages there, and the rich manufacturer sitting tight and doing nothing. Or cutting costs and throwing more men out of work. Starvation breeds revolution, Futherby, and I've heard tales as an American might make some of your care-for-nothing artistocrats shake in their shoes."

"My dear Mr. Warren!" The lawyer's protesting hand stopped him in full spate. "To me, if you must, but for God's sake be careful what you say!"

"You think I'll be clapped in the Tower for treason, like Sir Francis Burdett."

"Not exactly treason. But I do think, Mr. Warren, that you should remember your somewhat awkward position as an American. Specially here, on the invasion coast. There's talk that Bonaparte is making a tour of inspection of his army in the Netherlands this autumn. It might mean anything. You don't know what it was like in 1804, when we expected to be invaded hourly. And now this talk of war with America—with *your* country, Mr. Warren—it might just give Bonaparte the chance he needs."

"You think so, too? I thought I was the only one."

"I do indeed. I'll be glad when winter really comes and the crossing is impossible for the small boats Bonaparte still has ready on the other side. By spring, let us hope things will be better."

Warren shrugged. "Or at least not worse. In the meantime, what do I do, as a possible enemy alien? Join the Volunteers, do you think?"

"I doubt they'd have you. No, I'd just keep quiet if I were you, Mr. Warren. Things are—one must face it—they really are a trifle awkward. Have you had any callers, if I may ask?"

"You can ask anything. And the answer is, no. Should I have?"

"It's an unusual situation." Mr. Futherby hedged. "In the normal way, I would have expected it, but you have been in town a great deal. And then, things were so oddly left. . . ."

"You mean, I am to be ostracised."

"I do hope not."

"We had better put it to the test, had we not? What do you suggest? A dinner party for the county? Now that Mrs. Penfold has the household so well in hand, I reckon she would positively enjoy that."

"Speaking of the Penfolds—" once again Mr. Futherby began his warning, and once again was interrupted.

"I'll tell you what I'll do," exclaimed George Warren. "I'll invite my cousins to dinner. Mrs. Warrender and that frumpish daughter of hers. I'm sure Mrs. Warrender can give me excellent advice as to how I am to go on in the district, if she only will."

"Yes, except . . ."

"Except what?"

"Well." Futherby looked miserable. "I'm sorry to have to say it, but from what I hear their social life has changed sadly now that they are housekeeper and governess up at the hall."

"Jehosaphat!" said George Warren. "I begin to think I don't want to know much more of your English society! Will it sink them beyond recall, do you think, if I invite them to dinner? Because I must certainly propose to do so."

After Futherby had finished his wine and ridden away, George Warren found himself, almost for the first time, wretchedly at a loose end in his new existence. So far, there had been almost too much to do. He had enjoyed doing battle with his head relative's creditors, and seeing to it that they got not a penny more than was their due. He had been equally entertained by the chicanery by which he and his new London friend, James Martin, had arranged to blind Mrs. Warrender with legal science and convince her that she was entitled to £500 a year of what should have been her own money. And then there had been the novelty of life in London and the challenge of trying to turn himself into a reasonable replica of an English gentleman. Until he had done so, more or less to his own satisfaction, he had not much wanted to try his luck in English society.

Now, he told himself bitterly, he was beginning to see the other side of the coin. The trouble with English gentlemen was that they had not nearly enough to do. He had earned his own living since he had been orphaned at fourteen and his uncle had given him a chance on one of his merchantmen. Taking it with both hands, he had made a fortune by the time he was twenty-one, lost interest in the mere business of making money, and been looking about for a new occupation when he had received the unexpected summons to England.

At first, he had thought he had found one. He had ridden the complete rounds of his estate by now, had ordered new roofs, new fences, new barns and been heartily thanked by a surprised and grateful tenantry. Busy with all this, he had not, until Lord Hawth cut him in the street and Futherby asked his question, much cared about the lack of social life, or if he had, had assumed that this was just part of the English pattern which he was not yet in a position to understand. Doubtless, he had thought, the calling season, like the grouse and hunting ones, had its definite opening date.

Was he really to be ostracised? Would even Mrs. Warrender and her daughter refuse his invitation? Resolved to put it to the test at once, he rang to order out his horse, then strode angrily upstairs to change into riding dress. He found Lucy Penfold in his room, very busy polishing shining brass andirons.

"Ooh, sir!" She dropped him a flurried curtsy. "You didn't half give me a turn. I was afraid you was one of the men!"

She really was quite remarkably pretty, with that apple blossom complection and the golden curls that never would quite stay under her cap. And today, doubtless warm with her work, she had loosened the lacing of her tight bodice, to reveal white skin never touched by the sun. "Ooh, sir!" She saw where his eyes were directed. "Whatever will you think!" She began to tighten the laces with trembling little hands. "Ooh dear, there's a knot!"

"Let me help you, child." She was tiny, and he smiled reassuringly down at her as his large hands joined her small ones at work on the knot.

"Ooh, you are so kind, sir. And clever!" Her clumsy hands pulled against his, and suddenly the whole bodice was open, revealing two perfect little white breasts, the nipples alert for his touch.

"You're very lovely, my dear." Had he really meant to help fasten that provocative bodice? If so, what were his hands doing now, and how did it happen that they were falling together onto the wide, soft bed?

She gave way for an intoxicating moment, then slipped, quick as an eel, from his grasp. "Ooh, no, sir!" she exclaimed, safe on the far side of the bed. "Whatever would my ma say?"

Chapter 7

The nights were growing darker as the moon waned. Soon, Kate thought gloomily, as she slipped a buckskin-clad leg over the window sill of her downstairs bedroom, she would have to give up the nightly rides she had so far managed to keep secret from her mother. And then, if the weather broke, she might well find herself tied by her own governess's apron strings until spring. Once the lanes were deep with winter mud, she and Boney would bring back all too obvious evidence of their truancy. As it was, James, who looked after Boney, had remarked once or twice that he was worried about the horse.

No. Whispering a greeting to Boney as she tightened the girths of one of Lord Hawth's old saddles, she told herself that she had better face it. Tomorrow, she and her mother were dining with George Warren. By next night the moon would be almost gone. This was almost certainly her last night ride till spring. It was a daunting prospect. She loved her mother. She loved the children. And yet she felt herself slowly stifling between the Dower House and the hall. Whatever she had imagined, when she made that rash proposition to Lord Hawth, it had not been this dim, domestic round. Had she expected orgies, she asked herself sardonically? Had she perhaps a little enjoyed the idea of them?

No. She made herself face it. It was worse than that. Her mother had been right. She had let herself dream her way into a schoolgirl's idiotic passion for her saturnine employer. It had been so pleasant, that first encounter, friendly, easy. Mad to have let herself dream that Kate might carry on the relationship Kit had started. And, after all, she had been warned. Hawth himself had said he was intending to marry. Lunatic to have let herself imagine, hearing no more about it, that his intended bride, like his mistress, had thought better of involvement with his bad-tempered lordship.

Though it had seemed understandable enough. Hawth was most certainly no lady's man. Abrupt courtesy was the limit of their rare encounters, and she and her mother had not so much as been invited to drink a glass of wine with him. It had been absurd, of course, to assume that because he had been friendly to Kit he would take some notice of Kate. It was all misery, and all very hard on the children. She would have liked to talk to him about them, and about Nurse Simmonds, whose influence, most particularly on Sue, she liked less and less. Only this morning she had found Nurse Simmonds in the main hall, where she had no business to be, flirting outrageously with Tom Bowles, up from the Tidemills on some errand or other.

It was no wonder if Sue was difficult and the others too quiet. Their father never sent for them, never asked how they were or how their lessons were going, never even spoke of them. He must—she collected Boney for the jump over the hurdles—he must have been very badly hurt by their mother. It was a pity this was a subject she could only raise in her alias as Kit Warrender, one she did not propose to risk with Hawth again. As Kate, she knew nothing about the children's mother, except that they showed no signs of pining for her. Which, she supposed, was exactly what Hawth was doing. How tedious of him. She turned Boney down the road to Glinde. A woman who would leave him for the tutor was so obviously not worth a second thought.

She had reached the priory ruins, the place where she usually turned back. Boney hesitated, and she gave him an encouraging kick in the side. When had she decided to treat herself to a pint of best ale at the Bell in Glinde? It meant a long ride, and she had not gone there since the move to the hall, but tonight she longed for the friendly anonymity of the Bell. She did not sleep anyway, these hot autumn nights; she might just as well be awake, cheerful and in company, as lonely in her lavender-scented cage at the Dower House.

It was late when she rode into the quiet streets of Glinde, and for a moment she regretted the impulse that had brought her. But the lights of the Bell burned bright enough down beyond the park gate. Her throat filled at a sudden memory of the first time she had gone there, the mad night when she had dressed up in an old suit of Christopher's and he had bet her that she could never pass herself off as one of their grandfather's bastards.

She had won the bet, of course. There had been a great deal of friendly chaff in the Bell, where Chris was obviously well known and liked. There had been more bets, inevitably, about the likeness between them. Change coats, and who could tell Chris from Kit? She caught back a half sob, remembering the first time she had been back to the Bell after her brother's death, and the strange moment when the landlord's jaw had dropped. For a minute, Brown had taken her for Chris.

The Bell was crowded tonight, and, her heart suddenly failing her, she wished herself back in the quiet of the priory ruins. Madness to have come. Well, she was mad . . . possessed . . . wretched. Enough of that. She looked in at the busy public bar as she passed its door and was surprised to see Knowles, Lord Hawth's bailiff, talking to another man whose face was somehow familiar. Of course, she had it: Coombe, the man George Warren had brought down with him and dismissed so summarily. How very odd. But she was in the snug now, glad to see that Brown himself was serving there.

"Master Kit!" He raised a friendly hand in greeting. "It's been a long time. Your usual?" He pulled an overflowing pint and handed it across the counter. "I'm right down glad to see you, sir, and that's the truth."

"Oh?'" There was something slightly disconcerting about this warm welcome.

"I surely am. It's about him." A jerk of his chin directed Kate's attention to a corner booth where she was amazed to see George Warren sitting alone. "Kin of yours, I reckon." It was not a question. "Been here most nights for a week or more. Something on his mind." Brown laughed quietly. "Someone. That little bitch Lucy Penfold, and him a Yankee without the sense to come in from the rain. Nor any idea of how talk runs in these parts. Word is she's holding out for marriage, the smart piece. Well," tolerantly, "he's only a Yankee, after all, and her mother *was* a parson's daughter. But it don't seem right, surely, not Lucy Penfold in Madam Warrender's place. Besides—" he leaned forward, elbows on the counter, to speak low—"I did hear Tom Bowles was a mite peeved over the whole affair. There's some of his men in the public tonight."

"His men?"

"*You* know." He completed the inadequate sentence with an expressive glance and a deep pull at his own beer. "I just wish there mightn't be trouble for Mr. Warren on the way home."

"You think there might be?"

"Well, Tom Bowles is a pretty powerful man in these parts, what with one thing and another, as you and I well know."

"Yes." Kate wished she did.

"And it's near dark tonight. A storm coming up, I reckon. And a lonely road back to Warren House. I suppose—" he leaned further forward and Kate knew he was coming to the nub of the matter—"if I was to make you known to him. As kin, see? You'd not feel like riding home with him, friendly like?"

"I?"

"Well, now, Master Kit, we both know they'd never touch *you,* surely. You ride with him, tip him the word to keep away from dark places, all's right. I don't want murder done anywhere near my house, or I'd not have spoken."

"Murder!"

"Well, what do you think? Tom Bowles don't play pretty. Ah, they're going now. He and his friends. Going to choose their ground, surely. The priory ruins, *of* course. And smugglers blamed when he's found, or wreckers, and trouble for everyone. But most particular for your cousin." He left her with it, and moved through to the other bar to call a cheerful goodnight. Two rough voices answered him, and Kate, unable to see or identify the men, racked her brain as to what she should do. She wished she did not believe Brown, but she did. George Warren was in deadly danger. If only she were equally sure that her company would carry automatic protection.

"I'm about ready to close up." Brown rejoined her. "Will I make you known to him?" His sharp glance was suddenly critical. "Or not?" And then: "Here he comes. One for the road, Mr. Warren?"

"Half, thanks. Your ale's stronger than we make at home. Good evening." He came out of his gloom to speak with natural friendliness to Kate, now the only other occupant of the snug. And then, puzzled: "We've not met, have we?"

For some reason, the half recognition settled it. Kate smiled, raised her mug in greeting and said, "No. It's the family likeness, I'm afraid. There are more Warrenders in the county of Glinde than ever show up in the Parish registers." She put down her mug and held out a hand. "Kit Warrender, cousin, at your service."

"Good to meet you." Her hand was warmly clasped. "I could just do with a cousin tonight. Thanks." He took his mug from Brown. "Pity it's so near closing time, but you'll join me till then?"

"Gladly." It was a relief to abandon the masculine pose against the bar and settle in the comparative darkness of George Warren's corner. But what, in heaven's name, was she going to do now? All this time, her mind had been scurrying round, snatching at expedients and letting them go again as useless. There was no help to be had in Glinde, and she could think of no pretext on which she could persuade George Warren into the safety of Hawth Park. Pretend to be ill? Ask him to escort her home? But what to do then? Besides, so far as he was concerned, the hall was not her home.

"Which way do you ride?" Warren asked the inevitable question as he settled back in his corner.

"Your road till you turn off to Warren House." There had been something horribly convincing about that casual remark of Brown's. The ambush would inevitably be at the priory ruins and George Warren's disaster attributed to an unlucky encounter with smugglers, or with the wreckers who also haunted this coast.

"That's dandy." George Warren's smile lit up his drawn face. He had aged and lost weight, Kate thought, since she last saw him. "I suppose," he went on now, hesitantly, "you wouldn't care to stop the night with me? One doesn't often meet a brand new cousin."

Now, here was a problem. "Good of you." Kate wished she had invented a home for herself. "But I'm expected." Where was she expected? Somewhere on the London road, the far side of Hawth Park. It was time she gave up this masquerading. Well, she thought as she finished her ale, if Brown was wrong, there might be two corpses found in the priory ruins tomorrow morning, and her masquerade over for good. A cold little shiver ran down her spine. Poor mother. How could she do it? And yet—how could she not?

"Shall we be going?" Warren rose. "Brown looks as if he'd be glad to see the back of us."

Confirming this, Brown bustled forward from behind the

bar to bid them goodnight, and then look from one to the other and ask casually, "You're not armed? It's coming up to the dark of the moon. *And* a storm brewing."

"And what's that to the purpose?" George Warren picked up his high-crowned beaver hat.

"Mr. Warrender will explain as you go. He's born and bred in these parts, and you'd do well to listen to him, sir, even if he hasn't the sense himself to ride armed in the dark nights. But then, he's well known in the district. You're not. Not yet." He moved a step back to look round the partition, presumably to make sure that the public bar was now as empty as the snug, then returned to say, "I'd be glad to lend you gentlemen my spare pair of pistols, just in case." He reached behind the bar and brought out two deadly looking little weapons. "I keep them ready loaded, in case of trouble; it's but to load the other pair when you've gone." And, as George Warren hesitated and Kate's heart sank still further: "I'd be glad if you'd take them, gentlemen. And bring them back at your leisure. *In* the daytime. And stay home, Mr. Warren, through the dark nights. I'm surprised that Futherby's not warned you."

"He did say something." George Warren reached out to take one of the pistols and weigh it in his hand. "I thought it a lot of nonsense. Besides, the moon's only waning, it's not really dark yet."

"Dark enough tonight." Brown handed the other pistol to Kate.

Thanks to Christopher's training, she knew how to handle it, and it did give an odd feeling of comfort to tuck it in the capacious pocket of his greatcoat. She had fired at a target often enough, but in anger?

"You won't need them, of course." There was a touch of scorn in Brown's voice, as if he had recognised her reaction. "Better safe than sorry, I always did say. Goodnight, gentlemen. The boy has your horses ready."

The town of Glinde was asleep now, with only a light here

and there in an upstairs window, and by mutual consent they rode silently down the narrow street until they passed the park gates and emerged into open country, with the wall on their right.

"Dark enough." George Warren looked up as the moon vanished behind scudding clouds. "What is all this talk about the dark nights?"

"Smuggling," said Kate. "It's the district's second livelihood. First one for many, in the winter when they're out of work. It goes on all along this coast. Well—no distance to France, and with the excise duties what they are, it's inevitable."

"And winked at?"

"I'm afraid so." It was a blessed distraction to be talking, rather than wondering what lay ahead in the priory ruins. "I doubt if much of the wine in your cellars at Warren House, or the tea in your caddies, ever saw a customs house." She remembered, suddenly, that puzzling extra consignment of the wrong tea. "Most of it goes to London, of course, for sale there, but we all get our shares."

"Shares? For what?"

"For turning our backs. Staying home in the dark nights, when they are running the goods. Saying nothing if one of our horses or waggons is 'borrowed.' Of course some people give regular orders, but we've never done that. We get it just the same."

"We?"

"The Warrenders." She coloured angrily in the darkness at her mistake. "The family." Time to change the subject. "I hope you find yourself happy here, Mr. Warren. It must all seem quite strange to you."

"It does. Happy? No. I reckon I'll be going back soon. Back where I belong. Back where I've friends."

"But the Warren! You'd never leave that!"

"Why not? I've got a house in Philadelphia. And friends. And a life. Sometimes, now, I wish I'd never left there. But what could I do? When your cousin, that poor young Chris Warrender, wrote and asked for my help in breaking the entail, it seemed my duty."

"What?" She could not believe her ears. "Break the entail? I don't believe it!"

"True, just the same." She could sense his shrug in the darkness. "The three of us—Charles Warrender, his son Chris and I—could have done it, Mr. Futherby tells me, all right and tight, according to your law, and I'd have been glad to. No hope now. I'll have to marry, get sons and grandsons, before it can be done. And there's a pickle."

"Oh?"

"I'm glad I met you. Blood's blood, after all. We're not close, but we're kin. I feel it, don't you? You're—easy to talk to. Not like that schoolmarm Miss Warrender. Do you know—" He was talking more and more freely, what with the strong beer, and the darkness, and the comfort of an easy listener—"I had thought, when I heard about her father and my inheriting, and all, maybe I ought to offer for her. Make things tidy. Good God! I'd rather marry one of those marble ladies on the frieze Lord Elgin brought back from Greece. Cold as ice, dull as ditchwater, haughty as Lord Hawth. That's my Cousin Kate. Oh—" It came to him suddenly. "Sorry. Your cousin, too."

"Yes," said Kate. "I—like her."

"Sorry I spoke. No doubt she's different with you. Treats me like something that shouldn't have happened. Well," fairly, "I reckon from her point of view, that's true enough. But where does that leave me? What am I supposed to do? Nobody comes near me. Nothing *to* do. Oh, they're coming to dine with me tomorrow night. She and her mother. Imagine that. The condescension of it. My first guests. Shall I give it them in their teeth? I'd like to see their faces. Specially that beanpole of a prudish governess."

"Give them what?" Kate was controlling her temper with some difficulty.

"News of my forthcoming marriage."

"Good God!" Kate remembered something Brown had said. "You can't be serious!"

"Know about it, do you? One thing I have learned, the weeks I've been here, everyone knows everything. Yes. Lucy Penfold. Pretty as a picture. Mother a parson's daughter. What's wrong with that? And virtuous. By God! There she is, in my house. I thought there was—what do they call it?—*droit de seigneur* still, here in England. Nothing of the kind! Or," ruefully, "maybe I'm not the kind of *seigneur* for whom it works. I'm going mad for her. She's always there. Whisking in and out of my room. Cans of hot water. Messages. 'Yes, sir.' 'No, sir.' Mainly, 'No, sir.' And that mother of hers watching me like a dragon." He was silent for a moment, then: "What do you think, boy? Sorry. Not really a subject for you, but you're all the worthwhile kin I've got this side of the Atlantic. I'm mad for her," he said again.

"You're crazy," said Kate. "Have you tried to talk to the girl?"

"Well, not to say talk. There's no chance, not in that house full of servants, God help me! And her mother, always on the listen. That's it, don't you see, that's just it! Engage myself to her, and I'd have a chance to get to know her. Surely, then, I'd get her to myself."

"Not this side of matrimony, if I know Mrs. Penfold," said Kate. "As for the girl, you're about in the head, cousin. Think again, I beg you. She hasn't two thoughts to rub together. Or only what her mother puts there. She's nothing but a tease, that one, a witless tease. And, I wouldn't wonder, cold with it, or how'd she manage?" Now, what in the world had put that idea into her head?

"Tried her yourself, have you!" George Warren's voice was angry. "I might have known. A young spark like you. But didn't get anywhere, did you?"

"Nor wanted to! What's that?" The priory ruins loomed up ahead of them, darker amid the darkness. And, somewhere to their right, came the unmistakable sound of harness rattling as a horse stirred impatiently.

"Trouble. Look!" They had rounded a bend in the lane to see a barricade dark across its chalk whiteness. Too close to jump and the lane too deep-cut for the horses to be able to get round it. "Cover me, while I clear it." But as Warren jumped down from his horse, the attackers were upon them, leaping down from the bushes above the lane. Kate, whose trembling hand had cocked her pistol at the first alarm, fired almost point blank at the man who had tumbled down on to the road beside her, and was amazed to hear him fall. But George Warren, caught between stirrup and ground, was now struggling with two other men who had come down on his side of the lane. What should she *do*?

"Ride for help! Back to Glinde!" George Warren panted it out as the three of them heaved and grunted in the narrow lane.

She could not abandon him to the unequal contest. Brown had been right. There was murder in the air. She could feel it. "Help's coming!" Anything to distract the attackers as she edged Boney forward, hoping for a chance to strike one of them from above with her now useless pistol. And then, suddenly, miraculously, realised that it was true. Horses were pounding towards them from the direction of Glinde.

If it was help? For an instant, the sounds of struggle ceased as all of them listened to the rapidly approaching hoofbeats. "Kit Warrender?" came a voice Kate thought she knew. "Are you there?"

"Yes." The horses were very near now, two of them, she thought, and saw one of the men who had attacked George Warren leap for the shadows of the hedge and vanish.

"Not you," growled George. "You're staying right here to explain yourself." A grunted curse from the other man suggested that he had him powerless. "Watch yourself, Kit," he went on. "Your man's stirring."

And what in the world was she supposed to do about that? Jump down from Boney and catch him in some kind of wrestler's lock? She edged the horse back towards where her victim was trying to drag himself up the bank, and at that moment, mercifully, two other horsemen rounded the bend in the lane and were upon them. Steel gleamed in their hands. "We're armed." Now she recognised the voice. It was the stranger she had encountered down at the Tidemills. The man called Ned Ludd. "Stay quite still, all of you." And then: "You're not hurt, Mr. Warrender?"

"No. Thanks to you. And you, Mr. Warren?"

"Nothing to signify." His voice came from the darkness of the barricade. "That was good shooting, cousin."

"Lucky shooting," she said, with perfect truth.

"So, who've we got?" said the man called Ludd. "Bring your man forward, if you would, Mr. Warren, and you, Bill, get the other, while I show a light." There was the click of flint on steel, and a tiny flicker of light from a taper made the surrounding darkness more absolute. "Let's see him, Bill. Never mind his leg. Ah," on a note of satisfaction, "just as I thought: Tom Bowles. And what might you be doing acting highwayman, Mr. Bowles?"

"That's my business," growled the shopkeeper.

"I fancy you will find it is mine, too. And the other man?" He leaned down to scrutinise the captive's blackened face. "Yes, I know you. I'll remember you. But I doubt if you're important. What do you say, sir. Shall we let him go?"

"Who are you?" asked George Warren.

"Shall we say a friend?"

"Not the law?"

"Well, no. If it's all one to you, sir, I'd as soon leave the law out of this. Tom Bowles laid for you, for his reasons. We've got him, we'll deal with him. He won't trouble you again, I promise you that. Nor you won't have any trouble if you'll just stay home in the dark nights."

"Oh," said George Warren. "It's like that, is it? What do you say, cousin? Shall we thank our friends and leave them to deal with their own problems in their own way?"

"I believe that would be best." Kate did not understand any of it, but every instinct urged her to be gone. Time enough in the safety of the Dower House to wonder about Ned Ludd's obvious connection with the smugglers. Any minute now, she thought, her teeth would begin to chatter with delayed terror, and then where would Kit Warrender's reputation be? She must get away. She must get home. "We owe you a million thanks," she told Ludd. "And I am sure you will know best how to deal with these men. It's very late. I will see you to your turning, Cousin George."

He laughed. "First we must clear this barricade." She could hear him shake his captive till his teeth rattled in his head. "Before I let you go," he said, "you will clear this for us."

Five minutes later the lane was clear. "We're for Glinde," said the stranger. "You're not coming, Mr. Warrender?"

"I think I'd best see my cousin on his way," said Kate.

"Very good." It was almost as if she had given him an order. "Don't worry about *him.*" Sam had loaded Tom Bowles on to his own horse. "They'll need a new shopkeeper down at Tidemills in the morning."

"You'll not—"

"Kill him? No need. 'No violence' is the word, and no violence it is. Goodnight, gentlemen both."

"What did he mean by that?" asked George Warren as they rode away. "'No violence is the word and no violence it is.'"

"God knows," said Kate.

"Don't you?"

"No."

"Oh," said George Warren, and rode on in silence until they reached the turnoff for Warren House. Then, drawing rein. "I rather think I owe you—and your friends—my life, Cousin Kit. Thank you. It was lucky for me we met tonight." And then, as the thought struck him: "Won't you dine with me tomorrow, to meet that cousin of yours you say you like?"

"I thank you, no." What next? "We don't meet socially," she explained.

"I'm sorry. Very sorry. Kit?"

"Yes?" How she longed to be safe away.

"Did you really mean it? What you said about Lucy Penfold?"

"Good God, yes. Make her talk to you, man. Listen to her, and then ask yourself if you want that for life."

"I will. Thanks, cousin. For everything."

Chapter 8

"I'm going to cut my hair."

"I beg your pardon?" Mrs. Warrender looked up in surprise from her breakfast chocolate.

"It's getting too tedious. All this pinning on of braids. And no need anyway. Lord Hawth never looks at me! I could dress in Christopher's breeches and I doubt he'd notice."

"The children would."

Mrs. Warrender was looking anxious again and Kate hurried to reassure her. "Not that I care whether our enigmatic employer looks at me or not. It's convenient as it is. But, to tell truth, mamma, I thought I might try and make Cousin George Warren notice me just a little when we dine there tonight. To get his mind off Lucy Penfold."

"A shocking affair," said Mrs. Warrender. "I thought better of Mrs. Penfold. But can it be true that the girl is holding out for marriage?"

"Deplorable either way. One really finds oneself compelled to be sorry for Cousin George. Is it true, do you think, that he is as much ostracised as we are?"

"Where did you hear that?"

"Oh, I forget. Nurse Simmonds perhaps. You know how

faithfully she brings the gossip back from Glinde. Someone certainly told me that we are to be the first guests since he settled at the Warren. So we must do justice to the occasion." A ruthless hand reached up and pulled off the braids that crowned her head, unloosing a tangle of curls. "It's grown! You'll have to cut it for me, dearest. Can you manage the Brutus do you think? Remember how you used to cut it for Chris and me?"

"And how you used to wriggle! I do indeed. We'd best hurry our breakfast if I am to do it before you go over to the children."

Arriving breathless and a little late in the schoolroom, Kate was greeted with cries of delight by her pupils. "Miss Warrender, I didn't recognise you," said Giles.

"Quite a transformation." Was there the hint of a sneer in Sue's voice?

"Darling Miss Warrender," said Harriet.

Only Nurse Simmonds, rising with her token curtsy, looked disapproving. "I hope you won't catch cold, Miss Warrender. Driving home in the dark tonight! Are you sure you are wise to go, miss? There's rumours running today."

"Rumours?"

"Something happened last night. No one seems to know what. But Tom Bowles has left the shop at Tidemills. Gone. Vanished."

"Vanished?" asked Giles.

"Run away, I expect," said Kate. "After that beating Mr. Warren gave him, I wonder he could show his face at Tidemills. His bullying days are done, that's for sure."

"Do you think so?" asked Nurse Simmonds.

"I think it's time lessons started," said Kate.

"I beg your pardon I'm sure, miss, for keeping you with my chat. And it is late already." With a meaningful glance at the schoolroom clock and another mock curtsy she left the room.

It was hard to get much work done that day. The children were almost as excited by the prospect of Kate's outing as if they were going themselves. It was a sad measure, she thought, of the dullness of their lives.

"May we come and see you when you're dressed?" begged Harriet, as Kate put on her pelisse for the walk across to the Dower House.

"I don't see why not, if you'd like to. I wouldn't be surprised if my mother had some of her spiced cookies for you."

"Good," said Giles. "Then I'll come too."

So Kate and her mother held their own little party before they set out. The children arrived while Kate was still dressing. The dark green sarcenet she had last worn the winter before to dine at Lady Beston's needed altering. She had lost weight, and the dress, a style of her own contriving, must fit to a nicety. Putting it on at last, she remembered the compliments she had received the first time she wore it, a lifetime ago, it seemed. "A peacock among doves," a poetically inclined young man from Hastings had called her.

Now, coming into the parlour where her mother, demure in widow's black, was regaling the children with orgeat and spiced cookies, she got a whistle of amazement from Giles, and a surprise compliment from Sue. "Miss Warrender! You look as if you'd stepped straight out of *La Belle Assemblée*."

"Clever of you." Kate laughed. "In fact, I did. It seemed to me it would make a change from all those miles and miles of muslin."

"It does." But Sue had reverted to her usual indifferent tone.

George Warren dined early, so it was still daylight when the carriage came for Kate and her mother, and the children begged to be allowed to run back to the hall by themselves rather than wait for Nurse Simmonds, who was supposed to fetch them but had not yet arrived. "Why not?" Kate thought they needed more independence than Nurse Simmonds would allow. She let Giles hand her into the carriage, bent down to urge them to run straight home, then turned to her mother as the coachman gave his horses the office. "I feel just like Cinderella going to the ball."

"Not much of a ball, I am afraid."

"No. Goodness!" Kate laughed. "What do you think Cousin George will be wearing? I do hope not those checked trousers!"

Cousin George had not wasted his time in London. He greeted them in impeccably modern trousers and an elegantly fitted coat. "Weston?" breathed Kate, as she and her mother took off their shawls in a new-papered room that had been a glory-hole in their time.

"Schultz, I think." Mrs. Warrender turned from the glass to look approvingly round her. "I couldn't have done it better myself."

"He must be rich as Golden Ball," said Kate. "Who would have thought it? I wonder Mr. Futherby never gave us a hint."

"Mr. Futherby is a very discreet man," said her mother repressively.

Their host was waiting for them in what had been Charles Warrender's study, or, to be exact, sulking room. Here, too, the change was astonishing. Brown paint and drab curtains had been replaced by white and gold in the style of Mr. Adam, and the room was brilliant with wax candles in sparkling chandeliers.

"I do hope you don't mind it too much." George Warren came forward to greet them all over again, his words for Mrs. Warrender but his amazed eyes for Kate in her dramatic green dress.

"Mind it?" Mrs. Warrender held out a friendly hand. "I congratulate you with all my heart, Mr. Warren. Who did you get to do it?"

"I wish you would call me Cousin George! To tell the truth—"he turned away from her to Kate, who suddenly wished she had taken the green dress in a little more drastically at the shoulders—"I did it myself. I have always thought it would be interesting to try one's hand at it. I got some of Mr. Adam's pattern books when I was in London, and this is the result." He clasped Kate's brown hand in his warm one.

"May I, in my turn, compliment you on your dress, Miss Warrender. It's just what the room needs."

"Straight out of Mr. Adam's pattern book?" asked Kate.

"Alas, Mr. Adam only provides the furnishings. Since I have had it done I have been feeling the need of company to fill my rooms. Ratafia, Mrs. Warrender? Miss Kate?"

"Could I have a glass of burgundy?" said Kate, and got a look of disapproval from Chilver, hovering in attendance.

"Burgundy? Yes, indeed, if you don't object to run goods. I have been having a great inquisition in the cellars today, and seem to have surprisingly little that bears the mark of His Majesty's Customs and Excise."

"Who has?" said Mrs. Warrender. "You are learning the customs of the country, I collect, Cousin George."

"I am indeed." He greeted her use of his name with a warm smile. "I had—"he paused—"a small adventure last night."

"Oh?" Mrs. Warrender smiled at him enquiringly over her glass, unaware of her daughter, suddenly rigid at her side. Why had she not prepared herself for this?

"I think you could call it an adventure. To begin with, I encountered a young kinsman of ours at the Bell in Glinde."

"A kinsman of ours? At the Bell?"

"Why, yes." Her amazement surprised him. "Young Kit Warrender." And then, colouring richly from neatly tied cravat to cropped hair: "Forgive me. I had not thought. You do not mind my mentioning him?"

"Kit Warrender," said Mrs. Warrender faintly. "No, no. Of course not. You met him at the Bell, you say?" This with a quick side glance for Kate.

"Yes. The landlord there, Brown, made him known to me. Charming young man. And not the milksop he looks, either, as I have cause to know. He rode part of the way home with me. Lucky for me that he did."

"Lucky?" Mrs. Warrender and Chilver were both now staring fixedly at Kate, who took a distracted pull at her burgundy.

"I should just about think so. We were ambushed. By some of your engaging local ruffians, I take it. I had occasion to deal with one of them down at Tidemills village the other day. He and a couple of his friends were lying in wait for me up at the priory ruins. Do you know, I think I might be fitting for my shroud now, instead of entertaining you ladies, if that young cousin of yours had not been with me."

"Our Cousin Kit?" asked Mrs. Warrender in a dying voice.

"Yes. No need to trouble yourself about him, ma'am. That's one can take care of himself. The landlord at the Bell had lent us a pair of pistols, see. Said the nights were getting dark, and we should not be riding so late. So, when they came at us out of the ruins, young Kit up and fires, cool as you please, and gets his man. Tom Bowles, it was."

"Shot Tom Bowles?" gasped Mrs. Warrender. "Our Cousin Kit?"

"In the leg. A dead shot, ma'am. Mind you, we'd still have been in trouble if a couple of strangers hadn't come our way from Glinde. That settled our attackers' hash for them, and they were grateful to be let go."

"You let them go?" asked Mrs. Warrender faintly.

"Surprises you, too, does it, ma'am? I confess it did me a trifle. More of your quaint local customs, I take it. But suits me well enough. I don't want any more enemies than I seem to have made already."

"Tom Bowles has gone." Kate decided it was high time she joined in the conversation. "I heard it this morning from the nurse up at the hall. Did a midnight flit, it seems, wounded leg and all."

"That's a comfort," said George Warren. "With him gone, I reckon I can go on riding where I will, without calling on our valiant young cousin for escort."

"Otherwise you would have been scared out of your wits, of course," said Kate, remembering that sweating, cursing fight in the dark.

"Why, naturally, Miss Warrender, a stranger in a strange

land. And, that reminds me, I would be greatful, ma'am—" he turned back to Mrs. Warrender—"if you could furnish me with young Mr. Warrender's direction. I want to see more of that young man."

"His direction?" Mrs. Warrender cast an anguished, appealing glance at Kate, who was having serious trouble controlling a fit of the giggles.

"Mr. Warrender's direction?" There was only one way out of this difficulty and Kate took it with raised eyebrows and her haughtiest tone. "Mr. Warren, you can scarcely imagine that my mother and I associate with young Mr. Warrender."

"You're the losers, then." He had thought her amazingly handsome when she first arrived, now decided that she was also amazingly disagreeable. "Oh, well," he went on, again addressing Mrs. Warrender. "I shall doubtless be able to get in touch with him through the landlord of the Bell."

"Doubtless you will," said Mrs. Warrender faintly, and let him take her arm to lead her in to dinner.

Here an even greater surprise awaited them. The dark and shabby room they remembered had been transformed into a Chinese pavilion, glowing in bamboo and gold.

"Good God," said Mrs. Warrender.

"Vulgar, isn't it?" George Warren looked down at her with a rueful smile. "My mistake, I am afraid, but I could not resist trying. I promise you, it shall not last long."

"No?" Kate was looking about her thoughtfully. "The funny thing is . . . I was at the Pavilion in Brighton once, for a concert. This is . . . different, somehow."

"Thank you." He turned from her mother to surprise her with a warm smile. "Dreadfully vulgar in execution, but at least my own design, based on what I saw in China."

"In China?"

"Why, yes. I made a couple of voyages to Canton with my uncle after my father died. Will you think me sunk beyond recall if I confess that I made my fortune in trade?"

"Opium?" asked Kate.

"No." Angrily. "Tea and silk." He stopped at the sound of a commotion in the hall and turned as Lord Hawth strode into the room, unannounced, travel-stained, seething.

"So!" His black look travelled from Kate to her mother and back. "You are entertaining yourself delightfully, I see. And being entertained." It was hardly a bow in George Warren's direction. "I thought I had left my affairs in better hands."

"Why, whatever is the matter?" The events of the evening had been too much. Silent tears began to slide down Mrs. Warrender's cheeks.

"Matter enough," said Lord Hawth as Kate sprang to her mother's side. "The children have vanished."

"What?" Kate looked at him, arrested, across her mother's drooping figure. "The children? Impossible! They were going to run straight home. They promised."

"Home across the park! In the twilight! One of them a young girl, almost a woman. And you let them go, though you knew their nurse was coming for them?"

"It was not twilight," said Kate, "and their nurse was late. They lead such dull lives, poor little things, I thought they might be indulged in this."

"Perhaps their last indulgence," said Lord Hawth savagely. "You did not, I take it, consider that the man Bowles from Tidemills was on the run? Look!" He had a piece of paper in his hand, now flung it on the table in front of her. "Look at that!"

"Oh, my God!" She stared, horror-struck, at the ill-written, worse spelled message. *The kidds is save fyve hunderd kepes them so.* She looked up at him. "I'll never forgive myself."

"Much good that is." He looked past her to George Warren. "I've come for your help, Warren, and your household's."

"Of course." He had reached out to take and read the message. "No instructions about the money?"

"No. He can't be far. My men are searching the park. If you'll have your land searched, then we can join forces down at Tidemills."

"Surely there first?" protested Kate.

"No." He hardly looked at her. "The obvious place. He's not quite a fool. Oh, my God, if he's hurt them, hurting them now! Sue, and Giles, and little Harriet . . ."

"Why!" Kate looked up at him in open amazement. "You care!"

"Care! They're my children, aren't they? Thanks!" To Warren, who had been giving swift orders: "I've stayed too long. There may be another message." A swift, savage, comprehensive bow, and he was gone.

"Excuse me, ladies." Warren was on his feet. "I must get out of this rig and join the search."

"What shall we do?" wailed Mrs. Warrender when he had left them.

"Go back to the Dower House," said Kate. "And pray."

"Back there? After what he said. Lord Hawth? Kate, we can't!"

"What else can we do? Besides, think, mamma. If it had been me, would not you have been angry? Blamed everyone? I . . . I . . ." For the first time she realised that she, too, was crying. "I had no idea he cared about them so much."

By the time their carriage was ready, George Warren had reappeared in serviceable country clothes. "You're going back?" He had apparently spared the time to think of their predicament.

"Of course," said Kate. "If they are found, they will need us. Lord Hawth will see that, when he thinks about it."

"I hope so." Doubtfully. "He was very angry. I'm only sorry . . . It seems my fault. Mrs. Warrender, if the worst should come to the worst, you will remember, will you not, that there is a home and a welcome here for you?"

She looked up at him through a veil of tears. "Thank you, Cousin George. And now, we'll not keep you. Come, Kate."

"Yes, mamma." Following her meekly to the carriage, Kate wished passionately to be Kit Warrender, able to join the search.

George Warren had been thinking on similar lines. "I wish

we knew where that cousin of yours is, that you don't associate with." His tone was disdainful as he helped her in her turn into the carriage. "He seems to know what goes on in the district. *He* would help."

Kate said nothing. There was nothing to say.

They drove back in wretched silence, both of them crying, neither of them able to reach for any hint of hope. What comfort could they imagine for Sue, and Giles, and little Harriet? And her fault, Kate told herself, over and over. Lord Hawth had been right to be furious, right in everything that he had said. How could she have been such a fool as to have let them go off by themselves, the day after Tom Bowles' disaster? She, who knew so much more about it than anyone? She, who had actually heard those original threats of kidnapping?

Betty Parsons opened the Dower House door for them. "The men are all out searching, ma'am."

"Of course. Is there any news?"

"Not that I know of. They've finished searching the park, that I do know, and have gone on down to the marsh and Tidemills village. It will be an all-night job, searching there."

And not much hope, Kate thought, as she followed her mother listlessly into the drawing room. She remembered all the secret places on the marsh where she and Chris had hidden as children. Bowles would know all the smugglers' hidey-holes and even with children's lives at stake, who in the village would dare betray them?

The answer stared her in the face. The stranger, Ned Ludd. Whatever he might be, he was a figure of power in the village. He had intervened last night, to save her and George Warren. Might he not again? Worth trying anyway, and anything would be better than to sit here, doing this woman's work of tears. And if the search was down the other way now, on the marsh, Kit Warrender had a good chance of getting unmolested to the Bell in Glinde.

She rose to her feet, pretending a yawn. "We're both worn out, and nothing in the world we can do. And we'll need all our strength in the morning. Hot milk, don't you think, and bed?"

"Kate, how can you? And those poor children . . ."

"Thinking about it won't help. If there was only something we could do."

"You're going out! I should have guessed! You're going out as Kit Warrender. Kate, I forbid it. As if last night was not bad enough! Shooting a man in cold blood and starting all this trouble!" And then, at sight of her daughter's face, "I'm sorry, love, I didn't mean . . ."

"But it's true," said Kate bleakly. "And that's why I'm going, whatever you say, so pray, pray don't say it. And anyway—" she managed a watery smile—"whatever else I did, mother, I didn't shoot Tom Bowles in cold blood. I was never so frightened in my life."

"And so you're going again?"

"You have to see that I must."

Mrs. Warrender's chin came up. "Then I'll help you dress."

No need to be quiet in the stables tonight. Every man on the place was out in the darkness, searching. Darkness. Clouds had covered the rag of a moon, and a light drizzle was beginning to fall. Lucky she and Boney knew their way so well. And where were the children, this damp, chill evening? There were caves under the cliffs at Glinde Head, reachable only at low tide. When she and Chris were children, they had heard blood-curdling stories of escaped French prisoners who had hidden there and been drowned by an unusually high autumn tide. Suppose . . .

She would not suppose anything of the kind. She would concentrate on getting through the priory ruins without letting her own terror and anxiety communicate themselves to her horse. The dark seemed extra dark, here where the ruined walls closed in around her. But tonight all was quiet, and she breathed a sigh of relief as they came out the other side of the ruins and a gap in the clouds let the waning moon show the white road that led to Glinde.

The town, too, was quiet. No signs of search here. There had always been a deep, tacit hostility between the old market town of Glinde and the brash new industrial village of Tidemills. She had thought Hawth quite right in leaving Glinde out of his calculations. There would be no shelter for a Tidemills law-breaker here.

The Bell, when she got there, was unusually empty. "They're all out searching," explained Brown, drawing her pint. "Shocking, ain't it? They'd a' gone anyway, I reckon, but Lord Hawth's offered good money *and* a reward. I'd be out, too, but for my Trafalgar leg."

"I'm glad you're here. Brown, you heard what happened last night?"

"Surely. Good thing you took those pistols of mine."

"And a very good thing that man Ludd came along when he did. You sent him." She did not make it a question.

"You know his name?"

"Surely." She lapsed into broad Glinde. "It's used freely enough. Ned Ludd." She spaced the words out for greater emphasis. "A very powerful man. I've seen him quiet those madmen down at Tidemills with a lifted hand."

"You've seen a great deal, Master Kit."

"Enough to know that the best hope for those poor children lies with Ludd. Will you get a message to him for me? Just saying that."

"I'll do my best, Master Kit, but don't you reckon too much on it. I did hear tell he'd gone back to London. He comes and goes so quick, it's the devil's own luck to catch him. But I'll do my possible, I surely will. I wouldn't want a dog of mine to be in Tom Bowles' hands, and as for those three children . . . Well plucked ones as ever I saw. And that Miss Sue almost a young lady. I do hope . . ."

"So do I." Kate swallowed a hard lump. "I must be going. I brought your pistol back."

"Best keep it a while," said Brown.

But the ride back was uneventful. Only, pausing before she took Boney over the gap in the park wall, she could see lights here and there, down on the marsh, to show where the search still went on. Hopeless enough, surely, until daylight. And yet—how could Bowles, with his wounded leg, have taken the children far? The answer was obvious. He had had help, doubtless the help of the two men who had been with him the night before, who must fear recognition either by George Warren or by Kit Warrender. The ransom, if they got it, would pay for their escape. And what would happen to the children?

It did not bear thinking of, and she could think of nothing else. It was a relief to find her mother sitting up for her, but there was no news.

And still none in the morning, when Joe, the man of all work at the Dower House, came back, heavy-eyed from his long night's searching, to eat a quick breakfast and go out again. "Tide's low," he explained. "We're to go through the caves under the cliff."

"Was it very high last night?"

"Yes, miss. Neaps."

No word from Lord Hawth, but Kate was interested to learn from Joe that a group of men from Tidemills itself had been chosen for the search of the cliff caves. "I was born there," explained Joe, "and my Aunt Sarah who's better than a mother to me lives there still. Lord Hawth got us together and told us what he wanted was his children. Nothing else."

"Sensible of him," said Kate.

"Funny thing." Joe was speaking with the freedom of extreme fatigue. "If this had happened when he first came, no one would a' lifted a finger. I reckon they like him now, down at the mills, without rightly knowing it. He's hard, but he's straight, that's Lord Hawth. You know where you are with him."

"I wish to God *we* did," said Kate, reporting this to her mother. "I'm not sure we shouldn't start packing our things. We're going to get our notice, mamma, like a couple of maidservants."

"No we're not," said her mother with surprising firmness.

"You're not being fair, Kate, and you know it. Lord Hawth's the soul of honour—he'd never—he was out of his mind with worry last night."

"Why, mamma, how you do start to his defence!" Kate flashed her mother a quick, bright, loving glance. "Just the same, I wish he would deign to let us know what's going on."

But the long day dragged glumly on with no word from the hall. "It's as if we were pariahs," said Kate. "And I don't even blame him. It's the way I'd feel. If they aren't found I shan't be able to live with myself."

"Don't, dear." But Mrs. Warrender did not try to offer comfort. There was none to offer.

"If only we could *do* something. But, do you know, I don't believe I dare go over to the hall and ask for news." And then, on a new note. "Mother, Kit Warrender could."

"No, Kate." Mrs. Warrender, too, had a new note, one of total finality. "You couldn't pass it off in the daylight, and you know it as well as I do. It would merely be to compound our disaster."

"Who cares about us!" But Kate knew her mother was right. Her appearances as Kit Warrender had always been in dusk or dark, by candle or lamplight. Daylight would inevitably expose her. "When it gets dark, then?" The light was beginning to fade already, the September evening settling into autumn.

"What use?" And then: "I'll send Betty Parsons. Now."

Betty came back breathless. "No news, ma'am, I'm afraid, but his lordship wants to see you and Miss Kate. He's just back from Tidemills. He looks dreadful, ma'am. At once, he says."

"Our dismissal, do you think?" asked Kate as they hurried across the park. "Not that it seems to matter, if only the children are safe."

"I know. But it won't be. Lord Hawth wouldn't do it."

"You sound very sure."

"I think I am. Remember what Joe said: hard but straight. He won't go on blaming you, Kate."

"But there will be no job for me, if . . ."

"Don't," said her mother.

A scared maid opened the big front door at the hall. "The men is all out, ma'am. He's in his study, his lordship. Get him to eat something, ma'am. He's had nothing, not since . . ."

Entering the study, Kate was reminded of that first time. Hawth might not have eaten, but he had been drinking. A slight flush along the cheekbones was the only colour in the sallow face that seemed to have developed new lines during the night and day of searching. His dishevelled hair and mudstained clothes, however, were very different from the flamboyant evening dress he had worn that other time. His greatcoat, tossed aside on a chair, suggested that he had come straight to the study.

"There you are at last." He put down his wine glass and rose to receive them. "You'll forgive me if I don't stand on points." He was addressing Mrs. Warrender, as if Kate did not exist.

"Of course. There's no news, my lord?"

"Another note. That's what brought me back. Thrown in at the Glinde gate. Instructions. The money's to be taken to the priory ruins tonight. It means he can't be far. Or the children, please God. He won't trust anyone else to come for it, and we know he's wounded. So . . . Mrs. Warrender, you must know this district as well as anyone. You've visited the poor, that sort of thing?"

"Why, yes."

"Then, think, ma'am. Remote houses, disused ones, sheds that might give shelter for a night or so. He's got a horse and waggon, we think, but he won't want to risk going far. He must know what kind of a search we're mounting. There has to be somewhere."

"He could have left the children somewhere else," volunteered Kate.

"He could have killed the children, Miss Warrender, and still come to collect the ransom." He looked through rather than at her as he spoke what had been in all their minds.

But she, too, was looking past him. "Oh, thank God!" she exclaimed as the secret panel slid open and Giles appeared, lantern in hand.

"Father," he said.

"Giles!" Hawth swung round, then strode forward to lift him gently down. "And Harriet!" He amazed himself as much as anyone by kissing her as he lifted her down in her turn. "And Sue! How in the world?"

"We were rescued," said Giles. "Oh, sir, it has been an adventure. We were scared at first, when they nabbed us. That stinking cart . . . and the shed . . . Sue and Harriet cried. I . . . I don't think I did." A defiant glance for Sue. "Only, you see, I knew him. It was Tom Bowles. I've been down to his shop with nurse. I said his name. He . . . he frightened me."

"You were right to be frightened," said Lord Hawth. All of the adults knew that whatever ransom he had paid, the children would never have survived after that fatally admitted recognition. "But how did you get away? What happened?"

"We were rescued." Sue took up the story. She was very pale, with traces of tears on her cheeks, and yet there was something about her, Kate thought, almost a glow. From deferred shock? From the relief of the escape? "They put us in a shed," Sue went on. "In the woods. Not far from the park wall. They had a way through. Father, you must have it closed up."

"Yes."

"They tied us up. Shut us in. Went away. It was dark. Black dark. I couldn't get to Harriet. She was crying. Well, I think we all were. And then, after a long time—I don't know how long—they came."

"Who?"

"I don't know. Strangers. Two of them. They didn't say much, just untied us. Got us out of there. It was quite near the priory ruins. When we came to them, I said, why not go back that way. Much quicker, and Harriet fussing. So they gave us a lantern and the chief one said that suited him.

Least said, soonest mended, he said, and we were to tell you so, Father, with his compliments."

"Whose compliments?"

"Ned," she told him. "Ned Ludd."

Lord Hawth had crossed the room to pull the bellrope. "Call off the search," he told the amazed girl who answered the summons. "And send for Nurse Simmonds."

"Didn't no one tell you, my lord? She's gone, vanished. Bed not slept in this morning."

"And no one thought to tell me!" The long night and day of anxiety erupted suddenly into rage as he turned on Kate. "No wonder you have been laughing up your sleeve at me all this time. No doubt you knew you would prove indispensable in the end."

"Laughing? I?" She had crossed the room to embrace the children and looked at him across Sue's shoulder, tears of relief streaming down her face. "Are you suggesting, my lord, that I was a party to this infamous business? Because, if so, I wish to hand in my notice. This moment."

"Father," said Sue.

And, "Kate," said Mrs. Warrender.

There was a long, strained silence, broken at last by Harriet, who burst into tears. "I want to go to bed," she wailed.

"And so you shall." Kate picked her up. "We will discuss this, my lord, in the morning, when you have slept."

"When I am sober, you would say? Very well, Miss Warrender, the morning let it be."

Chapter 9

Much though they disliked it, each for her own reasons, Kate and her mother had to spend that night at the hall. The children simply would not be parted from Kate, and Mrs. Warrender gave orders for their old room to be made ready.

"I should consult his lordship, ma'am?" Parsons had returned from the search, haggard with lack of sleep like the rest of them.

"I wouldn't if I were you," said Mrs. Warrender. "Send him some food to the study and let's cross our bridges in the morning, Parsons."

Morning brought no news of the fugitives. "I suppose once they found the children gone they took to their heels." Mrs. Warrender was sharing nursery breakfast with Kate and the children. Harriet and Sue had both had nightmares and Giles was very quiet. As for Kate, she looked as if she had not slept at all, and her mother thought she probably had not, torn as she was between rage with Lord Hawth and concern for the children.

Parsons, who had brought the nursery breakfast himself,

reported that Lord Hawth was still asleep. "He was worn out, miss. Not himself last night."

So the servants knew all about what had happened. It was inevitable, and merely another last straw. The furious thoughts chased themselves round and round in Kate's head. Hawth had actually hinted at some kind of complicity between her and Nurse Simmonds. She longed to tell him of her visit to Brown, the message to Ned Ludd which had surely been responsible for the children's release. But that was to tell him of Kit Warrender, and she would rather die than do that.

The morning dragged, with hardly a pretence at lessons, and Kate was reading aloud to the children when a footman appeared to summon her to the study.

"Just me?" She flashed a glance of appeal to where her mother sat working by the window.

"Yes, miss. He said so quite particular."

"Oh, me!" Kate rose to her feet, cast a depressed glance at the pallid reflection in the glass, managed a wavering smile for her mother and prepared to leave the room.

"I want to come, too," said Giles.

"And me." Harriet jumped down from her chair.

"I'm afraid not, bless your hearts." Kate found her eyes suddenly filled with tears.

"Well, if he sends you away, tell him we'll go, too," said Giles.

"You're keeping Lord Hawth waiting, dear," reminded Mrs. Warrender.

"And that would never do." The children's demonstration had given Kate back a little spirit. She wiped a brisk hand across her eyes and made her way to the study.

Lord Hawth was waiting for her, standing impatiently at the study window. She had seen her father on too many mornings-after not to recognise his state at once. She could almost have felt sorry for him if his bad temper had not been so obvious.

"Sit down, Miss Warrender." He kept his own place by the window. "I think I have to beg your pardon." He had clearly rehearsed the short speech and it came out with a kind of angry lack of conviction. "If I said anything, last night," he went on, "that might suggest I thought you connected in any way with the children's abduction, I wish to apologise and withdraw it unreservedly."

"Thank you, my lord." Her tone was as formally colourless as his.

"Good." He was glad to have it over. "Parsons tells me that Nurse Simmonds was seen several times with Tom Bowles. We must assume, I think, that she has gone with him."

"Good riddance," said Kate.

"Yes. You will stay, of course."

"Of course?" She considered it, then: "Yes, my lord, I will stay. The children need me. You have not asked how they are this morning."

"I have not asked *you,* Miss Warrender. Will you be surprised to hear that it was on my instructions that Parsons served the nursery breakfast? He tells me that Sue and Harriet had nightmares and even Giles looks far from well. I can see for myself that you have not had much sleep. I rely on you to see that things go on as quietly as possible for the next few days. I would be grateful if you and your mother would stay here, at the hall, until the children are quite recovered from their experience. I have written this morning to a cousin of mine—a Miss Lintott—suggesting that she make her home here until the children are grown up. When she arrives, you and your mother will be able to return to the Dower House."

"Thank you." She made him an angry curtsy. "But surely you'll not need us if your cousin is to take over here?"

"Not need you! Good God, you don't know my Cousin Lintott. As helpless a female as ever drew thread. But she will add some touch of respectability to the children's situation."

"Thank you again."

"You persist in misunderstanding me, Miss Warrender. You know as well as I do—" He broke off. "Damnation! What's the use!" He picked up his gloves. "I am leaving at once for Brighton, so you will not be troubled with my company."

"Nor he with ours," Kate summed it up for her mother. "He'll stay away, I take it, until the threadless cousin is safely installed. We're not respectable enough, it seems, you and I!"

"Kate, dear, be reasonable. We're not kin, that's all. He's right, and you know it."

"Nothing will make me like it. If only there was somewhere we could go!"

"But there isn't, Kate, and anyway you know we can't possibly leave the children now. And—" she put a pleading hand on Kate's—"he did apologise. Think what that must have cost him."

"I should say! You should just have heard him." At last she could laugh at it. "Getting each word out as if it choked him. I wish the Prince Regent joy of his company, if he continues in his present mood."

Lord Hawth had indeed left the hall in a combination of hangover and rage that took him flaming across the downs to Warren House, where he felt in honour bound to stop and thank George Warren for his help in the search for the children. The surprising result of this visit was a growing friendship between the two men. One of its bases was a strong, shared, tacit dislike for Kate Warrender, and George Warren made no attempt to reinstate his ruined dinner party. Riding with the Glinde harriers, shooting with his new friend, who often spent the night at the Warren rather than return to Brighton, he forgot to be homesick for America and had not much time to pursue Lucy Penfold either. In fact, he found himself less and less inclined to do so. For one thing, sight of her blonde prettiness somehow always put him in mind of Miss Warrender, handsome and disagreeable in dark green. For another, he soon noticed the ogling glances Lucy bestowed on Lord Hawth.

"Fetching little hussy," said Hawth one bright October morning when they had encountered her in the stable yard. "What do you reckon to do about her?"

"Do?"

Hawth laughed. "Quite right. None of my business. But you maybe don't understand how gossip runs in these parts. Word is, you're thinking of marrying the girl."

"Do you know," slowly, "I actually was." The past tense said it all.

"Would you like me to take her off your hands? The mother's a tartar, I believe."

"No thanks. I'll deal with it. Funny thing." George Warren ran a meditative hand along his horse's saddle as he prepared to mount. "I heard a rumour you were contemplating marriage yourself."

"Not a word of truth in it," said Hawth cheerfully. "Oh, I know there's talk. No wonder. I started it myself. Thought it would make things easier for those cousins of yours, coming to live at the Dower House."

"Thoughtful of you."

Hawth gave a bark of laughter. "Not really. Or . . . enlightened self-interest. Don't want a hell brew of scandal on my own doorstep, specially not where the children are concerned. They've trouble enough as it is, poor little bastards."

"Nothing you can do for them?"

"You mean marry their mother? I thank you, no. Money they'll have. That's of course. I expect they'll do well enough. Spunky lot. I tell you, I was proud of them that night they were kidnapped. Stood up to that. Stood up to me. Young Sue came home and told me to have my park wall repaired. I've done it, too. Deuced inconvenient for the smugglers, but I can't help that."

"You mean you knew about the gap?"

"Of course I knew. Everyone knew. Used all the time. I

reckon Tom Bowles is more afraid, now, of his smuggling friends than of the law."

"He was one of them?"

"Naturally. A key man, I've always thought. Well, stands to reason a good deal of the stuff is run by way of the Tidemills. Keep a store untidy enough, which God knows Tom Bowles did, and who's to tell run goods from legal? That reminds me, high time I found a new storekeeper for the Tidemills. One of my responsibilities as landlord, it seems. Would you like me to offer the job to young John Penfold? He's a quick scholar, your Futherby tells me, can read and write and reckon with the best of them. And he'd have a house with the job. Take his mother and sister off your hands."

"Oh, *yes,*" said George Warren. And then: "Thanks."

"Don't thank me. Thank Futherby. Manages us all, that man, and for our own good, which is hard to bear. I suppose it will mean young John Penfold gets mixed up with the smugglers, but that's his worry. Oh—" very casual—"I promised the children I'd take them down to Tidemills one day this week, now I'm back home, let them watch the mill at work. They've deserved a treat, and even little Harriet can ride that far, I understand. Care to join us? A deuced dull family party, but the mill itself is worth seeing, and I'd be glad of your company. After all—"he laughed his grating laugh—"you ought to own the place. Do no harm for those radical workers down there to see the two of us on good terms."

"Yes. Yes, I'd like to come. Thanks." But George Warren, who was slowly beginning to learn his way round the intricacies of British society, wondered if Hawth had other motives beside the openly acknowledged one for this rather surprising invitation. Did he think an American interloper good enough for his bastard daughter?

He was surprised, and, surprisingly, disappointed to discover that Mrs. Warrender and Kate were not to be of the Tidemills party. Joining it at the hall, he found the two ladies there waiting to see off the little cavalcade. "You're not coming, cousin?" He wished he knew, or dared use, Mrs. Warrender's first name.

"We are not invited." Kate Warrender answered for her mother. "I wish you will help Sue keep an eye on little Harriet, Mr. Warren. She is young for such a long outing."

"Disapproving again, Miss Warrender?" Hawth had come silently up behind her. "We will take good care of Harriet, I promise you."

"I'm glad to hear it," she said.

The little cavalcade set off in the best of spirits, the children in high twig over this outing with their father. All but Sue, thought George Warren, riding beside her while Lord Hawth shared his attentions between the two younger ones. George had met the children often enough in Glinde to notice that Sue had changed since the kidnapping. She had been a child. Now she was a young woman, and, he thought, not a happy one. Well, that was understandable. She was old enough, now, to be aware of her anomalous position, and aware, too, he was afraid, of her father's plans for herself and him.

What did she think of them? Impossible to tell. Anyway, he did not want to know. She might be a young woman. She was most certainly not the young woman for him. It was an odd thing, but, as with Lucy Penfold, when he looked at Sue's pensive withdrawn face, what he saw was Miss Warrender, handsome, haughty, intolerable in a dark green dress cut too low by Philadelphia standards. No doubt about it, her presence and her mother's would have made this party less insipid. Tired of saying polite nothings to Sue and getting paid in his own coin, he left her with an apology, and the groom, and spurred his own horse to join Hawth and the younger children. "Have you heard anything of young Kit Warrender?" he asked.

"Not a word. He comes and goes like a will-o'-the-wisp, that young man. I'm sorry. I owe him my thanks, Brown tells me, for sending word about the children's plight to that mysterious Ned Ludd. And there's another man I wouldn't mind meeting! Talks riot and revolution at my mill one day, and turns round almost the next to rescue my children. Not that I'm not grateful. And to Kit Warrender. Elusive young devil."

"You're not of a mind with his cousins?"

"The Warrenders?"

"They think him beneath their touch. Miss Warrender as good as told me so."

"Just like her." But he was distracted by little Harriet, who was beginning, visibly, to tire, and whose pony was starting to take advantage of her. "Devil take it if Miss Warrender wasn't right," he said. "It's a deuced awkward habit of hers. Now what's to do?" They were still about half a mile from the village. "Ride on and let the child rest at the inn, or cut our losses and turn back?"

"It looks like rain." George Warren was beginning to wish he had never come. "I think we had best turn back."

"I'm cold," said Harriet, through chattering teeth, and settled it.

"You'll come back and take a nuncheon with us?" said Hawth when they reached the turning to Warren House.

"I believe not, thanks." He was glad to escape the sad little party, and Hawth recognised it with a grimace.

When he rode up at last to the door of Hawth Hall, with Harriet held awkwardly on the front of his saddle while the groom led her pony, he found Kate and Mrs. Warrender waiting for their party. Inevitable, and infuriating. It was raining quite hard now, and all three children were wet and subdued. He carried Harriet indoors and deposited her at Kate's feet. "You were right and I was wrong," he told her, without pleasure.

Busy drying the child's tears, Kate did not answer.

"So tedious of it to rain," said Mrs. Warrender. "Such a bright morning. One would never have thought it."

"I would have, if I'd had any sense," said Hawth.

"Bed, I think." Kate picked Harriet up.

"She's too heavy for you. I'll take her." But Harriet clung

to Kate, crying harder than ever, and Hawth muttered an oath and went back out into the rain.

Half an hour later he arrived, soaking wet, in his curricle at Warren House. "I'm off to Brighton. Care to come too? The Prince Regent's still there. They're an amusing crowd, for a while."

"No, thanks." George Warren was in the estate room, poring over some papers. "I asked Futherby for a report on the tenant farms. He's just brought it. It's . . . interesting."

"Oh?"

"They're in terrible shape. What kind of a man was Charles Warrender? No improvements, old fashioned methods, land wasted on unnecessary fallowing, fields full of something called charlock. Plenty of apples and no cyder press of our own. Hops and no oast house. What do you think of the Suffolk ploughs one hears about, and those new thrashing machines?"

"I can't say I know much about them, except they're unpopular with the men. Lord Egremont's got a thrashing machine over at Petworth. Suffolk ploughs too, I believe. If you are thinking of coming out as an improving landlord, maybe you had better come to Brighton and meet him."

"He'll be there? That's something else again. I'd dearly like to meet him. And not just to talk farming. There's a painter visits him, a man called Turner. I saw some pictures of his at the Academy. I'm sadly tempted to buy one. Gives you—I don't know—kind of a feeling of England. And as for meeting him—I'd like that!" He looked embarrassed suddenly. "I paint a little myself."

"Good God," said Lord Hawth, shocked.

But he took his surprising new friend to Brighton just the same and thought himself bold to introduce him to Lord Egremont. The result was another surprise. Beginning with Turner and landscape painting, the two men were soon deep in discussion of something called the Romantic Movement about which Hawth neither knew nor cared. There was a Mr. Wordsworth, it seemed, who lived in the Lake District, of all barbarous places, and had published, with a friend named Coleridge, a volume called *Lyrical Ballads* that Warren had read in America. "I thought some of it dull enough stuff," he said, "but some of it is quite out of the way. I've been wishing to travel up to Westmorland to meet Mr. Wordsworth, but there's been so much to do."

"You'd better come and visit me at Petworth," said Lord Egremont. "I've a painter friend of theirs, Mr. Hayden, at the house, and, who knows, we might persuade Mr. Turner to join us and paint you a landscape. They come high, you know."

"Five hundred guineas," said Warren cheerfully. "I do know."

Summoned to dine with the Prince Regent at the Pavilion, Lord Hawth returned late and a trifle foxed to find George Warren busy packing. "Tired of Brighton already?" he asked, pouring himself a superogatory glass of port.

"On the contrary, I find it delightful. We've nothing to touch it at home. I must get a house here next summer. I hope you'll be so good as to advise me. But Lord Egremont proposes to return to Petworth tomorrow, and has invited me to go too, to meet Mr. Hayden and look at his Suffolk ploughs."

"An irresistible invitation," said Hawth dryly. "And will you read poetry together in the evenings?"

"I'm sorry." George Warren flushed fiery red and looked suddenly very young indeed. "Forgive me. It's outrageously rude of me when you have been so kind as to bring me here."

"Nonsense." Hawth recovered his temper. "Brought you here to meet Lord Egremont, din't I? He's asked you home to his house of the muses, han't he? Course you must go. Besides, suits me, to tell truth. I'm closing the house here. Had meant to leave it open for you, but now . . . The Prince returns to London in a few days. He's asked me to go too. There's trouble brewing in the north. Food riots . . . machine breaking. Well, no wonder, starvation wages and the quartern loaf up again. If only our party were in office, we'd soon have things in better train, but His Highness feels he cannot change his ministers while his father still has a chance of making a recover. To find himself saddled with a Whig government might prove fatal to the old King, the doctors say. Unfortunate. A Whig government would have managed things better with your country, too. I'm afraid the news from there is hardly promising."

"Well, no wonder," said George Warren, "when you can do no better than send a young fool like Augustus Foster to negotiate for you. He's made you an enemy a minute since he reached Washington."

"He's kin to the Duke of Devonshire."

"And what's that to the purpose? A fool's a fool, whoever's his cousin."

"Not exactly cousin," said Lord Hawth. "Mistress's son. Beg pardon! Second wife's!"

"You British," said George Warren.

In the end, he stayed over Christmas at Petworth, enjoying the informal hospitality and lively talk at the great house, and the curious native rituals with which the British celebrated the twelve days of Christmas. He met Mr. Turner and admired his paintings of Petworth Park, but did not, in the end, decide either to buy or to commission one. He had a curious fancy to add a portrait by the famous Thomas Lawrence to the family gallery at Warren House. An absurd idea, of course. He certainly did not want a portrait of himself, but it had irked him that Charles Warrender had not added a picture of his pretty young wife to the family gallery. In character, of course, but a pity just the same. What would happen, he wondered, if he were to ask Lawrence to do one of his striking portraits of Mrs. Warrender—or Mrs. Warrender and her formidable daughter? A mad idea, but tempting, just the same. After all, they *were* his cousins. An only child, he had lost his mother before he was five years old and had never quite managed to cope with the prim Philadelphia girls. One of the great advantages of life on board ship had been the masculine society, but Petworth House had taught him that mixed company could be wonderfully pleasant too, if one only knew how to go on. He was rather tempted to go to Mrs. Warrender for lessons.

Returning home to Warren House just after Twelfth Night, he found a budget of bad news awaiting him from Philadelphia. His friends there wrote anxiously of President Madison's anti-British message to Congress early in November, and the domination of the war hawks in the country. One and all, they urged him to come home, apparently convinced that if war should, as they gravely feared, break out between the two countries, he might be thrown into prison, as British visitors to France had been in 1803.

It was a very curious thing, considering how unhappy he had been during his first months in England, but he did not want to go home. What, indeed, was home? Surely, it was where one had a job of work to do. In Philadelphia, he had been merely concerned with making money. At Warren House, he seemed willy-nilly to have acquired a host of responsibilities.

Mr. Futherby welcomed him back with enthusiasm and a long list of problems to do with the estate. Told that Warren had ordered two Suffolk ploughs and one of the new thrashing machines, he looked grave. "The ploughs may do well enough," he said. "But I have doubts about the thrashing machine. There is a curious spirit abroad. I don't much like it, and am all the more delighted to see you home, Mr. Warren."

"What kind of a spirit?"

Mr. Futherby looked nervously round the quiet study. "Revolutionary, Mr. Warren. They had a Tree of Liberty in the mill yard down at Tidemills this Christmas. Drank all kinds of toasts. And made speeches. 'Death to the aristocrats!' That kind of thing."

"Dear me," said George Warren. "Am I going to be burned in my bed?"

"Oh, no, not you, sir. You're popular down there. For one thing, you knocked out Tom Bowles in fair fight. For another, you're an American. A revolutionary yourself, in their eyes. They almost look on you as one of them. Well, they're not fools. They know how close the two countries are to war. They feel it, in their pockets and their bellies. Your non-importation act hits them as hard as the French war. And it's the radicals who oppose the war. You heard, I've no doubt, how Sir Francis Burdett contrived to catch the Speaker's eye when Parliament met the other day, and made a strong anti-government speech. And anti-war. Both wars."

"Yes." Warren laughed. "You don't sound to have much order in your Parliament. But, Futherby, if the hotheads down at Tidemills don't intend to attack me, you can't mean—"

"Hawth Hall," said Futherby. "If you're in touch with his lordship, sir, I wish you would suggest he come home. There's something going on down at the Tidemills. I had young John Penfold to see me yesterday. A badly frightened man. He wants Lord Hawth home so he can give up the shop. Get permission to move away, with his mother and sister. He wouldn't give a reason. Said it was as much as his life was worth."

"But why you?"

"He don't trust Hawth's man Knowles. He wouldn't explain that either. He knows something that's fretting him good and proper, that boy. So, if you should be writing Lord Hawth and felt like saying a word. And . . . Mr. Warren?"

"Yes?"

"You've not heard anything of young Kit Warrender since you got back? He seems to fit into it somewhere. John Penfold was asking for him, too. I did make bold to speak of it to the ladies up at the Dower House, but got cold enough looks for my pains."

"I dare swear you did. No, I've not seen Kit Warrender since he saved my life last autumn. Seems to have left the district, and I don't blame him, treated as he is."

"Not to say left," said Futherby. "He's been seen, here and there, but nobody seems to know where to lay hands on him.

So if you should run into him, down at the Bell maybe, I wish you'd give him the word."

"What word, precisely?"

"Well, that's a bit of a puzzler, isn't it? Maybe just to ask him to drop down to Tidemills and see young Penfold? Careful-like?"

"I'll certainly do that. If I should meet him. And I'll write Lord Hawth today. I'd meant to anyway. I owe him a thank for my introduction to Lord Egremont. What should I say?"

"Ask him to come home, sir. I don't much like to think of the ladies at the Dower House, and the children at the hall, and nobody to look out for them but a parcel of johnny-come-lately servants. Not Parsons, of course, but I don't reckon much to the rest of them."

"I'll tell him," said Warren. "And I must call on the ladies."

The ladies, at that very moment, were involved in the nearest thing they ever got to an acrimonious argument. It had been raging off and on ever since Futherby had called, asked his question about Kit Warrender and told them about John Penfold.

"I won't allow it," said Mrs. Warrender.

"But I think I ought to," said Kate.

"It's too dangerous. And, besides, how would you go? I'm not sending James down with Boney this time, to have you risk suffocation in that secret passage and worse down at Tidemills."

This was unanswerable. Since the gap in the wall had been built in, Kate's private way out of the park was closed. Without her mother's help, she could not possibly manage the masquerade, and she was beginning to recognise that her mother really did not mean to help. "I know," she said at last. "Why didn't I think of it sooner? We must send for John Penfold to come here."

"Here?"

"Yes. Here to the Dower House. Tell him, if he wants to

meet Kit Warrender, he can do so, secretly, here. It's no affair of his if young Kit manages to spirit himself into the park without going through any of the gates. Anyway, why should he know?"

"True enough," said her mother. "You really think we should, Kate?"

"I'm sure of it. Since Lord Hawth chooses to stay in London, enjoying himself and doubtless winning other people's fortunes at Brooks's, someone had better take a hand before we are all burned in our beds. I didn't half like the sound of what Futherby had to say."

"No more did I," said her mother. "I'll tell Futherby when next he calls."

"That may be too late," said her daughter gloomily. And then, seeing her mother's blanched face: "I'm a fool, dearest! They'll never do anything while the weather's so bad, and the nights so dark. I'm just—blue-devilled, I suppose."

"And no wonder," said her mother. "It's been a dull Christmas, I'm afraid."

"Dull! If it weren't for the children, I'd go hang myself. And mother—"

"Yes?"

"I'm worried about Sue. She'd always been difficult, but there's no understanding her these days. One day over the moon, the next, glummer even than I am. There's no rhyme or reason to it."

"Anyone would think she was in love," said Mrs. Warrender.

"In love? But it's not possible? Who does she see, poor child? Who do any of us see?"

"One of the men?"

"Never! She's too much pride. Besides, I would have noticed."

"Of course you would. Oh, well, I expect she is just suffering the pangs of growing up. And into not too easy a situation, poor child."

"I wish Lord Hawth would come home," said Kate.

But when a carriage drove up to the Dower House through pouring rain later that afternoon it was George Warren, not Lord Hawth, who jumped out and hurried up the steps to the house. "I shall send a message to Penfold by him," said Kate.

"He'll be surprised."

"I can't help that. It's too good a chance to be missed." What she had not given herself time to think about was George Warren's inevitable reaction.

"You can get Kit Warrender here?" he said. "Splendid. May I come and give him the meeting. I've owed that young man a thank since last autumn, but he's as elusive as Jack-o'-lantern. Or that General Ludd who's giving such trouble in the north. When shall I tell young Penfold to come?"

"Tomorrow night," said Kate. "I'll need time to get word to Mr. Warrender. And I'm sorry, Mr. Warren, but you must see your being here would only increase the risk to John Penfold. I'll give your message to Mr. Warrender."

"Very well." Reluctantly. "If you think so. Then, if you would ask him to call on me on one of those night rides of his. Or, better still, give me his direction and I will call on him."

"I've told you before: I don't know that," said Kate. "I shall just send a message."

"A very mysterious young man."

"No doubt he knows his own business."

"Do tell us how you enjoyed yourself at Petworth House." Mrs. Warrender plunged boldly into the ensuing silence. "Lord Egremont is quite a modern Mycenas they say."

"Yes. An admirable host, even when he's not at home. It's wonderfully civilised, your English country-house life. The mixture of regime and freedom, of conversation and exercise, is done to a marvel. I wish I thought I could achieve something like it at Warren House."

"It would certainly make a change," said Kate.

And, "You are not taking these war rumours too seriously then?" said her mother hastily to fill another conversational gap.

"You mean, I am not thinking of going back to America? No, ma'am. It's true, my friends all urge it. They think war between our countries as good as certain—or as bad. But I seem to be fixed here. There are so many things to do. Futherby and I have all kinds of agricultural plans for the spring. Besides, I have invited a couple of poets to stay."

"Poets?" asked Kate.

"Yes. I don't imagine you know their work. Nothing like Sir Walter Scott. A plain Mr. Wordsworth and Mr. Coleridge. And their wives, of course. I don't suppose they'll come, but I met their friend Mr. Hayden at Petworth House, and he said he did not think they would be affronted at being invited."

"I don't suppose they would," said Kate. "But do you *read* their poetry, Mr. Warren?"

He laughed, struck an attitude, and began to recite:

> "It is an ancient Mariner,
> And he stoppeth one of three.
> 'By thy long grey beard and glittering eye,
> Now wherefore stopp'st thou me?'

Do you wish me to go on, Miss Warrender?"

"You mean you could?"

"Not the whole poem, as yet, but I'm perfect, I think, in the first three parts. There was plenty of reading time, sailing to China." He laughed. "Don't look so frightened, I'll spare you."

"I do hope your poets come," said Kate. "But of the two, I think I would really rather meet Mr. Wordsworth. Shall I recite his 'Lines Written Above Tintern Abbey' to you, Mr. Warren?"

"I wish you would call me Cousin George," he said. And

then: "And what *do* you think of Sir Walter Scott, Cousin Kate?"

"Well," said Mrs. Warrender, when he left at last three quarters of an hour later, "Who would have thought it?"

"Yes." Kate laughed. "I am ashamed to say I did not realise they had books in America. And I'll never get over those trips of his to China. What a surprise he is. But how awkward about his wanting to meet Kit Warrender!"

"He took your refusal very well, I thought," said her mother.

"Yes," said Kate. "Which gave me the most lowering feeling that he meant to surprise us with a visit tomorrow night. Or meet Kit Warrender on the way!"

"But he wouldn't," said her mother.

"No, he wouldn't, would he," said Kate. "So what, precisely, do we do about that?"

Chapter 10

George Warren had promised to let them know if John Penfold was not able to come, so no news, next morning, was good news in a way. "At least it means we will get it over with before Lord Hawth returns," said Kate.

"You think he will be back soon?"

"He's bound to learn there's trouble down here. That man hears everything."

"Well, being a magistrate, I suppose he would."

"Being a magistrate, you would think he would stay home a bit more."

"Dull for him, with only the children, after his life in Brighton and at the London clubs."

"Nothing to stop him keeping open house like Lord Egremont. After all, he's got a gem of a housekeeper, and all things handsome about him."

"I sometimes wonder whether that's not the difficulty," said her mother on a faint note of apology.

"What do you mean, dearest?"

"Why, I have thought he was afraid it would be too much trouble. Or that it would be—embarrassing for us."

"Lord Hawth! Afraid of making work? Or embarrassing

us! Mother, you must have windmills in your head! He never thought about anyone but himself in his life. Look at the way he treats those poor children! For a while, after that kidnapping scare, you would have thought they were his dearest possession, and then off he goes, with hardly a 'good-bye,' and sends you word to buy them their Twelfth Night presents. It's no wonder poor Sue looks so peaked. She set a good deal of store by his notice."

"I hope it's only that," said her mother.

Lessons stopped early these late January days when night fell about four o'clock and even a full moon was lost behind storm clouds. Since the kidnapping, Kate always had a qualm of conscience when she left the children behind at Hawth Hall with no company but Lord Hawth's elderly, dreary, superannuated cousin, who bored the children, as Giles shamelessly put it, "quite beyond permission" with her endless lamentations for her snug lost life in Bath.

Hurrying home to the Dower House and changing into a coat and breeches of olive drab whose jacket had been cut a little large for her brother and therefore never worn, Kate congratulated herself that, as a caller, Kit Warrender would not be expected to wear evening dress. She would never manage to carry off her impersonation in knee breeches and silk stockings. As it was, she went quickly round the drawing room blowing out all but one candle in each of the holders on the walls. "We are economising," she told her mother. "Patriotically."

"Did you get down without any of the servants seeing you?"

"Yes. And have told Betty to say I've a migraine headache and must not be disturbed on any account." She moved over to disarrange the curtain that concealed a long French window. "I'm an unorthodox young man." She turned to smile across the room at her mother. "I think I must have come on foot across the park and in at that window. A good thing it's stopped raining." She looked down at one of the shining boots her brother had outgrown.

"Scandalous," said Mrs. Warrender. "What in the world

would Lord Hawth think if he knew I was entertaining a young man by myself?"

"A cousin, remember. No need to refine too much upon it. And you, a highly respectable widow. Now if it was me! I collect I must have invented my migraine headache to avoid this shocking meeting. Unhandsome of me, was it not, to abandon you to it?"

"Oh, Kate, you'll be the death of me. You are actually enjoying yourself!"

"One might as well," said Kate, and froze quickly into a masculine posture, foot on the fender, half-turned from the door. The servants, she knew, were her greatest hazard.

But Joe was too much surprised at not finding his mistress alone to do more than gawp at her as he announced that young Mr. Penfold was asking if he might see her.

John Penfold was a badly frightened young man. "I'm right glad you're here, sir," he told Kate, after the first greetings. "You've got some influence with those madmen down at Tidemills! Can you persuade them to lay off me? Just till Lord Hawth gets back and I can try and get him to let me settle on some other part of the estate. Without his good word, no parish will have me, but if I stay at Tidemills, I'm a dead man, and then what will happen to my mother and poor Lucy?"

"A dead man?"

"Yes, sir. Could I speak with you alone, sir? Excusing me, ma'am?"

"Come into the next room." Ignoring her mother's horrified expression, Kate led the way into a little book-room that opened off the drawing-room. "Yes?" She leaned negligently against the back of a chair, grateful for the half darkness of the room, which was lighted only from the drawing-room door.

"They want to twist me in, sir! To make me one of them. They're all in it, down there! Blood-red revolutionaries, with smuggling as a cover. And they need the shop, see, to stow the run goods. There's nowhere else down at Tidemills. They've been at me and at me since I took over the shop, but, lucky for me, the weather's been too bad for any goods to be landed. They've given me one more week, and then it's join them or die. They mean it all right, sir." Kate had given a little exclamation of disbelief. "Look!" He held his right hand into the stream of light from the door, and Kate, leaning forward, could see the red weal of a burn across its back. "They did this to convince me, they said. Took me to the forge. Held it against a red-hot ploughshare. Promised me a slow death if I wouldn't join them. They surely mean it. And what they'd do to my mother and Lucy don't bear thinking of. Please, will you speak for me, sir?"

"Not to *them,*" said Kate. "It would be to sign your death warrant."

He groaned. "You're right. I hadn't thought!"

"But I'll send a messenger to Lord Hawth."

"No need!"

Kate started at the sound of Hawth's voice from the doorway. Entirely occupied with John Penfold's alarming story, she had not noticed the stir in the room next door. "I seem to have arrived pat on my cue," Hawth went on. "Good evening, Mr. Warrender. You pay your calls at odd hours."

"Well—" Kate instinctively withdrew a little further behind the sheltering chair—"come to that, my lord, so do you. And I, after all, am of the family. Besides, Mrs. Warrender sent for me."

"So she tells me." Hawth's tone was dry. "What I do not rightly understand is why."

"It's John Penfold." Kate hurriedly told him the young man's story.

"Twisted in!" Hawth interrupted at one point. "The whole secret society rigmarole? Did they tell you how it was done?"

"No, my lord." Penfold sounded more frightened than ever. "That was for next week."

"A pity." He listened in silence to the rest of the story, and said at last, "Well, it's clear you can't go back there. Unless I can persuade you to let them twist you in, and then keep me informed of their plans?"

"I couldn't, sir! I plumb couldn't!" Penfold held out his

burned hand in mute witness. "Besides, there's my ma and Lucy. What would become of them, happen I was caught? Or if I don't go back tonight, for that matter."

"That's easily answered." Hawth was at his most decisive. "I'm having you arrested, right now—let's think—for poaching? Caught in the park, what else could you be doing? Who caught you, I wonder? Did you, Mr. Warrender?"

"No," said Kate hurriedly. "I did not!"

"Then I must have. On my way home. What a fortunate thing I chose to drive myself and leave my man to bring on the baggage. Single-handed I arrested you, brought you here to the Dower House as the nearest place, and was very much surprised at finding Mr. Warrender paying too late a visit to his cousin. Convenient, though. You can help me escort my poacher over to the hall, Mr. Warrender."

Good God, what next? "I'm sorry!" Kate racked her brains for an excuse.

"Impossible." Mrs. Warrender had appeared in the doorway. "My cousin and I still have business to discuss. Family business."

"Family fiddlestick!" Hawth's temper snapped. "And talking of family, where's that daughter of yours who should be here chaperoning you?"

"Kate is unwell, my lord," said Mrs. Warrender with some dignity. "And I am long past needing a chaperone."

"Balderdash," said Lord Hawth. "And why in the name of God are we standing here talking in the dark? There's something very odd about this whole business, and I mean to find out what it is."

"I'm glad to hear it," Kate cut in. "It's time someone did. And took a little care for my kinswomen, and those children of yours you so cheerfully leave unprotected over at the hall, with God knows what revolutionary hellbroth brewing down at Tidemills." She laughed. "I've a better idea than poaching for you. Did you not catch young Penfold in the act of setting fire to one of your hayricks?"

"Of course I did. An excellent notion. That will fox our radical friends down at Tidemills."

"But that's a hanging matter," protested John Penfold. "Or transportation at the very least."

"Well," said Hawth thoughtfully, "I'm not entirely sure that transportation is not the answer to your problems. Don't look so scared, man. Not to Australia. But what of America? I had thought to smuggle you away to one of my other estates, but you and your mother and sister are something of an unmistakable trio. What do you say to a few comfortable days safe in Glinde gaol, while I get Mr. Warren to help in arranging your passage to America?"

"The three of us, my lord?"

"Of course, fool. Didn't I say so?" And then: "Good God! Another caller. What kind of a house do you keep, Mrs. Warrender?"

"Yours," she replied succinctly and retreated into the other room to welcome George Warren.

"I was riding late," he explained. "I was anxious about you. Is all well here?"

"Well!" exclaimed Mrs. Warrender. "It depends what you mean by well. My daughter's ill. I've a house full of unexpected company. And it's very late."

"Miss Warrender ill—" began George Warren, but Lord Hawth had emerged from the book-room to greet him.

"The very man. I need your help." As he began to explain John Penfold's predicament, Kate saw her chance, and took it. Penfold had followed Hawth into the drawing room. She slipped behind the curtains of the book-room's long window, pulled it silently upwards and climbed out into the darkness. "A very unorthodox young man," she told herself as she made her way quietly round the side of the house, praying that Joe had been too busy with visitors to lock up. She was in luck. The side door had not been bolted.

Ten minutes later, after the quickest change ever, she made her entrance into the drawing room, every inch the demure young miss in dotted muslin. Nobody noticed her come. John Penfold was standing awkwardly in a corner of the room, while Hawth and Warren loomed furiously one on each side of her mother's low chair.

"The insolence of it!" said Lord Hawth.

"Young whippersnapper," said George Warren.

"Without so much as saying good-bye to his hostess, apologising for his late visit!" Hawth, it seemed, was still harping on the late visit.

"Gentlemen," said Mrs. Warrender with some dignity, "I beg you will let me look after my own affairs. If I do not care to take affront at my young cousin's behaviour, I fail to see why you should do so on my behalf. No doubt he had . . . affairs of his own."

"A wench, no doubt." Hawth gave his short bark of laughter. "One last meeting with Lucy Penfold. The young dog."

"My lord!"

"I beg your pardon, ma'am."

"Mother!" exclaimed Kate reproachfully, and all eyes turned on her. "What in the world? Three gentlemen, at this time of night?" And then, "No. Two gentlemen and—it's young Penfold, isn't it? But it's after ten o'clock!"

"There's trouble, dearest. Oh, but I'm glad to see you," said her mother with complete conviction. "Are you really better? Lord Hawth and Mr. Warren are about to be so good as to take young Penfold away."

"Take him away? But they were shouting at you, mamma." She looked reproachfully from one abashed gentleman to the other. "I don't understand."

"They're a little put out," explained Mrs. Warrender. "Your Cousin Kit was here and did not stay to give Mr. Warren the meeting."

"*Another* gentleman! You amaze me. And it past bedtime, too. As for Cousin Kit, we all know he's a law unto himself."

"A very ill-mannered one," said Lord Hawth.

"*He* has some excuse."

"We're keeping the ladies from their beds." George Warren took the hint. "I'll walk over to the hall with you, my lord, to give colour to your 'arrest.' Though I must say he looks a timid enough arsonist."

"Arson?" exclaimed Kate. "John Penfold? Nonsense!"

"Hush, dearest," said her mother. "I'll explain later." She

rose to her feet. "I'm most grateful to you gentlemen for coming to my help, and poor young Penfold's, but it is late and my daughter's unwell. I will bid you goodnight."

The story of John Penfold's arrest, caught in the act of firing a rick and by Lord Hawth himself, was a nine days' wonder, and if there were people down at Tidemills who thought Penfold had done it on purpose, preferring transportation to the risks he was already facing, they kept their thoughts to themselves. Since Lord Hawth chaired the bench that tried him, the sentence of transportation was a foregone conclusion. The neighbourhood said it was good of Lord Hawth to arrange for Penfold's mother and sister to pack up and follow him to London, and after that everyone forgot about him.

"They're safe off to America." George Warren called on Mrs. Warrender and Kate a few weeks later. "A cousin of mine will look out for them in Philadelphia."

"I'm so glad," said Mrs. Warrender.

"Lucy Penfold will be missed," said Kate.

"The village Circe. To tell you the truth—" George Warren turned from Kate to her mother—"I'm relieved to see the last of that girl. Since she moved down to Tidemills, my men servants seem to have had constant reasons for visiting the village. And bad blood among them, too, I'm afraid."

"Poor child," said Mrs. Warrender.

"Poor child! Poor young men, I think. I like a happy household, ma'am, and I had one, until that minx moved in. I shudder to think of the swathe she will cut through our simple Philadelphia young men."

"You consider yourself simple, Mr. Warren?" asked Kate.

He laughed. "Not so simple as I was, Miss Warrender. I flatter myself I am learning, a little at a time, slowly. You've all been wonderfully patient with me. I suppose, in five years or so, I may have some real idea of how to go on in British society."

"You mean to stay and give it the trial, war or no war?" asked Kate.

"I believe so. Will you speak up for me, Miss Warrender, if

there is talk of throwing me into prison as my friends back home seem to expect?"

"Into prison?" exclaimed Mrs. Warrender. "Whatever made them imagine that?"

"They seem unable to distinguish between British behaviour and French, ma'am. Because Bonaparte still holds the unlucky British tourists who were in France when the war broke out again in 1803 they think you will behave the same."

"What nonsense," said Mrs. Warrender, "and with Lord Hawth on the bench, too."

"You think Lord Hawth can do no wrong, mamma?" asked Kate teasingly.

"I think he has a great deal of sense," said Mrs. Warrender.

"I wish it would bring him home," said Kate.

"You're anxious about something?" George Warren asked.

"About Sue, a little." She was surprised to find herself telling him. "She's been moped since Christmas, and worse still since Lord Hawth's last visit. Miss Lintott says she spends hours reading in his study."

"Well," said George Warren, "if you had to spend your evenings with Miss Lintott, what would you do?"

"I know," Kate agreed wholeheartedly. "It's just like Lord Hawth to send us down that pattern of dullness and then leave us to endure her."

"Poor woman," said Mrs. Warrender. "She can't help being a dead bore."

"She doesn't try," said Kate. "If she tells me about her 'cousin the Archbishop' once more, I shall go into strong hysterics."

"She thinks me beneath contempt," said George Warren cheerfully. "I must confess, it is the greatest comfort to me."

"What a delightful young man he is," said Mrs. Warrender when he had taken his leave. "I would never have thought that dreadful day when he first arrived that I would grow so fond of him."

"He seems to be bearing Lucy Penfold's departure with a good deal of philosophy," said Kate.

"I always thought that a parcel of rumour and malicious gossip."

"You're so charitable, mamma!"

"I try to be, but I must confess that Miss Lintott puts me quite out of patience from time to time."

"And no wonder! You'd be a saint else. Do you think Cousin George knows she talks of him as the American boor?"

"I expect so. He and Lord Hawth don't have many secrets from each other these days."

"I know. Is it not surprising!"

She would have been even more surprised if she had known that George Warren had ridden home and begun immediate preparations for a trip to London. He had been thinking of going for some time, but it was what Kate had said about Sue that had decided him. Something, he thought, was going on at Hawth Hall, and it was high time its owner came back and took charge.

Welcomed as a valued client at Fladong's Hotel, he changed quickly into the rather casual evening dress he favoured and strolled round to Lord Hawth's townhouse in Piccadilly. But his lordship had gone down early to the House, the butler told him. He rather thought he had an appointment before the session began.

"I'll join him there," said George Warren.

"You'll let me order you out the carriage, sir?"

"For that distance? Ridiculous."

"Then not across the park, sir. Not in the dark. Not after those bloody murders before Christmas."

"Oh, very well." He knew it was good advice. The days of the Mohawks might be long past, but there was always a risk of footpads in parks and quiet streets at night, and only the other day, on the Home Secretary's bill for a nightly watch in London, Parliament had debated the alarming rise of violent crime in the country.

Arriving safely at Westminster, he found the lobby of the

House unusually crowded. "What's to do tonight?" he asked the usher who took his message for Lord Hawth.

"It's Lord Byron, sir. His maiden speech is expected tonight, on Mr. Secretary Ryder's bill."

"Capital punishment for frame-breakers, eh? I'd like to hear that."

"You'll be lucky to get in, sir. He's drawn quite a crowd, has Lord Byron."

Lord Hawth, hurrying out to greet his friend, confirmed this, but managed in the end to find him a corner where he could hear but not see the famous Lord Byron make an impassioned plea against the hasty introduction of capital punishment for this new crime. Describing the distressed state of the poor in his own district, the poet-lord turned on his fellow peers: "When a proposal is made to emancipate or relieve, you hesitate, you deliberate for years, you temporize and tamper with the minds of men; but a death-bill must be passed off hand, without a thought of the consequences!"

"It won't do any good." Hawth met George Warren after the bill had been adjourned over the week-end on the motion of Lord Lauderdale. "Government will push it through in the Lords as they have in the Commons."

"You're against the bill?" asked George Warren, surprised.

"We Whigs all are. It will only inflame passions that are hot enough already. Besides, faced with the death sentence, magistrates are hesitant to find defendants guilty. It defeats its own end."

"I wish I had heard Lord Liverpool speak for the bill. Are things really so bad in Nottingham?"

"It's almost a state of war. There are more troops serving there than on the Peninsula. I was with Ryder before the session. He is afraid of the infection spreading south. God knows, there are enough agitators here in London."

"And young Penfold's experience at Tidemills is hardly encouraging. He and his family are safe on board ship, by the way."

"Good. And what's the news from Glinde?"

"Nothing to signify. And yet, I don't know. . . . There's a feeling in the air. What in the world induced you to let Jewkes at the Ship install that brother of his at the Tidemills shop? They're two ruffians together if ever I saw such."

"Better the devil, you know," said Hawth cheerfully. "After young Penfold's experience, I did not want to put another innocent man at risk. We know all about those two Jewkes brothers."

"So the smuggling will continue?"

"Oh, yes. For a while. Until we're ready."

"We?"

"A manner of speaking." Hawth changed the subject. "Have you visited the Dower House lately?"

"Yesterday. I took the ladies the news of the Penfolds' safety. To tell truth, that visit is partly why I came to town."

"Oh?"

"I wish you would come home. It's not only Tidemills that troubles me. I think there's something going on at the hall."

"Something going on? What can you mean?"

"I don't rightly know. It's since you were last down—since that business of young Penfold—Mrs. Warrender don't look well, and Miss Warrender is anxious about your Susan. Says she does nothing but mope in your study. I said anyone would with that whey-faced cousin of yours loose in the rest of the house."

"The children had to have someone." Hawth defended himself.

"You come home and see what it's like," said George Warren. "I saw your Susan in Glinde the other day. It's true, what Miss Warrender said. She doesn't look well. And so much older. I was, well, surprised. They need a mother, those children of yours, Hawth."

"Thanks!" said Lord Hawth. But the remark went on echoing strangely in his mind.

Chapter 11

The two men drove down to Glinde together a couple of weeks later, George Warren having passed his time contentedly enough between Lawrence's studio, the House of Commons to hear an unsatisfactory debate on the Orders in Council on a motion moved by Mr. Brougham, and Covent Garden where the ageing Mrs. Siddons was making too many last appearances.

"Her voice is going, I'm afraid," Warren told Lord Hawth as they set forward across Westminster Bridge on a fine morning of mid-March. And then, "It's a fine prospect!" He was looking downriver to the distant view of St. Paul's as he quoted:

> "Ships, towers, domes, theatres, and temples lie
> Open unto the fields, and to the sky;
> All bright and glittering in the smokeless air.

I don't quite know what made Mr. Wordsworth call it smokeless," he went on, observing morning smoke from dozens of urban chimneys.

"Wordsworth wrote that? No wonder the *Edinburgh Review* don't care for his poems. But as to the smoke, I expect he came to London in summer. It's better then."

"But the river stinks."

Hawth laughed. "You're not a true romantic either."

"How can one be, in the world as it is? London always saddens me. So much luxury, and so much wretchedness."

"Don't say you're coming out as a revolutionary now." Hawth, who had slowed his horses to let his friend admire the view, whipped them up and took his curricle rattling down the other side of the bridge. "That's all I need!"

"Liberty, equality and fraternity? Not on the French style anyway. But as an American, I suppose I'm revolutionary by definition. Your people seem to think so down at Tidemills."

"Then for God's sake be careful what you say."

"There's trouble, isn't there?" George Warren had seen little of his friend in the last two weeks but knew that he had spent a great deal of time at the Home Office.

"There may be. We're afraid of it." As once before, he did not identify the "we." "There are alarming reports from all over the country. Not just Nottingham, though it's more open there. But secret meetings, twistings in, conspiracy. Oh—" he anticipated George Warren's objection. "I know they've a right to be discontented, what with the war, and your non-importation act. Prices rising, wages falling. And it's true, too, what you say, the rich do go on seeming rich, though God knows there are bankruptcies enough."

"But those are among the middle classes," said George Warren.

"True again! We aristocrats seem to have the gift of survival. That's what makes us so unpopular. If trouble comes, be sure it will be to us that it comes."

"I hope you're not including me among the aristocrats," said George Warren.

"Oh, you're an enigma. But you're a landowner, too. You may find the revolutionaries think you tarred with the same brush as the rest of us."

"Revolutionaries! But you can't seriously think—"

"My dear man, the country's like tinder. One spark and it could be aflame from end to end. And there are so many irritants. You weren't in town when the House debated the move to give the four Princesses £30,000 a year between them. Nor for Mr. Bankes' bill against sinecures. There was some hot talk then, I can tell you, and every word of it reported in the public prints."

"Yes, I read of it. And some pretty strong words about your friend the Prince Regent and that expensive secretary of his, Colonel McMahon. What was it Mr. Lyttleton said? Something about the Prince's system of unprincipled favouritism—" George Warren stopped, obviously embarrassed.

He got a harsh laugh from Hawth. "'Hemmed in with minions,'" he quoted. "'Among whom, if there is a man of note or talent, there certainly is not one of any character.' You were afraid I might have taken that to myself? Well, so I might, six months ago. Not now. I'm no friend of the Prince Regent's now, nor he of mine. He's shown his Tory colours too clearly. When I think of the hopes we Whigs nourished a year ago when the Regency bill was passed! We expected to be in office by spring! All exploded now. Prinney tried to get Lord Grey and Lord Grenville to join the Tory government the other day, but they saw through his tricks. At least, thank God, we're a united opposition."

"You don't think," suggested Warren diffidently, "that you may do more harm than good by your attack on the government? I mean, you talk of a spark igniting the country. Some of the things your people say, both in the House and out of it, are quite inflammatory. I had no idea you spoke so freely in your Parliament."

"Thought you Americans had a monopoly in mud-slinging, did you? But it's true enough, one sees it all the time on the Bench. The strong words of a Burdett or a Brougham, meant for emphasis in the House, may delude some poor ignorant wretch of an illegal trade unionist into thinking they will back him in his violence."

"And they won't?"

"Of course not! We Whigs want a change of government, not anarchy."

"You're really serious about the danger?"

"I'm serious all right," said Hawth grimly. "And the worst of it is that there's evidence suggesting the focal point of the trouble is somewhere down in the county of Glinde."

"In Glinde! But I thought the worst outbreaks were up North."

"Yes, so far. But we fear a giant conspiracy for a national uprising. Think of the number of troops we have had to send up north to keep the peace. If trouble were to break out down south—or, worse still, all over—we'd be hard put to it to find the men to fight it. And the militia not over reliable. And as for special constables—well, you know what they are like."

"I wouldn't want to count on them for the defence of Warren House against the mob."

"Precisely."

"But what makes you think the centre of this conspiracy you speak of lies in Glinde?"

"A very curious thing. You remember the riot down at Tidemills last autumn?"

"I do indeed. The one young Warrender quelled for you."

"Yes. Naturally, in my capacity as magistrate, I sent a report on that to the Home Office. They sent for me posthaste when the trouble started up north."

"Oh?"

Lord Hawth steadied his horses for a sharp turn in the road. "Yes. Because I had reported that the stranger who acted as ringleader down at Tidemills had called himself Ned Ludd. Well, you know what they are calling the northern rioters now?"

"Luddites. For that mysterious General Ludd. I see. Ned Ludd. You think it began down in Glinde?"

"Seems so. And then quieted down as suddenly as it had started. As if, perhaps, someone had decided not to call attention to themselves. I could not understand, at the time, why, after so violent a beginning, things settled down so easily at Tidemills. And then there was that odd business of Ludd's intervening to save the children. I was just grateful, I suppose, at the time. Now, I'm not sure. We begin to wonder if Ludd might not have had his own reasons for wanting things quiet at Glinde. I'm coming back on the Home Secretary's direct orders. We must know what is being planned, and he thinks the best hope for that is down at Glinde."

George Warren laughed. "And I thought you were coming because I told you I was anxious about your Sue."

"You said more than that. You said you thought something was going on at the hall."

"Yes, I did. But I'm not dead sure what I meant. It was just a feeling I had. Absurd, really, to have made so much of it."

"We're at a point where we must take note of such things. These are bad times."

"It's hard to believe." They were out in open country by now, driving past spring-green fields and between hedgerows laced with primroses and with blue-and-white violets. It was indeed hard to believe that violence lurked in this placid countryside.

"I was in France in '89," said Hawth. "Starting on my grand tour. It was about this time of year, a little later perhaps. I remember the corn was green in the fields as we drove across Normandy. A rich, beautiful country. Oh, there were gibbets, I remember, men hanging in chains. I'd never been to Tyburn. . . . It shocked me, but I never imagined what was coming, that dark tide of blood that began with the fall of the Bastille that summer. I was in Paris then. I remember the sky red with its burning. I've never forgotten it, never will. Nor what came later. We must not let it happen here."

"What do you think of Kit Warrender?" They had driven in silence for a while and George Warren had been following his own line of thought. "He always seem to be about when there is trouble!"

"And damned elusive the rest of the time," agreed Hawth. "I intend to have a word with that young man."

He dropped George Warren at his own house and arrived, unannounced, at the park gates just as dusk was falling. He had done this on purpose. If George Warren was right in his suspicion that something was, as he said, "going on" at the hall, a surprise arrival might achieve some revelation. Now, on an impulse, he drew up his horses, jumped down from the curricle and told his groom to walk them slowly up to the hall. "I've given them a hard run of it. I'll take the cut across the park. Don't hurry them, mind."

Too well trained to show his surprise, the man obediently climbed up into the driver's seat while Hawth set off at a brisk pace along the path that led through the woods near the Dower House and then past the stables to the hall. Reaching the turnoff for the Dower House, he hesitated for a moment, curiously tempted to go there first. But it was at the hall that Warren had suspected trouble. Besides, he was hot and sweating from the long day's drive, in no case for paying calls. He took the right fork and walked briskly on through the woods towards the stables, whence he could already hear the sounds of evening routine. Buckets clanked, a horse neighed. It all sounded peaceful, rural. George Warren had undoubtedly been imagining things, but just the same he was glad to be home.

Now he heard something else, nearer, this side of the stable wall. An exclamation. A scream? A woman's voice. The sounds of a struggle. He was running. Kidnappers? Again? The children? He came silently out of the woods with the light of the setting sun in his eyes and stopped at sight of Kate Warrender struggling furiously in the arms of his bailiff, Knowles.

"Vixen!" said Knowles as she bit the hand that was trying to force her face upwards for his kiss. "I said marriage, didn't I?"

"Marry you?" His grip had slackened and she pulled furiously away, her colour high, her shoulder-length curls dishevelled, handsomer than Hawth had ever seen her. "I wouldn't marry you if you were the last man on earth."

"No?" Knowles' voice was ugly with anger. "I'll make you

sorry you said that, Miss Vixen. And grateful for marriage. On your knees you'll beg me." A pistol gleamed in his hand. "We are going for a little walk, you and I, Miss Warrender. Down to the woods in the dark. When we come back, you will be a thought tamer."

"I shall scream." She took a step away from him.

"You won't, you know." The pistol moved a little, threatening. "Such a sad accident it would be. Poor Mrs. Warrender." He moved a slow, confident step towards Kate, and Hawth, who had been struck rigid by sight of the pistol, moved silently out of the shadows and caught his wrist in a grip of iron. "Good evening, Miss Warrender." He locked his left arm around Knowles' neck. "Mr. Knowles is about to apologise to you. He is out of work, and in no position to offer marriage to anyone."

"My lord!" Knowles had stopped struggling when he recognised the implacable voice of his employer.

"Just so." Hawth took the pistol from his lifeless hand and let him go. "You will make up your books tonight, hand them in and leave tomorrow. But first, you will apologise to Miss Warrender."

"She led me on," said Knowles. "She should be grateful. A mere governess to a pack of bastards. . . ."

"That will do," said Hawth. "You may go. Miss Warrender will accept your apology in writing."

"You'll regret this!"

"I doubt it." He turned his back on the bailiff, dropped the pistol in his greatcoat pocket and offered his arm to Kate Warrender. "Let me escort you home, Miss Warrender."

"Thank you." She was trembling. "For everything. I'm ashamed." The hot blush had faded slowly, leaving her whitefaced, her dark eyes sparkling with rage and unshed tears.

"It's I who should be ashamed," he told her. "That this should happen to you on my land, my servant. My apologies, Miss Warrender."

"Thank you." She was recovering herself. "You really mean to dismiss him?"

"Of course."

"I'm sorry." She hesitated. "And . . . he'll talk."

"I'd thought of that. You must marry me, Miss Warrender."

"I beg your pardon?" She withdrew her arm and turned to face him.

"I said, you must marry me. Oh—"impatiently—"I didn't mean to do it like this. But I came home to ask you, just the same." And when, exactly, had he made up his mind to that? "It's obvious we can't go on as we are. You and your mother ostracised at the Dower House. My Cousin Lintott making life intolerable at the hall. Young Sue in trouble of some kind, Warren thinks."

"In short." She was white as ivory now. "Your times are out of joint, my lord, and I must marry you to set them right?"

"Oh, I'm sorry. I suppose I should have spoken of love, of flaming passion. If I had had time to con a speech, I might have done so. But you must see, Miss Warrender, that you need protection."

"The protection of your name? Very like those poor children of yours! A name, a position, without love. I thank you, but, no, my lord."

"Absurd!" He was angry now. "I offer you everything you need, for yourself and your mother: safety, a household, a title—if you care for such things—and all you can do is talk like a young miss about love. I thought you had more sense! Oh, I know you have a previous attachment. Your young cousin told me that before we so much as met. I don't ask love from you, why should you expect it of me? Your own lover don't do much for you, by all I can see. If he had come forward like a man, last year, it would be something else again." A sudden thought struck him. "Good God. I'd never thought. *Is* it that ramshackle cousin of yours?"

"That, my lord, is entirely my own affair. Now, if you please, I would like to go home."

"Of course." He took her reluctant arm again and felt it trembling still. "I shall speak to your mother," he said.

"No!"

"Yes. I should have in the first place. We'll talk again of this. When I have her consent."

"No!"

"I shall speak to her tonight."

She turned her head to look him up and down. "You are in no state to call on a lady."

He burst into one of his fits of harsh laughter. "Well, now I have heard everything. I was, I take it, fit to rescue you from your would-be ravisher."

"My lord, please." She turned to him, suddenly pleading. "Think no more of this. I am grateful for what you did—for your offer—flattered. Believe me when I say so. And believe me, too, when I say it cannot be. Please, please, my lord, don't speak to my mother."

"I shall speak to her tomorrow," said Lord Hawth. "What you say to her is your own affair, but tomorrow I shall ask her permission to pay my addresses to you in form."

"If you insist on doing so, I can only refuse them, in form. But I do beg you to think again of this. We would not suit, my lord, you and I. Pray—pray think of it overnight. I am sure by morning you will agree with me."

"Oh, I'll think of it," he said.

At the hall, things seemed quiet enough. Inevitably, the scene with Knowles and Kate Warrender had delayed Hawth so that his curricle had arrived first and he was expected. Parsons showed him into the morning room that Miss Lintott had made her own and she greeted him wanly from the sofa where she was reclining.

"Dear Mark, so impulsive! I collect you forgot to send a message announcing your arrival? You find us all at sixes and sevens here, and no time to send for Mrs. Warrender from the Dower House. You'll have to take pot luck for tonight, I am afraid."

"Send for Mrs. Warrender! I trust you would do no such thing." Why did the suggestion make him so angry?

"Well, she's the housekeeper, isn't she? Her job to cater for unexpected guests."

"I am hardly a guest, cousin. And if I know anything about it, Mrs. Warrender has this household running so smoothly that my arrival will disturb no one but you. How are the children?"

"Well enough, I think. To tell truth, I scarcely see them. And not through my fault either," she surprised him by anticipating his comment. "I'm afraid they find a poor invalid like me a dead bore, and do their possible to keep away from me. I suggested only the other day that Susan might care to take dinner with me, but, oh, no, she prefers nursery supper, thank you, and long hours reading in your study. She *said* she had your permission."

"And so she had. A child who wishes to read should be encouraged."

"But your books, cousin! I found her reading *Roderick Random* the other day!"

"She won't come to much harm with Smollet. I'd rather she was reading him than sentimental trash like Richardson or Mackenzie."

Miss Lintott sniffed. "She reads them, too."

"What time is nursery supper?"

"Good gracious, how should I know? Their governess makes all that kind of arrangement, and very high-handedly she sets about it, too."

If only he could say, "Their governess is about to become my wife." Well, in a day or so, no doubt, he would be able to. In the meantime, he moved towards the bellpull by the door. "If you do not know, we had best find out," he said. "I'll send for the children."

"Not here, cousin, I do beg of you. My sensibilities are shattered enough with the shock of your unexpected coming, without having a parcel of noisy children inflicted on my privacy."

He bit off a sharp retort. Experience had taught him that this would merely bring on one of her attacks of hysterics.

"Then I will leave you in peace and send for the children to my study."

"You will probably find Susan there." Miss Lintott applied herself to her vinaigrette to suggest that the interview was at an end.

Susan was reading *Clarissa Harlowe.* Deep in her book, she had not noticed the stir of Hawth's coming, and looked up in amazement when he appeared in the study doorway. "Father!" She jumped to her feet, surprised, and, could it be, frightened? She also looked quite amazingly older. Grown up, in fact. A young lady.

"Susan!" He could not remember ever to have been alone with her before and was almost as taken aback as she was. He had never pretended to be an affectionate father, but what did you do when your daughter turned into a young lady and made you a timid curtsy? "How are you?" he asked. "In looks, I can see."

It won him a shy smile and a blush. "I'm well," she said.

He did not really think she looked it. There were dark smudges under her blue eyes, and her newly formed figure was too elegantly slender for real health. He thought he could have spanned her waist with a hand. And that was not the kind of thought to have about one's daughter. "Do you get out?" he asked.

"Oh, yes. Miss Warrender makes us go out for a walk every day."

"She has to make you?"

"I like to sit in here and read," she said. "You don't mind? You did say . . ."

"Of course not. But you should be riding."

"That's what—" she paused for a monent—"Miss Warrender says."

"Then why not?"

"There's nothing my weight in the stable," she explained, her fair skin colouring all over again. "And Giles has outgrown his pony, too."

"Damnation! Why did no one tell me?"

She hung her head. "Miss Lintott said we were lucky to be here. We mustn't be a trouble. She and Miss Warrender had . . . had an argument about it."

"Miss Warrender should have written me."

"Miss Lintott said it wasn't her place," said Susan.

"Damn Miss Lintott. You'd better dine with us tonight, Susan, or I may say something to her that I will regret."

"And then she'll have hysterics." Susan had indeed grown up. But why did she still look so anxious ? "Father?"

"Yes?"

"Will you be using the study, now you are home?"

"Of course. But you may take whatever books you like."

"Thank you." She looked miserable. Frightened? What in the world?

"You need somewhere of your own." He thought he had it. "The children disturb you. I'll talk to Mrs. Warrender about it in the morning." Comforting to be so sure that Mrs. Warrender would know what was best to do. Well, if all went as he expected it to, she would be more or less the children's grandmother. What a very strange thought.

Dinner was not a success. A neat meal of two courses and several removes justified Hawth's confidence in a staff trained by Mrs. Warrender, but he was the only one who did justice to it. Miss Lintott had a regime of her own and picked daintily at potatoes drenched in vinegar, explaining that they were all that her poor constitution would stand. And Susan was not much better. Helped lavishly by her father to the breast of one of a pair of chickens in tarragon sauce, she pushed the food about her plate, sipped at her claret and coloured scarlet when Miss Lintott told her not to put on airs to be interesting. "I have to diet myself," said that lady, "because of my wretched state of health, but such megrims in a child of your age are quite the outside of enough. I'd have been whipped if I had made such an exhibition of myself as a child."

"I'm not a child!" Susan disproved this by bursting into a flood of tears and rising, with a mute apology, to hurry from the room.

Miss Lintott never took dessert, and the depressing meal was soon over. Left alone over his port, Hawth did not linger. Knowles should have turned in his books by now, and he meant to go through them at once.

Since he had made his intentions known, he was surprised to find Susan in the study, curled up on the hearthrug, *Clarissa Harlow* dropped from her hand, fast asleep.

"Father!" She jumped to her feet and looked wildly round as if she had just come out of a nightmare. Or into one? "It's you?"

"Who else? And high time you were in bed. Take your book with you, if you wish, but do not read any more to-night."

"No, father." She made him a timid little curtsy. "Good-night," she said.

"Goodnight, Susan." He felt an odd temptation to drop a kiss on the tumbled golden curls, but restrained it. She looked quite frightened enough as it was. "You had better take a glass of hot milk to bed with you," he told her. "You ate nothing at dinner."

"I'm not hungry." She made her escape and left him more convinced than ever of the wisdom of his proposal to Miss Warrender. Stupid of him to have plumped out with it in the aftermath of that scene with Knowles. No wonder she had refused him, but of course when he made his proposal in form, with her mother's permission, her answer would be quite other. He turned, in a very bad temper, to Knowles' books.

Chapter 12

Kate and her mother always walked over to the hall together after their frugal breakfast at the Dower House. Passing the scene of yesterday's encounter with Knowles and Hawth, Kate wondered for the hundredth time whether she should have told her mother about it. She had passed a sleepless night, tossing and turning in her bed, thinking of Knowles, of Hawth's amazing offer, and the still more amazing fact that she had rejected it out of hand. There had been a time, after their first dramatic encounter, when her answer would have been very different, but not now . . . not now. Strange, and almost shaming, to have changed so totally in the course of just one winter, but then, there were reasons.

"I wonder how long Lord Hawth will stay this time," said Mrs. Warrender, when they came in sight of the hall, ugly in morning sunshine. Inevitably, news of his arrival had come with their breakfast.

"Two days?" Kate shrugged. "Three? Long enough so that I can get him to arrange about ponies for Sue and Giles, I hope. Sue looks worse and worse. She eats nothing. I'm worried about her."

"Growing up, poor child," said Mrs. Warrender. "And not in easy circumstances, I am afraid."

"Far from it," Kate agreed. "With Lord Hawth for a father! I dislike that man more and more."

"Why, Kate!" Her mother was deeply shocked. "How can you! And so kind as he has been to us, so thoughtful for our comfort, our convenience."

"The benevolent despot," said Kate crossly. "Making the lives of his slaves endurable."

"Slaves? Katharine Warrender, what kind of talk is this?"

"Subjects, then! The Hanover of Glinde. Thoughtful for our comfort, indeed! When was he ever thoughtful for anything but his own? George Warren's worth ten of him! He listens when one speaks to him."

"Sensible of him," said Mrs. Warrender. "He has so much to learn."

"And Hawth knows everything? He certainly behaves as if he did. Pasha Hawth! As for George Warren, admit, mamma, that he learns fast. Futherby says he has done more for the estate in this one winter than papa did in all the years he held it."

"Well, that's not saying a great deal," said Mrs. Warrender sadly. "But, it's true, Futherby will be glad to see him back."

"I wonder if Hawth's people will." Kate remembered Knowles, blushed and was silent.

Parsons was waiting for them. "My lord's compliments, ma'am," he said to Mrs. Warrender, "and he asks if he may call on you in your room at your earliest convenience."

"Oh! Why, yes, of course." Mrs. Warrender sounded fluttered. "It's very good of his lordship to ask . . . to come to me. Tell him . . . tell him I'll be ready for him in five minutes. And tell the chef, please, Parsons, with my apologies, that I will see him as soon as I can."

"I already have, ma'am," said Parsons.

"Thank you. I should have known you would have. Oh, Kate!" She grasped her daughter's hand as they turned down the passage that led to their rooms. "Do you think it's trouble?"

"Why should it be, dearest? Don't forget, he can't manage without us." Too late now to warn her mother about what had happened yesterday. What a fool she had been to hope that Hawth would change his mind overnight.

"I wish you would stay!"

"I can't, mamma. The children are expecting me. And Hawth is not." She felt a wretch, leaving her mother all unprepared, but what else could she do?

Alone in her comfortable, chintz-furnished room, Mrs. Warrender took off her pelisse and turned to the glass to tweak the cap into place over still golden curls. One light hair had fallen on the black sleeve of her dress, and she removed it with distaste before turning to make sure that all was tidy on her work table. Her accounts were in order. She had nothing to fear from this unexpected visitation. She feared it just the same. Or—was it exactly fear?

Lord Hawth tapped on the door just five minutes later, and she welcomed him in shyly and offered him the big chair by the desk while she herself subsided nervously on a rosewood sewing chair.

After the first greetings, he was silent for a moment, looking round him. The newly lit fire crackled in the hearth. Spring flowers in vases explained the faint perfume he had noticed when he entered the room. A tapestry frame tilted towards the light of the bay window caught his eye with its bright colours and, with an apology, he moved over to look at the brilliant embroidery of flowers he had never seen. "Striking," he said. "Your own design?"

"Oh, yes." She blushed vividly. "I have been doing them forever. I meant—they were for the dining chairs at Warren House."

"I see." He remembered George Warren's Chinese dining room and found himself extraordinarily sad for her. But there was nothing to say—nothing he could think of. He moved back to her big desk and sat down at it, noting the neat piles of papers, and on a far corner, as if relegated, a little pile of books. A Bible, a prayer book and, surprising him, a volume of Mr. Pope's poems.

"You read Pope?"

"Yes. Kate doesn't like him. She and Mr. Warren keep talking of Mr. Wordsworth and Mr. Coleridge, but they don't write couplets like Pope's."

"No, indeed." She had given him the opening he needed. "It is about Miss Warrender I am come to speak to you."

"Oh?" She leaned forward, tense now, her hands tightly folded in her lap.

"She did not tell you?"

"Tell me?"

"I asked her to marry me yesterday."

"You—" She turned so white that he thought for a moment she was going to faint. "You? And Kate?"

"She did not tell you. Forgive me for surprising you so. She refused me, you see. Well, I was too sudden." If Kate had not done so, he would not tell Mrs. Warrender about Knowles. "I told her I would speak to you today. Ask your permission to pay her my addresses."

"And she told me nothing!" She drew herself up with a small dignity that touched him. "Forgive me, my lord. You have indeed surprised me. I never suspected . . . never imagined. . . ." She looked up at him gravely. "Do you love her, my lord?"

"Love?" Impatiently. "What's that to do with anything? I need a wife, Mrs. Warrender. You're not a fool. You must see that as well as I do. Oh, I'm more than grateful for all you and Miss Warrender—Miss Kate—have done for me and for the children. But I still have a house that is no home. Am exposed to the absurdities of that cousin of mine. And then there are the children. Even I can see Susan's not well. I haven't seen the other two, but my cousin complains of them a good deal."

"Well," said Mrs. Warrender, "Miss Lintott . . ."

"I know! I was every kind of fool to invite her, but having done so, how can I get rid of her, short of marriage? She gave up her apartments in Bath to come here."

"And the waters suited her so well." Mrs. Warrender could not help a smile.

"The supreme sacrifice. And how she does remind one of it." How easy Mrs. Warrender was to talk to. "So—you see how I am placed. Produce a Countess of Hawth and I can pension off Miss Lintott with a clear conscience. And just think how delighted the children would be."

"That," said Mrs. Warrender, "is hardly a sufficient argument for matrimony. Besides, I thought . . . You gave us to understand, last year, that there was someone else . . . someone in London?"

"I'm afraid I invented her." Lord Hawth actually sounded guilty. "It made things seem easier at the time," he explained. "I feel every kind of fool now."

She gave him a long, thoughtful look. "You meant it to stop Kate getting ideas?"

"I was an idiot! I feel it now. Of course," he exclaimed. "Idiot that I am! Miss Warrender still thinks me engaged elsewhere. No wonder she refused me. Will you tell her, ma'am? Explain for me?"

"I think it would come better from you." She was surprising him as much as her daughter had done.

"Mrs. Warrender." He rose and took a swift turn over to the window, where he stood for a moment gazing down at the brilliant embroidery. "Can it be that you object to my paying my addresses to your daughter?"

"Object?" She had turned gracefully in her armless chair to follow him with her eyes and he noticed how slender she was, her dress black against the chair's light chintz. "I have no right to do that, I think. It is—it must be between you and Kate." She spoke low and hurriedly, her eyes now downcast to gaze at the hands that writhed together in her lap. "You say she refused you yesterday? My lord, I do not know what to think. To tell truth, I have wondered, been anxious, once or twice this winter, thinking, circumstanced as we are, that she might be beginning to care for you." She looked up, straight at him. "I thought it impossible," she said simply. "I still do."

"But why?"

"Lord Hawth and his governess? You'd be laughed at, my lord. You would not like that."

"A lot of fools!" But he had thought it himself. "Besides, a Chyngford and a Warrender. You know how our families stand in the county. And if you think she cares for me—"

"Oh, no," she said more calmly. "She doesn't. She told me so this morning. I did not understand it then. I was wrong, I think. This winter. Must have been. I don't understand her, my lord."

"Then you are in no position to speak for her."

"That's what I said. She's grown up, knows her own mind. Of course, if you wish to speak to her again, you must do so, but, my lord . . ." She hesitated, her colour fluctuating.

"Yes?" He moved nearer to stand beside her chair and look down at the anxious little face and the twisting hands.

"A marriage without love is . . . is . . ." The hands writhed in her lap. Then she looked up at him squarely with blue eyes that held a tear each. "It's hell on earth," she said. "For your own sake, for Kate's, if you don't love her, don't ask her. Don't do it."

"But I have asked her. I told her I would speak to you. I am committed."

"Then it was not much use coming to me, was it?" She whisked the tears away with a lacy handkerchief. "Naturally, I would not dream of withholding my permission. It is, in every worldly sense, a brilliant connection for Kate. Whether it would be a happy one is another matter. You are both high spirited, my lord. Obstinate, if I may say so. Proud. If you loved each other, I think you might be very happy. If not it does not bear thinking of."

"Oh, love! Are we back to that again! You're a grown woman, Mrs. Warrender, not a girl moping over a romance. You know as well as I do that not one marriage in a hundred is made for love."

"And I know what comes of it. So does Kate. I doubt she'd have you if she did not love you."

"Then if she does?" He was triumphant now, but not in the least happy.

"I hope you don't break her heart for her. I don't think I could bear that." She spoke it softly, slowly, with finality.

Now she had shaken him. But he had committed himself. That fact remained. "Of course," he said, "if you are aware of a previous attachment. I did hear something last autumn. That cousin of hers, perhaps?"

"Good God, no!" For a surprised moment he wondered if she could be laughing at him. "In love with her cousin?" She *was* laughing, almost hysterically. He hated hysterics in women, but she was making a gallant effort to control herself. "Oh, no, my lord." She looked up at him at last to say gravely, "I can give you my word for it that Kate is not in love with her cousin."

"Then I will ask her again," he said, and felt a Rubicon crossed. "You will wish to speak to her first."

"Will I? What should I say? That you do not love her, but wish to marry her for convenience' sake? I would rather you said it for yourself, my lord. This is not a case in which I feel I can advise her."

"You surprise me. I thought you cared for her."

"Of course I care for her. That's just why—" she rose to her feet with the quiet dignity that always surprised him—"I think we have said all that we profitably can on this subject, my lord, and now, if you will forgive me, I have work to do."

Thus firmly dismissed in his own house, he went crossly off to the study and rang the bell. Best get it over with. And that, he thought, was a very odd way to contemplate proposing marriage.

Receiving his summons in the schoolroom, Kate sighed and put down the Latin grammar she and Giles had been studying. "I shall expect you to be perfect in the fourth conjugation when I return," she said. "And Sue, if you will help Harriet with her reading?"

"Miss Warrender," said Giles eagerly, "will you ask him about ponies for Sue and me? So we can all go out together again. You said you would."

"If I can." Making her way down the network of passages between schoolroom and study she thought how much easier the children's lives would be if she should accept their father. But she was not going to do so. How strange it seemed.

She had made no concessions to the possibility of this interview when she dressed. Her governess's grey was demure as usual, her hair swept severely back off her face as she wore it in the mornings. A quick glance in a glass in the main hall told her that she was neat as a pin and white as a sheet.

"Miss Warrender." He rose to greet her. "It is good of you to come."

"You sent for me."

"The domestic tyrant? If you really think me that, Miss Warrender, you know how to set about reforming me. I have just been speaking to your mother." He was into it now and no escape.

"Yes? And what did she say?"

"She gave me her permission to ask for your hand in marriage."

"Just like that?"

"Well, no." Why was he saying this? "She read me a lecture, Miss Warrender, about marriages without love. But she gave me her permission."

"I see." She sounded as if she did. "And you still wish to offer for me?"

"Of course."

"Having made up your mind? Or having committed yourself?"

"Both! Neither!" What a devilish gift these two women had for getting under a man's skin. "I told you yesterday, Miss

Warrender, that I need a wife. Nothing has happened since I got home to change my mind."

"I should think not indeed," she said with lively sympathy. "Miss Lintott in hysterics and Sue in the doldrums. Why not cut your losses, my lord, and go back to town."

He gritted his teeth. "May I have an answer, Miss Warrender? I have asked you, formally, to be my wife. Must I go down on one knee to do it?"

"I don't think that will be necessary. But in view of my mother's remark, do you not think some kind of a statement might be in order?"

"You mean, I am to say I love you, whether I do or not?"

"No. Just if you do. And, I think, if you did, there would be no need. So is it not a fortunate thing, my lord, that I do not love you either, and we can part friends, with no harm done."

"You mean, you are refusing me?" His pride was lacerated and his heart leapt with relief. It was all very confusing.

"Precisely." She held out her hand. "Shake hands on it, my lord, and admit you are as relieved as I am to have this interview well over. You have done me a great honour, and I thank you for it, but we would not suit, you and I, and in your heart, I think you know it."

He took her hand in both of his, and for the first time felt real regret at her refusal. "I'm sorry," he began.

"Don't be. It wouldn't do. We both know it. May we, please, forget all about it and be friends?"

"Your mother says it's not that cousin . . ." He was still amazed at her refusal.

Her eyes blazed suddenly. Then: "My cousin Kit?" She laughed lightly and shook her head and two curls escaped from their bondage and fell on either side of her face. "No, it's not Kit."

"But what will happen to you?" Surprising to find, after her renewed refusal, how much he cared.

"God knows. But for the time being, I hope you will let me

continue as governess to your delightful children. And that reminds me—" she brought the conversation firmly down to earth—"Sue and Giles are desperate for ponies. Lord Hawth, do you think . . ."

"Incorrigible woman!" But he could not help laughing. "I do think. I talked to Susan a little last night. I have already given the orders. Will you be prepared to ride out with the little nuisances, Miss Warrender?"

"Indeed I will. May I tell them? May they come and thank you?"

"Not now. I have to finish Knowles' books."

"Oh." For the first time in the interview, she blushed, and he remembered how her mother's colour had come and gone. "Knowles. I am sorry. Will you miss him very badly?"

"From what I have seen of his books, Miss Warrender, I shall miss him very pleasantly. Pray do not let that lie on your conscience."

"I won't. I never did like the man. In fact—" she stopped.

"Yes?"

"I—I don't trust him." She had realised, in the nick of time, that she could not tell him of that strange, wild suspicion of hers based on her sight of Knowles and Coombe sitting so sociably together at the Bell on the night George Warren was attacked. Had they had something to do with the attack? Or, equally possible, equally strange, with the rescue? They could not have been in either party, but might they have been behind one of them. And if so, which? She had fretted over the problem all winter, in the enforced inactivity of the dark, wet nights. If only she could have discussed the problem with George Warren, but to do so would have meant admitting to her masquerade as Kit Warrender, and how could she do that?

"Well, no wonder." Lord Hawth had taken her remark at its face value. "After yesterday. And as to his books. . . . Whatever he has been doing this winter, it's certainly not the work he is paid for. I think I shall have to stay at home for a while and look into things for myself. You will not mind it?"

"Why should I? Oh—my lord!"

"Yes?"

"One other thing. Giles is almost beyond me in his classics. About that tutor . . ."

"What a wretched father you think me. And rightly. No ponies, no tutor. I am glad to be able to tell you, Miss Warrender, that your classical labours are almost over. I engaged a most suitable man only the other day. He comes next week. A classics scholar, I was lucky to get him. I would have thought him fit for better things, but he tells me his health has been indifferent this winter and he will be glad of a period of country retirement. As for the ponies, I'll lose no time. Susan should be riding more and reading less."

And whose fault was that, Kate thought angrily as she took the remark for dismissal and left the room. Nothing went right that day. Returning to the children and announcing the imminent arrival of the new tutor, she realised that she had not even thought to ask his name. Oh, well, there would be time enough for that, but it made her feel a fool *vis a vis* the children, and she did not much like that.

She was glad when the long day was over and it was time to put on her pelisse for the walk back to the Dower House. Her mother finished her work in the course of the morning and usually went home for lunch, and Kate, saying the daily farewell to the children, suddenly found that she did not much look forward to the walk back across the park. Absurd, of course. Knowles was gone, but just the same . . .

"Miss Warrender." One of the footmen was waiting outside the schoolroom door. "His lordship said I was to walk home with you."

"Oh." She found herself swallowing a lump of tears. Why was this unexpected thoughtfulness on Lord Hawth's part such a last straw?

Arriving at the Dower House, she found that her mother had a caller. George Warren was sitting in the comfortable living room that looked out over herbaceous borders towards the park.

"Miss Warrender." He rose at sight of Kate and, surprisingly, blushed. "How are you? And the children?"

"Well, thank you." She bent to drop a kiss on her mother's cheek and saw that she, too, was blushing.

"Look what Mr. Warren has brought us," said Mrs. Warrender. "That book we saw noticed in the *Critical Review. Sense and Sensibility*. Do you remember?"

"Yes. How kind of Mr. Warren." She looked down at the neatly bound volumes. "And giving us a binding, too. You should not have troubled, Mr. Warren."

"I like buying books," he said, and rose to take his leave.

Alone with her: "What in the world, mamma?" Kate turned to her blushing mother.

Mrs. Warrender's blush deepened. "Kate, do you know, I really believe the poor young thing has taken a boy's fancy to me. What *am* I to do?"

"Discourage him," said Kate.

"I did my best." Defensively. And then, with an effort: "Kate, did Lord Hawth speak to you today?"

"Yes, indeed, and with your permission, he told me. I've a crow to pluck with you over that, mamma. Why did you not tell him how much I dislike him?"

"I did try. But how could I make him believe it when I don't myself? How could you?"

"Such a *preux chevalier*," said Kate bitterly. "You may enjoy lying down and letting him walk over you, but it is more than I do."

"You did not quarrel with him?" asked her mother anxiously.

"I did my best to, but he does not care for me enough to quarrel. No need to look so fretted, love. We're not out of work. We parted on the best of terms, my Lord Hawth and I, as master and governess. Oh—there's a tutor coming next week. Did you know?"

"No, What's his name?"

"His lordship did not trouble to tell me."

Their dinner that night, normally so cheerful, was a silent

meal, each of them deep in her own thoughts. Afterwards, Kate sat down as usual at the upright piano to play to her mother as she worked at another chair cover, but soon rose to her feet with a long, angry concluding chord. "I'm out of sorts! Blue-devilled. Forgive me. I'll take my bad temper to bed."

"Kate." Her mother pulled her down for a long, loving kiss, then looked up at her anxiously. "You're not regretting? You'd not like me to say a word to Lord Hawth?"

"Regretting? Lord Hawth! Are you out of your wits?"

"Just worried," said her mother.

Chapter 13

The new tutor, John Winterton, came a week later, and Kate, who found silent fault with most of what Lord Hawth did these days, could find no fault with him. The only mystery was why he should choose to bury himself in the deep countryside to teach a small boy his Latin verbs. Tall, dark and athletic-looking, he was anything but handsome, having had his nose badly broken in what he ruefully described as "a bit of trouble" at Harrow. He also had an ugly scar down one side of his face, and a weakness in his right arm for which, he said, the exercise of riding was the very thing. The children's new ponies had arrived a few days before he did, and he was soon their daily companion, ranging further and further afield with them as they got used to their new mounts, and the evenings lengthened.

"But why don't you go too?" asked Mrs. Warrender, when Kate came glumly home straight after nursery lunch.

"Because I am not invited." Kate looked out at the garden, where quickly shifting patterns of sun and shade spoke of the chancy brilliance of an April day.

"But, Kate, you surely do not need to stand on points with the tutor! If you wanted to go, you should have said so."

"He made it impossible," said Kate crossly. "And the children don't care. He's all in all to them since he came. Even Sue looks better. It will serve my autocratic Lord Hawth right if he finds he has another tutorial romance on his hands."

"Perhaps that is what he wishes," said her mother. "After all, poor Sue. . . . She can't look very high, placed as she is. I did wonder, last autumn, whether Lord Hawth might not have built some hopes on George Warren."

"If he did, he has been disappointed." Kate's laugh was a little off-key. "The way that young man dangles after you is a perfect scandal, mamma. I had no idea he was such a frequent visitor."

"He says I am teaching him how to go on in English society." There was just the hint of a stress on the word "says."

"He does, does he? Well, who better? Only, you're not going to break his heart for him, mamma dear?"

"Good God, no!" Her mother laughed. "You're right, of course. He has convinced himself, just a little, I think, that he nourishes a passion for me. A boy's folly, that's all. He'll get over it. Poor thing, he knows so little about women. I'm getting very fond of him, Kate. He's interested in things—poetry . . . painting. I even like hearing him talk about his agricultural plans. You have no idea how knowledgeable I am getting about turnips and fallowing."

"Wicked one! Just so long as you keep your pretty little head, mamma! No wonder you are in such looks. I like you in that lavender coloured jaconet. I'm so glad you have decided to come out of full mourning."

"It's two years since Christopher was drowned." Mrs. Warrender sounded almost defensive.

"And you do not mourn for papa? Quite right. Mamma?"

"Yes?" Her mother looked up quickly at her change of tone.

"Have you ever thought that with my £100 a year and the

£500 of yours that so miraculously escaped from papa's debts we could set up housekeeping for ourselves?"

"But why?" Her mother looked at her in amazement. "Are you not happy here?"

"Happy!" exclaimed Kate. And then: "Are you?"

"Why, yes, I think so. It's good to be useful. I thought you felt that, too. Just think how the children have come on in the course of the winter!"

"To such a point that they can do very well without me! And Mamma, think what will happen when Lord Hawth finds himself a bride. It won't be long, I wager, now he's on the catch for one. Next trip to London and some charming young schoolroom miss will snap him up, and it will be marching orders for you and me. How much better to find ourselves a genteel little apartment in Bath. Or maybe Tunbridge Wells? Cheaper there, and not so far to move? And go, before we are pushed?"

"But, Kate," wailed her mother, "I don't want to go!"

"Mamma dear." Kate, who had been standing all this time, gazing out at the spring green of the garden, turned and came over to put both hands lovingly on her mother's shoulders and look searchingly down at her. "It would be better. You must see that. For both of us."

"I don't know what you are talking about!" But Mrs. Warrender had blushed crimson, and turned with a mixture of relief and dismay as Joe appeared to announce Mr. Warren.

His pretext for the call was a copy of *The Memoirs of a Female Dandy* which he had just received from London. "But I am afraid you will think it sad enough stuff, ma'am." He handed it to Mrs. Warrender. "Imagine the heroine dressing up in men's clothes and parading about the country so! All very well in a Shakespeare play, perhaps. Doublet and hose might have acted as a disguise, but imagine a modern young lady in buckskins and top-boots!"

"Shakespeare wrote for boy actors," said Kate crossly. "And Lady Caroline Lamb masquerades often enough, they say, as one of her own pages. I envy her. To be able to ride astride for once instead of sitting perched up sideways like a bundle of old clothes!"

"Lady Caroline Lamb may," Warren said with some firmness, "but if I had a sister, as I wish I had, I should most certainly not wish to see her tramping about the countryside in men's clothes, exposed to God knows what in the way of insult. Still less riding astride! I am surprised you even see fit to mention such a possibility, Miss Warrender."

"Shocked you, have I? Poor Mr. Warren! Do you find us British females so very free-spoken?"

"Well." He spoke to her but smiled at her mother. "A little surprising, perhaps. My fault, of course. Our Philadelphia young ladies don't mix with the gentlemen quite the way that happens here. I like it," he hastened to add. "Only—" he turned ruefully to Mrs. Warrender—"I don't quite know how to go on."

"We'll do our best to teach you," said Mrs. Warrender.

"Much use we'll be," said her daughter. "Shut up here like a couple of nuns. But, Mr. Warren, surely your mother . . ."

"Died when I was a child?"

"Oh! I'm sorry." And then, irrepressibly: "Don't tell me! You were brought up by a maiden aunt."

"Precisely. My mother's sister. I loved her dearly. She and my father both died of the smallpox when I was fifteen. That's when I went to sea with her brother, my uncle. Not much female companionship there, Miss Warrender." Once again he turned to her mother, who had been making small noises of sympathy. "May I show you my aunt's picture, ma'am?"

"I should like it above all things. But, where . . ."

"Here." He reached into his pocket, produced what looked like a watch and flicked it open.

"She's beautiful," said Mrs. Warrender as she and Kate gazed at the delicate miniature.

"So is the painting," said Kate. "Who in the world did you get to do it? It looks like one of Mr. Cosway's."

George Warren laughed. "You flatter me, Miss Warrender."

"You did it yourself? At fifteen? I don't believe it!"

"Kate," said her mother.

But Kate had already blushed fiery red and held out a hand in apology. "Forgive me, Cousin George. My wretched tongue! I'm in the dismals today, but that's no excuse for being rude to you. My occupation's gone. The children are out riding with that paragon of a new tutor, who, by the way, I suspect of having been involved in several duels. How else could he have got that weak arm and scar on his face?"

"Hawth did not tell you?" Warren looked surprised. "Winterton was with the 19th Division at the storming of Ciudad Rodrigo in January. You did not know he was an army man? He does not talk of it much. The wounds he got at Ciudad are likely to make him a civilian for life, and he's wretched about it. But I would have thought Hawth would have warned you."

"Warned is the word," said Kate angrily. "It would have saved me from making a complete fool of myself." She rose and took an angry turn across the room, muslin skirts swishing. "No doubt he's told the children all about it. Of course they dote on him! As for me, I may as well go lead apes in hell!"

"Like Beatrice?" George Warren surprised her by picking up her quotation. "You are a little like her, now I come to think of it. She's always been one of my favourite of Shakespeare's heroines."

"You have a weakness for shrews? I should be grateful, I collect, that I do not remind you of Katharina in *The Taming of the Shrew*! I have no doubt she would have made an admirable governess if the opportunity had offered itself."

"Kate!" said her mother again.

"My dear Miss Warrender—" But Kate cut short his protest with a rather blind curtsy and left them.

She did not reappear till supper time, when her dark-circled glittering eyes hinted at tears and forbade questions about them. "You had a pleasant visit, I trust, with our surprising cousin?" she asked, competently carving and passing her mother the breast of a cold squab. "What new talent do you think he will reveal next?"

"Oh Kate," sighed her mother. "You are hard on that nice young man."

"Nice?" She laughed, off-key. "Just the word! Scrupulous, you would say. No sister of his would ever go jauntering about the country in buckskins and topboots. If, of course, he had a sister. Lucky for her he hasn't! Did you notice how careful he was not to sully our delicate ears with the word 'breeches.' No doubt, if pushed to it, he would have talked of 'inexpressibles!' Oh, mamma, dearest little mamma, do let us go to Tunbridge Wells!"

"That's enough, Kate! I don't want to go." Mrs. Warrender's firm reply surprised her daughter as much as if she had let off one of Mr. Cosgrove's rockets in the dining room.

Kate was quiet after that, and withdrew to her room as soon as she decently could. Intolerable day. Fool that she had made of herself. "'No sister of mine,'" she quoted angrily as she moved over to the window to draw back the curtain and let in a flood of moonlight. "'Still less riding astride!'" Over at the stables a horse whinnied impatiently. Boney, fretting, as she was, for freedom? "Riding astride!" Why not? And plague take the lot of them. She moved quickly to the chest where she kept her brother's clothes. Kate Warrender must listen to what the gentlemen chose to tell her, and make a fool of herself when they left her in the dark. Kit Warrender could go where he pleased, do what he pleased, say what he thought.

She made herself wait, candle out, in the dark, until she had heard her mother pass her door, pause for a moment, and then go on, with a little sigh, to her own upstairs room. Then she heard Joe go heavily round locking up. At last, silence. It was early still, but they kept daylight hours at the stables. She dressed quickly, glad to find that Christopher's clothes still fitted her after the long, lazy winter, opened her window quietly and was out in the welcoming moonlight.

Delighted to see her, Boney stood quietly to let her saddle up and they were soon safe outside the stable yard. Where next? Tonight, there was not room for her to breathe in the park. Luckily, she need not stay there. The children had found the new gap in the park wall when they were out primrosing, just before Mr. Winterton's arrival. It lay heavy on Kate's conscience that she had not told Lord Hawth about it, but how could she seek a private interview with him? Anyway, tonight she was glad of her ommission. The gap was on the London side of the sea gate, very handy, she thought, for the smugglers, and very handy, tonight, for her. She and Boney would shake out their megrims on the London road. No fear of meeting anyone, since the little used country lane was a short cut to London only for the village of Tidemills and for Hawth Hall itself.

As always, the smugglers had been considerate, and the gap was neatly filled in with brushwood and hurdles, equally easy to remove or to jump, but safe to keep deer in and sheep out. Should she, after all, tell Lord Hawth in the morning? Things had been quiet at Tidemills since John Penfold had left. Thinking of the mob law reported from other parts of the country, the arson and frame-breaking, she thought it might be best to leave well alone.

Reaching the lane, she paused where it forked. She had forgotten how darkly overgrown the way to London was. A pity, she told herself, to leave moonlight for shadows. Besides, it would be awkward going, and she would be in a fine pickle if Boney were to slip and hurt himself. Liar! She shook her shoulders angrily, and Boney moved uneasily, recognising her mood. She was afraid of that dark lane. What had happened to Kit Warrender?

It had been a bad day. A bad two days. A picture of George Warren hanging on her mother's words flashed before her eyes. Kit Warrender could pay a call on him tonight. Lord, she was tempted. He had said, several times, how much he would like to meet her cousin again. They would sit and talk over a glass of wine, as she had that first night with Lord Hawth. Kit Warrender could air opinions that his Cousin Kate must not venture. Kit could even consult George Warren about that gap in the park wall.

No! She shook the reins and turned Boney's head towards the long, moonlit slope that led down to Tidemills. Madness even to think of going to Warren House. She *was* mad, she sometimes thought, but not so mad as that. She would ride down over the hill as far as the outskirts of the village. Moonlight gleaming on the great bend of the Glin as it wound down to the sea showed it full tide. The mill would be hard at work and the shift would change at midnight. She must keep well away from the village itself, but the easy ride, with the moonlit view of marsh and sea, was just what she needed.

It was soothing to let Boney find his own clever way down the chalky track while she looked ahead at the great shining curve of the sea between the two dark headlands, Glinde Head and Chyngford Point, that formed Glinde Bay. Lights on Glinde Head to the east showed where night watch was being kept, as always, at the barracks. Were they watching, as she found she was, the dark speck out towards the horizon that gradually defined itself as a small ship of some kind? Probably not. These moonlight nights were for fishermen, not smugglers. Someone from Tidemills had doubtless decided to stay awake through his off-shift and go out for a spring catch of herring or mackerel. God knew they needed the extra food badly enough to stay awake for it. She must speak to Lord Hawth about conditions down at the mills. "They're close to starving, miss," Joe had told her. "My Aunt Sarah says she don't know why things is so quiet. She don't like it, she says. Her man don't say nothing, and she don't ask. But there's meetings still, regular, she says."

Kate sighed and pulled at the reins. She could hear a door bang in the village now, and a man's voice came up to her in something between a shout and a curse. The new shift must be getting ready to go to work. She was quite as near as was safe. Besides, she had suddenly had a mad idea. All part of the general, moonlight madness? It was going to be difficult for Kate Warrender to speak to Lord Hawth in the morning. But suppose Kit Warrender were to call tonight? Lord Hawth might listen to him, when he would not to a woman, and particularly one who had just refused him. It must be near midnight, but Hawth sat up to all hours. Should she? Dared she?

On the thought, she had turned Boney and kicked him into a brisk trot up the hill, moonlight from over her shoulder making the way easy. Kit Warrender could knock up old Ben, the lodge keeper at the sea gate, and insist on seeing Lord Hawth. Kit Warrender could tell him about the new gap in the park wall, and about the state of things at Tidemills. He would listen to Kit.

Enjoying the idea, she was too deep in imagined talk with Lord Hawth to hear the other horse until it was too late. Horse and rider emerged from the thicket where the paths forked and came swiftly down the hill towards her. Absurd to feel such a sudden start of pure terror. And nothing to do but brazen out the meeting.

"You ride late." The rider pulled in his horse as they met. The capes of his coat were pulled well up, and his hat down over his face, but moonlight and his cockney accent revealed him to Kate as a stranger.

"So do you." With the moon almost behind her, Kate hoped to present nothing but a black silhouette.

"From Tidemills?"

"I've been there." The right answer? The wrong one?

"What's doing there?"

"Nothing. The night shift's just going in."

"And you?"

"None of your business." And as she spoke realised that she had let him outmanoeuvre her. He had edged the horses round so that moonlight struck clear across the side of her face.

"Mr. Warrender! You're here already! The General will be

mortal glad to hear that. He's coming down tomorrow, sent me on ahead. He'll want to see you straightaway. Where are you for now?"

"Glinde." What could this all mean?

"Of course. Well then, there'll be a message for you at the Bell, soon as the General gets here. Things is moving at last, I reckon. Not long now. Goodnight, sir." He rode swiftly away down the track towards the village. And, from it, the ruthless clamour of a bell announced that it was midnight already, and the shifts changing. Too late now to call on Lord Hawth. Besides, if she did, what in the world could she say? "Not long now." The words rang in her head, echoing the brutal bell, as she rode slowly homewards. "Not long now," and, "You're here already," and, "The General will be mortal glad." What did it mean? What could it mean? She must think it over before she said or did anything.

The stranger reached the village, as he had intended, long enough after the second shift had gone in so that the street lay quiet again after the weary bustle of the changeover. Lights, here and there, showed where tired men were taking time to eat a meagre bite of bread, and maybe a bit of musty bacon, before they fell on their pallets and into the stupor of exhaustion. Children, waked by the commotion in the sordid one-room houses, cried and were irritably hushed by their mothers. Fathers must sleep and wake again, fresh enough to earn the family pittance.

At the Ship, he was expected. Jewkes, the landlord, had heard his horse come down the quiet street and was there on his doorstep to greet him. "You're true to your time, Brother Jenson. Here, you, Pete, see to the gentleman's horse, and then off to bed with you. I closed early." He led the way into the empty bar, where abandoned beer mugs and a strong smell of tobacco told their own tale.

"They didn't mind?"

"Mind! Course they minded. But they mind me, too, and no mistake. Your usual?" He moved behind the bar and reached for a squat, black bottle.

"Thanks." Jenson had thrown greatcoat and shabby hat on

a table and settled with a tired sigh on a bench by the fire. "A long day."

"And not over yet. What's the news from town?"

"Good and bad. The word's still, 'Not long now.' Devil take me if I know what they're waiting for. There's trouble all over in the north. Manchester, Leeds, Huddersfield. Even Carlisle. General Ludd's done his work well. So why must we hang back, down here in the south, and starve to death like clods?"

"Soon now, I reckon." Jewkes had poured a stiff draft of gin. "That will warm you. Something to eat?"

"No, thanks. I stopped for a bite in East Grinstead. At a brother's house. They're ready and waiting there. Getting impatient, too. I tell you, man, it don't make sense. With the spring, things will ease up, stands to reason. Things growing again, a bite of greens from the garden, a hen laying, maybe. Things is ripe and ready now. Take the time, I told the General, take it when it comes. It won't stay for no one."

"And what did he say?"

"'Not long now,' damn him. And, 'wait.' Like he's said all winter. Well, true for him, *up* to a point. They've sent so many soldiers up north, they're stretched mighty thin round London. But they know it. Talk of a new barracks building in the Regent's Park. A new one in Brighton, too."

"They won't be built in time," said Jewkes.

"Won't be built at all, if the Whigs have their way. A great cry of waste of public money. Francis Burdett's to speak against it in the House."

"Will he come out for us, do you think?"

"The General says that's partly what we are waiting for. Him and his friends. To declare themselves. I don't want them. I don't trust them. Lot of bleeding aristos. Use us and hang us, ask me."

"Did the General?"

"Ask me? Does he ever? Keeps his own counsel, does the General. Have to wait for a sign, sez he. When the mail coaches don't run. That's the day. But what's to stop them running? That's what I want to know."

"The General, of course. That's mebbe what he's waiting for. It's the mob will stop the coaches, but what's to get the mob out? That's the question, ain't it? London mobs ain't like no others. It takes more than a simple cry like 'bread or blood' for them. You ought to know that! You cobblers have always seen further than most, but you stay pretty quiet, mostly."

"Waiting," said the other man bitterly. "Jist waiting." He held out his mug. "I'll thank you for the same again. You're not joining me?"

"No." Jewkes took the mug and rose to his feet. "I've not touched a drop since the General first came, last autumn. He made me promise when he twisted me in. 'There's too many temptations in your line of business,' he says. 'You stay sober, Jewkes, and listen,' and, by God, I have. When's he coming down?"

"Tomorrow, he said. Meeting at the usual time 'n he wants to see young Warrender first. Funny thing, I thought he wasn't due till tonight."

"No more he isn't."

"But I met him. Half an hour ago. Just outside the village. Riding to Glinde, he said."

Jewkes turned to look at him, bottle in one hand, mug in the other. "And what did you say?"

"Nothing much." Jewkes' tone had frightened him, and it showed in his voice.

"That's no answer. *What* did you say?"

"Let me think." He reached out a shaking hand for the replenished mug. "Nothing, really. Something about riding late. I didn't recognise him at first, see, not till I got him round with the moon on his face. Then, of course, I knew him, called him by name. Told him the General would be glad he's safe back." He stopped, aware of something dangerous in the listening silence.

"Go on." Jewkes' voice grew more deadly as it grew quieter.

"Let me think." Reluctantly. "Of course! Naturally, I told him the General was coming, would want to see him tomorrow. There'd be a message at the Bell. Nothing wrong with that, surely," he said into the menacing quiet.

"You think not? And what else?"

"That was all, I reckon." Some inner caution advised him to say nothing of his last, hopeful remark.

"Not quite all, I think." A sharp man, Jewkes. And no mistaking the threat in his tone. "Go on, man. It's important."

"Just something about 'Not long now.' Just what I said to you."

"Enough." Jewkes took the half empty mug from his reluctant hand. "Enough to send us out again. And fast. You met him when?"

"Half an hour ago? Mebbe less."

"Riding towards Glinde?"

"I told you. But what is all this?"

"Trouble. Not your fault, mebbe. Trouble just the same, and not a moment to lose. Pete!" His shout echoed through the quiet house. "Rouse out this instant and saddle up for us. You—" he turned on Jenson—"wait here. I'll fetch my brother. Then we're off."

"But where to?"

"Hawth–" He paused, looking thoughtfully at Jenson. "No. You've had a long ride. Go to bed. Your usual room. My brother and I can manage."

"I don't understand."

"No reason why you should."

Tired, Boney jibbed at the more difficult jump over the brushwood barrier from the uphill slope. After putting him at it unsuccessfully for the third time, Kate resigned herself to the inevitable, tied him to a tree and went to work to clear a path for them. Idiotic not to have thought of this on the way out, but she had been in no state for clear thinking. Struggling with the tightly packed bundles of brushwood, she told herself that she might just as well report the gap in the wall to Lord Hawth in the morning. This would have to be Kit Warrender's last venture on the marsh.

The opening made at last, she led Boney through and felt hideously tempted to ride home and leave the gap unblocked. That would certainly ensure that Lord Hawth learned of it. But he and George Warren had recently bought a flock each of two different kinds of merino sheep. Hawth's were in the park, Warren's in the long meadow. They must not be allowed to mix. She sighed, tethered Boney again, and went to work with aching back and bleeding hands, only to stop, head up, listening, at the sound of horses, ridden fast, coming from the direction of Tidemills. What in the world? Some disaster down there? She moved over to quiet Boney, glad that she was safe inside the park boundary and out of sight of the lane.

Two horses? Three? Coming dangerously fast up the long hill. In a moment she would know whether they were heading for Glinde or London, and be able to go back to her exhausting task. Lord, she would be glad to be safe in her comfortable bed.

There was something hypnotic about the oncoming drum of hooves. She listened tiredly, a soothing arm round Boney's neck as he bent to crop at spring grass, then suddenly threw up his head and whinnied. Too late, starting into full awareness, she heard the horsemen sweep straight across the lane to come crashing through the half-built barrier and pull their horses to a trampling halt.

"Mr. Warrender?" A familiar voice. Whose?

"Yes?" It must be smugglers. No reason to be afraid, surely? But she was. There were three of them and they had already formed their horses into a close circle round her and Boney.

"We need you." Again, there was something teasingly familiar about the broad Glinde accent.

"Need me?" If she had been in the saddle, she would have made a wild attempt at escape, but standing there, with them looming over her, she knew herself helpless.

"Yes. Down at Tidemills. There's trouble there. A meeting after the night shift. They talk of marching on the hall. You quieted them last autumn. You're the only hope now."

She had recognised him at last. "It's Jewkes, isn't it? From the Ship?" And knew it for a mistake the moment it was spoken. The blow caught her on the side of the head. She had an instant of blinding pain and panic, then nothing.

It was dark. Her head hurt. She hurt all over. Her hands were stiff. From shifting the brushwood? No, more than that. They were tied, and so were her feet. She was trussed, helpless. Jewkes. She had recognised him, and, idiot, said so. Trying to move made her head hurt more, and was useless. She lay very still and tried instead to think.

Total darkness. Not a glimmer, not a hint, not the faintest streak of light. A cellar? The air was fresh and cool. Thinking made her headache worse. There were no cellars at Tidemills; the ground was too swampy. Hard to imagine a room in any of those shoddily built houses that would be totally impermeable to moonlight.

The air was fresh and cool. Something familiar about it. Of course. The tunnel. They had not gagged her. Scream? If that would have helped her, she would have been gagged. They would have thrown her in at the lower end of the tunnel, too far either from the house or from the lane for her voice to carry. How did they know about the tunnel? Why had they done this to her? How did she threaten them? And—what did they intend?

Absurd even to ask herself that question. Obvious what they intended. She had been left here, helpless, to die. It concentrates the mind wonderfully, Dr. Johnson had said. So: concentrate. Look for hope. Hope? The children. They knew about the tunnel, too. When she was missed, in the morning, might they not think of it? In the morning? How long had she been here already? And why should they look here? Boney would be found somewhere else, somewhere miles away. It would look as if she had had an accident. Search would concentrate there. What would her mother do? Oh, poor mother! Would she tell them that it was a young man they must look for? She writhed a little in her bonds. Had Jewkes, tying her up, recognised her for what she was? Or had he known all the time? Should she be grateful that she was lying here, unviolated, merely to die, at her leisure, of starvation? Or would he come back? Would one of them come? On the thought, she heard something. The stone at the tunnel's mouth being moved? Jewkes? The throbbing in her head beat a wild crescendo. Footsteps. Very quiet, careful . . . still no light. She tried not even to breathe. Useless, of course. They knew she was here. Very close now. Something struck her head and the pain of it exploded her into unconsciousness once more.

Chapter 14

"Kate! Kate!" The voice came from far away. And long ago? Impossible. She must have slipped from unconsciousness into dream. A happy dream; let it continue. Christopher's voice. "Kate! Wake up! There's no time!"

Her hands and feet were free. What kind of a dream was this? She stirred a little and opened her eyes. Light. The flickering light of a candle. And, bending over her, holding it, unmistakable, Christopher.

"Chris!" Hardly more than a breath, but he heard it and bent closer.

"Kate! Thank God! I was afraid for a moment. How do you feel?"

"My head aches. It's nothing. Nothing compared to this! Chris, you're alive! It wasn't you! That body—oh, Chris!" The thoughts battered against each other in her aching head. Chris alive. How wonderful. But how strange. And yet it explained so much. Chris and the smugglers . . . It was for him they had taken her. So—Chris and the revolutionaries: Chris and Ned Ludd. She put a hand to her throbbing brow.

"Christopher, what have you been doing?"

"Earning my living."

Bravado, and yet a note of constraint in his voice. And no wonder. Her thoughts were clearing now. Clearing painfully. "And left us to mourn you all this time? Poor mother! How could you?" She struggled a little and let him help her up to sit, her back against the cold wall of the tunnel. "Chris, why?"

"No time for that! Not now. It's not safe. They might change their minds. Come back to finish you off. Jewkes is capable of anything."

"Jewkes!" This was stranger and stranger. "You know?"

"I saw them riding away. Him and his brother. Heard them coming, luckily. Hid in the bushes up where the path turns off to Tidemills. Heard that brother of Jewkes' say they should have made a job of it. Didn't know what he meant of course. Not till I fell over you."

"But what were you doing? How did you know about the tunnel?"

"There's no *time,* Kate. And, look, the candle's almost burned down. We've got to get out of here. Can you stand, do you think?"

"I'll try." With his help, she struggled to her feet, and stood, shivering all over, one steadying hand against the tunnel wall.

"That's right." Holding the candle in his left hand, he supported her with his right arm and began to help her forwards.

"But that's the wrong way!" She held back. "Why not to the hall, Chris? So much safer."

"Not for me. Not for either of us, if we are seen together. Kate, you must trust me, do what I tell you. I've not hidden, all these years, for nothing. I can't let it go now. Besides, it would be death. For us both. Come." As he spoke, he had been urging her down the slope of the tunnel.

Still she held back. "You promise you'll explain? Word of a Warrender?" Strange to find the childhood oath come so readily to her lips. With it, the full truth came home to her and tears of happiness filled her eyes. "Oh, Chris!"

"Ah, Kate! You've no idea how I have suffered through the long silence."

"How *you've* suffered! But *you* knew! What do you think it has been like for mamma and me?" She stopped, faced him. "Chris, I must have your promise that you'll explain."

"Oh, I mean to," he said. "I need your help. But first we must get away from here. Ah—" They had come to the tunnel entrance and he reached down to feel for the hinged stone.

"You've done that often! Why?"

"Hush!"

The stone had swung outwards to show the priory ruins, still and strange in the moonlight. Judging by its angle, she could not have been unconscious for long. But by what miracle had he come to find her? The cool night air was reviving her by the moment, and with strength, the questions came flooding. But not to be asked. Not now. He was right about that. She let him lead her silently to where a horse stood tethered to a tree, and help her into the saddle. She swayed a little and he put a steadying arm around her, holding the reins in the other hand. "It will have to be the gap, I'm afraid," he whispered. "Can you manage so far?"

It seemed an eternity before they got to the gap, but at least this was still unblocked and Chris was able to lead the horse through and turn its head towards the short cut to the Dower House. They had never been in Hawth Park as children, but now he seemed to know the way as well as she did. Knew about the gap. Knew Jewkes. Knew altogether too much. She made her plan, decided the vital questions and let him lead her on, still in total silence, still swaying a little in the saddle, until they came to the edge of a copse, and a moonlit view of the Dower House.

She leaned down to him from the saddle and spoke quietly. "If I scream," she said, "they will hear it in the house. If you don't want to be discovered, you will explain. Now."

"Kate!" She had surprised him. "But you're hurt, you're tired. What you need is your bed."

"And what *you* need is time to decide what lie to tell me. So, hurt I may be, tired I may be, but you are going to make a round tale of it now, Chris Warrender, or, word of a Warrender, I'll scream and rouse the house."

"You wouldn't?"

"Oh, wouldn't I!" Strange, and despite everything pleasant to feel them slipping back into the old relationship of older sister and wayward young brother. "Chris! I'm afraid it's a scrape, a bad one. I helped you out of enough before. Won't you trust me now?"

"I suppose I'll have to," he said ruefully. "But it's a long story, Kate. You ought to be in your bed."

"So the less you argue, the better. Besides, you don't want dawn to find you here. They get up early in the stables, and there will be a hue and cry after Boney. What are we going to say, Chris? I don't suppose you know what they did with him?"

"No." It had been the right appeal. They were conspirators together, as they had been so often in their childhood. "How many set on you, Kate?"

"Three."

"That's it, then. I only saw the Jewkes brothers. The third man must have taken care of Boney. I've been glad to hear you rode him, Kate."

"Don't flannel me, love." But she said it lovingly. "What do you think they will have done with him?"

"It depends what they want thought, doesn't it?" He too had obviously been thinking hard during the silent return. "But, first, why did they do it, Kate? What happened?" They had halted there in the dark verge of the copse.

"I was riding down to Tidemills. I go out at night sometimes. Dressed like this."

"I know."

"You know a great deal!"

"Yes. But the question. What happened that made you a threat to them?"

This was not the little brother she had protected. This was

a man, and he must be answered. "I met someone," she said. "A stranger. As I came back from Tidemills, just before the shift changed. He recognised me, called me Mr. Warrender."

"Ah! And then?"

"Said something about the General, whoever he is. Coming tomorrow. There would be a message for me—for you, I suppose—at the Bell. And then, as we parted, something about, 'Not long now.' "

"And told Jewkes of course. About meeting you. And he knew I hadn't landed yet."

"Landed?"

"From France." Impatiently. "I'll tell you about that later. No time now. I was afraid Jewkes might have guessed there were two Kit Warrenders. I'd been wondering what to do. Hoped you would have the sense not to risk it again. Crazy thing to do!"

"How was I to know it was a risk?' She began, sadly, to feel how much he had changed, this beloved, freakish brother of hers.

"By using your wits! Surely, that first time, when Ned Ludd—General Ludd, he calls himself now—when he got you a hearing down at Tidemills. It must have made you think. Wonder. Lord, I laughed when I heard about that. And very well you did, too, by all accounts, and very useful you've been all winter. Confusing things, giving me cover. But you must have wondered."

"Of course I did. I thought it must be one of grandfather's . . ." She hesitated.

"Bastards," he said cheerfully. "I knew you weren't stupid. Let's just hope that's what Jewkes thinks *you* are. He certainly lost no time in coming after you tonight. Where did they catch you?"

"Inside the park wall."

"That's bad. And then?"

"I called him by name. That did it. I suppose. They knocked me out. When I came to, I was in the tunnel—left to die."

"Horrible. And they must know, too, if they carried you there. Who you are. What you are. Thank God it was no worse. But—" he seemed to shake himself—"that settles it. What they did to you. Murder, or as good as. Bad as."

"Settles what?"

"Kate." He reached up to gather both her hands in his. "I need your help more desperately than you can imagine. Can I trust you?"

"Yes."

"I'm sorry. I shouldn't have asked. But I've been leading such a shabby life. Kate, you're not going to like it."

"I know. I saw that at once. But I still don't understand. Just explain, and I'll try to. After all, you're the only brother I've got, and, oh, Chris, I'm so glad you're alive."

A tear dropped on the hands that held hers, and he bent to kiss them. "If we can only spare mamma."

"Yes. So, tell, Chris."

"It was a game at first. Almost. And one that paid. That was it, you see. Father kept me so short. *You* remember! All of us. Skint on food, on clothes, on everything, while he dropped thousands at the gaming tables. So when I joined the Volunteers and got the offer, I . . . I jumped at it, Kate."

"What offer?"

"There was a man sitting by when we were sworn in. Watching. Said nothing. Afterwards, he met me, by chance, in the Bell. Asked if I was game to take on dangerous work for extra pay."

"And you said?" This was not what she had feared.

"'Yes.' Of course. He gave me his name and an address—*not* his name, in fact, as I learned later. Said I was to send him reports. The behaviour of my fellow recruits, anything out of the way that went on in the district. That kind of thing."

"A government spy." She had heard of them, had hardly believed they existed. Did not much like the thought of them now. But at least it was for the government that he had worked.

"Well, yes. It was good money, Kate. Made all the difference. And useful work. They needed to know. At least that's what I thought. At first."

"Oh?"

"Then . . . he sent for me. The first man. Mr. Smith. To London. All expenses paid. You remember that time I went?"

"Yes." She and her mother had wondered, anxiously, how he had afforded that first trip to town.

"He put it to me then. More money. Much more money. And a future safe for me afterwards. If—"

"If what?"

"If I would disappear. Join the radicals, who, they began to suspect, were revolutionaries. Find out, from within, what they planned. A chance to serve my country, he said. Maybe to save it from the kind of blood-letting they had in France."

"You took it, of course." It would have been irresistible to the young man, half boy still, kept dangling idle at home.

"Yes. Kate, I honestly believed I'd be able to let you and mamma know. It was only after we'd carried out the 'drowning'—they were waiting in a boat, of course, to pick me up—that they told me I must tell no one."

"Whose was the body?"

"I don't know. Some dead French prisoner I imagine, from the gaol, who looked enough like me. That wasn't my business. My job was to get in with the radicals."

"And you did."

"It was easy. I was Kit Warrender, you see. A bastard. With a grudge against society. They approached me. Welcomed me. Twisted me in. And then—"

"Yes?"

"I began to realise that I *had* got a grudge against society. That they were right, and my masters in London wrong. They were brothers. Stood for each other through good times and bad. Wanted nothing but their rights. The right to a living wage, Kate, and a decent existence. 'Life, liberty and the pursuit of happiness.' They were good to me, talked to me, gave me books to read. Trusted me. Not Jewkes and his kind. The leaders, up in London."

"So what did you do?" She was shivering now, not with cold.

"Joined them. In heart as well as in show. Oh, I didn't tell them about the other thing. Went on sending in my reports, but harmless ones."

"And taking the pay?"

"I had to live!"

"How *did* you live?"

"Smuggling mostly." He said it with bravado. "It's their cover, you see."

"Cover for what?"

"That's just it. Kate, you must try to understand. See it as I did. Their plans were so reasonable. At first, they thought they would be able to keep the Prince, make him King, with a real Parliament, freely elected. But then, when he became Regent at last, had his chance to throw out the Tories and did not take it, they saw that would not do. Had to change all their plans. It's to be Princess Charlotte now. Queen Charlotte, when they take over."

"But she's only a child!"

"Young enough to be taught. The radicals have always backed her mother, as you know. Once they had young Charlotte in their hands, they would educate her as a true constitutional monarch. Lord knows, she's been taught little enough so far, by all reports."

"But her father? The Prince Regent? All his brothers? And sisters! They come first in line."

"Oh, I don't know." Impatiently. "That wasn't my business."

"I see." She saw enough to freeze her blood. "So when is this to happen, this fine, bloody, democratic revolution of yours? Soon, I take it. That's what the man meant by 'not long now.' That's why I was a danger to them."

"Yes. I don't know what will start it. I don't think anyone does but the General himself. He'll be Prime Minister, of course."

"Very democratic," she said. "That's settled already?"

"Well, yes. That's it. That's just what I began to see. And

then, they sent me to France. That's where I got back from tonight."

"France?" It was all extraordinary.

"To arrange for a shipment of arms. Naturally, the French said they'd help, to have an end to this wretched war that's draining the lifeblood from both countries. Only, when I got there, I began to see there was more to it. You remember how well I speak French? Our people had always used interpreters before. I heard things I wasn't supposed to. And then began to see things . . . to put two and two together. Kate, if it starts here, the French will come. In the general chaos. Take over. Oh, the Emperor's making a great noise about attacking Russia, but what do you think he was doing when he went to the Netherlands last autumn? His invasion fleet's still there, ready, waiting. Part of General Ludd's plan is for mutinies in the army and navy, don't you see? Has to be."

"Dear God! And then the French will come! Chris, what are you going to do?"

"I hadn't decided, till I found you, killed, as I thought, by Jewkes and his brother. I'd even thought of telling them. Trying to make them see their danger. No use. Not now. I'd be a dead man, and nothing achieved."

"The General then? When you see him tomorrow?"

"Kate, he wouldn't believe me. He's . . . I don't know who he is in real life . . . I suppose it doesn't matter. But as General Ludd, he's a man of one idea. He couldn't be shaken in it. Not now. Not after he's got so far. He'd just brush me aside, and go on. You've got to help me, Kate."

"How?"

"To meet Lord Hawth. I'm almost sure he's another government man. They don't tell us about each other, but he's turned up mighty pat when there's been anything doing. Even if not, he's a magistrate, the obvious man to turn to." And then, as if sensing her hesitation: "No need for him to know about you. When did he last see you as Kit Warrender?"

"Ages ago. And only twice. Chris!" She began to see it all. "You arranged that. Set it up. Set *me* up. Persuaded me to wear your clothes, go with you to the Bell, establish your alias for you. You had it all planned!" And all the risk it involved for her. She had to face that.

A light dawn wind brushed the side of her face. Above them, in the trees, the birds were beginning to stir. "There's no more time, Kate." He avoided the issue. "You've got to help me get in touch with Lord Hawth. Tell him you've had a message. That I must see him. Alone, in secret, in his study, first thing in the morning. When it's safe, he must open the door in the panel. I'll spend the rest of the night in the tunnel."

"Suppose Jewkes comes back?"

"I'll have to chance it. Besides, he'd have done so by now, if he was going to. It's almost morning. Kate, I must go."

"May I tell mamma?"

"No. Not unless you want me dead indeed. Tell no one. Not Lord Hawth. Not who I really am. Just say that Kit Warrender wants to see him." He reached to pull her down and kiss her. "Can you manage from here?"

"I'll have to to. But, Chris, when will I see you?"

"When it's all over. 'Not long now,'" he quoted. "And if we all survive. Kate! One more thing. It's here they mean to land. The French. Here in the bay." He lifted her down from his horse. "What will you say about Boney?"

"God knows. But I'll think of something."

"I'm sure you will. And, Kate, be careful. We have to assume they know who you are. Jewkes knows. I'll do my best to convince him you're no danger to him, but, meanwhile, be careful."

"Trust me, I will! And you too, Chris. If we should lose you again . . ."

"I take a lot of drowning." He swung into the saddle and rode swiftly and silently away through the trees.

Left alone, Kate made herself think only of what was most urgent. Boney. Aching in every limb, she dragged herself to the stable and opened the main door and that of his box. The grooms could make what they would of it in the morning.

It was almost morning now. Streaks of light, to the east, beyond the park, where Glinde lay, spoke of day beginning to break. It would only be a few hours before Betty knocked on her door with her hot water. Safe in her room at last, she made herself write a quick note to Lord Hawth, dropped her clothes anyhow into the chest, fell into bed and was asleep.

Lord Hawth had sat up late over a bottle of burgundy and the estate records, which Knowles had left in chaos. His temper had not been improved by a timid visit from his daughter Susan, who had tried, for some extraordinary reason, to persuade him to pay a late call on Mrs. Warrender. Some nonsense about Miss Warrender having gone home unhappy that afternoon . . . about suggesting that she should join the children on their afternoon rides. Of all the absurdities. Did the child seriously think that she could make him her messenger? And to Miss Warrender of all people. He had refused, ungraciously, he thought afterwards, and had thought, too, afterwards, that Susan had perhaps been trying to make him behave like a father.

He had gone to bed in a very bad temper, slept little in consequence and been justifiably furious when he was waked at what seemed like crack of dawn by a terrified servant.

"What in the devil's name?" He sat up angrily in bed.

"It's a message, my lord. Urgent. From Miss Warrender."

Urgent? From Miss Warrender? Hell's teeth, had she changed her mind and chosen this extraordinary means of telling him so? If she had, she should learn her mistake, and fast. Marry her indeed! Had he ever really wanted to? He opened the note as the frightened servant drew the curtains and let in a stream of morning sunshine. It was short and to the point. "My lord. I have had a message from Kit Warrender. He asks to see you urgently and in secret, on a matter of life and death. He is awaiting you now, in the secret passage.

When you are alone in your study, and the doors locked, summon him, and he will explain." It was signed, without periphrasis, "Kate Warrender."

Urgent! Secret! Secret passage, even! A message from melodrama. He crumpled it angrily in his hand, then thought again. "You!" The servant had been hovering nervously.

"Yes, my lord?"

"Hot water at once. Breakfast in ten minutes. In the study. For two."

"Yes, my lord." And then, greatly daring, "My lord?"

"Yes?"

"Mr. Spinton is not up yet."

"To hell with Spinton. Do you think I can't dress myself, idiot?"

Fifteen minutes later he entered his study at the unprecedented hour of nine o'clock and waited impatiently while a couple of footmen produced a lavish meal that did credit to Mrs. Warrender's training of the chef. Dismissing the servants, he locked the study door and moved over to open the panel. "Good morning, Mr. Warrender. You are an early caller."

"My apologies." Warrender looked exhausted and, perhaps because of this, Hawth thought, a good deal older than when they had last met. He stepped down from the tunnel entrance and Hawth saw that he was stiff with fatigue and cold.

"Here, man, come to the fire. You're frozen!" He half filled a cup with coffee, added a generous dram of brandy and passed it to his guest. "I trust you don't dislike brandy as much as you do claret."

"Claret? Oh, no," said Warrender vaguely. "Forgive me. I've had a night of it."

"And are starving, no doubt. I always seem to be giving you meals at odd hours, but I can offer you a decent piece of steak this time." He was investigating covered dishes. "Or some ham and eggs?"

"Both, thanks," said Warrender. "You're right. I'll make

better sense when I've had something to eat. I came back from France last night, sick as a dog all the way, always am. You're saving my life." He had finished the first cup of fortified coffee and handed it mutely over for replenishment. "Perhaps the brandy separately this time?" This was a man, not the boy Hawth remembered.

"France?" he said. If, as young Warrender's words suggested, he had been dangerously to and fro from there all winter, it was no wonder it had aged him. "What news from France?"

"That's why I'm here." He paused to deal with a large piece of steak and spoke inelegantly round it. "D'you know Mr. Smith?"

"Mr. Smith?" Hawth had been pouring brandy into a glass, now paused and looked thoughtfully at his guest. "Which Mr. Smith, pray?"

"Mr. Smith at the Home Office. Oh, he might call himself something else when he talks to you. He's a man of many names, and, I suspect, several faces. He employed me. The face I know is sallow, with an old fashioned tie wig, but I saw him once at the opera looking ten years younger, with his own hair, cut in a crop."

"You are observant, Mr. Warrender."

"A man needs to be in my line of business."

"And that is?"

"Spying." Defiantly. "As, I would think, you must have guessed."

"It did seem likely. And, yes, I asked some questions, after I had the pleasure of meeting you last year, and was told to mind my own business."

"Good." Food and brandy between them were bringing colour back to young Warrender's cheeks. "You knew where to ask. So you are the man I need."

"Let us assume so." Lord Hawth helped himself to a modest portion of ham and eggs. "And proceed without delay to the discussion of just why you need me. The news from France, of course?"

"Yes. I speak French."

"I congratulate you."

"You don't understand!" Colouring angrily, he looked more like the boy Hawth remembered. "I went as one of their emissaries."

"Their?"

"The revolutionaries. I heard more than I was meant to. It's not just revolution, my lord, as they think. Even General Ludd's been fooled there. Bonaparte plans to invade while the country's in chaos."

"Indeed," said Lord Hawth. "You interest me vastly. Tell me more, my friend, and have some more to eat."

"Thank you." Still wolfing his food, Warrender detailed the revealing phrases he had overheard and understood.

His host watched, and listened, and said at last, "So, first revolution, then invasion. And the landing here, in the bay."

"Yes."

"You've told your friends, the revolutionaries?"

"No!" He had been careful to say nothing to suggest that he had ever thought of throwing in his lot with theirs, and this question shook him. "I came straight to you."

"I am flattered. But, in fact, by way of Miss Warrender. What does she know of all this?"

"My cousin? Why, nothing, of course. A woman . . ." He had said nothing to betray his real identity, or suggest the existence of two Kit Warrenders.

"A devoted woman," said Hawth dryly. "You got back from France last night, you say? And I was roused at what I still consider a barbarous hour by her note? A romantic rendezvous, Mr. Warrender? What a melodramatic life you lead, to be sure. You will think me quite Gothic, I have no doubt, but I cannot say I quite like to think of my children's governess keeping midnight assignations, even with the most romantic of cousins. I think I must have a word with Miss Warrender."

"Oh, no." Now the young man looked very young indeed. "It's not like that at all, my lord. Forgive me, I can't explain. Not my secret."

"Then, of course, I must not ask about it. Besides," said

Hawth to his guest's heartfelt relief, "we have more urgent matters to consider, have we not? Miss Warrender can wait. I will take your news to London today. I think I can find your Mr. Smith, or someone else who will do as well. But, tell me, what is the signal?"

"That's what nobody knows. No one but the General."

"And you are to see him tonight or tomorrow. Do you think he will tell you?"

"I doubt it," said Warrender. "He keeps his own counsel."

"Wise man. Can I give you a little more steak? No? Then I think we should put an end to this agreeable occasion. But first, how will I get in touch if I should need you?"

"I could come back." He gestured towards the tunnel entrance.

"Do you know, I would much rather not. You will think me odd, no doubt, but I have it in mind to have that panel nailed up. But there must be someone with whom I can leave a message. Miss Warrender, perhaps?"

"*No!* I tell you, she must be kept out of this."

"I incline to agree with you. Well, then?"

The young man threw out his hands in a helpless gesture. "I have played a lone hand, my lord."

"Wise. But at this point, inconvenient. I have it! George Warren. He has said several times since you saved his life last autumn that he would like to meet you again. You are kin, I suppose, after a fashion. I leave it to you to think of a pretext for getting in touch with him that will satisfy your revolutionary friends. Call there tomorrow, or better still, today, renew his acquaintance for his servants' benefit, and arrange to keep in touch."

"He can be trusted?"

"Yes. I'll see him this morning, on my way to London. Warn him to expect you. And now—" he rose courteously to his feet—"I dislike hurrying you, but I think . . ."

"Yes." He picked up his hat and greatcoat. "My lord?"

"Yes?"

"You do not wish me to come back here?"

"No." But was that what the young man had first meant to say? Watching the panel close behind him, Lord Hawth stood thinking for a few minutes, then unlocked the door, rang the bell and proceeded to give a volley of orders.

Arriving late because Kate had overslept, the Warrender ladies met him in the hall. "Thank you for your message." He did not sound grateful as he glared down at Kate. "I am leaving at once for London. But before I go, I should perhaps warn you that I have given orders for the panel in the study to be nailed up. You will keep no more assignations with that cousin of yours there."

"Assignations? I?"

"Nor anywhere else, if you wish to remain in my employment. "Ma'am—" his tone softened as he turned to Mrs. Warrender—"may I have your word that you will not admit Kit Warrender to your house?"

"Admit Kit Warrender? But, my lord—"

"No time for argument. I trust *you* ma'am." And with that and a curt bow he turned on his heel and left them.

"What in the world?" Mrs. Warrender turned to Kate, who was still gazing furiously at the closed front door.

"He must be mad." Kate made her escape to the nursery wing.

Chapter 15

"Miss Warrender's horse? In my stables?" George Warren, too, had been roused early by an agitated servant.

"Loose in the yard. Barnes swears he locked up as usual last night, but the gate's ajar this morning." Chilver was sweating with anxiety, and, incredibly, his waistcoat was buttoned awry. "I've made bold to send a message to the Dower House, sir."

"Quiet right. They will be anxious. Thank God, I paid a late call on Mrs. Warrender yesterday. Miss Warrender was there, so at least we know she is safe."

"Yes, sir," said Chilver woodenly. "The horse has a man's saddle."

"Borrowed by the smugglers! Of course. Oh, well, it's not the first time, and I suppose it won't be the last."

"It was moonlight, sir."

"Yes, that's odd." George Warren had learned a great deal about the smugglers' habits during the winter. "But can you think of any other explanation, Chilver? Why are you looking so anxious, man?"

"I'll be glad when the boy comes back," said the butler.

"You didn't send back the horse?"

"He's dead lame. Thrown out a splint, Barnes thinks."

"Oh, poor Miss Warrender. Tell Barnes to look out something we can lend her."

"Yes, sir." But Chilver's expression did not lighten.

"What's the matter with you, man? I've told you Miss Warrender was at home last night! And you go on looking as if we were about to attend her funeral." But however incomprehensible, the man's obvious anxiety was catching. He threw off the bedclothes. "Send me my man, and order breakfast in ten minutes. I'll ride over myself."

"Thank you, sir." It was what Chilver had wanted.

But George Warren found he could not eat his kidneys and bacon. Chilver loved the Warrenders. Chilver had been anxious beyond concealment. Something was very wrong indeed. But what? He made himself drink coffee, without tasting it. Miss Warrender had been out of sorts yesterday, had almost quarrelled with him, and had then withdrawn to leave him alone with her mother. Which, surely, was what he had wanted?

Was it? He drank more coffee and found with disgust that he had put cream in it. What was the matter with him today? Absurd to have let Chilver infect him with his own ridiculous fancies. Miss Warrender's horse had been borrowed and lamed by the smugglers. That was all there was to it. He gave up the pretence of eating breakfast and strode out to the stables to look at Boney himself.

"Not so much a splint," Barnes had decided. "More it looks as if someone had took and fetched him a blow on purpose."

"But why in the world do that?"

"To spite Miss Kate, mebbe?" His face showed that he regretted the words as he spoke them.

"Who in the world would wish to do that? But at least the hock should mend?"

"Oh, yes. Poultices for a day or two, and old Boney will be good as ever." He ran an affectionate hand down the horse's spine. "Good to have the old warhorse back in the yard."

"Warhorse?"

"He was Mr. Christopher's, sir, first of all. He rode him with the Volunteers. Miss Kate, she only took to riding him after poor Mr. Chris was drowned."

"I didn't know. Fetch out my hack, Barnes. I'm riding over to the Dower House to tell Miss Kate not to worry, and offer to mount her in the meantime. What have we she could ride?"

"Miss Kate, she can ride most anything, sir," said Barnes.

Warren met Lord Hawth's curricle where the lane forked for Glinde. After the inevitable exchange of surprised greetings, since both of them were up impossibly early for anything but a day with the Glinde harriers, Warren put the question that plagued him. "Is all well at the Dower House?"

"Since they heard you had Miss Warrender's horse? Yes."

"Damn that boy." Warren's exclamation concealed a surge of relief. Fool to have let Chilver infect him with his absurd fears. "He was supposed to come straight back!"

"He's Parsons' nephew," said Hawth, as if that explained everything. "I was coming to see you. Can you spare me a moment? If you are on your way to the Dower House, I should tell you that the Warrender ladies are already at the hall."

"Stupid of me," said George Warren. "Naturally, they would be. But where are you off to?"

"London. A word with you first? Walk the horses, Bob." He handed the reins to his man and jumped lightly down from the high perch of the curricle. "In private."

"Yes?" Warren dismounted, looped the reins over his arm and walked beside Hawth, a little way back down the lane towards his own house. "You're sure all's well at the Dower House?" he asked, when they were out of earshot of the boy.

"God knows," said Hawth. "Something's afoot, and no mistake. Miss Warrender's keeping assignations with that cousin of hers, Kit Warrender."

"I don't believe it!" Warren's hand reached for a weapon that was not there. "You'll withdraw that, my lord!"

"I wish I could. I don't much like it myself. My children's governess."

"My cousin!"

"Devil take your cousinship." And then, recognising that Warren's rage matched his: "I'm sorry. You're right. I apologise. No right to speak of a young lady, member of your family, like that. But I'm plagued beyond permission! I need your help, George."

"Help?" He could not help being mollified by this first use of his christian name.

"Urgently. There's trouble brewing. No time to go into it. Will you trust me as I am trusting you?"

"Oh, I think so."

"Good, Then, listen." He described young Warrender's visit as succinctly as possible. "I'm off to London with this to the Home Office," he concluded. "When Warrender calls on you, arrange some pretext to keep in touch."

"Everyone knows I've been wanting to meet him again," said George Warren.

"Just so. I've sent a note to Captain Grange at the barracks. If trouble threatens before I get back, go to him. But, please God, it won't. General Ludd must be coming down to make sure of the arms young Warrender brought over. Presumably nothing will happen until he gets back to London."

"Yes." George Warren had impressed his friend by his quick grasp of the situation. "If Ludd's the only one who knows the signal, he almost has to be there in person."

"I would think so. So—we've a little time. I wish to God I knew just where Miss Warrender comes into it."

"Innocently, I am sure."

"I hope you prove right." And on this sombre note they parted, Hawth to make record time to London, and Warren to go back to his house and await his visitor. It went against the grain with him to do so. It was odd how badly he wanted to go up to the hall and see Kate Warrender. Just the sight of her face would be enough, he was sure, to dispel the unpleasant miasma of doubt with which Hawth's story had surrounded her. No. Not just Hawth's story. She had been in a strange mood yesterday. Something to do with Kit Warrender? He would not believe it. There must be an innocent reason for her connection with him, and he would not dream of insulting her by asking for it. Still less would he mention her name when young Warrender paid his call.

But the long day dragged by and there was no sign of Kit. Maddening to be confined to the house by the chance of his coming, but there it was, and he must resist the temptation to pay a quick afternoon call at the Dower House just to make sure that all was well there. He did, however, send over a horse for Kate and received a note of thanks in her spiky unmistakable hand. She was his "most grateful Cousin Kate." He liked that. He found he liked it very much.

Kate *was* grateful. She had got home in a towering rage from the hall, to find George's note and the boy from Warren House patiently walking a handsome thoroughbred up and down in the stable yard. "The pick of his stable," she told her mother. "At least Cousin George does not jump to the worst possible conclusions about me."

"Kate, dear, are you not refining too much upon poor Lord Hawth's behaviour?"

"'Poor Lord Hawth!'" If he does not think me fit to have the care of his children, why does he not out with it and say so!"

"I don't understand," wailed Mrs. Warrender, not for the first time. "What's the matter with you two today? You look like death and insist there's nothing wrong with you and Lord Hawth flies up into the boughs for no reason. I *wish* you would tell me what is going on, Kate."

"Mother, I can't. It's not my secret. I promise you, it will all be cleared up soon, and then—" She stopped. Then everything would be changed. Tossed this way and that by the night's amazing events, it had taken her a while to realise the full implications of her brother's survival. No need now for that set of apartments in Tunbridge Wells. When the crisis was past and Chris was able to make himself known, George

Warren would have to pack up and leave Warren House. His tenure as heir in tail would be over. He would go back to Philadelphia, and she would never see him again. The little note of thanks that pleased him so much took her an hour and a half to write.

"At last!" George Warren held out a friendly hand as Warrender was ushered into his study next morning. "I've been badly wanting to meet you again, and thank you for saving my life."

"It was nothing."

"On the contrary, it was my life. But what's the news?"

"We've a little time. I was down at Tidemills all evening. General Ludd was there—you know about him, I take it?"

"Yes. Hawth told me it all."

"Good. So you know about the consignment of arms I brought."

"Yes?" It was an odd thing, but George Warren found his young visitor a disappointment. He had liked him so much at that first meeting, been so grateful for the courage that had saved his life, and now . . . What was it about him? Something tarnished? Something just a little shabby? The hectic flush of a gambler who has just risked everything on a throw. Well, natural enough, perhaps, considering the desperate life he had led all winter, but disappointing, just the same.

"They're not for here. The arms." Warrender sounded a trifle impatient, as if he suspected his host of not paying full attention. "They have to be shared out and laboriously smuggled up to London before anything can happen. He was arranging that last night. The General." He took a deep draft of the claret Warren had poured for him.

"By the usual channels, I take it." With an effort, George Warren kept his voice friendly.

"Yes. I'm taking one load. Tell Hawth I'd take it kindly if he'd have a convincing job made of my 'capture.' I want to live to fight another day."

"To spy another day." Warren could not resist it.

"Call it that if you like." The young man's colour rose. "And tell me where England would find herself today without my 'spying.'"

"Fair enough." George Warren threw out a hand. "My apologies. It's a dangerous enough game you are playing, God knows. You'll keep your cousin out of it!" He had not meant to say this.

"My cousin? Oh, Kate. Well, of course. Hardly woman's work—eh?"

"Then perhaps a pity to have involved her to the extent of that note to Lord Hawth." He found himself disliking this young man more and more. "Hawth's jumped to some quite unpleasant conclusions, you know. It might even lose her her place."

To his amazement, his guest burst into a fit of laughter. "Lose her her place! Oh, that's rich! Tell Lord Hawth, with my compliments, that there is no need to fret himself about a place for my Cousin Kate. I'll find her one."

"You?"

"Not the way you think!" Warrender was struggling to control his mirth. "No, no, Mr. Warren, I don't propose to marry my Cousin Kate, but by God I'll make a place for her just the same, and no one will be more surprised than you."

"You talk in riddles." Warren did not try to keep the distaste out of his tone. "And about a lady I admire."

"Admire her, do you? That's better still. But I'd cut it out if I were you. Quite above your touch, is my Cousin Kate, and so I warn you. Your touch!" He dissolved once more into helpless laughter. "Oh, poor Cousin George." He reached out for the bottle, refilled his glass and drank. "I have quite other plans for Cousin Kate. Countess of Hawth, don't you think? Pity about that note, though. Thanks for telling me that. I'll make it right for her, never you mind how. Oh—and if you were planning to pay a call at the Dower House, as no doubt you are, you might give her a message from me, since my company is so compromising. Privately, if you will. When the old lady is busy with her housekeeping. Tell her, all's well, and she has nothing to fear."

"Fear!" exclaimed George Warren angrily. "What should she have to fear?"

"What, indeed?" laughed young Warrender. "With such a *preux chevalier* to leap to her defence."

"I think—" Warren rose—"that I will wish you a good day, Mr. Warrender. You will have to vist me again when you know the plans for moving the arms to London, so we must continue to appear friends, but we will not, if you please, discuss Miss Warrender. Or her mother."

"Oh, very well." Sulkily. "Just so long as you give Kate my message."

Left alone at last, George Warren took a hard pull at his wine, and his temper. Sad to have been so disappointed in young Warrender, but absurd to have let him make him angry. He was a spy, a nobody, and what he said about Kate Warrender mere bragging. But it had come uncomfortably close to home just the same. Why had it got him so exactly on the raw? Because of Mrs. Warrender. Her daughter should not be spoken of in such slighting terms. If only he had the right to protect them both. Impossible, of course. Once or twice that winter, watching Mrs. Warrender's fair head bent over her embroidery, he had been tempted to take the plunge. To ask her to be his wife. But, somehow, something had always stopped him. Not something: she had stopped him herself. So subtly, so gently, that it had taken him a while to recognise what she was doing, she had made it impossible for him to propose to her.

It left him free. If that unpleasant young man was right, and Hawth made Kate his countess, neither she nor her mother would ever need protecting again. As for him, he would go back to America. He wished he had never left.

And now, when he was not sure that he wanted to, he must call at the Dower House and deliver young Warrender's odd message. To the future Countess of Hawth? It seemed extremely probable. He could only hope that they would be happy together.

"You're going to the Dower House, sir?" Chilver was waiting to open the front door.

"Yes?"

"May I make so bold as to ask you to give Miss Kate a message for me?"

"Why, yes." He had lived in England long enough now to know just what an extraordinary request this was.

"Thank you, sir." So did Chilver. "It's to say, sir, please, will she be careful. Not walk over to the hall alone. Stay home at night. There's something going on," he added. "Isn't there, Mr. Warren?"

"Yes. And the less said about it the better. But of course I'll give your message to Miss Kate. I'd thought of saying very much the same thing to her myself. Though she would hardly be going out at night."

"No, sir," said Chilver.

Entering the comfortable little living room at the Dower House, George Warren thought neither of the two ladies looked well. Both were pale and heavy-eyed, as if from lack of sleep, but the pallor, which merely accentuated handsome bone structure in Kate's face, made her mother strike him, for the first time, as a woman much older than himself. What a fool he had been, and how grateful he was to her. He took his usual place by her chair and looked across the room at Kate, elegant in dark green. Had she grown more handsome, or had his idea of female beauty changed in the course of the winter? She would make a striking countess.

He must give her young Warrender's message, and Chilver's. His chance came when Joe appeared to announce a messenger from Lord Hawth, and Mrs. Warrender excused herself to receive him. "Miss Warrender." He moved across the room to stand over her chair, and she looked up at him, sudden colour flooding her face. "I have a message for you."

"A message?" The colour drained away, leaving her

drawn, anxious. She must think it came from Hawth. "From your cousin," he hastened to explain. "I don't much like to be its bearer."

"Pray, don't trouble yourself on my account, Mr. Warren. I can see that my kind employer has already told you my character is quite gone. He thinks I have been using the secret passage for assignations. He means to have it nailed up, to prevent me . . ." Her face changed, darkened, as if at some new and unpleasant idea. "No," she exclaimed. "Impossible!" And then, with an effort: "Forgive me. A message, you said?"

"I wish I was your brother!" Now, what in the world had made him say that, and why had it turned her whiter than ever? "At least I am your cousin," he went on, "and I take it unkindly that you are calling me Mr. Warren again. Miss Warrender, if you should ever need help . . ." Idiot. Lord Hawth would look after her.

"Thank you. But this message?"

"Reassuring enough. Kit Warrender asked me to tell you that all is well and you have nothing to fear." His tone inevitably betrayed what he felt about the strange message.

"Kind of my Cousin Kit," she said lightly. "And there I'd been looking under the bed of nights."

"Just what I said." He was relieved she took it so. "What should you fear, Miss Warrender?" And then, remembering: "Though in fact, I have another message for you."

"Another?"

"From Chilver. He waylaid me as I came out. Asked me to warn you to be careful. Don't go to the hall alone, he says, don't go out at night."

"Out at night?" Mrs. Warrender had rejoined them. "Why in the world would we be going out at night, with no invitations, and it the dark of the moon anyway."

"Poor old Chilver," said Kate. "He always was a worrier. But a good friend, too. Tell him to be easy, Mr. Warren. Joe takes me to the hall these days, and one of the men brings me back. Lord Hawth insists on it."

Naturally Lord Hawth did. Bad enough to have his future countess acting governess to his bastard children without letting her risk reputation walking alone, even in his own park. Warren rose to his feet. "I have been keeping you ladies from your work. But before I go, what news from Hawth, ma'am?"

"He returns tomorrow." Now it was Mrs. Warrender's turn to blush, and he raged inwardly at himself. Could he actually, with his crazy attentions, have got her to care for him in the course of this devilish winter? "He asks me to send you a message. He'll call on his way home tomorrow evening."

"What a great many messages." said Warren, making his unhappy escape.

"What in the world did he mean?" asked Mrs. Warrender when he had gone. "And as for Chilver! What's got into the man? The effrontery of it! To send a message by his master."

"George Warren didn't mind," said Kate.

"I'd like to hear what Lord Hawth would say if Parsons were to send us a message by him."

"My gracious, so would I!" Kate was delighted with this change in the line of her mother's thought, and half listened while Mrs. Warrender planned the dinner that would welcome his lordship home to the hall. She had much to think about. What precisely had Christopher meant by his message? Presumably that he had managed to convince the Jewkes brothers that she was no risk to them, but the message combined oddly with Chilver's anxious one. She had a pretty good idea of the fright Chilver must have had when Boney was found in the Warren stables. One of the few people who knew about her impersonations of Christopher, he must have jumped at once to the conclusion that some disaster had befallen her. Well, so it had. She only wished she could see the end of it. In the meantime, she found herself paying more regard to his message than to Christopher's. Chilver she could trust absolutely. And Christopher?

She made herself face it. This long lost brother of her had come back a stranger, one she must love but could not trust.

Something had been working at the back of her mind ever since Hawth had accused her of using the tunnel for assignations, and had suddenly surfaced when she was talking to George Warren. Chris never had explained what he had been doing in the tunnel when he had found her. She must hope to God that she had not guessed right.

Chapter 16

"It's all very fine and dandy," said Jewkes the publican, "but can we believe Kit Warrender, that's what I want to know? He's her kin after all; wrong side of the blanket, but kin. He just might tell a tale to protect her."

"It's possible." The man they called General Ludd was sitting with the Jewkes brothers in the closed bar of the Ship. "And too important to be ignored. You're sure of your facts?"

"Facts? They shout at you, surely. One riding up the track before the ship was so much as in harbour and the other could have landed. Besides, I *told* you, General. We caught him. Her," he amended. "Miss Warrender from the Dower House. Seems she's been play-acting as her cousin all winter. We did a bit of asking, once I started to think."

"Once she'd got away," said the General.

"How was I to know young Warrender used the tunnel, too? And he did swear up and down, like I told you, that she knew nothing, just didn't understand what had happened to her."

"Precisely," said General Ludd. "If you had only left well

alone in the first place, there'd have been no trouble. Now, she's bound to start wondering, and we can't afford that. I don't like violence, *as* you know, but we can't risk our whole plan for one girl. Listen."

"He's got a head on his shoulders, and no mistake," said the elder Jewkes admiringly when the General had left them. "Make a dandy first minister he will. All planned as neat as one of Lord Wellington's battles, even down to the drafting of the note, and the hand that's to forge it. Send her with the decoy run, and make sure she's caught and killed. All neat as ninepence and no blame to us."

"I just wish we knew the date we're to rise," said his brother.

"But he's told you and told you, the General has, that no one knows that, not even he. He'll choose his time when he's ripe and ready. The mail coaches won't run, there'll be risings all over the country. We take the mill, the hall and Warren House, hold the damned aristos as hostages, and wait for word from London. It will be the same all over. Christ, I'd like to be in Brighton and see them pick up fat Guelph from his whore's arms. Or Petworth to help sack Egremont's little love nest."

"But the General said, no sacking, no violence."

"What the General said, and what may happen, brother Seth, is two things. Not our fault, surely, if there's a bit of resistance—*as* there's bound to be—and a few get hurt."

"And the women?" asked his brother.

"The General said they wasn't to be touched."

"Yes, he did, didn't he." Seth's ironic tone matched his brother's.

"We'll go for the Dower House," Jerkes senior summed it up. "Pity that high-nosed Miss Kate won't be there, but the old lady's quite an armful. Lord, won't they be having themselves a time in Brighton."

"You don't think *anyone's* going to heed what the General says?"

"Well," The publican put his finger to the side of his nose.

"What do *you* think? There's a long score to be settled; a long tale of hunger and hardship, impressment and the cat. What do you reckon Brown at the Bell's going to do, that lost his leg at Trafalgar and got no pension, no prize money, nothing?"

"You reckon Glinde will be in it too?"

"I tell you, everyone's going to be in it. It's just no one speaks of it till the time's ripe."

"Then we'd best start quick for the Dower House and the hall," said his brother. "Or they'll be there first from Glinde. How'll we manage? Mail coach stops at Glinde. They'll know first when it don't come. I do surely want to be first at the Dower House."

"And the hall. Fat pickings there, too. I reckon we'd best have someone waiting where the Glinde road turns off from the Brighton one. Shepherd up there will do it. He's twisted in, all right and tight. Glinde mail coach runs along with the Brighton one up to there. They pass regular as clockwork, ten to five in the morning. One gets to Brighton at quarter past six; the other to Glinde, half past."

"How'll Shepherd let us know?" asked Seth.

"Now, that *is* a question. Reckon we'd better build a beacon up on Chyngford Point. Shepherd can watch the road from there. Black as pitch, 'twill be, that early in the morning. He'll see the coach lights, hear them blow up for the change in Lewes."

"But he won't," objected Seth. "That's just what he won't see. If the coaches don't run."

"Hell!" Jewkes senior scratched his head. "You're right. Well, he gives it twenty minutes, like the General said they was to in Glinde, then he lights his beacon. We'll see it here; they won't in Glinde, hill's between."

"Someone will have to watch down here, too," said Seth.

"We'll take it in turns. You and I and young Pete. And whatever the General says, we'll lead the attack on the Dower House and the hall. The hands can have the mill. I'm after better pickings. There's old Mrs. Warrender and the girls at the hall. Shall we toss for them, or take it in turns?"

"You've surely got your head screwed on all right," said his brother admiringly. "No need to toss; there'll be plenty for all. When should we start the watch, d'you think?"

"Let's see. Arms off to London tomorrow night. Take a few days through the deep lanes. Got to give the General time to get them handed out. He keeps his counsel, does that one. He may mean to send some of them up north. So, say a week. And now, we'd best get thinking about Miss Nosy Warrender."

"I hope it's not too late already."

"You surely do forget to listen to what the General says. Didn't you hear him say she'd not want to tell on account of having to admit that she'd been fossicking about the country in breeches? Give us a bit of time, the General says, and I reckon he's right *as* usual. But let's get going, just the same."

Betty Chilver gave Kate the note when she got back from the hall next afternoon. "I'm in dead trouble" commanded Christopher's bold scrawl. "Help me out this once, for the love of God, or I'm done for every way. Blown up. Sunk. I'm to guide a party of Volunteers tonight. Across the park. Can't do it. Do it for me? Meet them at the gap in the wall. Take them across to the Lewes road. It's life or death, Kate. Mine." And then the unmistakable signature, the cross he had always used for Christopher.

She had never wanted to do anything less. But how could she refuse? In the dangerous double game he was playing, any false move might so easily mean death. There was desperation in every line of the short note. And no one she could consult. Not without betraying Chris. He had saved her life. She owed him this. He must have his chance to serve his country, regain his place in society, become himself again. If she must stand in for him this once more, well she must.

Less used to her than Boney, George Warren's horse, Firefly, resisted her first attempts to saddle him up and get him out of the stable, and she was afraid that she might be late for the rendezvous. But once clear of the stable he took her swiftly and surely along the familiar track to where the party of Volunteers were waiting for her. A quick greeting exchanged, she wheeled Firefly to ride beside the lieutenant in charge and guide the little party across the park to the other gap, the one that gave on to the road from Glinde to Lewes.

She had never been this way in the dark, and she did not much like it, nor yet the slow pace set by the taciturn lieutenant, but when she protested at this, he gave a quick, gruff explanation. This was an exercise in timing. The men were carrying loads to simulate smuggled goods. She could leave them at the Lewes road and make good time back across the park. "If that's your way, Mr. Warrender," he said in the rather rough local accent that had surprised her from the first. But then, with the long war grinding on so slowly, all kinds of people were being accepted for the Volunteers, and this young man had doubtless risen to his lieutenancy most creditably, by merit alone.

It was very dark, with rain in the air, a proper smuggler's night, she thought, and wished herself safe home in her bed. This must be her last appearance as Kit Warrender. She would give him up, hand the part back to her brother with relief, and, oh, she would be glad when this night's work was done!

They reached the gap at last and there was the usual business of clearing a way through it, the men working and cursing under their breath, while the lieutenant and Kate sat their horses and listened. "Come a little this way," said the lieutenant quietly when Kate thought the gap must be almost cleared. "There's something I want to give you. A note. Quiet-like so they don't know."

"Yes?" She edged her horse beside his up along the park

wall a little way, glad that she was to get some kind of explanation from Chris.

"Here!" He held out something that showed faintly lighter than the darkness.

"Thanks." But between them, somehow, they fumbled it and the paper fell to the ground.

"Damnation!" said the lieutenant. "I'm sorry, sir." He turned his horse away, apparently taking it for granted that it was Kate who would dismount and search for the note.

She did so with extreme reluctance, anxiously aware that Firefly was both a taller and more restless horse than Boney and that remounting was not likely to be easy. But first she must find the note. Firefly had moved a little, wanting to follow the lieutenant's horse, and she had to lead him back along the wall by the reins looped over her arm. And as she did so, she heard a body of horsemen approaching at a gallop down the road from Glinde.

"Scatter!" The lieutenant had heard it, too, but why the surprising order, which she could hear being swiftly obeyed, some men leaping on to their horses, others running for it into the darkness. And she was dismounted. She pulled Firefly nearer the wall, hoping to use it as a kind of sideways mounting block, and as she did so was aware of movement in the darkness behind her. Someone come to help? She turned quickly towards them and so missed the blow that had been levelled at her head, and received it instead on the arm that held Firefly's reins. Sick with pain and shock, she lost the reins and stood swaying on her feet, a helpless target for the next blow. But it did not come. Another man had emerged from the darkness and set upon her attacker. As she listened, still in shock, to the grunting, desperate fight, the troop of horsemen came storming down the road. A quick order and they were through the gap. No question but that these were dragoons from the barracks. So—who were her companions?

A lantern flared, and an officer and two troopers came up the wall, alerted by the continuing sound of the struggle beside her. "Separate them," said the officer, and, to Kate: "And you, stand still if you value your life."

She could hardly have done anything else. The pain in her arm was excruciating, but she must not faint. To do so meant inevitable discovery. She stood, silent, swaying, fighting for consciousness, and watched half-seeing as the two troopers separated the fighting men and brought them forward to the light.

The officer leaned down to scrutinise their faces and let out a satisfied exclamation. "Jewkes of the shop," he said. "Red-handed, God bless all informers. And who else have we? You—" to the other man—"who are you?" And, as he hesitated: "No use, man. I know your villain's face well enough, just can't place it."

"Sam Chilver, sir, but no villain." Kate started as the remembered voice penetrated her flickering consciousness. What centuries it seemed since she had encountered Sam and the stranger, that first time, and Sam, Chilver's cousin, who worked on Warren farm, had recognised her by Boney.

"No villain?" sneered the officer. "Then what the hell were you doing helping a parcel of smugglers run their goods through Hawth Park? We've picked up enough already to make it a transporting matter." He turned to Kate. "And you're the elusive Mr. Warrender, if my informant's to be trusted, which it really seems he is. Delighted to meet you, Mr. Warrender, and escort you where you belong, to Glinde gaol. We've wondered about you often enough. Now you're beyond any protecting."

"We'll see about that." Kate assumed a bravado she was very far from feeling. Her thoughts in a whirl, she tried to make some kind of sense of what had happened. The "Volunteers" she had led had been smugglers in disguise. And they had expected to be attacked, had proved it by the speed of their escape. A trap set for her, by Jewkes. And by Christopher? His note. She would not believe it. A forgery? Possible. That bold hand would be easy to imitate, and she had not seen it since his "death."

That must be it. Jewkes had recognised her, knew her for a threat. That first blow had been meant to kill her and leave him free to escape with his gang. It was only by good luck and Sam Chilver's intervention that she had survived. As it was, she was in trouble enough, caught red-handed with a gang of smugglers. At all costs, she must stick to her male alias as long as she could.

It was going to be difficult. She put out her good hand to support herself against the wall, and fought off another fit of faintness.

"Sir." Sam Chilver spoke again to the officer. "Mr. Warrender's hurt. Jewkes attacked him from behind. I saw it. Let me help him, sir. I doubt he can ride."

"When thieves fall out, eh?" said the officer. "Very well. Mr. Warrender, your word not to try and escape?"

"Willingly," said Kate. "And my word for Chilver, too. It's true: my right hand's useless." She turned to Sam Chilver. "Thank you," she said with feeling. "On the head, I think that blow would have killed me."

"I think it was meant to," he said.

"That's enough," the officer interrupted. "Talk can wait for the morning and the magistrate."

The magistrate. Through the agony of the ride to Glinde, with Sam Chilver beside her, steadying her in the saddle, she kept coming back to the two questions: which magistrate, and what should she do? For her mother's sake, for Christopher's, for her own, even for Lord Hawth's, she must try to keep the secret of her real identity as close as she could. But what hope had she?

Chilver leaned nearer to her, on the pretence of steadying her in the saddle. "Don't fret, miss," he whispered, "as a gentleman, you've a right to a cell to yourself."

"Don't leave me, Sam!" Thank God, he was an old childhood friend from the days when she and Chris had been free of the farm.

"Stop your whispering there," came the officer's sharp command.

Half-conscious when they clattered into Glinde, Kate heard Chilver speak up roundly for her right to a cell to herself. "My master, Mr. Warren, is a good friend to Mr. Warrender," he told the officer. "And so is Lord Hawth. They won't be best pleased if he don't get treated with courtesy until I have had a chance to say my say and prove him innocent."

"Innocent!" sneered the officer. "And guiding a parcel of smugglers on their way to the deep lanes! But, just the same, for tonight he shall be treated as the gentleman he isn't."

"Thank you," Kate managed it with difficulty. "I'd like Chilver with me, please. My word still holds."

"No need," said the officer. "Get out of Glinde gaol, you'll be clever."

Alone at last, "Let's see that arm," said Chilver. "You ought to have the doctor, miss."

"Sam, I can't." They both knew it must mean discovery. With a nervous glance at the door, she let him help her out of greatcoat and jacket, but the pain as he removed this tighter sleeve was too much at last, and she fainted.

"Miss! Miss!" Chilver was shaking her good shoulder, gently. "They'll be here any minute. We must have you in your coat again." She must have passed from faint into sleep, and found herself lying now, comfortably enough save for the throbbing of her arm, immobile in a sling, the greatcoat acting as blanket.

"Not the jacket, Sam. I couldn't."

"No need. The greatcoat will be well enough. Over the sling, see." He helped her to sit up, shakily. "It's good news, miss. Nothing broken; nothing but a terrible great bruise. You were lucky, and no mistake."

"Lucky!" She looked around the dismal little cell. "What's lucky about this?"

"We're alive, ain't we?" It was unanswerable. "And you'll get us out of this. I know you will, one way or t'other. I'm counting on you, miss. You'll speak for me? I've been wanting to get free of them ever since I saw what bloody business they meant, but how could I, not twisted in as I was? Now you'll save me, miss, won't you? I knew it for my chance, the minute I recognised your voice."

"I hope I can, Sam." She wished she shared his confidence.

"Hell and damnation!" Reaching home very late the night before, Lord Hawth had given strict orders that he was not to be disturbed, and here was Parsons actually shaking him awake. "What the devil?"

"It's Mrs. Warrender to see you, my lord. She says it's urgent. I hope I did right to wake you. She looks dreadfully, sir."

"What time is it?"

"Early. She wouldn't come, sir, if it wasn't . . ."

"Urgent. Tell her ten minutes, Parsons. Give her breakfast, if she's not had it."

"I doubt she'll take it, sir, the way she looks."

"Well, try." Impatiently, as he swung his long legs out of bed.

He found Mrs. Warrender sitting in his big chair in the study, her hands twisting together, her face drawn as if with pain. The breakfast he had ordered stood untouched on the table beside her. "My lord." She jumped to her feet as he entered the room. "Thank you for coming so quick. I'm sorry—"

"No need." He took both her cold hands in his. "I'm yours to command. What is it?"

"Kate." She had been crying but checked it with a gallant effort and looked up at him, the two last tears creeping unheeded down her pale cheeks. "She's disappeared."

"Disappeared?" She was shaking all over, and he pushed her gently back into his chair. "When?"

"Last night. Her bed's not been slept in. My lord, I think I must tell you . . ." She paused, her hands writhing together.

"Eloped, by God! With that cousin of hers. I should have known. Last night, you say? It's a long start, but I'll do my best. You can count on me. Did she leave a note? Any clue as to where they've gone?"

"No! My lord, you don't understand." She had been trying in vain to interrupt him.

"I think I do," grimly. "A fine fool I've made of myself. And she of me. Don't *cry,* ma'am. I've said I'll help, and I mean it. I'll catch them, never fear. Bring her back to you, make him do right by her if he don't mean to."

"I'm *not* crying!" At last she managed to intervene. "It's not what you think, my lord. Please . . . please *listen!* Try to understand. Poor Kate . . ."

"Poor Kate, indeed! Making you so unhappy. I . . . I . . ." And then, furiously: "What is it, Parsons?"

"I'm sorry, my lord." If Parsons had looked anxious before, he looked almost frantic now. "It's that new lieutenant from the barracks, with prisoners. Taken last night. He wants your lordship to commit them for trial." Oddly, Parsons was looking not at his master but beyond him, to where Mrs. Warrender sat in his chair. "It's young Mr. Warrender," he said, "Sam Chilver from Warren Farm and Jewkes from the shop at Tidemills. Taken red-handed with a gang of smugglers in the park last night. The lieutenant says. He asks for an instant committal, my lord. Wants to get back to barracks."

"Young Warrender! Impossible!" Following Parsons' gaze, Hawth turned just in time to catch Mrs. Warrender as she fell fainting from his chair. "Tell the lieutenant I'll see him in five minutes." She seemed featherlight in his arms. "Send for Miss Lintott. No! Fetch my daughter! And Betty Parsons from the Dower House." He carried his fragile burden upstairs to his own room and laid her on his bed. She was breathing more easily now, a little colour coming back to her cheeks. "Ah, Sue." She had appeared, breathless, from the nursery wing. "Mrs. Warrender's fainted. Take care of her? Sal volatile? Burnt feathers? I rely on you. Betty Parsons is coming, but I have to go. I'm needed as a magistrate. It must come first." Was he explaining to her or to himself? "Take care of her, Sue."

"What happened, father?"

"There's trouble. No time now. I have to go. That young cousin of hers has been arrested."

"Kit Warrender?" For an extraordinary minute he thought Sue was going to faint, too. Then she came towards him, hands outstretched. "Father—"

"No *time,* I said. And look to your patient, child. I rely on you."

"But, father—"

"*No!*" Hurrying downstairs, he tried to order his surging thoughts. Kit Warrender arrested. So, where was Kate? Waiting for him somewhere, presumably, poor girl, so no urgency about her. And Kit? Did this mean that he had actually thrown in his lot with the revolutionaries after all, or, more likely, that they had smoked him at last and arranged for his arrest by the new lieutenant from the barracks, who must be ignorant of the general warning out to keep hands off him. Either way, for Kate's sake, or rather for Mrs. Warrender's, he must arrange to see the young man alone and find out where Kate was.

It was disconcerting to find the clerk of the justices awaiting him in his study and happily consuming Mrs. Warrender's uneaten breakfast. "I thought you'd be needing me, my lord." The man was pleased with himself. "It's a fine haul. Three of the villains at once. I always did think there was something deuced havey-cavey about that young come-as-you-please Warrender."

"Did you? Yes, Parsons?"

"It's a note, my lord, urgent, from East Grinstead."

"Good God! Yes, of course." Taking the note, he remembered for the first time in this crowded morning that last night had been the one when the revolutionaries' arms were to start on their run to London and be "surprised" by soldiers from East Grinstead posted along the various routes

Kit Warrender had indicated. Warrender had expected to be with one of the parties, so what the devil was he doing planning an elopement for the same night? Had he meant to show a clean pair of heels to the lot of them, taking Kate Warrender with him? He opened the note. "Safely housed," it read, adhering to the code they had arranged. But that should mean that Kit Warrender had been captured and safely isolated from his revolutionary companions. Stranger and stranger. "I'll see the prisoners now," he told Parsons. And then, to the clerk: "I may need to see young Warrender alone. Reasons of state."

"Deuced havey-cavey," said the clerk, but he said it under his breath.

The prisoners were awaiting them in the high, glum "baronial" hall that even Mrs. Warrender had not tried to make habitable.

"Lord Hawth," the lieutenant saluted smartly. "Three arrant villains for you. I've given my deposition to the clerk. If you'll excuse me?"

"One moment." Hawth was looking beyond him at the three prisoners standing against the wall. "No one told me Mr. Warrender was wounded." Young Warrender was leaning against the man who must be Chilver, the sling on his right arm showing under the greatcoat whose collar was pulled high round a white face.

"Does it matter?" The officer shrugged. "He'll be worse than wounded presently. And now, if you'll excuse me?"

"Gladly." He knew the man was disappointed at not being congratulated, but was busy reading the deposition. It made out a damning enough case. He looked up, saw young Warrender swaying on his feet and caught a glance of appeal from the man who was supporting him. It decided him. "I'll see Mr. Warrender alone," he said. "Bring him to my study."

"But he's dangerous, my lord," protested the clerk.

"He hardly looks it." He turned to one of the two constables in charge of the prisoners. "Bring him along. Gently there."

With an effort, young Warrender pulled himself upright. "I can manage, my lord. I've given my parole already. And so has Chilver here."

"Chilver?"

"Yes. He works on Warren Farm. He saved my life. The butler's cousin." The words came with difficulty. "I'd be grateful for a word alone, my lord."

"You shall have it." Ignoring the protests of clerk and constables, he led the way to his study, where he found Parsons anxiously hovering. "What the hell are you doing here?" And then, seeing the prisoner clutch the back of a chair. "Glad you are. Brandy, Parsons. Quick!"

"Thank you." Again the voice was muffled. "But—burgundy?"

And, surprisingly, "I have it here," said Parsons, filled a glass half full and put it in the prisoner's shaking left hand.

"Oh, sit down, for God's sake." Hawth threw himself into his own chair, remembering briefly that Mrs. Warrender had sat there earlier. "Help him, Parsons."

"Yes, my lord." Parsons took back the glass, from which the prisoner had had one enlivening draft, found an armless chair and helped him into it gently as a woman might. "And for you, my lord?"

"Nothing. Go and find out how Mrs. Warrender is. Send for the doctor if necessary. I'll ring when I want you."

"Mrs. Warrender!" exclaimed the prisoner as Parsons withdrew. "What's the matter?"

"She's ill, as well you should guess. Now, quick, before anything else, where is Miss Warrender? Is she compromised beyond recall? Because, if so, you'll marry her as fast as I can get a licence, even if you do leave her a widow after your trial."

"Thank you." Could the prisoner possibly be laughing at him? "But it will not be necessary, my lord. You thought it an elopement? You've not much confidence in your children's governess, have you? What did Mrs. Warrender say to that?"

"She fainted."

"Oh poor—" A pause. "Who's looking after her?"

"My daughter and Betty Parsons. If it's any concern of yours."

"Could I have some more burgundy?" The first glass had brought a faint flush to the pale cheeks.

"Burgundy?" Pouring it, he remembered. "You drank brandy last time." Something had been puzzling him ever since his first sight of the prisoner. Wounded, of course, but smaller, slighter, surely? "You're not . . ." he said, and then: "Who are you?"

The flush deepened. "I owe you an apology, my lord. Several, I am afraid." A half defiant pull at the burgundy. "I needed that. Thank God you got back from town. It was the best news I ever had when I heard we were being brought here. I don't know what I'd have done if it had been one of the other magistrates." A shaking hand pushed away the concealing coat collar from the face. "I *am* Kate Warrender, my lord."

"What?"

"I was afraid you would not like it."

"Like it! Do you expect me to!"

"Don't say, 'My children's governess.' Or, if you must, say 'ex-governess.'"

"Just so. But—" He had been thinking in a whirlwind. "There are two of you. Two Kit Warrenders."

"Yes. I'm . . . sorry."

"And the other one?"

"My lord—" she leaned forward, a pleading left hand outstretched—"I can't talk about him. Not yet. Believe what you will."

"You expect me to get you out of this scrape and then give you my blessing while you run off with this good-for-nothing cousin of yours? Well, Miss Warrender, you may be interested to learn that he was arrested last night, too. That's why I began to wonder about you."

"Arrested?" The flush ebbed from her face and left it fine-boned with exhaustion.

"Oh, he'll be protected, your lover, as I suppose I must protect you."

"Your children's governess?" The defiance came out faint and pitiful enough.

"No, your mother's daughter. But to do so I must know what lunacy took you out last night, guiding a parcel of smugglers across the park."

"I believed them to be Volunteers, my lord." She had thought hard while she awaited his pleasure in that cold hall. "I had a note—from the other Kit. A forgery. It *has* to have been a forgery." Was she trying to convince herself as well as him? Reaching with her good hand into her greatcoat pocket she pulled out the note and handed it over.

"His hand?" He read it quickly.

"I thought so. Now, I'm not so sure. But he always signs like that."

"And you should know, I take it."

"Oh, God!" He was obviously still convinced that she and Chris were lovers. "If I could only explain."

"It is a shade unfortunate," he said.

Chapter 17

"All's well, ma'am." Parsons had found Mrs. Warrender being ministered to by his daughter Betty. "My lord is seeing Miss Kate alone. She'll tell him. She'll have to."

"Yes. Thank you, Parsons. I don't know how I'd have borne today without you. Bring her to me as soon as you can."

"Of course I will. Don't you fret yourself, ma'am. His lordship will contrive all for the best, you see if he doesn't."

"He'll be very angry, Parsons."

"Well, yes, ma'am."

"What am I doing here?" She looked round Lord Hawth's spartan bedroom, one of the rooms in the house that she had not dared touch, except for a thorough cleaning.

"His lordship brought you up, ma'am, when you fainted."

"Oh." She sat up shakily in the bed. "Help me to the morning room, Betty. Miss Kate will expect to find me there. And, Parsons, tell Lord Hawth I am better. Thank him. But what are we going to *do* about Miss Kate?"

"Don't fret, ma'am," he said again. "His lordship will manage."

His lordship, still very angry, was confronting Kate with the same problem. "If you weren't hurt, I'd make you wait in the tunnel till dark." He had been furious when he got back and found the panel not yet nailed up. "And serve you right. As it is—wait here." She heard the click as he locked the door after him.

In the cold hall, he gave his orders quickly, impatiently. "Mr. Warrender's not well," he told clerk and constables. "I shall keep him here for the time being. Oh, yes, I'll be responsible. "He brushed aside the senior constable's objection. "As for these two. Committed for trial at the next assizes. Yes, Parsons?" Ignoring a movement of protest by Sam Chilver, he turned to greet the butler who had just entered the hall. "How is Mrs. Warrender?"

"Better, sir. She's in her own room, wishful to see you."

"I'll come at once." It would do Kate Warrender no harm to be left for a while to her own thoughts.

Susan was hovering in the hall. "Father?"

"Yes?" Impatiently.

"How is he? Mr. Warrender. They say he's wounded."

"He'll not die this time." And then, alerted by the way her colour came and went: "What the devil do you know of Mr. Warrender?"

"I love him, father. I've promised to be his wife."

"His wife?" He was speechless for a moment as he faced this new complication. "But how in God's name?"

"It was he rescued us, last autumn, when we were kidnapped. He and two other men. We promised not to tell . . ." She dwindled to a stop before his furious gaze.

"One meeting?" And then, as memories fitted themselves together in his mind. "*No!* That's what you've been doing in my study. 'Reading' forsooth! Assignations! Your mother's daughter. He came through the tunnel. No wonder you haunted the study when I got home. You were afraid he'd come on me by mistake. I wish to God he had. I'd have seen to it he remembered the day."

"Father," White as death, she nevertheless stood her

ground. "Let me see him. Just for a minute. Please . . ."

"No!" Why had this new complication decided him to protect Kate Warrender, or had he decided already? "Go to your room, Susan, and stay there until I send for you. One thing only I will promise you. So far as I am concerned, Mr. Warrender will come to no harm. As for your crazy promise to marry him, we will discuss that later, when I have a better chance of keeping my temper. But, in the meantime, begin learning to forget him."

"But, father . . ."

"No!" With the key of the study door in his pocket, he stormed down the hall to the morning room, where he found Mrs. Warrender making a gallant pretence at doing her accounts. "Well!" He slammed the door behind him. "A pretty fool you have made of me among you!"

"My lord!" She had jumped to her feet at sight of him. "You know?"

"Miss Warrender has just condescended to enlighten me."

"How is she, my lord? She's wounded, Parsons says."

The black brows drew further together. "Parsons, of course, has known all along. And how many other of my servants?"

"Only Betty. Please, my lord. Is she . . . is she badly hurt?"

"No! She's curing herself with a glass of burgundy in my study. Locked in." Ever since the discovery, an undercurrent of his mind had been surging round those first meetings with "Kit Warrender," the things he had said, the fool he had made of himself. "More than she deserves," he said now. "But, for your sake, ma'am, and a little, I suppose, for my own, I mean to protect her from the results of her own folly. I don't much want to look the kind of ass I feel just now."

"Oh, please . . ." Once again he was aware of her gallant effort not to cry. "It was only high spirits, poor child."

"High spirits! Guiding a gang of smugglers through the park!"

"I don't believe it."

"Fact, ma'am."

"She'll explain."

"She has. Whether I believe her . . . Oh, some of it. But for the moment the question is how the hell we get her safe home to the Dower House without a discovery. Oh, forgive my language."

"Don't mind it," said Mrs. Warrender. "I don't. I wish I was a swearing woman myself. But as to getting her home—and I do *thank* you, my lord—I've been thinking about that. What's to stop Kit Warrender escaping by the tunnel?"

"Maybe she already has."

"Not if she gave you her word. Just give me an hour, my lord, and then send her along it. I'll be ready to smuggle her home."

"You're not well enough." And then, recognising her set look: "But you're right. The best way for all of us." He badly wanted to tell her about Susan and the real Kit Warrender, but there was no time for that now.

It took all Kate's courage to grope her one-armed way down the tunnel, but at least the effort blanked out that last swift furious confrontation with Lord Hawth, who had seemed, for some reason, angrier than ever. Well, she could hardly blame him.

"Quick!" Her mother and Betty Parsons were waiting for her at the appointed place, and Betty helped her off with her greatcoat, wrapped a swathe of material round the betraying buckskins and draped a cloak gently over the ruffled shirt and the right arm in its sling. "Now you'll do well enough," said Mrs. Warrender, "for a girl who's been kidnapped."

"Kidnapped?"

"For all the world like the children. It was the best I could think of. Everyone knew you had disappeared, you see. Can you think of a story? Masked villains? Ransom threats? A gallant escape?"

"I expect so," said Kate wearily. "Oh, mother, what a mull

it all is. I'm sorry!" If only she could tell her mother about Chris, but she had promised. And it was not over yet.

"Never mind, dear. At least you're alive. For a while, I was afraid . . ."

"You were right to be," said Kate.

"Gone! And didn't even ask to see me!" Susan turned on her father like a fury. "I don't believe you!"

"I don't care what you believe." And yet, angry like this, she reminded him, almost for the first time, of himself. "Mr. Warrender apparently values his life above his love," he went on, thinking as he did so that it was unfair.

"His life?"

"Caught with smugglers, child. Hanging or transportation for certain. The sooner you forget him, the better."

"But, father—" Once again, she was interrupted, this time by Parsons to say that Mr. Warren was asking for his lordship urgently.

It was a relief. What should he say to this daughter of his? How warn her that, so far as he could see, the man she loved was carrying on a simultaneous affair with her own governess. Because, the more he thought about that, the less chance he could see of any other explanation for those two damning notes. Kate Warrender could set up his appointment for Kit. Kit could send Kate out into the dangerous night. A forgery? Perhaps. But she had gone. Cousin? Lover? Both?

"Hawth!" Warren's tone was urgent. "Thank God you're home. I've had a message from young Warrender, asking the two of us to meet him at my house. He was arrested last night, he says, but expects to be free this morning, as planned. Should arrive any minute now. Says there's no time to be lost. Says you're the only person will believe him. Will you come?"

"At once." He was glad of the excuse to get away from the hall and its problems. Mrs. Warrender could be relied on to take care of her daughter—and of his, if necessary. And he had a word or two to stay to young Warrender. Meanwhile, was he going to tell George Warren about Kate's impersonation of her cousin? He thought not. And he was sure he was going to say nothing about Susan. He must contrive to speak to young Warrender alone. He had still not quite made up his mind whether he shared Kate Warrender's conviction that the note that had nearly lured her to her death had been a forgery. "What do you make of young Warrender?" he asked now, suddenly, out of a silence.

"Odd you should ask that." The going was bad after a heavy rainstorm and the two horses were making a cautious way down the slippery chalk lane. "I liked him immensely the first time we met. Well . . . he saved my life. But when you sent him, the other day, I was disappointed somehow. Something—a little shabby about him? Do you trust him?"

"That's just what I wish I could decide." Hawth could not help a little spurt of pleasure at the idea that Warren, too, must have begun by encountering the pretence Kit Warrender, that he, too, had been fooled and would, presently, feel it. Or need he? Why should he ever know? More and more, he was certain that he must keep both Kate's secret and Susan's. Warren would never know that it was a woman who had saved his life.

Chilver was awaiting them at Warren House. "Mr. Warrender's just come, sir," he told George Warren. "He's eating a luncheon." And then, turning eagerly to Lord Hawth: "My lord, Miss Kate? Has she been found?"

"Miss Kate?" exclaimed George Warren. He turned furiously on Hawth. "Missing? And you didn't tell me?"

"A storm in a teacup," said Hawth, and then, qualifying it. "Well, not precisely." What a blessing Mrs. Warrender had insisted on rehearsing their story so carefully. "She was kidnapped last night."

"Kidnapped! And you call it a storm in a teacup!" George Warrens' eyes blazed in a face suddenly white.

"Very incompetent kidnappers," said Hawth urbanely.

"She freed herself in the night, came safe home to the hall in the morning, none the worse. Or not much," he amended, remembering that Kate would have her arm in a sling for a few days. "We've had a busy morning at the hall," he went on. "Another cousin of yours has turned up, George." Once again he was grateful for Mrs. Warrender's insistence that they must have a story ready.

"Another?"

"Another Kit Warrender, believe it or not. Caught smuggling in the park last night and escaped from my study this morning."

"Kit Warrender? Escaped? But he's here!"

"I said, another. Like as two peas, though. Same nose, same name. Well . . ." He looked up at a portrait of an eighteenth-century Warrender over the chimneypiece. "There's the nose. What was *his* name?"

Warren laughed. "Christopher. Odd to find it gracing the bastards surely?"

"Maybe their mothers had hopes."

"So you mean—" George Warren had been working it out—"they may have been working together? The two of them? That's why—I did think he had changed the other day."

"Exactly." And that, Hawth thought, was quite as far as it was safe to go. "Let us see what your Kit Warrender has to say for himself."

"Not mine," said George Warren. "I prefer the other—the younger one."

They found Kit Warrender in the dining room making formidable inroads on a side of beef. "Good morning." He raised his glass to them. "Forgive me if I don't rise to greet you. I am making amends for a deuced uncomfortable night. Damned hard beds in the East Grinstead gaol. Damned good claret, Cousin George. Glad you've not drunk it up yet."

"You know it?"

"Well, of course. Member of the family, what? Talking of

family—" he turned sudden and sharp to Hawth—"what's this about my Cousin Kate? Missing? What happened?"

"She was kidnapped." Hawth paused, waiting for a reaction.

"Kidnapped! My . . . Kate? And you do nothing?" He was on his feet now, finishing his wine as he rose.

"All's well," said Hawth. "She rescued herself, like the capable young lady she is. No need to interrupt your luncheon on her account."

"Thanks! You might have told me at once." The young man carved himself another huge slice of beef and sat down again. "You keep a good house, Cousin George."

"Thank you." Warren's tone was dry as he poured wine for Hawth and himself. "You wished for an urgent meeting," he said.

"Did—and do. I've news of the landing, gentlemen."

"The French?" said Hawth.

"Just so. The French. All ready and waiting for the word, while Boney makes great faces at the Czar."

"And the word?"

"Started on its way last night. That's all I know. But enough, wouldn't you think?"

"How do you know?" asked Hawth.

"Had it from a girl. Clever child. Knows when and how to listen at a keyhole."

A girl. Hawth found he was clenching his teeth. Kate Warrender? Or his daughter Susan? Keyholes! But there was nothing to be learned at the hall. Or was there? He turned to Warren. "Forgive me, George, but I think perhaps I should have a word with Mr. Warrender alone."

"Certainly. If there's a lady in question." Warren rose to his feet. "Should I be taking any action in the meanwhile?"

"Yes. Warnings to the barracks—Glinde, Brighton, Lewes, Hastings—to be passed on. And—" he had pulled out his pocket book and was writing fast—"this to the Home Secretary in London. If the landing's so soon, they must be ready for trouble there, too. I doubt they'll dare spare us more troops. Oh, and send a messenger to the Tidemills, George? Someone inconspicuous to report what's doing? I'm afraid of trouble anyway, after Jewkes' arrest last night."

"Jewkes arrested?" Alone with Hawth, Warrender filled his glass and gave him challenging glance for glance. "You appear to have had an eventful time of it down here, while I was getting myself captured in a good cause on the way to East Grinstead."

"Yes. Jewkes of the shop was caught red-handed with a smuggling party in the dark. A decoy for the arms movement, I suspect. Some inferior tea and brandy. And an attempt on Miss Warrender's life."

"What?"

"She was guiding them. Dressed like you. Because of a note from you. She thinks it a forgery."

"She's right. You've seen it?"

"Yes. But that's not all. I have to speak to you, Warrender, about my daughter."

"The devil you have!"

"I ought to thrash you. You're not worth calling out. Maybe I will when this is all over. In the meantime, you will not go near either Miss Warrender or Miss Chyngford."

"Proper squire of dames you think me, don't you? Very well, I will concentrate, for the time being, on my inamorata in East Grinstead. Ha!" He had seen Hawth's quick breath of relief. "Afraid it was one of them, were you? Don't have much confidence in females, do you? Thought of Mrs. Warrender? She might have as good an ear for a keyhole as the next one. No flies on my Cousin Warrender. My lord!" He was on his feet, alerted by Hawth's expression of naked rage. "All a jest, I assure you. Merely a jest."

"In the worst of taste," growled Hawth. "But no time for that now. If you wish to qualify for the reward you're promised, you will do as I bid you. Stay away from the hall and the Dower House. And one word to anyone about Miss Warrender's escapades, and you might as well leave the district at once."

"Oh, I think I'll stay," said Kit Warrender.

"You'll have to stay hidden anyway. There's a warrant out for your arrest, remember. Warren believes there are two of you bastards, but I doubt the rest of the district would take that."

"Damnation," said young Warrender. "You mean to say I've got to go into hiding just when things are coming to a head? Plague take that Kate. Trust her to believe a lying message and get us all in this scrape."

"You will refer to the lady as Miss Warrender."

It got him a roar of laughter and a curious look of, surely, satisfaction. "Of course I will," said Kit Warrender, "for the time being." He rose to his feet. "I suppose I shall have to escape again. Very incompetent lot it makes you seem, don't it? Thank Mr. Warren for me, would you." He moved over to the big window and threw it open.

"Oh, no you don't." With one stride, Hawth had him by the arm. "I've no time for you now, nor for the thrashing I'd like to give you. But don't delude yourself I'm letting you go. You are going to stay here, under house arrest, until the crisis is past and I can decide what to do with you."

Once again the young man surprised him with a roar of laughter. "House arrest here at the Warren? Oh, that's rich! I like that! Specially now poor Cousin George has made the house habitable. With a chef like his, who cares about house arrest? Besides, you may be right, I'm not sure how safe my life would be in these parts just now. House arrest will be very pleasant, and so you may tell my Cousin Geoge."

"You mean you'll not try to escape?"

"Good lord, no. I know when I'm well off. You may take care of the crisis, my lord, while I lie up snug here. Pray give my kind regards to Miss Chyngford *and* Miss Warrender." He burst into another fit of laughter as Hawth suppressed an oath and left him.

Joining Warren in his office: "I'd like to take a horsewhip to that young man," Hawth said.

"I know just how you feel. What are you going to do with him?"

Hawth gave a harsh bark of laughter. "Put him under house arrest here. I'm sorry, George."

"He'll stay?"

"He's delighted to. Compliments to your chef. Have the messages gone off?"

"Yes, indeed. But Hawth, what are we going to do? If the French land here in Glinde Bay, we're lost, and by what that young man said they may do so any night. And the troops up at Glinde barracks gravely under strength since that last detachment was sent north."

"I know," said Hawth. "They can do little more than mount a token resistance. So the French must not land."

"And how do you propose to prevent them?"

"I've been thinking about that ever since we first heard of the threat, and I think I have the answer. I am going to invoke another of our quaint local customs, George. Did you know that as well as smuggling the good people of Glinde also have a penchant for wrecking?"

"Wrecking?"

"Yes. If we can find out when the French are coming, I think I can guarantee that they wreck themselves on Chyngford Point. Those that manage to get past the Channel Squadron, which we must hope has been alerted by now. They'll be steering by the light on Glinde head, you see. They won't be the first, I can tell you."

"Good God. What happens?"

"The wreckers light a bonfire on Chyngford Point and put out the light on Glinde Head. And, as a result, instead of beaching nice and snug in the bay, a ship steering by the light will hit the long cliff at Chyngford, and break up for sure. The wreckage washes into Glinde Bay with the tide, and the wreckers hardly have to wet their feet."

"Jehosaphat," said George Warren. "But how will we know when to light the bonfire?"

"I've been working that out. If the word started on its way last night as young Warrender says, it can't reach France till tomorrow. They'll be as ready as possible, but there must be some delay. We'll keep watch from the night after."

"Best build the bonfire today."

Hawth laughed. "That's the wreckers' business, and you can rely on them to know it. I think they do it at the last moment, our climate being what it is."

"You mean you will leave it to them?"

"Oh, I think I must." He rose to his feet. "Enjoy your prisoner, George. I must go and see a friend in Glinde."

Chapter 18

Up on Chyngford Point the evening air struck cold. Mist in the valley was creeping slowly up the cliff. Soon it would be quite dark. But the two riders who approached from the direction of Glinde seemed to find their way without difficulty. Only, reaching the top of the cliff, they stopped, surprised, looking at the huge bonfire ready built there.

"Right handy," said one.

"Yes, but who?"

"Best find out. You that way, I'll go this."

They found the shepherd crouched in his hut in the lee of the cliff top and began systematically to bully an explanation out of him. Yes, he looked after the beacon. No, he would tell them no more. "I'm more sceeart of them than I be of you, see."

"We'll see about that. Wreckers, of course."

"Surely," said the shepherd. "Who else?" He made as if to rise from the ground where they had thrown him.

"Not yet, friend. Their names?"

"No!"

"Yes." A blow underlined the word.

"No!" Another blow felled him to the ground again, where he lay very still.

"He's not moving! You hit too hard."

"I never." But the old shepherd was unconscious.

"What will we do?"

"Leave him and say nowt. Nor will he, I wager."

Hearing that the beacon was built and ready, Hawth sighed with relief and went to call on George Warren. It was good to get away from the hall, where everything was at sixes and sevens. Miss Warrender, it seemed, was suffering from nervous prostration after her "kidnapping," and her mother stayed at home to nurse her. Miss Lintott was furious, quarrelled with the chef and then grumbled at the bad dinners that resulted. Worst of all, Susan went about the house like a hunted animal, cowering away when her father tried to speak to her. She had heard, of course, of Kit Warrender's confinement at Warren House. She had not, Hawth was sure, heard anything from him directly, and was suffering accordingly. And serve her right, he thought, but there would be time for all of that when the danger of invasion was past.

Mounting his horse, he was tempted to go by the Dower House and make sure that Mrs. Warrender was not wearing herself out nursing that tiresome daughter of hers. But it might mean meeting Miss Kate, and he did not much want to do that until he had decided what to do about her, and that, like everything else personal, must wait.

"Two days, since the message went," said George Warren. "Do you think the French will come tonight?"

"It's possible. Boney's a hard master. They'll have been ready."

"Still no word from London?"

"An acknowledgement. As we feared, no troops for the moment. One consignment of arms got past the trap set for it. They are on full alert up there. Still don't know what to expect. Frankly—" with a wry smile—"I'm not sure the Home Office quite believe in the French invasion. God knows, young Warrender begins to seem an unreliable enough source. And they've plenty on their hands up there, with the whole royal family to be protected. The chance of a new Gordon riot, or worse."

"Just as well you've made your own arrangements."

"I think so. How's your guest by the way?"

"Enjoying himself, I think. There's something very disconcerting about that young man. I feel, all the time, that he is laughing at me. And moreover there's something wrong with Chilver."

"With Chilver? What in the world do you mean?"

"I wish I knew. He *can't* be involved in any of this."

"Of course not. I thought he looked far from well. He's an old man."

"He seems one, all of a sudden. Oh well . . ." He shrugged it off. "Do we watch tonight?"

"The wreckers do."

"You trust them?"

"In this case? Absolutely."

George Warren sighed. "It's a mad country, yours. If I live here the rest of my life, I won't understand it."

"I hope you will."

"Live here? Or understand?"

Hawth laughed. "Both, I suppose. As for watching, I'd be glad if you'd come and spend these nights at the hall. There's a turret with windows all round. One can see both Glinde Head and Chyngford Point. Dine with me and we'll share the night. I've got young Winterton on guard at the Dower House, turn about with the man there, just in case someone should decide to try another attack on Miss Warrender."

"I'm glad to hear it."

It was a rough night, with a strong east wind bringing cold rain across the Channel to throw it against the upstairs windows of the hall. "I doubt they'd chance it in this," said George Warren as he and Hawth settled down in the turret room that had been part of the first Lord Hawth's Gothic folly.

"But if they do," said Hawth, "they've a damn good chance of eluding the Channel Squadron, however much they may be on the lookout. It must be a foul night at sea."

"How will the wreckers know if they are coming?"

"Oh, they have their methods, into which I do not choose to pry. Wrecking and smuggling and fishing all go together on this coast."

Warren took an anxious turn across the room to peer once more out into the blackness and listen to rain beating on the leaded panes. "Then will Jewkes and his friends not know about the wreckers' plans?"

"I took care of that. There's been bad blood between Glinde and Tidemills for a long time as you must know. My connection is with Glinde. Mind you, if there should be a wreck here in the bay I'm afraid there may be fighting over the spoils."

"Glinde against Tidemills? Charming lot of local peasantry you have, but at least it may distract their minds from thoughts of revolution. And from Miss Warrender. Has there been a report from the Dower House?"

"All quiet," said Hawth. He yawned and shrugged and filled their glasses. "I'll toss you for first watch, George. Duke or darling?"

Down at Tidemills, watch was being kept, too, from a top attic window of the mill itself, the only place in the village to command a view of Chyngford Point. Jewkes the publican was sharing the watch with his son Pete, grumbling because none of his fellow conspirators had been prepared to turn out. "It may not be *likely* it'll happen tonight, and the mail coaches not run," he told his son, "but it's possible, ain't it? Arms should be in London now. When the General decides to act, he's quick. And the quicker the better, ask me, so we can get your uncle out of Glinde goal before they move him." He made a pillow of his coat and stretched out on the floor by the brazier they had brought with them. "Damn this weather." He pulled his huge turnip watch out of his pocket and handed it over. "Wake me at quarter to five, and if you fall asleep Peter Jewkes, I'll kill you."

After midnight the weather eased, and George Warren, who had won the toss and chosen the first watch, found it possible for the first time to see the light on Glinde Head, and even, from time to time, the flash of lights from the barracks below it, where presumably watch was also being kept. Waking Hawth at last for his turn, he remarked on this, and asked how the wreckers would contrive to put out the light with the barracks so near.

"You can't see the light from the barracks," said Hawth. "It's one of our more comic bits of military planning. There was to have been a martello tower up by the light, but what with one thing and another, it never got built. I'm not sure Trinity House wanted it."

"Trinity House?"

"They run the lighthouses—it's a Trinity House man up there now, feeding sperm oil to Rumford's multiple wick burner." He stopped short. "George, can you *see* the light?"

"I could." George Warren, who had been looking towards Chyngford Point, hurried across the room to join him. "No, it's gone. Could it have just gone out?"

"Unlikely." With one accord they crossed the room to look out the other way. "It stands to reason the man on the point would take his time from the one on the head. You can relight a lamp that goes out by accident. It's hard work quenching a beacon. So we give it a minute or two." He moved back across the room. "No sight of a light," he reported.

"Nor here. The wind's getting up again. I wouldn't want to try and light a candle up on Chyngford Point, still less a bonfire."

"And heaven help the poor French, if they are out there," said Hawth. "They won't stand a chance."

"The poor French?" Warren's tone was half friendly, half

mocking. "A good thing young Winterton's not here to listen to that!"

"Oh, he'd understand, I think," said Hawth. "It's not the French are our enemies, but Bonaparte." He gripped his friend's arm. "George, look!" A light was gradually growing to the west, where the point lay.

"Dear God," said George Warren. "It's really happening."

"Looks like it." Hawth bent to trim the wick of the lamp and replenish the fire. "Let me fill your glass, George. No chance of more action for an hour or so. And this waiting comes hard!"

"Yes. Thanks." He took the glass and moved back to the window. "Lord, what a blaze. You wouldn't think the French could mistake it."

"Beating across Channel, on a filthy night, expecting a light? What would you think?

"I suppose so. And meanwhile your friends the wreckers are getting ready to receive them. You didn't warn the barracks?"

"How could I, George? And betray my friends? You and I will have to do the best we can to protect any Frenchmen who should survive. Not many on a night like this, I fear."

"Fear?" Once again George Warren took him up on it.

"They're men, George. With wives . . . children." Now he was gazing out towards the blaze on the point. "Any sign of life at the barracks?" Moving across the room, he paused to glance out of the window that faced directly south, down to the bay. His voice changed, "George, come and look! Something's happening at Tidemills."

"Tidemills?"

"It's dead south from this window. Look!" He stood back and Warren took his place and saw small points of light flickering against the black dark.

"Torches?" he asked.

"Yes. But why?"

"They must have seen the beacon," said Warren. "I suppose they'd know what it meant."

"Yes. But so soon? They must have been watching."

"The wreckers and the smugglers were in closer touch than you thought."

"I suppose so." But he said it doubtfully. "I've made a fool of myself so many times just lately that I can believe I've done it again, but I'd have sworn—" He broke off. "Look!" The flickering lights had now martialled themselves into a group. "Wouldn't you say they were coming this way? Not to the shore?"

"Yes," said Warren gravely. "I would. You think—it's the beginning."

"It has to be. What else? Thank God we were watching." He turned from the window. "They *are* coming this way. Up the hill. But not fast, thank God." He threw it back over his shoulder as he started at breakneck speed down the steep stairs. "I'm for the servants' wing to rouse out the men. We *must* meet them at the top of the hill, where the lane forks. It's the only place to hold them."

"Yes." Warren had paused to take one last glance southwards. "Have you a boy you can spare?" He followed Hawth quickly downstairs. "Some of them have branched off along the coast path."

"To your house? An organised attack on all of us? The beginning, for certain. Here, you!" A servant had come blearily through the green baize door. "Over to the stables, rouse the men there. The first one ready's to ride hell for leather to Warren House. Tell Mr. Warrender there to be ready to defend it. The second to the barracks. Tell them the mob's out from Tidemills. We'll hold them as long as we can."

"The Dower House," said Warren.

"I've sent a man to warn Winterton. Told him to rouse the ladies and get them over to the hall. Easier to defend, if it comes to that." More and more servants were assembling now, most of them armed. "A good thing I made them all join the militia," said Hawth, and addressed them briefly. "The mob's out from Tidemills. We've got to stop them at the top of the hill or not one of your wives or sweethearts is safe. Parsons, you will stay here. Mr. Winterton and Joe will be bringing the ladies over from the Dower House. If the worse comes to the worse, you'll defend them here."

"Yes, my lord. Thank you. I'll do my best."

Warren listened with admiration as Hawth swiftly allocated the best riders to the available horses. "The rest of you, run," he concluded. "We'll hold them till you come."

It had all taken a dangerous amount of time, but at least a faint lightening of the pre-dawn sky made the going easier along the well-kept drive to the sea gate. They found the lodge keeper there, ready and waiting at the gate, having been roused by the messenger to Warren House. "Have you heard anything?" Hawth reined in his horse for a moment.

"Not to say heard, but a while back I thought mebbe there was something. What do I do if they come, my lord?"

"Lock the gate and hide in the woods, you and your wife. But I pray they won't come." He was through the gate and taking his horse at dangerous speed down the lane towards the corner where it forked for Tidemills. And now, unmistakably, they could hear a mixture of singing and shouting from somewhere down the hill towards Tidemills. "Good," said Hawth. "They don't expect opposition or they'd come quietly. Surprise will be on our side."

"It had better be." George Warren looked back at the too small group of mounted servants.

"This is the place!" Hawth reined in his horse at the point where the lane to Tidemills sloped steeply away to their left. He made his dispositions quickly. The two best marksmen in the party dismounted on his orders and climbed the banks on either side of the lane. "Don't fire till I give the word. Aim for the leaders. And try to disable, not kill. You and I at the front, George, the rest of you spread out behind there, ready to back us up. The others will form our last line, when they get here."

"When," said a footman, but he said it under his breath.

They could hear the rioters very close now, singing raggedly a song with a refrain of *Blood, blood, bread or blood.* The lights of their torches showed as a glow above the little wood that masked the turn of the lane. "They'll have them in their right hands," said Hawth. "Won't be expecting a fight here."

Blood, blood, bread or blood. The refrain sounded suddenly much louder as the first torches came into view. "Hush," said Hawth quietly, "they won't see us for a minute more." He nudged his horse gently forward and Warren suddenly realised why he had chosen an elderly grey whose colour would stand out in the dark. "Halt!" His shout echoed strangely between the two bodies of men in the high-banked lane.

For a moment, the first torch-bearers paused, but then inevitably moved forward again, pushed by the mass of men behind them, jostling together in the narrow lane, torches flaring dangerously close, but the singing dwindling into silence.

"Halt, or we fire!" Hawth shouted again into the hush.

"Be damned to you, Hawth!" Jewkes the publican came forward at a rush, his torch raised to strike Hawth.

"Fire!" The shots from the bank cracked out as Hawth gave the order and Jewkes fell to the ground, to be trampled over by his own followers. In the sweating, cursing struggle that followed firearms were useless. It was sword against torch or cudgel, with the advantage of height on the horsemen's side, but that of sheer mass on their opponents', who came forward it seemed endlessly, fighting their way up the lane over the writhing bodies of their wounded friends.

And some of the horses were beginning to panic, terrified by the torches that were thrust at their eyes. Or were their riders encouraging them to panic? Certainly their numbers were rapidly diminishing, when Warren, parrying a cudgel stroke that might have felled him, heard the welcome sound of horses, hardridden up the lane from Glinde. The messenger to the barracks must have had wings, he thought, parried another stroke, and edged his horse over to where he could see Hawth laying about him with the flat of his sword. It had got much lighter. It was becoming possible, disconcertingly, to see how few of their party were left.

The rioters, who had withdrawn for a moment, saw it, too. "Come on boys," came a shout. "One push and we're through, and then who's for the hall and the Dower House!"

"Huzza," came the answer, and, "Bread or blood," they shouted, "Blood, blood, bread or blood," as they came on again, slow but steady, up the slope.

Up at the hall, Kate and her mother were sitting shivering over a newly lighted fire in the morning room. "If only someone would come," said Kate, not for the first time.

"We must think no news is good news," said her mother patiently. And then, also not for the first time: "Kate, I wish you would change."

"No!" Kate adjusted the ruffles of her shirt-sleeves. "I'd rather be killed as a man than raped as a woman. Besides, who knows? Kit Warrender may still carry some weight with the rioters. Anyway—"she laughed wickedly—"it was worth it all to see young Winterton's face."

"Your reputation's quite gone," said her mother.

"Darling mamma, it's my life I'm worrying about, not my reputation. That's gone anyway. Let's just survive this and then I'm your most obedient spinster for the waters in Tunbridge Wells."

"Yes, dear," said her mother without enthusiasm. And then: "What's that?"

"Bad news, I'm afraid." John Winterton had entered the room, carefully looking away from Kate's buckskinned legs. "The servants are coming back. The foot party met the riders, fleeing."

"Coming back?" Kate jumped to her feet. "But, Mr. Warren? Lord Hawth?"

"Vanished, they say. I don't like the sound of it." He was addressing himself to Mrs. Warrender, rather as if Kate did not exist. "I'm afraid the rioters must have captured them, or worse. Ma'am, I'm sorry to say it, but I think we should prepare to evacuate the hall."

"Evacuate?" asked Kate. "You mean we should run away?"

"Hide in the woods," he said, again to Mrs. Warrender.

"Lord Hawth left me responsible for your safety. I can think of no better way."

"And let them burn the hall as well as the Dower House?" asked Kate dangerously. "How many men have you, Mr. Winterton?"

"It makes no difference." He turned to her with a kind of desperation. "They've run away once, they will again. I tell you, we cannot hold the hall."

"Let me talk to them," said Kate. "They know me. Kit Warrender."

"I don't know what you are talking about," said Winterton. "He's under arrest, down at the Warren. I tell you, ma'am," he turned back to Mrs. Warrender, "we must rouse the children and hide them in the woods. I said we should have got them ready in the first place. If you won't do it, I'll send one of the maids."

Left alone, the two women looked at each other with a kind of mute despair. Then: "I don't believe it," said Kate. "'Vanished,' he said. As if they had run away!"

"Impossible. But in the dark . . . killed, Kate?"

"I *won't* believe it. Not both of them. Not together. Oh, mamma." Silently, she reached out to take both her mother's hands in her own.

"Oh, Kate." They exchanged a long look of complete understanding.

"How long have you known?" asked Kate at last.

"That you loved him? Longer than you have." Mrs. Warrender managed a shaky laugh. "Longer than he has, come to that."

"But it's no use!" Kate took a furious stride to the window and pulled back a curtain to look out. "No use for either of us. Let's face it, just once, together. If they survive this—and we do—we must go, mamma. Anywhere. Away!" And when had she dismissed Christopher and Warren House as a possible refuge? How strange, and how sad, but she had done so.

"Yes," said Mrs. Warrender. "And if they don't, who cares what happens to us?"

"Not I!" She pulled back the curtain. "Listen! There's someone coming. Horses. It *must* be them!"

"Unless the rioters have taken theirs."

"I won't believe it. And, even if it's true, the place to meet them is at the front door. It's light enough now for them to see us, to know what they are doing. And to see I am armed. It's our best hope, I promise you. Much better, and more bearable, than cowering here, waiting for the worst. And might give Winterton time to get the children away, if it should come to that."

"Yes. I'd not thought of that." Mrs. Warrender dried the tears that had been trickling quietly down her cheeks and rose to her feet.

"Bless you." Kate picked up the pistol she had never returned to Brown, made doubly sure it was loaded and ready, and led the way to the front door. Winterton must still be in the nursery wing, but a little group of menservants were huddled in the front hall, being harangued by Parsons.

"There's someone coming." Kate ignored the men's amazed glances. "Throw open the door, Parsons. We'll meet them on the steps. No need for torches. It's almost light outside."

"They'll see how few we are."

"They'll listen to me. I hope. Besides, listen! It's only a few. Two perhaps. His lordship and Mr. Warren? Needing help? Quick! Do as I say, man!"

Slowly, reluctantly, without any help from the other men, Parsons threw open the big doors. Kate took her mother's arm to lead her firmly out on to the steps. And saw two horsemen emerge from the park shrubbery. "Thank God." At the sight of Hawth and Warren she uncocked the pistol and handed it to Parsons.

"You're safe?" Hawth sat in the saddle for a moment, swaying slightly, looking up at the two figures on the steps. "They've not been here?"

"No, no," said Kate, and looked beyond him to George Warren, who was staring at her in amazement. And horror?

Time for all that later. "You're not hurt? Either of you?"

"Nothing to signify. It's all over, I think." He laughed sardonically as he strode into the hall. "A miracle. The same beacon seems to have alerted both rioters and wreckers. We were having a hard fight of it, George and I, with the rioters—and not much help from my men!" An angry look round at trembling servants gave point to his words. "When along came the wreckers from Glinde, so we just stepped quietly aside and let the two gangs fight it out between them. I wonder how long it will take before they recognise each other, join forces and go down to watch for the French in the bay."

"The French?"

"They had planned a landing tonight. Thanks to the wreckers' beacon, they'll be landing any time now, but not the way they meant. We must get down there, George, and see what we can do for them. You'll look after things here for me, Winterton. I'm glad you kept your head and didn't run for it."

"Not my doing, my lord." Winterton spoke up from behind Kate. "It was Miss Warrender said we must stay."

"Where *is* Miss Warrender?" asked George Warren. "And what are *you* doing here?" to Kate.

"I'm . . ." Kate began to attempt the impossible explanation, then turned, astonished, as warm arms were thrown around her from behind.

"You're safe! You're here! Oh, thank God!" cried Susan. And then, recoiling: "But you're not! You're not you!"

"No," said Kate apologetically, "I'm afraid I'm not."

"It serves you both richly right." Hawth had dismounted by now and joined them at the top of the steps. "You!" He turned with fury on the gaping servants. "Back to your duties! The night's work is over, no thanks to you. Now get out of my sight, for the pack of poltroons you are." He turned to take Mrs. Warrender's hand. "They've behaved themselves? The servants?"

"Behaved?" She looked up at him in wide-eyed surprise.

"Yes." Kate understood him. "I was afraid when they came

back that they might take it into their heads to throw in their lot with the rioters. That—" she turned to Winterton—"is why I thought flight would be madness. Show fear, and a bull attacks."

"You were right, Miss Warrender, and I owe you an apology." Winterton had Harriet and Giles on either side of him, and the children were staring wide-eyed at Kate.

"It's Kit Warrender," said Giles.

"No, it's not, silly," said Harriet. "It's our Miss Warrender in . . . in fancy dress. You look splendid, Miss Warrender!" She held up her face to be kissed and Kate bent to give her a strong hug. Then, looking up, she met George Warren's amazed eyes squarely. "Kit Warrender," she held out a hand. "At your service, Mr. Warren."

"Two of you! But it was you!" He took her hand in his own cold one and bent to kiss it. "*You* saved my life that time! But . . . but *why,* Miss Warrender? Why the masquerade?"

"'No sister of yours?'" Kate began to quote him bitterly, but was interrupted.

"No time for explanations," said Hawth. "You seem to have forgotten, George, that your house may be in flames by now."

"*Not* his house." While all attention had been centred on Kate, the front door had opened once more and Christopher had entered and stood for a moment surveying the scene. Now he took a leisurely step forward. "Well, mamma, no welcome for the prodigal?"

"Christopher!" She flung herself into his arms. "You're alive! You're safe! But Chris—" She drew away a little to look up at him. "How? I don't understand."

"It's a long story." He turned, dismissing her, to George Warren, who was still gazing at Kate. "The Warren's safe, by the way. The servants seem to care for you. They fought like tigers. Apropos: I must thank you, Cousin George, for taking such good care of my house. The chinoiserie is not quite to my taste, but we'll let that pass. There, child!" Susan, who had stood for a few moments staring from him to Kate, now threw herself upon him. "Calmly, please." He held her off with one hand and his mother with the other. "Mother, may I make you acquainted with my future wife."

"You may not." Lord Hawth was biting back rage. "This is neither the time nor the place for such a proposal. I am to take it though that you are, in fact, Christopher Warrender?"

"Oh, I'm Warrender, all right. Just ask my mother and Kate."

"You knew?" Hawth turned his furious glance at Kate.

"Of course she knew." Christopher spoke before Kate could. "An ally in a thousand. A woman in a million. My sister Kate."

"It's not true!" Aware of furious glances from both Hawth and Warren, Kate turned to her brother, white with rage. "Tell the truth, for once in your life, Chris Warrender. Tell them I only found out the other day, when you rescued me from the tunnel. And tell them, if you dare, what you were doing in it."

"Visiting my future wife, of course." He turned the full blaze of his charm on Hawth. "You'll get used to it, sir." A proprietary arm round Sue made his point for him. "I'm not such a bad *parti,* after all. Warrender of Warren House."

"Be quiet, Christopher," said his mother. "You're only making bad worse, as you always did. How could I have forgotten?" She was looking past him, very gravely, at Sue's white, defiant face. "Come, dear." She held out a hand. "Come and tell me all about it." And then, to Hawth: "I apologise, my lord. For my son. May we discuss it later? It's time the children were in bed. And high time you made yourself presentable, Kate."

"Presentable?" Kate looked ruefully down at herself. "A little late in the day for that, is it not?"

"No time for all this talk." Hawth took a long stride towards the door. "What must be discussed can wait till the morning. I'm for the bay. Are you coming, George?"

"Of course." But he was still gazing at Kate.

"And so am I," said Chris.

Hawth looked him up and down. "If you insist."

Chapter 19

"Well!" As the door closed behind the three men, Mrs. Warrender looked thoughtfully down at Susan, who had thrown herself sobbing into her arms. "I suppose we are safe enough now," she summed it up. "But perhaps you would be so good as to go the rounds, Mr. Winterton? To make sure. And send someone over to the Dower House? For fear of stragglers."

"Yes, ma'am. Would you be wishful to go with him, Miss Warrender?"

"To make myself presentable?" she asked bitterly. "Not yet, I think." She still had Harriet by the hand. "First I must put these brats back to bed."

"Oh, Miss Warrender, must we?" asked Giles. "It's been such an adventure." He laughed. "You called us hellborn brats that first time we met you. That *was* you, wasn't it? Brought us home through the tunnel! Miss Warrender, what a trump you are! I'll never forget the way you stood up to papa that night."

"Nor shall I," said Kate. And nor would he, she thought, leading the younger children firmly off to the nursery wing, while her mother withdrew with Susan to the morning room.

Giles and Harriet were surprisingly obedient, a powerful argument, Kate thought, for "Kit Warrender." But Kit was dead and gone, she told herself, leaving the quiet nursery, and Kate must face his consequences. She let herself quietly out by a side door that gave on to the path to the Dower House. It was time to end the masquerade. When the men came back from the bay, the discredited governess must be ready, meek in muslin for her dismissal.

Indoors, candles had still burned, prolonging darkness, but out here dawn mist was rising, translucent, from the park. A glow in the east heralded the sun. It would be a fine day. Fine for what, Kate asked herself bitterly, then reached quick for the little gun that still nestled in her greatcoat pocket. A horse was coming through the shrubbery, ridden fast. Idiot to have come out alone.

But the figure that rounded the bend in the drive was George Warren's. He pulled his horse to a skidding stop at sight of her standing there, pistol in hand. "More trouble?" he asked.

"No." She coloured and was about to replace the pistol in her pocket when he reached down to take it from her.

"Best uncock it," he said. "Better still, let me keep it for you, Miss Warrender. Our troubles are over now, I think. All's quiet at last, down on the shore. But you should not be out alone." He dismounted and looped the reins over his arm.

"I'd rather be alone." Enraged at her unwonted stupidity over the pistol, she felt herself blush harder than ever as he took it from her and dropped it safely in his own capacious pocket. In a moment, God help her, she would be crying. "Please!" She tried to pull away from the hand held out to her.

"Nonsense." A firm hand under her elbow turned her round to face the way she had come. "You're coming back with me, Miss Warrender, to drink a glass of burgundy and get ready for the last act of our melodrama. Hawth's in a black rage, I warn you. I've never seen him so bad. You can't leave your poor mother to face it alone. That brother of yours! Enjoying every moment of it. Was he always like this?"

"Ah, poor Chris! Our fault, I think. We loved him so, mamma and I. And he could always talk one round. I was much older, of course."

"An old lady," he agreed gravely.

"I feel like one now. I suppose we spoiled him between us. Father was so hard on him, you see. Wouldn't pay for a commission . . . left him to run wild here in Glinde. No wonder if he fell into bad company. To tell you the truth, when he told me his story, I was glad it was no worse."

"I can see that. But I'm afraid it's a shabby enough game he's been playing, just the same. Both sides at once. And that poor little Susan. I *knew* there was something wrong there. More shame to me. I should have done something."

She looked up at him, her eyes clouded with tears. "How do you think I feel, who didn't see? Her governess—responsible for her. I don't see how I can face Lord Hawth."

"But you will." He spoke with warming confidence. "And so will your splendid mother. Only—I think we should get back and warn her just how angry Hawth is. Prepare her."

"Yes. She'll be grateful." Kate made an effort to free her arm from his, but it was held tight.

"I doubt it," he said. "People seldom are. Interfering's the devil! Oh, forgive my language. It's the fault of that fetching rig of yours."

"Fetching!" She turned on him, glad to let tears burn into rage. "Don't mock me, Mr. Warrender! You told me long since what you thought of women who masqueraded like this. No sister of yours, you said, jauntering about the countryside in . . . in . . ."

"Breeches," he said helpfully. "So that's what you meant, earlier on, when you made that fulminating remark about my sister. To tell the truth, it baffled me at the time. My dear Kit, if I may call you that this once, let me confess to you that I had quite forgotten those unlucky comments of mine. I do remember now. I was a young prig then. I've grown up since. You came out strong in defence of Lady Caroline Lamb, did you not? May I say that I do not think you resemble her in the least." They were nearing the hall now, and his arm, firm through coat and greatcoat, drew her to a halt. "This is goodbye, Kit," he said. "Kate. Odd to think I loved you first as Kit, and never knew it. Even let myself think for a crazy while it was your mother. And now, too late. I'll be a laughing-stock tomorrow, Kate. Your brother has made that richly clear. And off to America the next day. Alone. Tell me, if I had spoken, if I had only spoken when I was still Warren of Warren House, might I have had a chance?"

"A chance!" Anger was the easiest way. "Thank you for the compliment, Mr. Warren! So you think me mercenary, as well as a vulgar masquerader. Well, it's over. The masquerade. If only it had never started. I wish you joy of America! As for me, I am going to take my tarnished reputation and my mother to Tunbridge Wells, whether she likes it or not. We shall have an extremely genteel establishment and play cards every night."

"Your tarnished reputation! You're not serious?" And then: "Damnation!" Lord Hawth and Christopher had rounded the bend of the drive, riding hard.

"All's well." Hawth flung it at Kate as they all moved indoors together. "Not a Frenchman survived the wreck. The military have things in hand now. Give Mr. Warren some breakfast, if you would, Miss Warrender, while I have a word with this brother of yours." He was holding his temper on a tight rein, aware as they all were of servants back in their usual functions. Servants, perhaps, who knew just how close they had come to changing sides, and consequent disaster, the night before.

Mrs. Warrender was alone in the breakfast room, where a steaming urn and covered dishes on the sideboard spoke of normal living recaptured. "Mr. Warren!" She jumped to her feet. "I'm so glad you are come. I don't know what to say to you, how to apologise. For what we have done to you . . . what my son has done."

"Not you." He took her hands in his. "And no need,

please, to apologise. Nor to look so sorry for me. I wouldn't have missed it for the world. I've enjoyed being an English landowner, every moment of it, but the play's over now. I shall go back to Philadelphia, back to business."

"Will you like that?"

He gave her a long, steady look. "No," he said at last. "Mrs. Warrender—"

"Yes?"

"Will . . ." He stopped. "Will he be good to you? Your son. To you and your daughter? Miss Kate speaks of going to Tunbridge Wells. As if . . . as if . . ."

"As if she did not trust her brother." Mrs. Warrender was white with fatigue. "As well she may not. Oh, Kate!" She held out a pleading hand. "Oh, *Kate!*"

"It's bad?" Kate flashed an appealing glance at Warren and put her arms round her mother.

"As bad as possible. Tunbridge Wells! It's not far enough, Kate. No." She turned as George Warren made as if to leave the room. "Don't go, Cousin George. You're family, after all."

"Thank you. Then pour me a cup of tea, ma'am, and drink your own. It's been a long night. Things will look better in the morning."

"It *is* morning. Where is Christopher?"

"With Hawth in the study."

"If possible, she went whiter still, but she poured his tea with a shaking hand, then made herself drink some of her own and urged Kate to do likewise. "We must be ready to face Lord Hawth," she said. "I'm so ashamed. Of Christopher. All he's done. To us all. To you, George. To poor little Sue. To Kate. No, dear—" as Kate began a protest—"let's face the truth about Christopher, for once. Don't pretend he didn't start you on that mad masquerade of yours, because I won't believe it. He needed you, did he not, for cover?"

"I'm afraid so."

"Without a thought of what it would do to you—to your reputation."

"Never mind that, mamma." Kate managed a cheerful note. "You *know* I enjoyed it! Just as Cousin George enjoyed being an English landowner. And when I think that Christopher will get the advantage of all your improvements, cousin, it's almost more than I can bear."

"That's the least of my worries," said George Warren. He turned to Mrs. Warrender. "Are you serious, ma'am? About Miss Kate's reputation?"

"Good God, yes. The servants know tonight. The whole county will tomorrow. Well—just look at her!"

"I have been," said George Warren. "With pleasure." And then, as Kate blushed fiery red: "I have told her already how much I have missed the young cousin who saved my life last winter. Kit Warrender. Kit will-o'-the-wisp. Kate!" He smiled at Mrs. Warrender. "You have given me hope, ma'am. If her reputation's really gone, if Tunbridge Wells is too near, perhaps there is hope yet for a landless man. What would you say to America? Mrs. Warrender, may I have your permission to pay my addresses to your daughter?"

"Oh, George, of course you may." She turned to him warmly, teacup in hand. "I was beginning to be afraid you would never realise . . ."

"That I loved her?"

"That she loved you," said Mrs. Warrender.

"Mother!" Kate had jumped to her feet when she saw how shamelessly her mother was guiding the conversation, but her attempt at flight was too late. George Warren had risen, too, and somehow got between her and the door.

"Another chance." His hands, very gentle, very firm on her shoulders, held her where she was. "It's not often one gets another chance. Kate!" A hand under her chin made her raise her head to meet his eyes. "Tell me it's true!" And then, reading her answer in her eyes, he smiled across her at her mother. "How did you know, ma'am?"

"Dear George, it was plain to see in both your faces."

"You see, Kate." Now his smile was all for her. "It's no use. Your mother's betrayed you. I always did want a mother."

"And are proposing for me to get one?"

"Of course, Kit Warrender. Besides, I might need my life saved again."

"By a boy in breeches?"

"By the woman I love. My wife, Kate?" And then, once more across her to her mother: "Excuse me, ma'am?"

"Dear George." Watching the long, slow ecstacy of that first kiss, Mrs. Warrender raised a secret hand to brush away a tear, but neither of them noticed.

In the study, things were not going so smoothly. Hawth had taken Chris Warrender straight there without a word spoken until they were alone behind closed doors. Then: "We've a great deal to discuss, you and I."

"Yes," Warrender sat down in Hawth's own big chair and swung a casual leg over the arm. "May I have some of your excellent brandy? It's been a long night. Thanks." He accepted the glass Hawth had angrily poured. "Here's to you," he drank. "And the Countess of Hawth."

"The Countess?"

"Why, yes. My sister Kate. You're surely going to do the honourable thing, my lord? The poor girl's compromised beyond redemption. You know that as well as I do. And who's responsible?

"You," said Lord Hawth.

"On the contrary, my dear man. I never asked her to come and live in my house and mind my children."

"She has lived in the Dower House. With her mother," said Hawth between clenched teeth. "We are not discussing Miss Warrender, sir, but your pretensions to my daughter's hand."

"Pretensions?" Chris Warrender had a laugh for it. "I think you will change your tune, my lord, after you have talked the matter over with young Sue. If I am not very much mistaken, she is in a fair way to making you a grandfather."

"*What*?" For a moment it seemed that Hawth would strike the smiling young face. Then, slowly: "I see," he said.

"I'm glad. And, no need to be anxious. I mean to marry her. It's not a bad match, if you dower her properly. And I'm fond of the chit."

"Dear God," said Lord Hawth.

"Only, as part of the bargain, you must make an honest woman of my sister Kate."

"Honest! You're not fit to touch her little finger."

"A very proper sentiment. I knew you'd come round to it, with time."

"On the contrary. If you must know, I proposed to Miss Warrender some time ago, and was firmly refused."

"Damnation! Fool of a girl! I might have known she'd spoil sport if she could. But I'll speak to her, my lord. Trust me to make her see sense."

"She's seen it. My offer does not stand, Mr. Warrender, and no interference of yours will revive it."

"You seriously think Sue and I are going to start married life with a houseful of female relatives? A sister with no reputation, a mother who's been acting housekeeper to a single man, and one with your name in the county? You'd better be careful, my lord, or I shall consider withdrawing my offer, and then where will your Susan be?"

"Better off, I shouldn't wonder. But do you actually delude yourself, Mr. Warrender, that you are going to be able to settle down and live in Warren House as if nothing had happened?"

"With a little backing from you—from my father-in-law—I see no reason why not. Warrender of Warren House. The people always looked forward to the day when I would succeed. You and Warren are mere strangers, interlopers. I'm Warrender."

"I wonder," said Lord Hawth. And then: "Yes, Parsons?"

"It's the lieutenant from the barracks, my lord. Prisoners for committal."

"Many?"

"Only three. What with the wreck, and those poor drowned Frenchies, and all the fighting on the beach, it seems most of the rioters got away. It's Jewkes, badly wounded, and his son Pete and one other man. And there's something else, my lord. I just heard the other Jewkes escaped from Glinde gaol in the commotion last night. He and Sam Chilver. I reckon someone let them out."

"I'm sure they did. How badly's Jewkes hurt?"

"He looks dreadful."

"I'll see them at once. No, in five minutes. Here." As Parsons left, he turned to Chris Warrender. "The less you are seen, the better. I suggest you hide in the tunnel you have used so disgracefully and listen to what they have to say about you. Then perhaps you will understand your position a trifle better."

Jewkes had been shot in the shoulder and then trampled over by his own supporters. White with loss of blood and clutching a makeshift bandage to his shoulder, he sank into a chair on Hawth's orders, and accepted a glass of wine gratefully. His son Pete stood anxiously beside him, but the third man kept to the shadows at the back of the room, hat pulled down and cloak muffled up around his face.

"He won't tell us his name, my lord," said the constable in charge. "He's gentry, or near to, by the sound of it."

"Is he so? We've never been so lucky as to catch General Ludd himself!"

"Not likely." Jewkes spoke up from his chair. "You don't catch our Generals so easy!" He was on the borderline of delirium, Hawth saw, and the wine was sapping his last restraint.

The chance was too good to be missed. "The General's in London, I suppose?" He made the question casual.

"Course he is! Seeing to it that the mail coaches don't run." And then: "Did they run? What with the wreck and all, I clean forgot."

"Hush your blabbermouth." The man in the corner took a furious stride forward and would have struck Jewkes if one of the constables had not intervened, and, in doing so, pulled away the collar of his coat.

"I know you," said Hawth. "I have it! You're Coombe; used to be George Warren's man of business."

"And Chris Warrender's before him," said Coombe defiantly. "He'll see me right. Tell you I only joined this riff-raff on his instigation, to help betray them."

"You did, did you?" Jewkes lifted blood-shot eyes to stare at Coombe. "I'll see you rot for that, if it's the last thing I do."

"You're going to die," said Coombe.

"That's as may be, but young Pete ain't. My lord—" He turned back to Hawth. "You'll be easy on my Pete? He could a' run with the others, I swear it, but stayed to help me, like the good boy he is . . . You'll not . . . you'll not . . ."

"Tell me about the mail coaches," said Lord Hawth, "and we'll see."

"It's when they didn't run, see. That's the signal. For the rising. All over the country. Only we wanted to beat Glinde to the hall. So, we had shepherd up the point with a beacon ready to light when the coach didn't pass. He lit it last night. Didn't he? *Didn't he?* Tell me, my lord, did the coaches run?"

"Course they did," said the constable. "Pack of nonsense and moonshine. What'll I do with them, my lord?"

"Oh, committed for trial," said Hawth wearily. "Let Jewkes' wound be cared for. And his son stay with him. You'd best keep the other man, Coombe, well away from them. You're answerable for his life, and it's not worth a moment's purchase if any of the revolutionaries get near him."

"That it ain't," said Jewkes with satisfaction. "And I warrant we'll catch him, soon or late, and Mr. Turncoat Warrender with him. You'll not forget, Pete? You'll not . . ."

"I'll not forget." Pete caught him as he fell from his chair.

"Well?" Alone again, Hawth opened the panel. "What do you think of your position now?"

"God blast that Coombe, Playing it both ways. Forged my hand to that note to Kate of course. I should have thought of that. He knows it well enough." Warrender poured wine with a shaking hand. "He'll not get a penny—" He stopped.

"I wonder just what you promised him. And *for* what? It was he, I remember, who advised George Warren so badly when he first came over. Your plan, I take it? It didn't work, you know. He's loved about the place. He's made work, built cottages, cared."

"Oh, God, your pattern landowner. I know! I've seen! So what do we do, your daughter and I?"

"I'm glad you ask it at last. I only wish I knew the answer. If I could persuade Susan to whistle you down the wind, I'd do so. Were it not for the child."

"Ah, yes, the child. That invaluable child. Had you thought that if it should be so obliging as to be a boy, we can break the entail on Warren House, George Warren, he and I?"

"I think you entirely shameless," said Lord Hawth.

"And starving," said Chris Warrender. "If you'll excuse me, my lord, I'll make an end of this improving conversation and find myself something to eat."

"You'll not leave the hall!"

"I most certainly shall not. I value my life, and am glad to see that you do, too."

But Hawth thought his bravado was wearing thin. Glad to be alone, he sat down to write a quick despatch for London. An urgent relay of riders must get it to the Home Office in time for guards to be set on the night's mail coaches. Incredible that after so much activity, it should still be early morning.

In the dining room, Chris Warrender found his mother, Kate, still in coat and breeches, and George Warren, all very comfortably consuming ham and eggs. They had been talking, even laughing. Now they were silent, looking at him.

"Well!" He had one of his challenging glances for Kate. "I should have thought by now, sister dear, you would have contrived to make yourself at least *seem* respectable. But how should I expect anything but idiocy from you! To have refused Lord Hawth! Are you about in the head, girl! I am doing my best to bring him round again, and then, as head of the family, I shall expect a more rational answer. In the meantime, pray go to your room and try and make yourself look a lady, if you cannot behave like one."

"That's enough." George Warren was on his feet, eyes flashing, fists clenched. "You are speaking to the lady who has agreed to be my wife. Otherwise, sister or no, I would think it my duty to call you out."

"You wife? *Your* wife?" Warrender dissolved into laughter. "Well, I'll be damned. Not quite the fool I thought you, eh, Kate? Pity about the title, mind you, but judging by what he's done to my house, Warren's a warm man. I hope you'll stop her jaunting about the countryside like that!" He had a scornful comprehensive look for Kate's trousered legs. "You'll be living under the cat's foot else. Probably will anyway. Which reminds me. I'm head of the family. Time you asked my permission?"

"I have Mrs. Warrender's."

"Thanks! But I'd like a word with you alone just the same."

"Very well. In the book-room."

"George?" Kate put a hand on his arm. "You won't fight him?"

"No need." He looked down at her, smiling. "He doesn't mean to fight me."

"Of course not. I've got some sense. Really, women . . ." Alone in the book-room, Chris turned to Warren with an assumption of good fellowship. "They've got no more idea . . ."

"We will not discuss the ladies."

"Oh, very well, but I trust you intend to give that old mother of mine a home, for it's more than I do."

"I'd not let her live with you—" He stopped. "Never tell me Hawth has consented to your marriage to Susan?"

"Quick, ain't you? Yes, he has, and for reason good. That's what we have to discuss, you and I, as men of the world. My Sue's in the straw. Course her father consents. Quick marriage, early birth, no trouble. And a million to one it's a boy. We Warrenders breed true. So—you and I and he together can break the entail. I never did fancy being tied down to the grind of a country gentleman. Seems you like it. Well then? With Sue's dowry and what you give me for Warren House we'll take ourselves off far as you please. No problem to anyone. Pity Boney's got such a stranglehold on Europe, but it won't last for ever. In the meantime, we'll find ourselves a corner somewhere. Sicily, maybe? Lisbon? And you and Kate can settle snug as you like at the Warren." He laughed. "You and Kate! Of all things. What a dance she'll lead you, my sister Kate."

"We are not discussing the ladies! As to your proposition, I like it. Futherby shall look into it, with the utmost discretion, as a future hypothesis. In the meantime, we will settle, among us, on a fair rent for the Warren, which shall be paid to you through any foreign banker of your choice."

"Foreign, eh?"

"I think you'd be wise to leave the country, for your own sake as well as for Susan's. And the less said about *that,* the better."

"Mustn't sully the ladies' ears? Nonsense! My mother spotted it at once, I could see. Always did have a sharp eye for a maidservant's condition."

"Hold your tongue," said George Warren.

Returning to the dining room, he found Kate and her mother still sitting over empty teacups. "All's well, love." He pushed back the ruffled shirt cuff and kissed Kate's hand. "It's not to be America after all. Will you be disappointed? You and I are to rent Warren House from your brother. Which I take it means he has given permission for our marraige."

"That's lucky," said Kate.

Warren laughed. "He said I'd live under the cat's foot." He turned to Mrs. Warrender. 'Ma'am, I hope I don't have to ask it, but you will come and live with us and protect me, will you not?"

Mrs. Warrender blushed, and smiled, and sighed. "Thank you, George, I will gladly."

"Good." He smiled at them both. "How pleased Chilver will be to have you home. I have only just realised why he has been looking so wretched. He must have recognised your son and been anxious for him."

"Or for you," said Mrs. Warrender.

Hawth spent most of the day in his study, dealing with the flood of messengers who reported the state of the wreck, the number of drowned Frenchmen and the injuries to the two parties of wreckers. These had been surprisingly slight, since everyone's first thought had been for booty, and even Jewkes was reported to have some chance of recovery. As for his brother Seth and Sam Chilver, they had vanished without trace.

"And I'm just as glad," Hawth told Warren, who had found him still busy writing. "I think this is a time for mercy to temper justice. Sam Chilver saved Kate's life; Seth Jewkes was his brother's tool."

"But what of the wreckers?"

"I've been discussing that with the commander up at the barracks. He says that there were genuine efforts made to rescue those of the Frenchmen who had any chance of survival. What with that and the fact that they prevented an invasion, he and I are inclined to let sleeping dogs lie."

"You mean, no prosecutions?"

"Just so." Hawth smiled his saturnine smile. "It's all to be hushed up. The rising, the French attempt at landing, everything. He took a bit of persuading, but he's gravely under strength; he doesn't want trouble any more than I do. You know how that kind of thing spreads."

Warren nodded. "Specially with this unknown threat still hanging over us from London."

"Precisely. If only we knew what it was that was to bring out the mob and stop the coaches. But General Ludd keeps his counsel well."

"Yes." Warren shivered, remembering that refrain of *Blood, blood, bread or blood.* "You think it will happen soon?"

"I'm sure of it. Don't you see, the French attempt at landing proves it. The rising in London, whatever is planned, should have happened first, so that we were already in trouble here when the French came. They must have got their signals crossed somehow, but they would hardly have been more than a day or so out. And Jewkes and his friends would only have kept watchs as they did if they expected the signal at any moment. I hope to God my couriers reach London in time to alert the authorities. Though mind you Mr. Ryder is pretty much on the *qui vive* already." He looked up as the clock struck. "Time to change for dinner. You'll stay the night, of course. I'm not letting Mrs. Warrender and her daughter return to the Dower House."

"No." George Warren had been waiting for his opportunity. "Hawth, I've something to tell you. I hope you'll like it, though I'm afraid it means you will lose your housekeeper. I'm engaged to be married."

"What?" The pen broke in Hawth's hands as he jumped to his feet. "Engaged . . ."

"Miss Warrender has done me the honour of accepting me."

"My dear man! I'm delighted. Congratulations. I hope she makes you very happy." It came out in jerks. And then: "You've talked to that brother of hers?"

"I've promised to pay him rent for Warren House at any foreign bank of his choice."

"Foreign? Thank you, George." They exchanged a long look.

"But that poor child. Susan. Should you let her?"

"I'm afraid so. She wants it. And in the circumstances . . ."

"Yes." Strange little creature. God knows what will come of it. But she wants it. And there it is. As soon as possible. And—we'll say no more about it." He rose to his feet. "Come, we must change."

Kate was putting on the green dress that Susan had admired, it seemed a million years ago. "Miss Kate?" Betty Parsons was fastening the back and Kate could see her anxious face in the glass.

"Yes?"

"I've a message for you. James said to give it."

"James?"

"Yes, miss. My intended. He and Sam Chilver are better nor brothers. You heard Sam got away, miss? With Seth Jewkes of the shop?"

"Yes. I'm glad about Sam. I'd meant to speak to his lordship about him. Still will, of course. And to Mr. Warren."

"I'm so happy for you, miss. That's a good man. And he'll listen to you, that's for sure. We knew you'd speak up for Sam. And of course everyone knows by now what was done for Johnny Penfold. But, miss, the message. Sam told James I was to ask you to get that brother of yours well away, and then not to fret. All that should know about you and him, does. Now Jewkes of the pub's as good as dead, things is going to be different down at Tidemills. They've had a fright, James says. And they don't like the French anymore than you and I do. That General Ludd had best keep away from these parts, surely. And, as for you, why, I reckon they kind of like *you,* miss. For what you've done, whatever that is."

"Thank you, Betty." However enigmatic, it was curiously reassuring, and she went downstairs, in glowing looks, to find George Warren waiting for her in the morning room.

"I hoped you'd be first." He had something in his hand. "This was my mother's." It was a ring of the palest, plainest gold, with one single, perfect pearl, and it fitted. "And these—" his lips just brushed her cheek as he produced the two leather jewel boxes—"are yours. Yours and your mother's. I thought it a night for decorations, and sent posthaste for Futherby. I forgot to ask him which was which!"

"Dear Futherby. And dear George." She picked up the smaller of the two jewel boxes. "I've missed them." Opening the box, she took out a small string of seed pearls. "Perfect," she said. "Fasten them for me, George?"

Miss Lintott, arriving upon this scandalous scene, let out a loud and awful sniff. "Men's clothes all day," she said, "and—"

"My wife to be," said George Warren.

"Congratulations." Miss Lintott addressed the one word to Kate.

It should have been a festive evening, with the two engaged couples to be toasted, but over it all hung the shadow of what might be happening in London. "I've sent James and another of the men in to Glinde," Hawth told Warren as the men sat over their wine. "He's to report at once when the mail coach arrives."

"If it arrives," said Warren. "Half past six in the morning, isn't it?"

Hawth laughed grimly. "Not the ideal time of day to start a revolution. Anyway, after last night's activities, there's not much spirit left at Tidemills. They know there are to be no prosecutions. They'll lie low, I think."

"No prosecutions? Not even Jewkes?"

"Jewkes died. This afternoon. Coombe will be sent to London for trial, and, presumably, spirited away by the Home Office if he can convine them that he was really playing their game."

"And young Pete?"

"I've had him released."

"High-handed." Chris Warrender had been very silent, drinking heavily.

"I think I am in a position to be. You'd best be grateful for it. Frankly, your position is not much better than Coombe's."

"Ah," Warrender smiled at him, "but he has not the advantage of being about to become your son-in-law."

"Let us join the ladies," said Lord Hawth.

By general consent, they all retired early, all determined to be up and ready for whatever news the morning might bring. Kate and her mother, sharing the room they had used when they first came to the hall, undressed in silence. Kissing her daughter goodnight at last: "I'm so happy for you, dear," said Mrs. Warrender.

"Oh, mother, if only . . ."

"It's no good, Kate, and we both know it. Impossible anyway, even before Chris . . ."

"I could kill him," said Kate. "And poor little Susan. I wish he'd not allow it." They both knew to whom the "he" referred. But Mrs. Warrender was pretending to be asleep, and Kate did likewise, and, equally, pretended not to hear the tears gallantly stifled in her mother's pillow. Neither of them slept much, and they were down, heavy-eyed, to meet the rest of the party over an anxious, early breakfast. Only Miss Lintott and Chris Warrender were absent, Miss Lintott seeing no reason to break her lifelong habit of breakfast in bed, and Chris perhaps feeling that the less he saw of his future father-in-law the better.

Pouring Lord Hawth's tea just as he liked it, Mrs. Warrender stopped, listening. "Someone's coming!"

"Fast," said Hawth. "Parsons, bring him straight here."

"Yes, my lord. At once." He returned a few minutes later with James, still in mudstained riding boots.

"They came, my lord, the coaches." James looked badly shaken. "But there's news. Word of mouth. No time for a Gazette. Mr. Perceval's dead. Killed in the House."

"The Prime Minister? Killed? How?"

"Shot, my lord. They don't know much. A man called Bellingham, that they did know. And the mob cheered him. Bellingham. They had to wait for the Life Guards before they sent him, double-ironed, to Newgate. Touch and go, it was, by the sound of it."

"But the mail coaches ran," said George Warren.

"Thank God they were prepared for it," said Hawth. "Is all quiet at Glinde?"

"Hardly a soul stirring. Sleeping it off, I reckon."

"Good. Thank you, James. Get some sleep. I wonder," he went on, after the man had gone, "Bellingham? Never heard of him. Could he *be* General Ludd?"

"We may never know," said George Warren. "But it does sound as if the worst of the danger is past." He stood up. "I think I'd best thank you for your hospitality, get home to Warren House and start setting things in order there. I want it fit to receive its mistress. Kate—" he smiled down at her—"you'll let me name an early day?"

"I don't know." She looked from him to her mother. "It's all so strange. Poor Mr. Perceval. And Mrs. Perceval . . . all those children. It doesn't seem right to be happy."

"It's good to be alive," said George Warren, "and not fighting off the mob. Come, love, see me to my horse and let me persuade you? Mrs. Warrender will stand my friend, won't you, ma'am? I was thinking." Diffidently. "You know the old west wing? We could make a kind of . . . kind of Dower House there for you, ma'am. If you'd just tell me what you'd like?"

"Too kind." She looked up at him, hollow-eyed. "You are everything that is kind, George."

"Damnation!" Left alone with her, Hawth, who had risen as Kate left the room, took two long strides to loom over Mrs. Warrender's chair. "A Dower House indeed! What's wrong with mine, pray?"

"I've been very happy there." She looked up at him pleadingly. "But you must see, my lord, without Kate . . . You've had more than your share of gossip and scandal as it is. And . . . " She stopped, horror-struck at what she had been about to say.

"Am like to have more. Goddamn that son of yours, ma'am."

"Poor little Susan," she said. "I'm ashamed, my lord. I . . . " She sniffed and smiled up at him. "I know you hate to see a woman crying. But I must just tell you once how ashamed I am. Of Chris. Of my son."

"Not your fault," he said. "That husband of yours. Ma'am, shall I tell you just once what I thought of *him?*"

"No. Please don't." She managed a watery smile. "I'd much rather not hear it."

"Gallant." He bent over her and she could smell wine, and

the cigars he smoked. "And like you. So you propose to dwindle into a mother-in-law, Mrs.—damnation, what's your *name* ?"

"You didn't know? Susan," she said.

"Susan, by God! Well, Susan, are you really going to leave me and my remaining children to the tender mercies of my Cousin Lintott?"

"What else can I do, my lord?"

"You know as well as I do. For God's sake, stop calling me 'my lord' and say you'll marry me. Make an honest man of me at last. Take me over, Susan. Make me over? I'm not much of a bargain, I know, and I know *you* do. I'm a bad tempered brute. I drink. I smoke. I swear. I doubt I can change, but, by God, I can try. I'm tired of myself, Susan. Please—"

"Because you need a housekeeper?"

"No, damn you. Because I need a wife. Because I love you! And didn't even know it till last night. When George Warren told me he was engaged, he said I was going to lose my housekeeper. *You.* I thought it was you. That I'd lost you. God, what a fool. You've every right to laugh at me. I've made a proper idiot of myself, have I not, proposing for your daughter. I just didn't understand . . ."

"I'm not laughing at you," she said.

"No, by God, you're not." He put a gentle hand under her chin and tilted it up. "You're trying not to cry. My darling love, cry if you want to, but, before you start, just say you'll marry me."

"Oh, Mark." She met his gaze steadily. "I ought not to."

"You call me Mark as if you always had."

"Well, I did once."

"What?"

She smiled up at him a little wryly. "You've quite forgotten. I thought you had. I . . . couldn't. Do you remember a party your grandmother gave? Bastille year. At the Dower House. We danced. We laughed. We walked out into the garden. It was moonlight. You kissed me. And then the next thing I heard you had gone on the grand tour. I married Mr. Warrender next year."

"Dear God! That was you? My nameless girl. 'Call me Susan,' you said. Susan with the golden hair. But you disappeared; vanished like a night shadow. What happened?"

She laughed ruefully. "My hostess had the headache. We had to leave early. I couldn't see you anywhere. To say goodbye . . . to explain. What could I do?"

"And so I lost you! A hostess's headache! I waited, Susan. For you . . . for the supper dance you promised me. It seemed like hours, standing there, feeling the fool I looked. In the end, I joined the other young bucks; drank myself stupid. I was to start on my grand tour next day. When I woke; head like a sawmill; the carriage was at the door. And—idiot—I got in and drove away. Infatuation, I told myself, as my head cleared. An unknown jilt; absurd; I'd forget you. I never did."

"You didn't recognise me when we met." Her smile took the sting from the words.

"Drowned in your widow's weeds! Besides, when I lost you, I banished you—did my best to. A haunt from the past. Lost . . . best forgotten. I tried very hard. But"—he leaned down towards her—"I called my daughter Susan."

"Poor child."

"We are not." Very gently, very firmly, he lifted her out of her chair. "We are not going to discuss our children."

"No, do let's not." She smiled up at him mistily. "Oh, Mark!"

Miss Lintott's tea had been cold and her toast burned. Dressing angrily and early, she hurried downstairs to give a piece of her mind to the housekeeper. Opening the dining room door: "Good God," she said. "Have you taken leave of your senses, cousin?"

His arms still firmly round her, the Earl of Hawth stopped kissing his housekeeper and smiled over her head at the intruder. "No, just come to them," he told her.

Note

I must plead guilty to some liberties with history in this book. The Luddites were a phenomenon of the north, not the south, but since their leader "Ned Ludd" was himself a fiction, I do not feel that I have stretched fact too far in letting him make a brief, first appearance in my imaginary county of Glinde. As for his identity with Bellingham, it is Lord Hawth that suggests it, not I. The Luddite riots were real enough, but Napoleon did not take advantage of them to attempt an invasion in England's bad winter of 1811–1812. It was probably just as well. The more I investigated, the more I found myself inclined to believe in the organised attempt at revolution that I thought I had invented. History is stranger than fiction after all.